The Game of Gods 2

~The Death of Champions~

Joshua Kern

Copyright

Other Books by Joshua Kern

The Dungeon Alaria

The Creators Daughter

The Well Within

The Well Within: Part 1

Stand Alone

The Ridden

Duologies & Box Sets

The Game of Gods: Arc 1 Duology Box Set

The Dungeon Alaria: The World of Alaria Arc 1 Duology Box Set

Contents

Prologue

The dark-cloaked game leader and god, Bob, watched as Brigit of the Tuatha Dé Danann grabbed Odin by the back of the neck and dragged him to the corner of the room while his birds squawked up a storm.

"What were you thinking?" She screeched as she batted away Muninn with her free arm. "Sierra is Kira's enemy. How are they going to work together?"

Odin focused his good eye and pulled her hand away from his neck. "You let me worry about that!" He said confidently as he stroked his beard. "I have a feeling that there is more to their tale than either of them knows. You just make sure that Kira doesn't kill her, and I'll do the same with Sierra."

Clearing his throat, Bob gathered the attention of the remaining gods and goddesses surrounding the table. "Alright then, we have two heroes chosen. The rest of you need to decide on your choices soon as well. Also, Earth is entering the second stage of the change. You all know what that means, so be prepared for the coming changes."

Hermes rapped his tanned knuckles on the table before stepping back, drawing all eyes to him. "When can we expect the stores and messaging system to come into effect?"

"Good question," Bob remarked as he shuffled through some papers quickly. "They will come into effect at the end of the week, on the day the game officially begins. You need to make sure you have everything arranged by then. People currently have no idea what to do with the things they get from looting the monsters. We need to give them something to do with it all."

A knock on the closed door of the room silenced him, as his covered eyes glowed with an unearthly light. "It seems a guest has arrived that I need to introduce. As many of you know, originally, we had no system for dungeons in place. What happened in Kansas City was a surprise to all of us, though I think we managed to salvage the situation." He moved away from the table and over to the door, opening it without hesitation. "I would like to introduce Alaria, the goddess behind the dungeon."

The room exploded with noise as everyone started talking at the same time. "There is no goddess by that name!" Odin yelled from the corner of the room where Brigit still held him in place.

Alaria looked at Bob with glowing mismatched eyes as she stood in the open door. He gave her a small nod. "It's true there is no goddess by that name on Earth. I am not a goddess of your world. I come from the world Alaria. When your little game began, a tunnel was somehow created to my world. I followed the tunnel, and a dungeon was created as the result."

Bob slipped past her as she continued to explain her presence, leaving the room behind as he hurried across the hall to another room. He had more to say to them, more that they needed to know. This was Alaria's moment; however, he would speak with them more once the confusion generated from introducing a new goddess to the world had died down. This new room held another grouping of gods, and the atmosphere was notably darker than in the first room.

"Is it time for us to start playing as well?" Set, the Egyptian god of chaos asked impatiently.

Bob settled himself into position at the head of the table before answering. "Yes, they are in the process of choosing their champions among the humans. You may make your selections from among the monsters on Earth. Each of you may choose a primary champion and a backup in case something happens to the first. The less intelligent the monster, the more you may control them. Now, who wants to go first?" His eyes glinted maliciously beneath his hood.

The dead disfigured hand of Hel raised itself, drawing everyone's attention to her frightful visage. Half of her face was a thing of beauty, while the other half was a dead rotting mess of congealed flesh and bone. "I already have a monster in mind." Her harsh, raspy voice announced.

Chapter 1

"GO, go, go!" Charles yelled as he jumped into the truck cab with wide eyes.

Kira twisted around and immediately saw what had him so panicked. Countless monsters were jumping from the top of the dungeon wall and down into the river far below them. They were too far away to tell if any of the monsters survived the jump, but the thick rain like fall of monsters left her heart racing and the gas pedal under her foot jammed to the floor.

In the back, Kira's younger sister Kate was clinging to a sleepy-eyed Alli while her parents huddled in the opposite corner.

The engine roared, and the truck began to shake as Kira pushed it to the limits in their rush to get as far away as possible as quickly as possible.

Clouds had begun to gather in the atmosphere with the completion of the dungeon and were roiling high in the sky. The wind began to pick up, whistling past the sides of the racing truck. The temperature outside plummeted by the second until their breaths began to mist and fog with each exhale.

Charles rolled down the cab window and leaned out as he withdrew coats and blankets from his inventory. Krystal took each of them from his hands and handed them out to her daughter and husband.

"We need to find someplace to get out of this!" Kira yelled at him, trying to be heard over the roaring of the wind and the open window. She had leaned over the steering wheel and was looking intently at the stormy clouds above them. The crackling of old hard leather stressing and breaking with every movement filled the cabin alongside the smell of old tobacco pipe smoke.

Alli pushed her tired and still adjusting body into an upright position. "I'll find a place for everyone to hide." Without waiting for a reply, she leaped out of the speeding truck and disappeared into its shadow. "I'll be going on ahead." Her words echoed in his mind although she had already left.

There was a flash of lightning that struck the dungeon wall behind them, followed by a crash of rolling thunder. In the back of the truck, Kate huddled together with her parents, each of them wearing the coats he had distributed and were wrapped together in a blanket.

The sky overhead continued to grow darker as the clouds joined together in a dark mass. The wind had started to pick up buffeting the truck constantly as it endeavored to push them off the side of the road.

Kira had the heater cranked all the way up as their white puffs of breath began to fog up the windshield and windows. Charles held onto the door, shivering from the cold as the truck continued to shake and rattle from the slowly degrading road. The last week had not been kind to any structure made by human hands.

Abandoned cars and trucks had appeared on the road again once they left the dungeon behind. Some of them were mere husks of what they had once been, while others showed the bloody aftermath of their owner's deaths. Tires that had been ripped from their axles and doors that had been torn from their frames littered the highway.

Kira's hands were white from the pressure she was exerting on the steering wheel as she concentrated on navigating between the rubble.

Charles kept his eyes on the sky as the clouds came together and started to change.

"You need to go faster!" He shouted as a tornado formed behind them with a speed he had never seen before.

The air around them screamed as the wind continued to pick up. The three people in the back of the truck were holding on to one another and hiding under a thick blanket in an effort to escape the chilling wind.

"I think I have found a place," Alli's voice suddenly intruded into Charles' mind, startling him. "I'll be back with you in just a moment. Going through shadows is fun!" The glee she was having with her new ability obvious as she appeared in front of them stepping out of the shadow of a car with a wide ecstatic doggy grin.

"Alli says she found a place for us, follow her," Charles commanded Kira as she slowed at the giant dog's sudden appearance.

Ahead of them, Alli stepped from one shadow to the next, her form fluid and quick as she remained ahead of the speeding truck. Charles kept his gaze fixed on the lengthening shadows as the clouds above covered the sun completely, leaving everything in shadow.

Kira was silent as she focused on the condition of the road and keeping their speed up. Behind them, the tornado had continued to form and was extending down to the ground with a distant roar. Slowing down too much could leave them in its path without enough time to getaway.

"Turn here," Alli told him as she stopped moving next to a small dirt turnoff.

They were just barely outside the city proper and already the number of buildings had dwindled to almost nothing. Wide empty fields replaced the skyscrapers and large sprawling parking lots filled with non-functional vehicles.

Charles pointed ahead of them to Alli. "She says to turn onto that dirt road."

Kira shifted into a lower gear, slowing as little as possible before spinning the wheel. The truck fishtailed as the people in the back were thrown around helplessly, a cloud of dirt spewed out behind them and then drifted away. The dirt road was bumpy as they sped down it towards a house and barn that could barely be seen in the distance. Alli ran alongside the bouncing truck, maintaining the same speed easily now that Kira couldn't drive as fast as she had on the highway.

The cabin of the truck was silent as they drew closer to the two-story farmhouse and a large red barn at the end of what was apparently a very long driveway. The force of the wind had fallen slightly once they were off the main roads, although the temperature had yet to rise at all. Puffs of white mist flew from their mouths with every exhale.

With a loud squeal of brakes, Kira stopped the truck in front of the barn and looked to Charles. "Open the doors. I'll store the truck inside and then we'll go over to the house."

Charles opened the door without delay and sprinted over to the large sliding doors. He had to reach into the small gap between the door and the wall to unlatch it before pushing it open. With a heave, he slid the door open on well-oiled and silent wheels.

Kira flicked on the headlights as she drove the truck into the dark interior of the barn. The yellow beams of light revealed the backside of an old military transport vehicle that had undoubtedly been sitting in the barn for years, judging by the cobwebs that covered it.

She pulled in behind the larger truck and turned off the ignition, plunging the barn into darkness once more. The only light in the otherwise dark building coming from the open door. In the back of the truck, Kate peeked out from beneath the blanket before pulling it to the side, unbundling herself and her parents. "Where are we?" She asked softly as she climbed from the truck and onto the dirt flooring. Outside the barn, the wind screamed past creating an awful howling noise.

Kira's mother stored the blankets in her inventory as she and her husband followed after their youngest daughter and climbed from the back of the now stationary truck.

Charles stood just inside the barn at the open door with Alli at his side, listening to the howling wind and watching the small decorative windmill in the yard next to the house spin ever faster. His arm was resting on Alli's back as he leaned against her, soaking in her warmth.

"We need to hurry, the storm is coming closer," She told him in a worried tone, her large head twisted to look at the distant spinning clouds.

Kira held onto her younger sister as she came to a stop behind Charles and Alli, noticing how much the wind had picked up just in the short amount of time that they had been in the barn. "We need to hurry!" She called back to her parents, trying to rush them along.

Alli stepped into the fierce wind, her silver hair rippling like a wave from the pressure. She turned to face the dark interior of the barn; her large pointy ears held flat against her head. "The house has a storm cellar we can hide in." She paused and looked at Charles, her head sinking slightly. "There are some people already inside, however, that we will need to share the space with."

Charles didn't respond as he followed her out of the barn and into the cold, windy air. He didn't really mind that people were there, he just didn't feel the need to help everyone because they were both humans. Holding out his hand, he grabbed hold of Kates' hand and pulled her along behind him. She grabbed onto her father's arm, who then held onto his wife.

Kira was the last person to leave the barn, taking the time to close and latch the door behind them. Alli waited for her to take hold of her mother's arm before leading them to the door inset in the ground to the side of the house. Each step was a work of effort against the wind as they struggled to push forward while taking small steps that kept them close to the ground.

Underneath Charles' hand, the door to the storm cellar was flung open as the wind ripped it from his grasp, sending it crashing to the ground with a bang, the hinges barely holding on. A scream of terror was heard from the cellar before he took his first step down the stairs.

"Calm down," He yelled. "We're going to be sharing this space with you until the storm passes."

"D-Don't come down, we're armed and we're not afraid to use them."

Charles sighed in annoyance before throwing a simple light spell into the darkened cellar. "I said to calm down!" He ordered the roomful of people as he stepped into view, the glowing orb of light he had thrown down silencing them.

Alli stayed by his side as he stepped off of the stairs and onto the concrete flooring, her size drawing muffled gasps from every person gathered there. Charles kept his arm on her shoulder to ensure that people didn't get any ideas of attacking her.

Everyone stepped back hugging the wall in fear of the giant dog and the man who had lit up the area in a fashion they had never seen before. Kate and her parents stepped into view behind him as Kira struggled to close the door above them. The wind was pushing against her efforts, making even her leveled-up strength struggle against the pressure.

Kira took in a deep breath and heaved with everything she had, the hinges twisted and screamed as the thick metal flexed and gave in. The door slammed shut, locking them in as the ruined hinges were no longer operable.

Kate hid behind Alli, her large silver body making it easy. Kira pushed past her, coming to a stop next to Charles. She folded her arms across her once white oil-stained shirt, her lean muscled arms and her scowling face stopping anyone from protesting further.

The crowd of people that were revealed under the harsh white light created by Charles' magic was dirty and ragged in appearance. Several of them were obviously married or part of a family in the way that they clung to one another. The still air in the cellar was rank with the stifling smell of sweat and unwashed bodies.

Charles stepped away from the stairs and headed for a corner of the room, leading his group to the now clear area. Above their heads, the old farmhouse creaked and groaned from the wind as it continued to pick up in speed until conversation was barely possible in the cellar.

Kate kept her hand on Alli while Kira followed behind her parents, glaring at the other group of people. The four of them settled down against the wall with Kira next to Kate and Alli stretched out in front of them like a protective wall.

One of the women stepped forward, her face tanned but dirty, making it hard to tell her actual age beneath the harsh light. "Hi, my name is Tara. This farm belongs to my family, or at least it did before everything happened. I don't know if anyone can own land in this new world." She looked down unsure of herself before seeming to firm her resolve and looking up again at them. "I know I shouldn't ask this of you considering the storm outside, but if you have any water or food, would you mind sharing it with us? There has been little drinkable water to be found recently and most of us haven't eaten in the last day or so."

Alli immediately turned her massive silver head to look at Charles, her large mismatched eyes pleading with him despite her not saying anything.

Charles sighed and gave in to her overly expressive eyes, pulling a 24 pack of water from his inventory. He only had three more 24 packs of water in there, he hadn't been worrying about water up to this point since he could just refill the bottles as needed. That wasn't something he would be able to keep doing, however, if more people joined them.

Tara's face went through several changes at the sight of the water. "How, what, where? Where did that water come from?" She finally settled on as she gingerly reached for the proffered water.

"My inventory," He answered simply.

"Our inventories don't work like that." She began once she had the water firmly in her grasp, where he couldn't take it back. "The inventory only allows one of each item per slot." She looked at the bottles of water. "Although certain items do count as just one thing, a box of bullets for example." She held the pack to her chest and closed her eyes.

Nothing happened.

Charles turned away from her and settled on the ground with Alli at his back. "I guess my inventory works differently than yours, don't make a big deal about it." In truth, he had already been through this a couple of times and knew just how different his inventory truly was from everyone else's. He wasn't going to hide that information, however, that didn't mean he was going to purposefully draw attention to it either.

The people on the far side of the room began making noise at the sight of the water. The thirst they had each been forcefully ignoring till now rearing its head with mouth-drying force.

Behind him, Alli bumped against his back, her eyes narrowing. "Give them some food as well, I know you have more than enough for all them and us."

Charles turned to look at her with a scowl on his face. "If I give food to every person, we come across it won't last very long." He whispered softly to her before sighing and turning around. With a careless move of his hand, a box was tossed across the floor to them. It was full of breakfast granola bars of various flavors and types; some were filled with fruit while others were grain and nuts. "If you're hungry, then eat those."

A few muffled sobs came from the people as they tore into the box of food and the bottles of water. The lack of tears, however, showed just how dehydrated they truly were. One of the bottles of water disappeared down Tara's throat without her letting a single drop escape her dry cracked lips. She greedily gasped for breath drawing attention to her stained dark blue long-sleeve shirt.

Alli nudged Charles' back again drawing his attention. "Fill their bottles for them, they need more water than just a single bottle of water each."

The house above their heads shuddered and creaked loudly, drawing everyone's attention and silencing the basement for several seconds.

"Do you have a pitcher or something with a spigot on it?" Charles asked Tara, disturbing the quiet cellar without even moving.

She pointed her hand to the corner of the room where everything they couldn't use had been piled together in one giant mess. "I think there should be something along those lines in that pile somewhere."

Kira and Kate were talking quietly on the other side of Alli as Charles climbed to his feet with a barely contained sigh of annoyance. He was only doing this because Alli had asked him to help them. The orb of light floated across the room settling itself over the mess in the corner while throwing the rest of the basement into shadows.

Charles dug into the pile, moving an old toaster to the side that had a plastic plate stuffed in it. Deeper within the pile, the sound of something scuttling around had him jerking his hand back for a second. Trying to ignore the entirely mental based feeling of bugs crawling over his skin, he reached back into the pile and shifted an old foam boogie board to the side. With the large item out of the way, a colony of cockroaches crawling over an old brown plastic juice pitcher with a spigot at the bottom was revealed.

The cockroaches flew into motion, scattering in every direction that would take them deeper into the pile and away from the human's questing hands. Charles flexed his hand and pulled the nasty brown pitcher into the light, wishing he had a gallon of disinfectant to bury his hand in afterward.

His mouth was twisted in a grimace as he held it between two fingers and used his cleaning spell to scour the grime from his hand and the pitcher.

Shocked gasps resounded behind him, reminding him that he hadn't had a chance to explain the fact that he could use magic to them.

Chapter 2

Charles turned around, deciding to ignore the muttering people for the moment. Moving over to the wooden stairs that went into the house, he set the pitcher on a step and filled it with water.

"You can refill your bottles with this," He told them gruffly, moving back over to Alli's side. His left hand rubbed the back of the glove on his right, his fingers questing over the raised edges of the swirling runes on the back. He was tired of fighting Alli's good nature and saw no reason he shouldn't give in this time. They were stuck in this basement until the storm passed at the very least. Truth be told he didn't actually mind helping other people, or at least he hadn't in the past. His issue with it now lay entirely in him just being focused on not getting sidetracked from reaching his sister.

Tara looked from him to the pitcher of water and back again. "Is it safe to drink?" She finally asked hesitantly, distracting Charles from his thoughts. Behind her, everyone was nodding their heads at the question.

Charles moved the orb of light to hang in the air above the water, before responding. "It's clean drinkable water, and the pitcher itself is clean now as well. Feel free to drink as much as you want, I'll refill it as needed."

Tara was the first to move, placing her empty bottle beneath the spigot and twisting the handle until the water flowed clear into the cheap plastic bottle. All eyes were on her as she brought the bottle to her lips and tipped the refreshing liquid into her mouth. Her first swallow was somewhat hesitant as she tasted the water and let it slide down her throat. Her eyes opened wide in approval as she squeezed the bottle in desperation, drinking it as quickly as she could.

The pitcher needed to be refilled a number of times before the people were no longer thirsty. Each of them was holding their slightly swollen bellies and groaning from having drunk so much. Charles felt a twisted sense of amusement at their pain since they had brought it upon themselves.

Behind him, on the other side of Alli, Kira and Kate were whispering softly while their parents slept, leaning against the wall with a blanket wrapped around them.

"Do you understand everything that I have told you so far?" Kira asked her sister quietly.

Kate buried her fingers into Alli's silvery side as she answered. "I think so, I remember some of it from the first night before the attack. What is this manual you keep mentioning though?"

Kira was glad her little sister was taking everything so well; she had been worried that she would be in denial. Kate had been laid up sick in bed, barely coherent since the attack that had almost killed her on the first night. "Open your inventory and then say 'manual', the manual was written by the gods," She used her fingers as quotation marks when she mentioned the gods. "It lists pretty much everything that you absolutely need to know in order to survive in this new world."

Kate opened her mouth to respond when a ding echoed in each person's ear, causing them to stiffen in dread. They had heard that ding that reverberated through the skull only once before, on the night of the apocalypse.

Everyone held their respective breaths as a new message flickered into being in front of their eyes.

To those who are reading this message, congratulations on surviving the apocalypse. The manual has now been updated with new pertinent information that will help you survive in the future.

That was the entirety of the message that had appeared before them. Charles closed the message with a snort and opened the manual as Kira and Kate continued their discussion. Kira was determined to keep her sister alive and knowing what was coming and how the new world worked, would be the thing that helped the most in keeping Kate alive in the future. The people around Tara started chattering before quieting down as well, each of them reading the manual.

The manual popped into existence in his hands, taking on the appearance of a leather-bound book. It was noticeably thicker now than it had been the first time he had read it. Flipping to the first page, he saw the odd inscription that had been written as a greeting for each person who decided to read the manual.

In this new world, death is not the end, it is the beginning of the cycle of rebirth. Every being releases their energy back into the world upon the expiration of their physical form. This energy helps the world and beings that lives on its surface to grow and become stronger. The strength and energy of those that have died will become the strength of those left behind.

It was an odd message from the gods that had changed their world, causing untold amounts of death and destruction.

Charles flipped to the next page which listed information on the effectiveness of weapons. It was a simple and short message, though it now held an addendum that seemed to apply to him.

Any weapons created before our return to the world lack the life energy known as mana. When we returned, mana once again began to infuse the world. Use of weapons that contain no traces of mana will have little effect on anything that has become infused with the energy. This means that guns and their ammo will be useless against those of a higher level. That said, any item or weapon created after our return will be stronger than ever before depending on the amount of mana the material has absorbed or had directly infused in it during its creation. The art of infusing mana must be taught by the sole person capable of using mana living at this time or one of his disciples.

A growl escaped from his throat at the mention of the sole mana user. It was talking about him he just knew it. When it became known that the sole user capable of using mana was him, he would have people constantly seeking him out. Some would want to use him for their own purposes, while others would want his help in other ways. Either way, this single mention of him meant he would need to start making plans for what he would do after he found his sister. He looked down at the book in his hands and turned the page, hoping that it was just a single mention.

It wasn't, nearly every page in the book mentioned him in some way. Everything, no matter how pedestrian it seemed could now be strengthened and made better through the infusion of mana during its creation. Then there was the information on classes, classes were generated according to the life you have lived and your actions. The only way to get a magic-based class was to already know how to use magic when you reached level 15, or to have fulfilled certain requirements. Either way, the only person who could teach them magic, whether it was before or after was him.

The later pages focused on information that was completely new and hadn't been in the prior version of the manual. There was a page dedicated to the growing of crops and how the mana in the air helped everything from grass to trees to planted crops grow faster and become more nutritious.

It was the last page that truly grabbed his attention and refused to let go, however.

> *It will take two weeks to the day from our return for the world to stabilize somewhat, at that time settlements can then be created. Each of these settlements can receive and send messages to any other settlement. In addition to the ability to send and receive messages, they will also possess a simple general store where daily necessities can be purchased, and items received from looting monsters can be sold. It is up to the inhabitants of each settlement to ensure that these places remain safe from the monsters that now roam the world. As the mana in the air grows thicker, new and dangerous monsters will come into existence alongside beings from myth and legends.*

The book in his hands snapped shut, the soft leather dulling the sound slightly. It disappeared with that sound still hanging in the air. Charles felt his hands clenching in anger at how the gods were going to forcefully use him. Just then another notification appeared in front of him.

The gods have issued you a new challenge, create a town in the location of their choosing. The location will be revealed after the first challenge has been completed.

His first thought to the message was to rant and rave at being jerked around by the gods. His second thought, however, was slightly calmer in nature, he couldn't forget the end goal here. Completing the challenges that the gods laid before him would allow him to sleep again. He found that he desperately missed sleeping, for whatever reason it seemed like his body no longer needed it, but his mind was something else entirely. His mind still needed that downtime to sort through everything and file information away into its proper location. Without sleep all of that was just building up in his head, distracting him and slowing his thoughts.

Drinking the potion, the gods had given him seemed to help, but he was always hesitant to drink it without injury. He never knew when they might need something powerful like that and not have it available. Besides, he was sure the potion was doing something else to him every time he drank it. The changes that his body had gone through were too drastic otherwise.

It was only when his mind had sufficiently calmed that he began to think through the new challenge and what it meant for him clearly. He was still being pulled around by the gods and whatever whims they may have but creating a town may not actually be a bad idea. He would have to change his mentality to do it, but it would actually serve to fix several problems he could see coming on the horizon.

Charles thought about the information on the page and what he had just been worried about before the new challenge from the gods had appeared. The creation of a settlement once he had found his sister might just be the thing he needed. It would ensure people could find him and the sheer number of people would keep them safe.

He had no intentions of helping every single person that wanted his help, but that didn't mean he wasn't going to give it at all, of course, that didn't mean he was going to help them for free either. His thoughts began to wander as various plans flitted through his mind before being dismissed in turn. The problem was where the gods would have him create their settlement; it was bound to become huge and would develop into a town or larger he was sure.

People would jump at the chance to learn magic, and he was the only person who could make that happen. It looked like the gods had plans for him, that didn't mean that he would go along with them willingly though. Not to mention that he didn't even know how to teach someone else how to sense or even use magic. He had a slight idea that he would need to try out sometime, but if that didn't work, then he had no other ideas at this time.

Across from his group, Tara was looking from her manual to him and back again, clearly thinking that he was the person it kept mentioning. Charles narrowed his eyes at her and shook his head, wanting to postpone the conversations that were sure to come as long as possible.

The house above them rumbled from a burst of fierce wind and dust fell liberally from the rafters as everyone stopped their reading and looked wearily upwards.

Kate squeaked in fear and Kira enfolded her in her arms protectively, letting the manual they had been reviewing fall from her hands. "It's alright, I'm right here and I'm not going to let anything happen to you!" She said fiercely as she held her younger sister. Kate had helped her through the darkest time in her life, and she would be forever indebted and grateful to her for that. She would do her best to protect and keep her safe, no matter what.

Another shudder went through the house and Charles waved away the orb of light he had created, throwing the cellar into darkness. There were a few scattered shouts from surprised people, but they all quieted down quickly as they prepared to get some rest.

Charles leaned against Alli's warm furry side, relaxing as the mental partitions in his mind sprang into action. His thoughts were filled with new ways to use and twist the magic he had learned thus far. The other partitions in his mind concentrating on the individual elements he had learned previously.

Sound faded away as he sank deeper into his meditations. The storm continued to rage until it finally blew itself out in the early morning hours, unnoticed by anyone as they slept huddled together.

Charles kept his meditations going until Alli stirred, feeling the movements of mana in his body as it spun and shifted with his thoughts. Ever since his understanding of mana had increased, he had been feeling the mana in his body strengthening and growing thicker. It was beginning to respond to his touch easier, feeling more malleable and willing to be shaped into spells.

He had begun to notice the subtle differences that existed when he cast spells normally versus when he used the glove to do it. The glove used brute force to take the mana from the air around him and shape it as he desired, making it less responsive to any changes he wanted to make. When he cast them normally using the mana flowing through his body, they were more receptive to being changed without increasing the cost explosively.

Alli shifted again and twisted to nudge him with the side of her head. "I need to go outside for a few minutes. Let me up."

Charles pushed off her warm side and moved over to the stairs that would let them out. The light trickling through the gaps in the closed-door guiding him, Alli climbed up the stairs beside him and pushed against the door. The hinges groaned and then screamed as the entire door popped from its housing and fell to the ground outside; the grass muffling its impact slightly.

The sound of the hinges tearing had awoken everyone in the basement and sent their heart rates into the stratosphere with terror that something had come for them.

The sky outside had cleared sometime in the early morning hours and shone blue and bright overhead. The ground was littered with branches and shingles from the roof of the house. Farther out the barn appeared to have a new hole in the roof but was still standing with the doors closed.

Alli stepped gingerly onto the grass before taking off around the side of the house like a shot. Charles shook his head at her and stretched, his back popping painfully several times. He tended to rarely move during his nightly meditations, and it made his muscles stiff each morning.

Charles stepped into the sunlight and leaned against a ragged leafless tree as he pulled up the quest that had been his goal since that first day, when he had woken to find a goddess in his bedroom.

The gods have issued you a challenge, join your sister in Pennsylvania!

A shiver of shock ran through him as he read the quest details, it had changed! The original message had read Massachusetts, not Pennsylvania. His sister was moving towards him and making better time than he was on top of that, not that he was surprised by that. His sister would never let something like the end of the world stop her. Her intellect was unmatched as far as he was concerned, the things she had created as a child still put some large companies to shame that had teams of hundreds working for them.

A coil of apprehension and dread that he hadn't even realized was forming released itself from his chest with the realization that his sister was still alive. A weight that had been growing heavier with every uncertain mile was released into the ether as he allowed himself to relax for the first time.

With a new destination in mind, Charles pulled the map he had found at one of the gas stations they had stopped at out and spread it flat on the ground. His finger traced the route they had taken thus far and stopped around where he thought they currently were. He followed the interstate further into the state until it crossed over into Illinois then Indiana and Ohio until it finally continued into Pennsylvania.

Flicking his eyes to the legend at the bottom of the map he noted the distance indicator and mentally began adding up the distance, stopping when it reached over 700 miles. He sighed in resignation and folded up the map; it was going to be an extremely long day, and that was without accounting for the inevitable monsters that would attack them.

The distance had decreased rapidly once he had met Kira. The amount of trouble encountered had also increased, however, maybe not the number, but the sheer size of the encounters had exploded. Kira stepped out into the morning light and walked over to him.

"I'm going to check on the truck. Make sure nothing damaged it during that storm." She stepped close to him and looked him in the eye. "Kate wants to talk to you about learning magic, be nice to her and know that if you make my sister cry, I will break your leg."

Charles winced and shuffled a step back knowing she was not joking in the slightest. "I read the additions to the manual, but I have to be honest. I have no idea how I'm supposed to help anyone learn to use magic." He held up his gloved hand. "The way I learned it is not exactly something anyone else can use." He sighed and let his hand run through his messy uncombed hair before pulling out his hat and covering his head. "That said, I do have one idea, but that's it. If that doesn't work, then I don't want to hear anything more on the matter. It's not like I was given a manual for teaching magic to others." He stopped, waiting, hoping that his words would trigger something from the gods. Nothing. He shook his head and looked at the imposing woman in front of him, the bracelet on her arm glinting in the sunlight. "I'll give it a try, but that is all I can promise at this time. And as for the other thing, you don't have to worry about me hurting her."

Kira glared at him for another heartbeat before her face softened and transformed into the barest hint of a smile. "Thank you, now I have a truck to go look at. Give me one of the gas barrels while I'm here. I'll make sure it's full."

A large fifty-five-gallon drum full of gasoline appeared before her. Kira bent her knees and wrapped her arms around the 350-pound drum of liquid and lifted it with a small grunt. Charles stared in amazement at the sight as she tottered off. He knew that she had been putting some of her status points into the strength attribute, but to see the difference it made firsthand was something else.

Alli trotted into view, her nose to the air as she sniffed the clean air. "I have never smelled air this clean before. There is no hint of smog or ash on the wind, just the smell of rain and vegetation."

Charles nodded in agreement, his eyes on the bright blue cloudless sky above. The early morning air possessed a hint of a chill leftover from the storm and early fall.

Alli shook her entire body and then stepped close to him, letting her side rest against his as they enjoyed the silent moment together. Over at the barn, Kira had placed the barrel on the ground and was in the process of opening the giant barn door. One side seemed to have come off the rail as she was forced to push it from the bottom near the ground. It squealed loudly piercing the otherwise quiet area with the grinding of the single wheel remaining on the rail at the top.

Charles flinched at the noise and Alli whimpered as she flung herself to the ground and threw her paws over her sensitive ears.

Chapter 3

Tara ran up the cellar stairs and saw Kira opening the barn door. "I've been meaning to fix that door for years now. Every time there is a storm, it somehow pops off the rails." She muttered loudly to herself. Standing there in the sunlight, Charles was able to get an accurate idea of her age for the first time. The lines around her mouth stood out in sharp relief against the sunlight, causing him to mentally bump her age into the low forties. "Why is she going into the barn?"

"Hmm? Oh, we parked our truck in there yesterday and she needs to look it over and make sure it survived the storm undamaged," Charles informed her as he scratched Alli behind her ears.

Tara stepped onto the grass from the stairs and hurried over to the duo. "I'm sure you saw the old transport truck when you parked in there?" Charles nodded that they had. "We've managed to keep it running throughout the years, the battery is dead on it right now and it is too heavy for us to push start it. Would you be willing to give us a tow until we can start it through compression?"

Charles crouched next to Alli and played with her soft ears as she relaxed, stretched out on the ground next to him. "Let's help them," Alli said unsurprisingly. He struggled to keep his sigh internal at Alli's predictable desire to help everyone she met.

"You'd have to ask Kira, she's the one who knows what the truck is and isn't capable of," Charles said as he stood.

Alli perked up and looked off into the distance. "I'll be back, there's something I need to check on." She stepped close to the tree and sank into its shadow vanishing without another word.

Tara stepped back in shock, unable to look away from the spot Alli had vanished from. "Where, what," She shook her head and blinked, her brows furrowed. "Did your dog just disappear into that shadow?"

"It's part of a class skill she acquired at level 15," Charles said, focusing on the horizon Alli had been looking at. Even with his increased eyesight, he couldn't see anything that would have caused her to leave in such a hurry.

"Right, classes. I read about those in the manual," She replied in a daze, her voice somewhat robotic. "The manual said nothing about animals gaining levels as well though."

Charles shrugged. "As far as I understand it, it makes no difference if you're human, animal or monster. If you are alive in some manner, then you have the ability to gain levels and increase your stats. Either way, I get the feeling Alli is special."

Kate appeared behind them, her shy eyes looking at her feet and her hands entwined anxiously. "Charles, can I talk to you?"

Tara took a step towards the barn as he nodded. "I'll go ask Kira then what she thinks on the matter." She informed him before hurrying off.

"Where's Alli?" Kate asked, looking around for the large silver dog that was nearly always by his side.

"She had something she wanted to look at and left a few minutes ago." He said as he leaned against the tree and waited for her to speak. He hadn't spent much time around Kira's younger sister, but from what he had seen so far indicated that she was an alright teen, if somewhat shy girl.

Kate breathed in deep and forced herself to relax as she breathed out explosively. "How much did Kira tell you when she came out earlier?"

"I can't say for sure, but probably most of it," He answered, neatly sidestepping the question by not saying anything concrete.

Kate breathed in and out with her eyes closed, her hands clenched at her side. Her face set in determination she opened her eyes and met his gaze head-on. "I want to learn how to use magic! Would you be willing to teach me how to use it?" She faltered halfway through and finished politely.

He looked the teenage girl over carefully before responding. "There are a few questions I'll want to ask you about that later. I have to be honest with you though. Currently, I don't know how to teach anyone how to use magic. I do have a single idea on how to start, but I have to be honest if that doesn't work then I don't even know where to begin." He held up his gloved right hand so she could see the silvery runes along the back. "The way I learned is not exactly available to anyone else."

Kate tilted her head in confusion. "Why not?"

Charles pointed to the meditation spot on the back of the glove. "See this spot here? When I press on this spot, I go into a special meditation trance that allows me to focus on and feel the mana that surrounds me and exists inside my body." Although in truth, the order he had learned to use his magic in was rather disjointed and impossible without the glove augmenting his abilities. He had learned to properly feel and control his mana after he had learned his first spell.

Kate's hand shook as she stepped closer to him and reached out to touch the meditation point on his glove. Charles saw what she was reaching for and extended his hand towards her.

"Is it alright?" She asked as her finger hovered just above the raised silvery rune.

"Sure, go ahead. I don't think anything will happen, anyway." He said raising his hand to meet her finger.

Against his expectations, Kate froze as a thin, translucent blue barrier appeared surrounding the two of them. The barrier could be seen by his eyes, but where it interacted with Kate and himself it changed, allowing him to watch the movements of mana in their bodies.

Charles stepped away from her breaking the connection. "Interesting, this may be easier than I thought then. I'll ride in the back of the truck with you today, we'll take it slow and make sure you can feel and control your mana first before we start on spells."

Kate wavered weakly in place as the light in her eyes returned and she ran unsteadily to the corner of the house. She fell to her knees as she began retching uncontrollably. Her eyes were bloodshot and her cheeks splotchy when she finally stopped and collapsed onto her back. She stared up at the blue sky; the morning dew-soaked grass clinging to her back and cooling her neck.

"Please don't break the connection like that again." She covered her eyes with her arm as she tried to explain. "When I touched the back of your glove, it was like my senses all expanded and I was seeing the world as it truly is for the first time. When you broke the connection like that, all of those expanded senses were forcibly cut and shoved back into my body."

Charles grimaced and sat on the ground next to her. "Sorry about that, I was just surprised that it actually did anything. I didn't mean to hurt you or cause you any discomfort."

Kate waved her arm weakly. "I know that, it's just something to keep in mind for the future."

Charles handed her a bottle of water. "How are your parents doing with everything?"

Kate swished and spat the water before answering the vague question. "Now that they're not having to worry about me dying on a cot while they look on helplessly, and now that Kira has rejoined us, they're doing better." She pulled blades of grass from the ground, not looking up. "Reading the manual with Kira last night helped me to understand certain things, but I'm worried about them not being able to handle the changes to the world."

"I think they'll be fine," Charles said as he threw a clump of grass at her. "They've survived this long. They know how the world works now as well. They may not be warriors, but that might not matter as much for much longer. After we find my sister, I have a quest of sorts that will change a number of things." He tried to comfort her with his words of their uncertain future.

The truck in the barn started with a distant roar before Kate could respond, settling into an even rumbling purr without delay. Tara ran from the barn and stopped as she saw the ruined upper floor of her farmhouse. Shaking her head, she dug her feet into the dirt and ran to the back of the house.

Charles heard a car door open and then slam shut seconds later. Tara reappeared with a bundle of thick wires with clamps on the ends, they were jumper cables.

"We don't need a tow with these!" She said excitedly as she ran past them.

Kate groaned and got to her feet trotting after Tara, the half-empty bottle of water clasped tightly in her hands. She weaved from side to side for several steps, seeming to still be slightly unsteady on her feet.

"I need to talk with Kira, and then I'll be back." She called back to him over her shoulder.

Charles went down into the basement, filling the water pitcher as he passed it. Kira's parents were leaning against the wall with their heads pressed together as they whispered quietly to each other.

"Kory, Krystal," He called out to them without moving from the stairs. "Kira has the truck started so as soon as she helps Tara get their truck up and running and Alli gets back we're leaving."

The two of them nodded their heads to let him know that they had heard him and then promptly went back to their own conversation. The other people in the basement perked up at the mention of the trucks and tried to get Charles's attention before he stomped back up the stairs ignoring them.

He had done his due diligence in helping them already and wanted to be on his way again as soon as possible. The morning chill had dissipated somewhat once the sun had risen higher over the horizon. He did not expect it to get truly warm, however. They were in the last couple days of September and while it wasn't cold just yet; the days had already become noticeably cooler.

He was slowly making his way over to the barn when he heard the whirring of the old transport truck's starter. It stopped and slowed to a stop without ever catching. It whirred to life a second time, again failing to catch on anything as he stepped through the open barn doors. Kira was standing inside the large engine compartment with a small red gas can in her hands.

"I just put a little gas into the intake to prime it a little. Try it again." She yelled to Tara, as she made sure she was clear of anything that might spin and hit her.

For a third time, the starter whirred to life, before catching once and then twice a second later. The engine shook as it struggled to start, and the gas she had poured into it caught with a belch of flame. Kira laughed as she leaped from the engine compartment to the ground and rolled once. Kate who had been sitting inside of their truck keeping the pressure on the pedal, stepped out and ran to her laughing sister.

Tara kept the revs on the larger truck high as Charles ran to the front of it and pulled the jumper cables free. He held them apart from each other as he slammed the metal hood down and then did the same thing with their truck. He glanced at the thick cabling and stored it in his inventory without another thought. He was sure they would find another chance to use it again in the future.

Charles slipped behind the wheel of their truck and slid the transmission into reverse. Kira looked up as he backed the old truck from the barn and took it out of view next to the house.

"I asked him," Kate whispered next to her ear, the hole-ridden muffler of the transport truck creating a near-deafening noise.

"What did he say?" Kira asked back, pulling her younger sister to her feet.

To their side, Tara jumped out of the truck's cab and pulled them into a tight embrace. "Thank you. Now that it's running, we can find someplace safe to go!"

Kate looked at the tanned and age lined face of the older woman. "Why can't you just stay here? You may not have food or water but at least it seems to be safe for now."

Tara gave her a slight smile, "That's exactly why we can't stay here, we've eaten all the food here and there was little water to be scavenged after everything stopped working." She released them and looked out into the distance over the sprawling green fields. "It's true that this area has been safe enough for some reason, no monsters have come closer than the road a couple of miles away. With no supplies though, being safe is a luxury we just can't afford any longer. Especially now that we have a way of getting around."

While they were talking, Kira was looking at the loud truck distrustfully. "It's too loud." She finally announced. "Monsters will be able to hear it everywhere and will come running."

As if to prove her point, the sound of Charles yelling sent all three of them scurrying outside the barn to see what the matter was. He was looking off toward the horizon, their truck at his back and angled down the driveway next to the house.

Krystal was holding onto her husband as they burst from the cellar and into the sunlight with everyone else right on their heels. Charles didn't acknowledge the presence of the other people, merely pointing into the distance. They could see a dark writhing mass had begun to appear and was heading towards them.

Charles turned to look at Kira and Kate, "It's time to go, make sure we have everything and then let's go!" He turned to stare at the people gathering outside the house and thought back to what he had read the night before. "Take these, they won't do much damage, but they might still save your lives." All the guns and ammo he had collected at the store appeared on the ground in front of him, stuffed inside several bulging duffel bags.

Kory grabbed a large rifle with a scope and placed an entire metal ammo can in his inventory. He noticed Charles raise an eyebrow and explained as he came to stand next to him. "I can't use magic like you, and I don't have the strength to wield a hammer, not like my daughter. This rifle may not do much damage, but for now, at least it is all I can manage."

Charles looked the older man over before asking him a question that had been bugging him since they first met. "What is it you used to do? You seem to be intelligent, but you have the calluses of a working man. Judging by the way you handle that rifle, you seem to be familiar with them as well."

Kory shrugged his shoulders and brought the rifle to his shoulder, using the scope to look at the horizon. "Not sure what to tell you. I'm just a normal guy who takes care of his family." He lowered the rifle to his hip and looked over to his wife. "I want you and Kate inside the cab with Kira, Charles, and I will take care of the monsters that chase after us."

Krystal was already pushing Kate into the small cab and didn't reply. On the other side of the truck, Tara reached for Kira's arm, causing her to flinch away and a hostile gleam to enter her eyes.

"Sorry, I didn't mean to scare you," Tara said as she raised her hands and backed up a step.

"You didn't scare me; I just don't like to be touched," Kira explained harshly.

"I thought she was getting better," Kory whispered softly to himself as he witnessed their exchange with sad eyes.

"I wanted to ask if we can follow you for the time being? Safety in numbers and all that?" Tara asked the angry younger woman, who in turn looked to Charles.

"I don't care if they follow us in their truck if they can keep up that is. We are heading for Pennsylvania where my sister is at the moment and will decide where to go after that." Charles explained as he climbed into the back of the truck. Kira looked at him strangely but didn't say anything as she slid behind the steering wheel and next to her sister.

Tara whistled sharply to get everyone's attention. "Listen up, everyone needs to get into the back of the transport truck immediately. We have permission to follow along with them, but if we fall behind that's it! Now move it."

As one the entire group ran towards the barn and the loud rumbling truck within.

"With the racket, their truck is making, every monster from here to your sister is going to be on our trail," Kory remarked as he placed the ammo can on the floor of the truck bed and began inspecting the ammo.

"I know, it'll be perfect," Charles replied with a malicious grin, as a thought on how to help them become stronger edged its way into his mind.

Kory shuddered slightly at that and focused on loading the rifle in his hands while wondering what the man his daughter had dragged into their lives had in mind.

Alli chose that moment to appear in the shadow of the truck, her tongue lolling out of her mouth with exhaustion. With what seemed to be the last of her energy she climbed into the back of the truck and collapsed, leaving little room for the men to move around in.

"Monsters everywhere," She told Charles tiredly. "I couldn't see much, there is just too many of them and walking through the shadows is more tiring than just running."

"It's alright, you did your best. Get some rest while you can. I'll make sure you're safe." Charles told the large silver dog. He scratched her behind her pointed ears as she closed her eyes and fell asleep within seconds.

The transport truck slowly backed out of the barn, the back packed full of people.

Inside the cab of their truck, Kira shifted the transmission into gear and drove them down the long dirt driveway. Detritus from the storm lay everywhere preventing them from getting too much speed until they reached the highway. Meanwhile, the oncoming horde of monsters was drawing ever closer.

Chapter 4

Kory cringed as the transport truck's engine roared, its ruined muffler enhancing the sound instead of muffling it in any way. He propped the rifle against his knees and leaned into Alli's warm fluffy side.

"That truck is making enough noise to draw even the deafest of monsters our way." He looked over to the grinning Charles. "So, why does it seem like that makes you happy?"

Charles let a firebolt form just above his hand, controlling the flow of mana to make sure it didn't go anywhere. "I'm excited because they can't reach us, so we are safe as long as we are moving." His grin widened. "In other words, we can attack them all we want without worrying for our lives. We're kiting them for easy experience."

"Kiting?" Kory asked curiously at the unfamiliar term even as he nodded in understanding.

"It's a gaming term used in MMO's. It more or less means to grab the attention of the monsters and then lead them on a chase, while your party members attack and whittle down their numbers," Charles explained as he let the firebolt disappear and crawled from the back of the truck bed to just behind the cabin. He rapped on the clear back window with his knuckles to get Kira's attention and then leaned over the edge of the truck to speak to her.

Kira rolled down the driver's side window while keeping her eyes on the road. "What's wrong?"

"Slow down some, I want to have the monsters close enough for me to attack them, but not close enough for them to attack us." He yelled into the cab, the rushing wind threatening to overpower his voice.

"What about Tara?" Kira asked, leaning as close to him as she dared while driving.

"I'm going to try to get her to drive in front of us for a while." Charles pulled away from the window and carefully stepped over Alli's exhausted body to the other side of the truck. Inside the cab, Kira pulled her foot back from the accelerator, letting the truck slow.

Charles waved his arms at the transport truck and Tara pulled alongside them as the stretch of highway cleared for the moment. Unfortunately, the growl of her truck was just too loud for her to hear anything he was saying. Holding up his hands in a stop motion he banged on the side of the truck and did the same motion to Kira.

As soon as the two trucks had stopped, he leaped from the back and ran over to Tara. "Take the lead for the next bit, Kory and I are going to be killing the monsters that chase after us, so keep the speed down as well. We're heading to Pennsylvania, so just keep heading in that direction." He told her as soon she had opened the door for him.

Tara looked uncertain but nodded regardless, "How fast are you thinking?"

Charles stopped to think, "Let's say between 40 and 50 for now. I've seen some of them move faster than that, but not many."

Tara's eyes widened at his casual declaration of the speed the monsters chasing them possessed. It was with wide panicky eyes that she slammed her door shut and pushed her gas pedal to the floor. The transport truck screamed at deafening levels as it started forward, its age alone preventing it from accelerating quickly and leaving them in the dust.

Shaking his head to dispel the ringing in his ears, Charles climbed into the back of the truck with Alli and Kory and smacked the closed tailgate once with his hand. The truck leaped forward with a less deafening growl of its own.

Charles felt his heart begin to beat faster as the monsters chasing them began to appear. Their short stop had let them get close enough to see even without his enhanced vision. Far off to the side, back the way they had come he could see more monsters converging on Tara's house and barn before it too slipped from view. It was a good thing that she had had that truck there waiting for them, otherwise, they would all be in the midst of dying and fighting for their lives right then.

Trolls, orcs and more were chasing after them, with the smaller races such as the goblins hanging onto the backs of the larger and faster monsters. Charles sent a surge of magic to his eyes as he let them focus on the new monsters. His analysis ability activated while the magic in his eyes allowed him to see everything clearly even at the extreme distance that currently separated them.

Gnoll Lv. 10

Appeared above the slavering head of the hyena faced monster that was running on all fours. Next to it was a large goblin-like monster that had light green skin shot through with deep angry-red streaks running all along its visible body.

Hobgoblin Lv. 12

Charles let the magic fade from his eyes after he had gotten the information he wanted. He wasn't sure if these new monsters were part of the ongoing changes the message had mentioned or if they had been here all along and they were just now running into them. Either way, it was obvious that there were more species of monsters out there that they had yet to see.

Next, to him, Kory sighted down the scope on the rifle and grumbled, "This old truck shakes too much, I'll never be able to hit anything accurately."

Charles was tempted to remind him that the rifle wasn't going to hurt them much anyway but decided that he needed to learn the lesson on his own. It was like they said, seeing was believing and until he saw with his own eyes how useless guns were, he wouldn't fully believe it.

There was one last thing that he needed to do before he started firing on the monsters chasing them. With a thought he brought up the information on the current members of his party. Listed at the top was Alli, then Kira and the rest of her family were listed below her. Exactly as it was supposed to be. By making sure that they were still in the party, he was ensuring that they would all be getting experience from what he and Kory were about to do. It wouldn't be the full amount, but it would be something. He knew from his time with Alli that he still received experience even when she was off hunting alone, which was most of the time.

These people were part of his group and they were helping him to get to his sister, he in return would help them to stay alive even after they parted ways. And the best way to do that was to raise their level, making them stronger and more resilient against attacks. They were stuck together for the foreseeable future, in any case, thanks to Kate wanting to learn magic.

Glancing down at his hands, Charles thought of how he wanted to attack them. He knew he needed to use his regular magic more. He couldn't depend on the magic in the glove to always save him. One gift from the gods had already been taken back by them, there was no reason to think that they wouldn't do it again.

He would be using his glove until that time. He needed to balance the two together. The more he used his magic without the glove, the more it grew. He knew this from his ability to heal growing as a result. He didn't want to neglect using the glove either though. It was a powerful tool and it would be a waste to ignore it, regardless of the downsides that came with it.

His left leg twitched at that thought, and he imagined that he could feel the rune that had been carved in his leg-pulling at his skin. It was a ridiculous thought that he forcefully ignored. Whatever the glove had done to him, the rune engraving was seamless with his own skin. It felt and looked different, but it reacted just like the rest of his thigh and leg.

Alli's coat of silvery hair that had darkened slightly when she had chosen her class, ruffled and moved as they sped down the highway. Charles leaned against her flank as he thought through what they were about to do. He was aware that he was doing something that was unlike him, but if the last few days had taught him anything, it was that he needed to be prepared. The experience and level-ups did him little good currently, but he was no longer alone, he had Alli, and Kira and her family. He needed to be thinking of making the people around him stronger as well, and this was the first step in the right direction.

Alli shifted in her sleep, throwing Kory against the wall and squishing him for a second before she breathed out and settled back into position. Kory grunted and relaxed against her side as well, following Charles's example.

"Relax while you can, it'll take a little while for them to get into range yet," Charles told him, keeping his eyes on the distant mob chasing them. The constant loud noise of the transport truck holding their attention and refusing to let it go.

Twisting his head, he could see Kate talking to her mother and sister with expressive hand movements. Seeing that reminded him of the request she had made of him to help her learn magic. Turning to look back at her father, he could see the concern and love the man held for his family and a sudden pang of loneliness went through his heart.

His parents had been distant, he had been an odd child growing up. The little things that everyone else seemed to understand regarding society and how they were supposed to act escaped him. He had caused them endless amounts of trouble and he could only assume that they had felt relief when he left home for college. His sister was different, she had understood him. She didn't have the same difficulties that he did with society and people in general, but she never turned away from him. It was because of her that he had done so well in college and beyond.

It was a rare week where they did not talk at least once; he had gradually learned to function like everyone else under her tutelage. Unfortunately, the damage had already been done in other ways, and he had never repaired the relationship with his parents. And now it was too late. One of the things his sister had impressed upon him was the value of introspection, by understanding his own emotions he was better able to understand others. It wasn't perfect or anywhere close, but it had made it easier for him to put himself in another person's shoes and understand them in some small way. He let himself wallow in his emotions for a few minutes. Taking the time to sort through and understand his emotions and regrets. He did not want Kira's family to experience regrets like this.

"Kate wants to learn to use magic, I'm sure you know what that will mean concerning her life in this new world," Charles finally managed to say once he had gotten himself under control.

Kory swallowed and nodded. "She's choosing to fight for a future where she can keep the people she cares for safe," His eyes were sad as he spoke. "She wants to take care of her older sister. Kate has always been there for Kira and she wants to continue to be the rock her sister can depend on. It makes me worried about what will happen if she ever grows to resent Kira for needing her like she does."

Charles looked into the cab and saw how closely Kate clung to her older sister while listening attentively to whatever she was saying. "I don't think you have to worry about that, just from me watching them it seems like they are as close as can be. Kate seems to be proud of Kira and cares for her too much to ever hurt her."

Kory followed his gaze, a smile filled with the love he had for his family blossoming on his face. "I know, it's one of those pointless fears that I just can't get rid of and as a result just always hangs there in the background. The three women in that cab are my entire world, and I don't know what I would do with myself if anything were to ever happen to them. I already experienced it once with Kira and it nearly destroyed Krystal and me." His smile shifted to one of sadness as he looked away from his family.

Charles kept his eyes on the line of monsters behind them and gave the man some space. He felt a flicker of uncertainty spear through his chest as, for the first time, he could see the entirety of the group chasing them. There was just too many of them, it was a veritable army of monsters.

When he had first come up with this now stupid idea, he had been thinking it would only be a hundred or so monsters. That was still a lot, but as long as they stayed on the road and out of reach it would have been doable with minor difficulties. They were not facing such a paltry number as that, however, unfortunately.

Charles quickly counted out a group of twenty monsters and created a mental segment of size based around them. Using that as the average, he began placing segment after segment struggling to keep them in order. It was no use; he had counted over fifteen hundred monsters before he had given up. A number that was just too high for them at this time. Maybe at a later time when he was more knowledgeable about magic and spells it would be viable. Currently, though, they would be overrun by the sheer numbers.

"There's too many of them," He told Kory as he got to his feet and went to the back of the cab. Knocking on the pane of glass at the back he motioned for Kira to roll down her window.

"What is it?" She called out, keeping her eyes on the road.

Charles leaned as far forward as he dared and yelled back. "Speed up and get us out of here, there are more than a thousand monsters behind us! We can't handle those numbers, take the lead from Tara and go as fast as possible."

Kira jerked the wheel slightly at the ridiculously high number, causing Charles to fall back into the truck bed. He held onto Alli as the truck accelerated, rapidly gaining on the larger transport truck in front of them.

Sitting up, Charles watched the pavement speeding by beneath them and the two-lane highway that was for the moment clear of all obstructions. Kira kept her foot to the floor, forcing the truck to accelerate and then pass the other truck. Tara looked at them with wide eyes as they passed, her muffler screaming and her own truck beginning to pick up speed behind them.

The sound of a loud roar somewhere ahead of them had Charles wincing at the pain that was to come as he began to channel energy into his glove. Behind them the monsters suddenly picked up speed, their mouths open and their tongues flapping in the wind as they began to desperately sprint.

Alli stirred from her sleep and lifted her head, her ears twitching every which way. "There are more of them to our sides," She finally told him. "It seems that they are going to try to surround us. I'm sorry Charles, there is nothing I can do to help. Using my ability earlier drained me more than I thought." Her mouth opened wide, and a yawn escaped from her muzzle.

Charles kept pushing more energy into his glove as he rested an arm on her head and scratched just behind her ears. "It's alright Alli, as long as Kira doesn't stop, we'll be just fine. As for the other thing, when you chose your class, it unlocked all of your class's abilities so that you could learn them. I'm actually surprised you can walk through shadows already. That is usually a higher-class ability in games."

Alli looked away from him, her head tilting towards the ground in embarrassment. "It seemed like the most useful ability to learn at the time, so it's the one I chose to learn first." Her voice was quiet in his head.

Another yawn escaped her mouth, as her voice became even softer as sleep overcame her once more. "It took everything I had just to learn it, might have been too soon after all." Her head slumped down onto her large paws, her eyes closed tight and her ears flat against her head.

Kory had been watching their exchange, unable to hear Alli's side of the conversation but able to guess to a certain degree what they had been discussing. "Her ability more tiring than she thought it would be?" He asked before putting the rifle away into his inventory along with the ammo can at his feet.

A banging on the side of the truck distracted him from answering for the moment. Both men turned around and saw Kira banging on the outside of her door with the palm of her hand, next to her Kate was twisted around looking at them. "The trees are ending!" Kira called back to them after her sister had whispered something to her.

Charles could see the trees in front of them beginning to rustle and sway as though a large number of monsters were rushing through them. "Don't stop, no matter what!" He yelled, before clambering to his feet and spreading his legs wide over Alli. Straddling her sleeping form in a bid to stay steady.

Visible sparks of electricity had begun to form on his hand, jumping from one finger to the next. He had continued to push as much mana into the glove as he could, taking the energy from his body and the air itself as he over-charged the prepared spell to dangerous levels.

The truck swerved as an orc with two knife-wielding goblins riding its back burst from the trees ahead of them and onto the road. Kira steered the truck with deft hands around the monster, while behind them Tara grinned and gripped her steering wheel even tighter. She smashed into the orc at full speed; her truck not even slowing as it rolled over the ugly monster and its companions. The transport truck bounced and shuddered as its tires settled back onto the ground.

On the road behind it, the orc pushed itself to its knees, looking at the smear of blood that denoted where it had come from. The goblins that had been hanging onto its back had popped like large bloody pimples when the truck had hit it. The weaker monsters dying instantly from the impact, while the stronger and relatively larger orc had received only minor damage.

Suddenly the woods were alive with monsters rushing the road in an effort to stop the fleeing humans. Charles looked back at the damaged orc and saw a large bear-like monster with an enormous metal sword clutched over its head. The sword swung down decapitating the orc instantly as the bear-like monster snarled at Charles, not even bothering to look at what it had just done.

A line of monsters swarmed the road obstructing his vision of the large sword-wielding bear for the moment. Charles felt time forcefully slow down as a gap appeared for a split second, and the large monster he had seen came briefly back into focus. His analysis ability activated without prompting from him, displaying information that he had never seen before.

?? Bugbear Lv. 25

Chosen Champion of an opposing god.

Then they were through, the line of monsters closing the gap behind them. Both trucks and their occupants had only just barely made it through in time. The trees that had been hiding the monsters so effectively ending abruptly, a clear sign of where humans had cut into them in the past.

The crack of guns firing repeatedly came from the other truck, as the people shook off their stupor and attacked. Bullets filled the air, and the distant tinkling of empty brass falling to the metal floor of the truck could almost be heard. Kory lifted his rifle as well and fired off several quick shots before stopping at the same time as everyone in the transport truck. They had witnessed for themselves that the bullets were doing no damage; the impacts were being shrugged off instantly.

The bugbear tilted his head towards the sky and roared in anger at having been denied his prey.

At the sound of the roar, Charles shook himself free from the stupor the information displayed had put him in and raised his hand. The time had come to try out the area attack spell he had learned before entering Kansas City. Lightning Storm it had been called with the description calling it a wide range attack spell. There would never be a better chance to try it out than he had now, the road behind them filled with monsters as the trees continued to empty their hidden threats.

He sent one last burst of mana from his own body into the glove and released the spell, aiming for a spot above the monster's heads. Charles could only watch stunned and frozen as the spell he had deliberately over-charged just for this moment came into being. This spell was different from his other spells as it did not originate from him. When he attacked with fire or lightning, it would leap from his hands. That was not the case with this spell, this spell merely took the energy from him and then formed at the designated location.

Concentric circles filled with runes he had never seen before appeared in the sky a split-second before being ripped asunder by the thickest bolt of lightning he had ever seen before. The bolt hung in the air above the road and the trees, splitting into flickering branches of electricity and then splitting again. In the time it took to process what had happened the spell had finished, and the bolt of lightning that had split and formed countless branches fell to the ground.

Everything went white as the monsters screamed and the trees went up in flames. Charles collapsed in the truck bed on top of Alli with a scream of his own. The pain he knew was coming had centered itself on his right arm and leg. A new rune was being carved into his leg, but something else was wrong with his arm.

Chapter 5

C harles was dimly aware of people talking to him and shaking his body. He had retreated into the depths of his own mind from the pain. He had known using an over-charged spell was not a good idea and using it on a new lightning spell was even worse.

He wasn't even entirely sure why he had done it. They had been safe; they had escaped. He could have probably released the energy he had been collecting without casting the spell. Seeing the words 'Champion' on a monster's info had shocked him and driven home the point that no one's life was their own anymore. They all belonged to the gods to do with as they pleased, and it apparently pleased them to make their lives' hell.

Notifications began to appear in front of his eyes, but he was still too deep into his own mind to notice them. The pain kept his thoughts from forming clearly, a heavy fog slowing everything to a crawl even in the depths of his mind.

Alli was the one responsible for helping him come back to reality. Her tongue was licking his face as she whined softly above him. Her mismatched eyes were wide with worry as she watched over the man who had saved her life and given her a chance to become something more.

Kory had a grim set to his mouth as he watched the road behind them. Kira hadn't slowed down after what Charles had done and now only an orange glow and smoke could be seen on the horizon marking where they had come. A fire had raged through the trees from the repeated strikes of lightning. The heat each strike generated drying out the trees instantly and turning them into kindling.

A short scream burst from Charles' throat as he came back to himself, his dried-out eyes blinking furiously.

"Charles? Charles, are you alright?" Alli asked him, desperately nudging him with her wet nose.

"Are we clear?" He asked raspily, his throat sore and the veins slowing receding back from the surface as his blood pressure went back to normal. His eyes lost focus as the notifications refused to be ignored anymore.

Congratulations, you have leveled up. You are now level 13; you have gained 5 status points for distribution.

Congratulations, you have leveled up. You are now level 14; you have gained 5 status points for distribution.

Just how many enemies had his lightning taken out for him to jump two levels? He scrolled through the rest of the messages and stopped counting after a hundred, noticing that more messages were still coming in as the fire killed indiscriminately. There was one message that was missing, however, there was nothing pertaining to Alli.

"You didn't level up?" He asked before pulling out a water bottle and drinking it dry in seconds. His leg twitched spastically, refusing to obey his commands as he sat up with a groan and a wince.

She laid her head against his chest and relaxed, seeing that he was mostly alright. "No, I looked at my status and noticed that the experience needed for my next level is equal to everything I had received to get to level 15."

Another groan escaped his mouth at that news, which meant that level 15 was meant to be the cut-off point. It was the level that the lowest villager would top out at in a game. In other words, everyone was still too weak. And it made him realize just how much stronger the champion he had seen on the road was. It had been level 25, while he had only been 12. There was no way he had killed it, at best all he had done was make it mad.

His entire body felt drained and his brain felt sluggish and his thoughts slow, casting a spell that he had over-charged to such a degree had left him empty. Shaking his head, he looked down to the flask of potion on his hip, weighing the benefits of using it against the changes that he believed it caused.

Kory, who had been quiet finally spoke up. "My level just jumped from 1 to 7, and I didn't even do anything. Just how many monsters did you kill in that attack?"

"A lot, and not enough," He answered simply, too tired to keep his eyes open any longer but unable to fall asleep due to the curse the gods had put on him. The problem was no matter how many he had killed with either his attack or the forest fire he had inadvertently started, was but a drop in the bucket. He had seen and counted over fifteen-hundred monsters behind them. The majority of them would have been too far away from both the fire and his attack.

He waited for his mana to come back slightly. The mana filling and pushing away the drained feeling he had. His mind slowly cleared, and he began to take stock of himself. His right leg still burned a little, but the spastic twitches had almost vanished. The problem was his arm felt different; it felt like something was missing.

Charles went back to the notifications to see what they said and stumbled on the answer buried amongst the experience gained messages.

Due to severe overcharging of a spell, the mana channels in your arm have been burned out. Traditional healing spells cannot fix this, only time has the possibility of mitigating the damage you have inflicted upon yourself.

Thanks to that particular notification he was instantly able to tell what was different in his arm, it felt distant almost numb. Having the mana channels burned away left the arm feeling like it belonged to someone else. Charles cursed the gods in his head. If, he had the proper stats for his level, then this probably wouldn't have happened. His body and his mana channels were unable to show the effects of his levels until he fell asleep. He was a level 14 stuck in the body of someone without levels.

With a sigh and fumbling fingers, he took the potion from his hip and unscrewed the lid. Alli was looking at him wordlessly as he prepared to drink the potion. He had expressed his concerns about it with her before, and while she didn't necessarily feel the same way, she was still concerned for him. It was undeniable that the potion changed the drinker, she just didn't think it was a bad thing.

The cap to the flask fell to the side, a leather thong attached to the lid preventing it from being lost. Charles breathed in deep, preparing for the burning pain that seemed to always come with drinking the potion. A wave of fire spread through his veins, burning away any impurities it found and changing everything in subtle unseen ways. Next came the flow of ice that soothed and calmed the ravaged nerves inside his body, healing everything as it passed by.

The feeling came back into his arm, as the damaged mana channels restored themselves slightly stronger than before. The last of the pain in his leg disappeared, reminding him that he needed to look at the new rune later. He had never seen the previous one until it had been completed, it would be interesting to see how it changed this time.

His fingers were steady as he replaced the cap on the top of the potion a while later, taking note of the countdown showing on the lid. He could only hope and pray that they wouldn't find themselves in a dire enough situation where they needed it before then.

Alli was looking at him closely, her head tilted to the side. She breathed in deep and spoke while looking him in the eye. "You smell different now, you smell slightly less human than before and more... something else. I do not think you should let any of the others drink the potion unless it is absolutely necessary. It's not a bad smell, it's just different than before." The voice in his head sounded puzzled as she tried to describe the change she smelled.

Alli's words only served to make him more leery of the potion as he placed it back on his hip and looked away from her. She may not have thought the changes smelled bad, but they were still changes that he might not want and had been done without his permission.

Pushing her head gently to the side, Charles looked at Kory who was watching him impatiently. "We need to stop for a moment. I should begin Kate's training as soon as possible."

Kate's father grunted and looked away before banging on the side of the truck with the palm of his hand. He motioned for them to stop and then jumped from the back as it slowed and stopped. The transport truck's brakes squealed as it followed their example and slid to a stop behind them.

The passenger door of the truck opened, and Krystal whispered into her husband's ear holding him in place.

"She worries that you are pushing yourself too hard to keep everyone safe at the expense of your own body," Alli told him, her ears angled toward the married couple even as her head remained low.

Kory shrugged and didn't reply to her, instead focusing on his youngest daughter. "Time for your training to begin, it's windy back there so make sure you're warm."

Kate slid across the cracked and worn leather of the bench seat with a wide grin and dancing eyes. Her father gripped her tightly in a hug and then released her, sliding onto the bench to take the place she had vacated.

Kate climbed into the back of the truck; her excitement palpable. She quickly scratched Alli behind the ears, causing her head to shift slightly as she tried to guide the girls' fingers into just the right spot.

Charles pushed back until his back was against the metal and glass of the cab opening a spot for her to sit in front of him. Kira waited for her younger sister to be seated in front of Charles, Alli supporting her back with her own before the truck started moving again.

Kate was almost vibrating with excitement as Charles extended his gloved hand to her. Kate took his hand in hers and lightly pressed on the same mark as before with her free hand at his nod. She inhaled sharply as the same translucent blue barrier from before sprang into being surrounding them. Charles took a moment to study how the mana looked in his right arm versus his left, noticing how the motes of lights that spread through his right arm were slightly smaller and more numerous.

Kate's eyes had flickered shut with the formation of the barrier, and her breathing had quickened as her eyes moved rapidly behind her closed lids. Deciding to trust his instincts, Charles closed his own eyes and dived into his meditations. The formation of his meditations linked his mind to hers and allowed him to take control and guide her thoughts.

Together they delved into the deepest parts of her body and mind, chasing the origin of the mana in her body. Outside their bodies, neither noticed as the temperature in the back of the truck plummeted and little wisps of mist blew out from their faces with each exhaled breath.

They chased the mana and finally found a core that exuded cold hovering over a small puddle of clear water. Charles slowly pulled them back through her body and mind before breaking the connection as gently as possible.

The sun hung high in the sky when he opened his eyes, barely noticing the chill that lingered in the air before it too vanished. He had to admit he was slightly confused; he had been thinking that people normally only had one element to work with. He being the sole exception, but Kate clearly had access to ice as well as a small amount of water.

He would have to take a look at himself later during his meditations, the exercise he had just done with her was not one he had ever done before. He had been following his instincts, but maybe there was something more behind it as well. The glove had been the one to guide his training early on, and they were connected through the glove for these sessions. It wasn't unreasonable to believe that it was still guiding him, and possibly her.

The truck slowed as Kira steered it onto an off-ramp, stopping in front of an old rest area. The brick building was well-taken care of despite its obvious age, and the abandoned cars and semi's in the parking lot would give them some gas and supplies.

"Well, we found your element at least, so now we know what direction your spells will take," Charles told the teenage girl as the truck came to a stop and was turned off.

Guns were thrown into a large duffel bag and then tossed over the side of the transport truck as their disgusted users got rid of the useless weapons. Not a single person in that truck had been able to do any damage to the monsters with their guns. Wearily each of the people in the back walked over and disappeared into the bathrooms, their shoulders slumped and their heads hanging low. Each looked close to giving up, the belief that they at least had the ability to defend themselves from monsters being taken away was the last straw.

One of the men came out of the male side with his arms full of toilet paper that he then passed to Tara. Taking the lead, she led a group of women away from the building and into the woods, a shovel grasped in her free hand.

"Follow them, and make sure there is nothing out there," Charles told Alli, patting her lightly on her flank. Her back curved as she stretched, her front legs straight and paws spread. She rubbed against his hand, shook herself and then leaped from the truck loping quickly after the group of women.

Charles picked up the duffels full of guns and ammo and stored them in his inventory. The guns may have been useless against monsters, but that wasn't the case for humans. He wasn't about to leave them with that group, not after seeing the look some of them had been giving him.

Kate and her mother trailed after the rest of the women as Kira moved over to the cars to begin the siphoning process. Charles withdrew the large drum of gasoline that they had been using along with the hand pump and began the slow process of filling both trucks with gas. Kory would take red canisters of gas from his daughter as she filled them and dump them into the barrel. Between the three of them, they were able to fill both trucks will gasoline and refill the gasoline drum before everyone was done using the woods or restrooms.

Charles stored everything back into his inventory and pulled up the quest for his sister, hoping that it had changed. Pennsylvania was a large state to go searching though for just one person, it was his hope that once they entered the state, it would give him another destination to go by. Closing the unchanged message; he started in surprise as Krystal rested her hand on his arm.

"I'll ride in the back with Alli and my husband. Why don't you and Kate ride in the cab with Kira? Maybe keep her company as you do whatever it is you were doing with Kate earlier." Her eyes were warm as she spoke to him, patting him twice on the shoulder she walked away without waiting for a response and joined her husband at the back of the truck.

He couldn't help but grin as she walked away. What she was trying to accomplish was obvious. She was trying to set him up with Kira. She seemed to believe that the two of them were closer than they actually were.

She had latched onto the perceived hope that her daughter had found someone. Seeing the mother looking out for her daughter sent a pang of envy through his chest that he quickly squashed.

Kate was looking at him curiously as he opened the door for her, no doubt she had heard what her mother said. "Your parents want to ride in the back, we'll keep Kira company while we continue your training." He explained while looking away from her inquisitive eyes.

Tara ran over to Kira and talked to her for several moments, her hands waving in the air as she did so. Kira took a step back holding her hands in front of her to keep the older woman at bay before turning and stomping away.

"Get in the truck, we're leaving!" She growled at him before throwing her door open and climbing into the truck cab.

Kate squeaked in shock and took her place in the middle of the bench. Charles turned to the woods and whistled loudly. "Coming," Alli yelled back to him, her voice in his head telling him that she had gone deeper into the woods than everyone else. He wasn't sure the distances involved with her telepathy ability, but he knew that he could hear her if she was within half a mile of his location. Anything farther than that and the sound of her voice would grow dimmer and quieter rapidly.

"Alli will be back in a moment," Charles told Kira as he sat next to her younger sister and closed the door. "Now why don't you tell me what's wrong? What did Tara say that made you so mad?"

Kate was looking at her sister closely, evidently keen on knowing the answer to that question as well.

Kira's hands gripped the steering wheel tightly, her knuckles popping from the pressure and her tanned skin going white. "She was talking about you! The ungrateful bi-" She looked over at her sister and swallowed the rest. "She seems to think that you are dangerous! You just saved their lives and there she was trying to convince me that we should go with them instead. Her little group of idiotic rejects have convinced her that it is more dangerous to stay with you than go it on their own!" She was quivering with rage by the time she had finished.

"That's just stupid," Kate said indignantly. "He's the only reason any of us are still alive, besides they all just threw their weapons away. How are they going to defend themselves now?"

Charles sighed and shrugged as Alli ran into view, the shadows in the woods seeming to cling to her for a moment longer than they should have. "They aren't, they're just going to have to pray that they don't run into any more monsters." A flare of anger highlighted his words at the end, he had been counting on them helping him establish the town. It was better to learn what kind of people they were beforehand, though.

Chapter 6

T he truck roared to life as Alli settled down in back, snuggling up to the two people with her. The tires chirped as they fought for traction on the dirty pavement. Kira cranked the steering wheel sending the back end into a fishtail, her parents held in place by Alli.

Tara stood off to the side, with the same look of defeat as everyone else in her group. Her shoulders were slumped and the keys to her truck dangled limply from her fingers as she watched them leave.

"At least they have a full tank of gas to get them somewhere safe," Kate said before turning to face the front.

Kira snorted and gave a short bark of laughter. "Not that it'll do them much good with their starter acting up. You heard the way it was whirring earlier as it refused to catch, that starter is almost done. They'll be lucky to get that monster of a truck started another couple of times."

"Oh," Kate said softly turning around to look behind them as the old rest area vanished behind a corner and some trees.

"Do you want to continue now or wait?" Charles asked her, turning to face the younger girl in a bid to distract her.

Her lips tugged up a little at the sides as she answered sadly, "We may as well continue now. I can see what you are doing, but I can't feel anything just yet."

Charles held out his hand to her before replying, "It may take a day or two before you can actually feel the mana flowing through your body. It'll take even longer before you can touch it and then longer again to be able to hold it in some way. Don't forget I've never taught someone any of this either, it could be easier or harder depending on the person." He paused as a thought entered his mind, "Actually you should have leveled-up a few times from the fight earlier, go ahead and put most of your status points into intelligence. You won't feel the effects until after you go to sleep, but the increase may help you understand everything easier afterward."

Kate's eyes lost focus as she quickly did as he said, "What's the average status for humans?" She asked after she had finished.

Charles laughed, waving away her hurt expression at his response. "Sorry, I promise I'm not laughing at you. I asked Kira the same question when we first met and she never answered me. I've been wondering the same thing ever since."

Kate turned to look at her sister who growled lightly in annoyance, "I can't say for sure, but I think the high-end is around 25 or 30 while everything else runs the gamut below that. Take my strength, for instance, before I put any points in it, it was at 26 already. Whereas my intelligence was 17, and my constitution was 30." She rubbed her scarred back against the cracked leather backing of the seat as she mentioned her high constitution numbers.

"What about empathy?" Kate asked quietly, her hand twitching before she reached out and gently rubbed her sister's back.

"I don't have that one in my list," Kira answered, giving her a small smile.

Charles cleared his throat. "I can actually answer that one to a certain extent. I have one for magic in my list. When I received that status, I was informed that certain stats can be added depending on the person, their abilities, as well as the class they choose. I would guess that empathy is an additional stat that was given to you and that you will receive the magic stat when we succeed in getting you to feel the mana in your body."

Kate looked thoughtful as she closed the screens that only she could see and focused on Charles. "Alright then, let's get started. I would like to be able to allocate my status points properly and I can't do that yet without the proper item in my list." Her hand continued to rub and gently scratch her sisters' back as she spoke.

Kira let go of the steering wheel with one hand and patted her younger sisters' leg. "I'm alright now, concentrate on learning what you can. I'm just going to keep driving."

Kate hesitated before nodding and turned to look at Charles as he stretched out his gloved hand to her once more. Her hand was steady as she reached out and touched the rune that controlled their meditations.

The barrier that came into being surrounding the two of them was a light pale blue, reminding her of the color of her element. Charles made the connection at the same time she did, that the color of the barrier mimicked her element. His final thought before closing his eyes was that he really needed to explore what it would show him about his own elements and abilities.

Diving once more into their joint meditation, he could feel something nudging gently at his mind, steering him on what to do next. Following the nudges and the promptings, he steered Kate back into the depths of her body, stopping only when they could see her elemental core. He reached out and touched the streams of thin string-like mana, shuddering as a wave of cold swept through his mind.

Kate followed his example and dipped a portion of her mind into the icy core. A light blue glow began to slowly infuse her being, starting with the part that was touching the core. The glow had only covered the smallest portion of her being when Kate pulled her hand away from his glove, forcibly breaking their connection.

The thin barrier surrounding them popped and Kate heaved in panicked gasps of air. "I couldn't handle any more than that." She hurried to explain to Charles, her eyes wide and bloodshot as she fought to get her breathing under control. "I felt the mana as it entered my being and began to join with me, it was overwhelming. I'll need to take it slow and let it join with me a bit at a time. I think I'll be able to properly feel the mana in my body when it is done."

Kira wrapped her sister in a one-arm hug, comforting her as her breathing slowed and she dropped off into an exhausted sleep.

Charles frowned as he watched them, his thoughts being pulled in different directions. Part of it on the notification that had appeared in front of his eyes, and part of it on what he was having Kate do. "I don't understand," He whispered to himself distractedly.

"What don't you understand?" Kira asked softly so as not to wake Kate.

Charles looked up, not realizing she had heard him. "The process she is going through to learn is completely different than what I went through."

"So, what's the problem? You already said that the glove was special, maybe what it is having her do is slightly more in line with the way someone would normally learn magic." She said keeping her eyes on the road.

"I think you're right. The glove is still adding its own element to the mix, making the process faster and easier to understand. That's not what I don't understand, however. I don't understand if I should or even need to do the same thing as I am having her do. I had her touch her elemental core, the core that will become the basis of her magic while I have never touched my own. I am left wondering if doing the same thing will help or hinder me." Charles was looking closely at the runes on the back of his glove as he spoke, hoping for a clue of some kind.

"Leave it for now," Kira began, her voice firm. "Right now, you have people to teach, if you do what she is doing who is to say it won't screw you up in some way. Wait until you've taught her and then maybe look at seeing and touching your own core."

Charles bit the inside of his cheek as he thought on her words. She wasn't wrong. What if touching his core sent him back to the beginning of learning how to use and control magic? He didn't really think that would be the case, but he couldn't risk it just yet. He had Kate to teach, a sister to find, a town to build somewhere, and more people to then teach. Maybe after all of that was over, he could look into the matter again.

"You're right," He agreed before turning to look out the window, effectively ending the conversation. In front of his eyes hung two notifications that he had yet to close.

> *Congratulations you have learned the spell 'Frost'. Frost is an ice spell that coats your enemies in a layer of icy frost slowing their movements. Frost can also be used to cool any beverage before drinking.*

> *Congratulations you have learned the spell 'Icy Lance'. Icy Lance is an ice spell that creates and hurls a lance made of ice in front of the caster. The thicker and denser the lance created the longer the range of the attack.*

The simple act of touching Kates core even briefly had taught him two new spells, in an element he hadn't even thought of meditating on up to that point. If he was truly meant to be the person who taught people how to use magic, then he would also be learning every single element at the same time.

He didn't necessarily have an issue with that; he was actually grateful to learn another way he could become stronger. The issue he did have, was how differently his magic and abilities worked than other people. He was too different, and he no longer believed that the glove was the sole reason. He was afraid or rather concerned about his future, about what people would think of him when they learned how different he was. Humans did not have a good history of accepting those that were different, he had already seen it to an extent with Tara and her people.

He could handle regular people avoiding him, but what if the people he truly cared for started to avoid him as well? Charles shook his head and turned away from the window, looking at Kira as he thought of a question that would take his mind off of the matter.

"Do you want to learn magic as well?"

Kira's eyes flicked over to him before returning to the road, her expression growing thoughtful. "I haven't given it much thought before. Would it even be worth it since my intelligence is so low?"

Charles shrugged, keeping his eyes on her. "I think it would be worth it, depending on what you learned. You may only have enough aptitude or magical ability to do a single attack but used in the right way it could save your life. Think instead if you were compatible with healing magic and were able to heal yourself or your sister in a time of need."

Her eyebrows furrowed as her fingers tapped on the steering wheel, "I would be willing to learn what my element is at the very least, depending on what it is, I may wish to learn."

"Tonight, before we all go to sleep, we'll take a few minutes and see what yours is then," Charles said quickly before she could change her mind.

Time seemed to pass quickly as Kira kept the truck speeding down the highway. When Kate awoke, she glared at a notification only she could see and muttered, "Need to sleep longer before the stats can take effect." Then she and Charles went back to meditating together. She would touch her core for as long as she could before ending the session and falling asleep for another thirty minutes or so. As a result, she made slow but steady progress that day, and Charles was able to understand how long it would take for a normal person to learn what he had in hours.

It was during a rest stop, giving everyone the chance to stretch and use the shrubbery that Kira walked away and laid down on the grass with a groan. "I need someone else to drive for the next while." She sat up and twisted, her back popping and cracking.

"I'll drive," Kory said as he came up from behind them and sat down next to his daughter.

A loud squeal of delight sounded from the back of the truck and Alli bounded into view, Kate holding tightly to her back. "I am going to explore for a few minutes," Alli told Charles, stopping next to him to rub her head affectionately on his chest.

"All right, just be careful and don't go too far." He gave her ears a quick scratch and then she was gone, Kate whooping in delight on her back.

"Will she be alright, riding her like that?" Krystal asked, stepping clear of the trees where she had been taking care of business.

"Alli isn't exactly the most comfortable ride, but it is safe to ride her," Charles informed them, remembering his own little journey on her back a few days before.

Kira frowned and looked away, her eyes growing distant. "Why are we going to Pennsylvania?" She asked suddenly.

"My quest says that is where she is, or at least was this morning." He told her while pulling up the quest information. The fact that it still read Pennsylvania had him more than a little worried. She had been making better time than him on her trip, and now she had been stuck in the same state for most of a day. Of course, that was assuming that he had even been her destination, maybe she had friends in Pennsylvania that he didn't know about.

"Where are we?" Krystal asked as a half-full bottle of water appeared in her hands.

"We're almost to St. Louis," Kira told her mother. "The number of cars and trucks on the road has been increasing as we get closer. I expect the highway will be packed as we get closer, forcing us to go off-road."

Kory stood up and looked towards the woods. "I'm going to go water a tree and then we can leave as soon as Alli and Kate get back."

"I'll ride in the back with Charles and Alli, Kate can stay in the cab with you two," Kira said without looking at anyone.

Charles shook his head at the excited look that flashed across the parent's faces before it was hidden away. He looked down at his hand and shivered before looking away, acting like he was looking for Alli. Having the mana channels in his arm burned out earlier had been frightening, painful, and made him more than a little scared of overcharging his magic again. The only reason he could still use his arm was because of the potion, the potion that he had decided was too dangerous to keep using.

It was true that he had done a lot of damage to the monsters that had been hunting them, but the price had almost been his arm. He needed to be more careful in the future, the world was still changing. It was likely that the truly powerful monsters had yet to even appear, and every time he did something stupid, he was risking his life along with everyone around him. What would he do next time they came across a similar situation? He needed to act smarter, not force more power through his weak body.

Kate had multi-colored leaves stuck in her wind-blown hair as Alli loped happily through the trees and stopped next to the truck. She had a grin spread across her face as she slid from Alli's back to the ground, her arms spread for stability.

"Let's go, everyone in the truck," Kory yelled, stepping into view from behind a tree.

Charles led the way as he climbed into the truck bed and put his back to the cab. Kate looked uncertain as to where she should sit before her mother motioned her into the cab next to her. Kira followed Charles into the back, sitting closer than he thought she would. The entire truck shifted as Alli climbed in with them, the suspension settling lower under her weight. Her head settled onto Charles lap as she watched Kira curiously.

"He's going to help me discover what my element is, and then I am going to decide whether or not I want to learn magic," Kira told Alli, seeing the way she was watching her.

"She doesn't like people touching her!" Alli reminded Charles forcefully.

"We need to be touching for this to work," Charles told Kira while watching her face carefully.

A shadow flickered deep in her eyes and vanished just as quickly as it had appeared, the slightest tremble in her hand as she brushed away a strand of hair the only clue that he had really seen it. "As long as I'm the one doing the touching, then it should be fine. I watched you with Kate. I only need to touch the runes on the glove, not you." She said in one long breath.

She's regressing, Charles thought as he looked at the pretty and slightly older woman. He had thought she had been warming up to him over the last few days but seeing her with Tara that morning and now this told him differently. He wanted to help her get past the damage that had been done to her so many years before, he just didn't know where to begin. He needed her to tell him, and she wasn't ready for that. Not yet, maybe not ever. She was too full of anger at the world and at herself. She had good reason to be angry and afraid. She was letting it control her, however, keeping her from moving on.

Charles extended his gloved hand to her while his free hand lightly scratched at the firm jowls' underneath Alli's jaw.

Kira ran her suddenly sweaty hands against her smudged and oil-stained tank top, before reaching for Charles's hand. He looked down as a beam of sunlight filtered through the trees and hit his hand just right to illuminate the runes on the back of the glove. It was the first time he had looked at them properly in the sunlight since that morning. Some of the runes had become darker, looking as though they had been put through the fire.

A notification popped into being, but before he could read it Kira's hesitant hand touched the meditation rune in the middle of the glove. Charles pushed thoughts of the darkened runes and the glove away for a later time as the thin barrier came into being automatically pushing his unread notification to the side.

Chapter 7

The barrier unfolded and twisted as it maneuvered, leaving Alli's head that was resting on Charles' lap outside the barrier. The barrier itself was a dark nature green like the middle of a forest, that exuded a sense of calm and serenity except where it was shot through with streaks of angry red. The streaks gave off a feeling of anger and resentment, vastly different from the cool and slightly detached feeling he had gotten from Kate's light blue barrier.

Charles watched the flow of mana in her body and located the place where it all met before spreading out once more. Letting the glove induced meditation guide him he dove into her being pulling her mind along behind him. Together they sped through the mana channels in her body, the way lit by motes of green and violent red mana.

Kira's elemental core, the part of her that gave her the possibility to use magic was on fire. Or at least part of it was. A vibrant green oak tree spread all around the room that contained her core, its branches were covered with thick leaves of the healthiest green he had ever seen. That was all on the right side.

The left side contained a fiery inferno that was actively trying to consume the rest of the tree.

With a shout, Kira broke the connection pulling her hand back to her mouth even as she scrambled to the side of the truck and hurled. "What was that? Why did one side feel so serene and peaceful, while the other side felt so violent and full of hate?" She finally gasped out, her hand wiping the last traces of her stomach contents from her mouth.

Charles handed her a bottle of water while he thought. This was only the second elemental core he had seen, but he'd had a thought when he first saw Kates about how the element was tied to a person's personality. For Kate, the feeling was that she kept herself aloof and distant; she was an icy person emotionally. He had dismissed the thought after seeing her interact with Kira, but now he found the thought coming back.

It was undeniable that Kira had issues with anger. She didn't like people touching her and was more than a little unstable. Was her core a reflection of that? Was the rage in her heart slowly eating away at the rest of her? More than that, how would she react if he was to tell her his suspicions?

"I think," He began, his mind scrambling for a way to explain his thoughts that didn't end in her pummeling him with her hammer.

"No, never mind I don't want to know, and forget about teaching me any magic." Kira hugged the side of the truck with her body, putting as much distance as she could between them.

Alli huffed and turned away from the woman, her head digging into Charles's stomach. "If all human females are as crazy as that one. Then I pity your chances of ever finding a suitable mate." There was a hint of longing in her voice that distracted Charles from what had just happened and had him focusing on the large dog in his lap.

"What about you? How are we going to find you a mate?" He whispered softly enough that only her sensitive ears heard him.

"I... I don't think we can," She replied sadly. "I'm too big and too smart, we'd have to find another dog like me first, and that's not even accounting for whether or not I would even like him." Her mismatched eye glistened wetly as she looked up at him before she closed her eyes. "That is the only thing I regret about meeting you and you saving my life. That I will never have the opportunity to have pups of my own."

Charles lifted her head and wrapped his arms around her, holding her tightly. He had never even considered what it was she might have wanted from life. He knew she was smart and more like a human in dog form, but it hadn't even occurred to him to ask her some of the most basic questions that he would have asked any other human.

He would have to fix that later after they found his sister and had some free time, he was going to have a serious talk with Alli. It was time to learn what she wanted from life, what her life used to be like and perhaps, more importantly, to learn just how much she had changed from that injured but already-intelligent dog he had found that first day.

"We'll talk about this again later; I promise you that." He whispered into her ear, "And I will do all I can to help you with whatever it is that you want."

Alli nodded and bumped her head against his chest. "I know you will."

The truck was only going 10 or 15 miles per hour as Kory drove on the cluttered highway. The roads had continued to become more clogged with broken down and abandoned vehicles the closer they got to St. Louis. Luckily the road they were on, skirted the city itself, instead of going through it like in Denver or Kansas City.

The truck trembled and bounced as they were forced to go off-road again to get around a pile-up that blocked the road. Charles had stopped counting after the fourth pile-up had forced them off the road. It was worth it to avoid the city, but his butt was no longer in agreement with the rest of him.

Off to the far right, buildings could be seen. There was a little smoke in the air, slowly drifting away on the wind. At their current distance though Charles could almost believe that the city had come through the apocalypse unscathed.

The tires echoed hollowly as the road transitioned to the bridge, leaving them in the air over the muddy river water. Luckily for them, and likely the bridge itself there had only been a couple of cars on it at the time they stopped working. Kory was able to steer them around those cars without a problem, crossing the bridge without difficulty.

The city they saw on the other side of the bridge was nothing like the buildings they had seen in the distance. It was a ruin, just like Denver had become. Factories along the river that had been hidden from view by the trees, were flattened heaps of rubble. Buildings everywhere had toppled into their neighbors, creating a devastating domino effect. The only saving grace was the lack of any major fires that had allowed the many people they could see moving in the distance to survive.

There was a distinct lack of monsters in the area that had Charles curious until he saw the water moving behind them. Tentacles stretched into the air, brushing the sides of the bridge before smacking back down into the water. Closer to the city another pair of tentacles extended from the river and smashed into the side of the building, crumbling it instantly.

The lack of monsters even on the far side of the city had Charles thinking that maybe the monsters were afraid of whatever was in the water. It was a thought to keep in mind for the future, for wherever he was tasked with building a town. Water was always a consideration, now he just had to consider what might be living in it and how the other monsters responded to it.

Some of the closer people looked up at the sound of the truck's engine, but few waved, looks of defeat mixed with weariness splashed across their faces. Kory resolutely kept his eyes on the road, purposefully refusing to look anywhere else. He knew that if he looked at any of these people in the eye, even if only for a second he would be tempted to stop and offer his help. Unfortunately, that wasn't the way of the world anymore. He didn't know these people, and he had to think of the safety of his family first. More importantly, though, he didn't have any help to give the people he could see from the corner of his eye. His own family was surviving on the generosity of someone else already.

Alli kept her head buried in Charles' lap and placed her paws over her folded ears, hoping to block the sound of people in need from penetrating. Her sensitive hearing made it an act in futility that had Charles clutching to her tightly.

The truck sped down the highway as quickly as it could, nobody inside wanted to linger near the desperate people.

Charles closed his eyes and brought up the partitions in his mind, letting the meditations distract him from the real world. Another partition had formed around the ice magic he had learned from touching Kates core. Without any specific spells in mind, each partition worked to delve into the mysteries of their particular magic. He paid little attention to them, however, as he focused on the movement of the mana in his body.

Before that morning he had to grab, pull, and coax, and anything else he could think of to get the energy flowing through his body to obey his commands. For all his effort, the only thing he seemed to be able to command it to do was to add energy to existing spells. He wanted to be able to freely manipulate the spell itself and add various effects to them. To do any of that, though, he first needed to be able to freely manipulate the mana in his body. That had begun to change that morning, after he had spent a night meditating and feeling the mana flowing through his body.

The potion from earlier had served to clear and refresh his mind, leaving it working better than it would after a full night's sleep. Concentrating on the energy in his body allowed him to see the thin streams of mana that extended from where his own core was hidden and wove throughout his entire body. The lines in his right arm had thickened, allowing for more mana to flow through them before he could damage them a second time.

Charles kept his eyes closed as he meditated, not feeling the passage of time and barely noticing when Alli shifted her head in his lap. He could feel the mana clearer the longer he sat there, and it, in turn, was more willing to obey his thoughts and directions even without the use of a spell.

The sun was touching the horizon when the truck stopped shaking and Charles finally opened his eyes. They were in a small one-stoplight town just off the highway. Two large truck-stops made up most of the town itself with one on each side of the highway. They had crossed over into Indiana hours earlier and had to have been nearing the midway point of the state at least.

"We need gas and may as well look for supplies while we are here," Kory informed them as he parked the truck in front of the truck-stop and stepped out. The glass windows of the single-story building were all intact, though they had been covered and blocked inside.

Kira refused to look at him as she leaped from the back of the truck and hurried away to look at the abandoned vehicles. Charles watched her retreat, annoyance flitting through him. He had done nothing wrong, so why was she avoiding him? Alli sprang lightly from the back and immediately began stretching, the back of the truck was just a little too small for her to be really comfortable.

He kept his eyes on the building, not trusting it to actually be abandoned. Someone had taken the time to cover and block the windows, the only reason he could think they would take the time to do that was that they were still there. Truck-stops like this were practically gold mines, they were in the middle of nowhere, but were large. The number of supplies they could hold was also a factor since they catered to long-haul truckers there was never a shortage of snacks and drinks.

If someone was willing to live on soda and beef jerky, then staying at an out of the way place like this was ideal. Charles held out an arm blocking Kate as she moved towards the doors. "Hold on. Alli, do you smell anyone inside or around the building?" He asked his silvery companion as she finished her stretches.

She stepped towards the building and sniffed a few times. "I smell a lot of death, it's old though. It's been there for at least a week." She sniffed again and sneezed. "Rotten and spoiled food, and a lot of patchouli oil."

Charles looked at her curiously. "How do you know what patchouli oil smells like?"

Alli pawed at the ground lightly before answering, "From you, when I became your companion, I inherited your knowledge of the world and how it worked."

He wasn't sure if he felt violated by that or annoyed that she hadn't told him any of that before, at the same time it explained how she knew so much. He rubbed the bridge of his nose as he thought.

"I want to talk about this more later, more specifically why you never mentioned any of this before."

To the side Kate and her mother were watching him, their expressions carefully blank.

"Uh, sorry about that. I was just checking in with Alli. She says nothing but death is in that building." Charles told them while scratching the back of his head.

Kate looked at the covered windows one last time before walking away to help Kira with the gas.

Charles pulled out Alli's watering tub, filling it quickly next to the truck. Moving back to the truck bed he opened his inventory and began pulling out sleeping pads and pillows, the sleeping bags were kept by those who used them.

In the time it had taken them to stop and siphon gas, the sun had crept below the earth, leaving only a few streaks of orange in the sky.

"I'll drive if you all want to get some sleep," He announced as Kira finished filling the truck with Kate.

Alli hopped in the back first, settling into position against the side, leaving just enough room for two people to sleep smooshed together.

"Let mom and dad have the back, I'll stay in the cab with you and Kira," Kate said with a muffled yawn as she reached into the back and scratched Alli's belly. Touching her core was an exhausting and long process, taking more out of her each time she did it.

Kira looked at him for the first time in hours, her eyes seeming to scour his face as though searching for something. Whatever it was she didn't appear to have found it, as she tossed the empty gas can at him and climbed into the truck.

Kate raised her brows at her sister before sliding behind the steering wheel and then over to her sister, taking the middle of the bench. She pulled out a blue pillow and rested it on her sister's lap, before laying down with her head on the pillow.

Kira lightly ran her hand through her sister's hair as they waited for her parents to settle in the back of the truck with Alli. Kate closed her eyes and seconds later was snoring lightly, already asleep and dead to the world.

In the distance, flying monsters could be seen taking to the air from the trees they had apparently claimed as theirs. Thankfully, none of them came in the direction of the highway, instead appearing to attack another group of flying monsters. The second group was of a different species, but even with Charles' enhanced eyes, they were at the very edge of what he could see.

A soft rap of knuckles on the back window had Charles starting the truck and steering them back onto the highway. Kira soon pulled out her own pillow and leaned it against the window, closing her eyes as she continued to ignore him.

Night fell as he drove on, a portion of his mind focusing on the partitions that were created whenever he meditated. The other portion of his mind noticed that the night sky had changed since the night before. The stars were still in their proper positions, and the moon still hung overhead. It was the color of the night sky that had changed, it now possessed a distinctly green tinge that glowed overhead. It was reminiscent of an aurora borealis, but everywhere.

Kate was asleep with her head on her sister's lap, the muscles and flesh underneath her skin shifting as the status points she had assigned earlier in the day began to go into effect. Her body was changing, becoming stronger and faster, while her mind expanded, allowing her to process and retain information easier.

Kira watched the changes come over her younger sister, her eyes focused on her and not the sky outside. "It's rather, freaky watching the changes happen in real time to her body while she was asleep." She said softly not expecting a reply and not getting one as Charles focused on the road.

He had been driving for some time when a notification appeared in front of his eyes, startling him into jerking the wheel. Kira peeked at him with a glare as he brought the truck under control and made sure the road was clear before reading the message.

The god who has claimed you as their champion on Earth has a message for you. 'Do not trust in your glove any longer, over-charging it as you did earlier not only destroyed the mana-channels in your arm but also created an enormous surge of energy as a result. This surge damaged some of the functions in the glove, so congratulations, you managed to damage an item created by the gods to be indestructible! Further use of the glove outside of training and meditation purposes, which were unaffected, will have random and varied effects. Use it going forward at your own risk! Also, beware of burning anymore of your channels. The mana channels in a human body belong in part to their spirit, burning them out in the manner you did

damages the soul. You were beyond lucky that they were
able to be healed this time, don't count on being that lucky
a second time.'

Charles closed the message with a soft, bitter groan. He was officially an idiot. He had one thing going for him, one thing that had allowed him to keep up with people far above his unleveled abilities. The glove, and now he had managed to somehow ruin it in a moment of stupidity.

The Ohio countryside passed in a blur, unseen by his regret-filled eyes. Charles found his mind going in odd directions as he skirted the capitol late in the night. He needed to find some way to fall asleep or go unconscious again, the first time he had been near death and in an incredible amount of pain. An experience that he was not exactly keen to replicate in any way. He no longer could rely on using the glove to keep him safe, he needed the full effects of his levels now more than ever. He needed to find some way to force himself asleep.

Charles pressed on the brake suddenly, causing Kate to tumble to the floor and Kira to bang against the hard-plastic console denting it with her face. They were nearly to the Pennsylvania state line, and in front of them, the highway had been destroyed by at least one passenger jet impacting with the road.

Massive pieces of the plane covered the highway, digging deep furrows into the asphalt where they had impacted and skipped across the ground. The plane itself had broken into three pieces, leaving its contents scattered everywhere and leaving the road impassable.

He was going to have to backtrack or find a way through the woods to get past the devastation the planes fall had created. He was thankful he was seeing the accident site at night and not during the day when the full carnage could be seen and not hidden by deep shadows.

"Alli," He called. "See if you can find us a route through the woods and around this mess."

The large silver dog poked her head through his open window and licked his cheek. "Back away so the little one doesn't have to see this." She melted into the night with those parting words.

Kira who was bleeding from a broken nose was glaring at him while keeping Kate from seeing the mess on the off chance the monsters had left a body in view.

With the twist of a key, the truck came to life, and he quickly turned it around, executing a rapid three-point turn in his rush to get them away.

Interlude

Bob slammed his hands down on the table. The arms of his cloak fluttered desperately to catch up and remold themselves around his arms. "Charles has no idea what he can do, and that special aspect of his is making it worse!" He had to grind out the word 'special', the rest of the gods were content to turn a blind eye away from oddities such as him and his sister.

"What about his sister?" The goddess of tinkering asked from the far end of the table. "Does she also contain this special aspect?" Her lips curled at the question.

"She does," Bob answered simply, his thoughts distracted by Charles.

"In that case, I choose the sister to be my champion in the coming game." The Hindu goddess Saraswati said firmly, throwing the entire table into yet another uproar. She was a goddess of learning and knowledge and choosing the sister made sense, regardless of her purported reason for doing so.

Alaria watched all of this happening from the sidelines, suddenly more grateful than she had ever been that she did not have to deal with a large number of gods on her world. It was only her and her husband. Their kids, while demigods and powerful in their own right, had no say in the running of the world.

Brigit of the Tuatha Dé Danann raised her hand as she looked around the table. "How did Charles damage the glove exactly? I looked at the glove when you ordered me to give it to him, it's an artifact level item. Artifacts like that glove or Kira's bracelet are supposed to be indestructible, it shouldn't have been able to be damaged by a lowly unleveled human."

Bob stared at the goddess while pinching the bridge of his nose. "We were just discussing that. It's because he's- "

"Stop!" Odin thundered, smirking at the woman who had beat him over his choice of a champion. Here was a chance for some petty revenge, the kind gods enjoyed the most. "Don't tell her, let her figure it out on her own."

Bob tapped the table as he quickly thought over the proposal. "I see no harm in doing that. Now moving on the shadow players have made their first move ahead of schedule I might add. They have already come to blows with Charles and his group. I have warned them repeatedly against interacting with the champions before the game has begun. They have chosen to ignore this rule and as a result, are being punished, you may choose a boon to give to our champions that will help them with their quests."

"Do we have to decide right now?" Shiva asked, all four arms folded across his muscle-bound chest.

The deep recesses of the hood on his cloak hid Bob's face as he grinned with smug superiority, everything was going according to plan. "No, the boon may be delayed until the game has officially begun in another few days."

Chapter 8

Charlotte

Charlotte kicked the tire of the old truck her boyfriend had procured and glared at him. "I thought you said we had enough gas! I'm pretty sure you said something along the lines of, 'Don't worry baby, this old truck has two full gas tanks.'"

Scott had the decency to look chagrinned as he shimmied under the rear of the truck and looked up at the dirty undercarriage. "Come on, don't be like that Char, you know I'm no good with anything mechanical."

"Don't call me that. You know how I hate that nickname." Charlotte kicked the tire again, causing some dirt to fall into Scott's mouth.

"There's a leak in the line connecting the second tank I think," He explained after he had finished spitting out the dirt and grime. "That particular line seems to be the only clean thing under there. Until we get that fixed, it's probably a good idea to just use the one tank."

Charlotte closed her eyes and leaned against the rust-brown hood of the truck. "That still leaves us out here in the middle of nowhere with no gas!"

"Don't worry. The professor will make sure the other group comes back for us with more gas. We have all the food after all." He comforted her softly as he rubbed her back. His practiced fingers kneading the spot between her shoulder blades that always tightened when she stressed about something. It tightened a lot.

Charlotte lifted her head and looked to the back of the truck that was indeed piled high with all the food they had been able to scavenge. Her eyes slowly lost focus as she remembered everything that had happened during the last week.

***

A thin line of drool ran from Charlotte's mouth to the lab table, where she had fallen asleep hours earlier. Her laptop was open and had finished running through the needed calculations so she could run her experiment one last time that night. Or, at least that had been the plan before she had fallen asleep, she never got the chance to review the information.

She wasn't the only person in the lab either; the semester was proving to be very lab-intensive already. Every night, the lab had people occupying the tables into the early morning hours.

A loud ding that reverberated through her skull woke her up in a panic, her heart rate shot through the roof as she slid off her stool and onto the linoleum flooring of the lab. She grabbed at her chest in fear as she gasped for breath.

All around her she could see people reacting in similar ways, grabbing their chests or their heads as they drew in panicky shallow breaths. She felt the pores in her body forcefully expand as an unfamiliar energy entered her and began changing her from the inside out. It was an odd but fairly pleasant experience akin to a deep tissue massage.

She was apparently the only one who thought that way as the people on the ground with her had their jaws snapped shut to prevent them from screaming. The veins all along their bodies bulged out from the increased blood pressure as the energy ran rampant through their bodies changing them in one tortuous swoop.

Blood seeped from pores and mouths as the eyes in many of the student's heads rolled back from the pain, the changes too much for their bodies to handle. They died in agony, from a myriad of causes, undiagnosed weak hearts, terror, blood loss, and more.

The noise in her head slowly faded, taking the strange energy with it and her heart-rate slowly went back to normal. Her body was aching from the energy forcefully changing her, the massage like changes leaving her feeling weak. The surviving students in the lab were left panting and crying on the floor. The pain they were feeling quickly faded away, however, as the last of the unknown energy fled their bodies, leaving them worn out and tired.

It was then that the message that everyone still alive at that point except her brother Charles saw appeared. A moment later all the lights across the globe went out.

Congratulations on surviving the change. The world as you know it has now been changed, we, the gods of old have decided to return and have as such wrought many changes upon the world.

Honestly, the message had been rather self-aggrandizing in her opinion, but that was gods for you. After she had read through each message that explained what had happened and then skimmed through the manual she had crawled from her lab, her dead laptop clutched under her arm. The hallway was a little brighter, with little beams of moonlight illuminating the area enough for her to feel confident in walking.

Outside people had been running around scared while she had hurried to the apartment she shared with Scott. She needed to make sure that he was alright, everything was secondary to that for the moment.

In the time it had taken her to get to their apartment Scott had managed to scrounge up some food and water for the both of them. They had talked it over and eventually decided that while they needed to go to Colorado where her brother was, Scott, being an orphan had no family to speak of, for the moment they needed to stay in one place. Both of them were convinced that whatever changes the messages had talked about were not over yet. There was more to come, and they were safe where they were. In the morning when they could properly see, they would decide what to do next.

They bolted and locked the doors and then just for good measure, stacked some heavy items in front of it as well. Then they curled up next to each other and fell asleep, exhaustion keeping the sound of screams and the many wails of pain from their ears and out of their dreams.

The world that greeted them when they woke late in the morning bore little resemblance to the one they had grown up in. There was no power for one thing and monsters now filled the streets, hunting down and devouring any and all people or pets that they found.

Charlotte discovered quickly that certain things were different from person to person. Scott had an additional attribute named 'Alchemy' whereas she had one called 'Magitech'. There was one more thing that set her apart from everyone else, something that they decided to keep to themselves for the time being. Her inventory had space for a hundred items and apparently was able to stack items that were the same.

It had been a lucky break when they had found a group of college students in their building banding together to escape the city. Their group had swelled in size as they found more survivors until they split into two separate groups. Each group would continue to look for survivors as they made their way out of the city and into the more open suburbs where they planned to meet.

Looking back on it, things had gone surprisingly well. There had been injuries and even a few deaths, but on the whole, their group had continued to grow in size saving more people. Each carried as much food and water as they could carry or stuff in their inventories along with their chosen weapon.

They discovered quickly that not only were guns not useful; they were also incredibly dangerous. It took concentrated fire from multiple people to injure the monsters, meanwhile, the loud gunshots would draw more to their locations. This actually turned out to be a blessing in disguise, she couldn't remember who had been the first to do it, but someone had picked up a monster's weapon in a moment of desperation and used it to attack. That had been the true turning point, where their weapons did little damage, the monsters' weapons were on a completely different level.

With every weapon they picked up, they were able to do more damage to the various monsters that attacked them. Weapons that modern logic told them should be better were dropped to the side of the road and forgotten as they walked on.

Certain groups of people seemed to avoid them when they saw the size of their group and it didn't take them long to discover why. They were scavengers that only cared for themselves, hoarders, that only wanted to take more to secure their own survival.

They managed to follow one group back to their hideout, and after subduing them had taken all their supplies. Then they continued on, each person in their group no matter their age understood that the world and society had changed and that they needed to change with it or die.

It took them two days to reach the suburbs, the other group was already there. Each group contained several hundred people, and each person contributed in some way as they worked to secure their new home. Worker groups were sent out to gather materials and a wall around their compound was quickly being erected.

Charlotte and Scott remained with everyone for an additional day, helping to secure the gathered people and learning as much as they could. More people continued to trickle in each day and on the day they had decided to leave, Scott's chemistry professor stumbled in.

Long story short, he wanted to travel with them since he knew Scott, several other people they knew from MIT decided to then leave with them as well. They managed to find some old trucks that needed minimal work. Scott and the professor created a chemical reaction that charged one of the batteries enough to start the truck. Then they were off, dodging monsters when they could, and fighting when they couldn't.

Progress was slow as they were forced to avoid the larger cities, taking the longer routes and wasting precious gas. Charlotte and Scott's levels jumped from 6 to 8 and then eventually to 9 as they continued to fight their way across the country.

The people who had decided to come with them adjusted to the sudden change in the world in different ways. The most notable were the ones who pretended that they now lived in a game and would come back to life when they died. That group was also the most outspoken on the matter of being able to learn magic. Supposedly they had tried everything they could think of or had read in their quest to learn magic. Inner meditation, check, trying to feel the world around you, check. The list went on becoming ever more ridiculous as the days passed without them making any headway.

Charlotte had her own ideas on the matter and that they needed to be taught by someone first. She believed magic did exist, there were too many myths and legends in the world that mentioned it for it to be anything but real. It had vanished somewhere along the line in the world however, and now it had the opportunity to return, humans were just missing the one person who could teach them how to use it.

That is how she found herself stuck in the middle of Pennsylvania with her boyfriend and a truck without gas.

***

Charlotte looked up at the slowly darkening sky, dark clouds had begun to fill the horizon earlier and were now coming towards them. She was starting to get nervous; the other group should have been back by now. They had been gone for several hours on a trip that should have taken a quarter of that.

Scott was sitting in the cab of the truck, drumming his fingers on the steering wheel as he waited impatiently. "I think we should start walking. I'm getting a feeling something happened to them," He finally said without looking at Charlotte.

"I've had that same feeling for a while now as well," She pointed to the trees that surrounded them, their leaves that had begun to shift from green to orange and red creating a beautiful tunnel of colors that the road cut through. "We haven't seen any monsters at all in this area, and we've been here for hours. That's not normal! When was the last time, we went this long without encountering a monster of some kind?"

Scott shifted his gaze to the tree's, her words sparking true. "Not since before the apocalypse." He opened the truck door and stepped out onto the hot asphalt next to her. "We should go now then while we can." He had filled out some since the first few days, he had been on the skinny beanpole side before he had begun distributing the points from his level-ups. He would never be a strong person, but Charlotte had to admit she liked the muscle definition he now showed.

A rusty sword made of some dark metal appeared in his hand, while two daggers appeared in Charlotte's. The goblins she had taken them from had been vicious blood-crazed little monsters, the stitches she now sported on her upper arm and inner thigh were proof of that.

The hiking boots she had stored in the back of her closet years before had been truly broken in by this point and hugged her feet without rubbing. Most of her inventory space had been filled with items she hadn't wanted to part with or things she hoped to be able to fix at some point in the future. It contained plenty of clothes, food, and water, but it also contained a number of laptops and lab equipment that was no longer functional.

Charlotte kept her eyes peeled for movement as they began to walk down the empty road, leaving the truck behind them. She walked with a slight limp as the stitches on her inner thigh rubbed against the rough material of her jeans, reopening the wound slightly.

Walking beside her, Scott noticed her limp growing more pronounced as they continued to walk, eventually noticing the red line of blood that had appeared on her thigh. He reached out and stopped her, his hand on her shoulder. "Char, there is no reason that you need to be walking while bleeding. I have plenty of first-aid supplies that we can use to clean and wrap the wound."

Charlotte sighed and stopped not even objecting to the nickname. It was time she told him anyway, why she hadn't wanted to stop and wrap her leg. "I didn't want to stop and wrap my leg because then you would see it."

"Why wouldn't I want to see it?" Scott asked, not understanding.

"I didn't want you to see it," She clarified. "It's infected, and the antibiotics I've been taking haven't done anything for it."

Scott turned to face her. "Why didn't you tell me?" His voice held a hint of the betrayal he felt at her not telling him something so important.

She swallowed thickly and raised her hand to his cheek. "There's nothing you could have done or can do. I didn't want you to worry about this."

"Even your hand is hot. How have I not realized that you had a fever?" Scott asked as he cradled her hand on his cheek, his stubble from not shaving for a week poking at their hands.

"Because I didn't want you to know." She sighed and pulled her hand back. "The antibiotics may still work; it's only been a few days after all." She said with a false smile, they both were smart enough to know the truth.

Scott pulled her off to the side of the road and after giving her a quick kiss ordered her to take off her pants. "I can at least make sure it's clean and covered for now." He announced as he pulled out several first-aid kits.

Charlotte held onto his shoulder as he meticulously cleaned her thigh with alcohol wipes, sprayed it with a thin film that would keep it clean and then wrapped it with a bandage. A tear that denoted him as the more emotional of the two falling from his eye as he looked at her red and inflamed skin.

"There," He said when he had finished. "That will at least keep it from rubbing against your pants and getting worse."

She smiled and pulled her pants back up, covering her thigh with the bloody fabric. "Let's go. I want to know what happened to them."

They walked close to each other, both feeling the need to remain close to the other person as they walked down the road. The trees were replaced by open fields and the fields then led to more trees, still, no monsters were seen or heard.

The Susquehanna river could be seen splashing against the banks through the trees as they drew closer to a small town. The road had been suspiciously empty of vehicles, providing them no opportunities to siphon gas and return with their truck.

The burned remains of a laundromat and a diner were next to the crisped husk of a gas station were the first signs of civilization they saw since leaving the truck behind. Next to the gas station was a small intersection that led onto a bridge covered in spots of darkened and dried blood, highlighting where cars had once stood but were now gone.

"Scott," Charlotte began as she took her first step onto the suspiciously empty bridge. "Where are all the cars?"

"Forget that," He began before dragging her next to the concrete wall on the side of the bridge. "I want to know what happened over there!" He pointed to the far side of the bridge, where cars now lined the river as far the eye could see.

In the far distance, what looked like a troll could be seen pulling another vehicle into position. Which led their eyes to the structure a little farther in. Just past the bridge was the remains of a small town and surrounding that area was a mismatched wooden wall. The wall was constructed from the bricks and wood siding of the houses that had been torn down and destroyed.

Charlotte hugged the wall of the bridge as she crept across, Scott doing his best to keep his taller lankier frame hidden as he followed after her. The shadows had begun to lengthen all along the bridge making their sneaking easier than it would have otherwise been.

They paused at the end of the bridge; their eyes unfocused on the area around them as they watched for movement. Several minutes passed by without them moving, taking in deep breaths they burst from the shadows and to the wall that now surrounded the decimated town.

Screams of pain could be heard farther in as they followed the wall looking for a way inside. The shoddily built wall offered plenty of handholds they could have used to climb over, but it also provided a number of gaps they could use to see through.

Goblins were tearing down buildings, a larger more muscled hobgoblin with red streaks covering his skin was ordering them about. In another section, a goblin leaned on a gnarled staff as it walked, a finger bone necklace clacking together with every step. Farther in they could see a hastily constructed tower with long steps, a goblin even larger than the other hobgoblins sat at the top, watching over everything.

They continued to skirt the wall, drawing closer to the source of the screams. It was Scott's professor that had been doing all the screaming. Their entire group was there in cages a little banged up but alive, more cages filled with what could only have been the town's inhabitants were next to them.

In front of all the cages on a large table was the professor, his shirt had been ripped from him, leaving his pale flabby skin to be painted in swirls of dark red blood. His arms had been tied to the corners of the table as had his legs, leaving him outstretched and unable to move. Blood dripped from his left arm, where a dark leather bracelet had dug into his tender skin.

They had found the members of the group but still had no way of reaching them, let alone being able to free them. Charlotte and Scott moved on when they saw that outside of the professor no one was being actively harmed. They needed to find a way in, and they could not do that while remaining in one location.

Night had begun to fall before they found a way in and with it any chance they had of sneaking in disappeared. The one gate they had managed to find was locked tight and guarded by several nasty looking goblins with bows. The wall itself was now patrolled constantly as well, leaving them with no opportunity to scale it. They would have been seen climbing the wall during the day and the patrols at night had robbed them of that chance.

Chapter 9

C harles kept the speed of the truck slow as he drove through the eerily colored woods. The greenish tinge of the night sky was warping the natural dark colors of the night. Alli had quickly found a route for them through the woods, an overgrown dirt road that hadn't been used in a very long time.

The truck jerked as the front tire on the passenger side dipped into and then out of a hole he hadn't seen in time. Kira for her part remained silent, one hand braced against the ceiling. Her eyes had refused to leave the night sky since she had woken earlier. He had to admit the change in the sky was remarkable and not something that he had been expecting in any way. It was a beautiful and poignant reminder that their world was changing in many different and unknown ways.

Alli loped in front of the truck showing him where to go. They followed her through the woods for over a mile before she turned and took them back to the road. The wreckage of the plane and ruined road left far behind them.

Charles pulled up the quest info for his sister while Alli settled herself into the back of the truck. He was in Pennsylvania now, if it was going to change and give him more information, then now would be the time to check it.

The gods have issued you a challenge, join your sister in
Danville, Pa!

A grin tugged at the corners of his mouth as he pulled out a map and began plotting the course. It was two-hundred and fifty miles away from the state line; he stuffed the map back into his inventory and shifted the truck's transmission into gear. It was time to find his sister.

***

There had been a distinct lack of monsters along the road, making Charles slightly edgy. Monsters had become a constant staple of this new world. They were everywhere, especially at night. Except for last night he hadn't seen or heard a single monster, in fact now that he was thinking about it. He hadn't really seen that many monsters since they ran into the Bugbear that had been a champion for an enemy god.

It had been nice at first, not having to worry every second. Now he was finding the lack of monsters to be even more nerve straining that the constant attacks he had suffered the first few days. The monsters were changing along with everything else, and that was more worrying than anything else he could think of.

Kira had eventually closed her eyes, cradling her sister in her lap as she did so. Alli was the one who kept him company during that time late in the night before the distant horizon could be seen lightening through the trees. He would whisper softly, and her sensitive ears would pick up his words without difficulty, her own words rolling through his head so that only he could hear them.

"What do you want out of life?" Charles asked after they had been talking for a while, his mind remembering what she had told him the day before.

Alli was silent for several moments. "I don't know anymore." She finally answered. "I remember some of the desires I had before I became your companion and started changing, but they're all distant now. Several of them just seem impossible for me."

"Like having children?" He asked pushing her towards the one thing she had mentioned earlier.

"Yes, like having children, it's more than that, though. The memories I received when our bond formed changed the way I thought in certain ways. You are a human, and that thought process has influenced my own way of thinking. For instance, I am a dog, we both know that. I should be attracted to my own species, but because of the way you're thinking, as a human, I now feel nothing but disgust at the thought of being with another dog."

Waves of sorrow coated her words and flowed dully through the companion bond, letting him know just how out of sorts she was feeling. The bond, in turn, let her know how her words affected him, the guilt he felt for changing her in such a way.

"How exactly did it work, you receiving my memories and thought patterns?" Charles asked, moving the conversation forward.

"Work," She corrected him gently. "It is still ongoing. As the companion bond continues to grow stronger, I receive more glimpses of your world before we met. With each burst of new information, the way I think shifts a little more, bringing my way of thinking closer to that of human in order to match the experience."

"And," He hesitated unsure of how he should frame his question. "You're aware of these changes as they're happening?" He dared to twist around and look at her through the back window. Her muzzle was pressed against the window, her eyes wide and glimmering beneath the brightening sky. The truck had drifted over into the middle of the road before he turned to face the front.

"Of course, I am, I can even choose to ignore them now, the first few times I couldn't. If I do so, then certain memories won't make sense, but

I'm not at risk of losing myself. I think that's what you're worried about isn't it?"

Charles bit the inside of his cheek as he thought over his reply. "I don't want you to change and stop being you. I guess hearing that it did change you, in the beginning, set me on edge."

"That's partly why I didn't tell you any of this to begin with. I wanted these changes, I wanted to better understand you and this world. The way I was before I wouldn't have been able to speak with you, or Kira when you were injured." She paused, and he felt another wave of sorrow pulse through the bond. "Just because I wanted this though, doesn't make certain aspects of it any easier to live with."

The truck swayed to the side as he heard her shuffling in the back. "I'm going to get some sleep; we can talk more on this later if you want."

Charles knew they weren't going to talk anymore on the subject, talking about the changes she had gone through caused her pain and that was not something he wanted to inflict on Alli. She meant more to him than she should, considering they had only known each other for just over a week. Everything they had gone through during that time cemented that bond and she had turned into the rock that kept him stable. He had a hard time thinking of her as a dog most of the time; she was more like his friend. Someone he could depend on; someone he didn't want to hurt.

So, he buried the remaining questions deep inside his heart and forgot them. Going forward he needed to be more aware that he didn't know everything about her or what she was going through. In essence, he needed to remember that she was female.

Kate shifted and opened her eyes, twisting as she stretched her arms to the roof. "Where are we?" She asked through a yawn.

A green sign beside the highway told him that Danville was only a few miles ahead. "We're almost there, just a few more miles." He told her, his heart beating faster at the thought of seeing his sister safe and sound.

A badly constructed wall made of clearly scrounged materials rose up in the distance as the truck turned a corner. A large store with the name missing, a single red 'W' hanging at an angle was just outside the walled area.

Charles pulled over and turned off the truck, hoping that no one had seen or heard them. He had a bad feeling looking at the wall. There was something off about it, and not just because of the random building materials. In the middle of the large area behind the wall, he could see a tall platform, with a throne-like chair in the middle of it.

He pushed his eyes harder, increasing the flow of magic to them as he struggled for details. Gradually, the form of a being too large to be a human came into view sitting atop the throne. Grimacing Charles shook his head, dismissing the magic from his eyes, the strain of drawing out that little extra making them ache from the pressure.

Kira stirred beside her sister and then inhaled sharply as she grabbed at her lower stomach. "We need to stop; I need to use the restroom."

Kate prodded at her sister's cheek. "We are stopped, we're there. Wherever there is, in any case."

Charles climbed from the truck as Kira burst from the door on her own side and into the woods that seemed to be everywhere in this part of the states. "Alli," He said softly. "It's time to find my sister and find out what is going on here."

Kate was talking softly to her parents as he crossed the deserted road and made his way over to what he could now see had been a grocery store. To the side of the building was a road that had been used as the dividing line for the wall. He used the wall of the store to keep himself out of sight. The cloudy sky and the early morning light casting shadows everywhere.

He couldn't see any gates or doors on the wall from his position, leaving him with no way inside, if that was even what he wanted to do. Alli stepped out of the shadow next to him, the dark inky shadows clinging to her body before melting to the ground and off her paws.

"I smell a lot of people inside, and even more goblins. There are a few other kinds of monsters here as well, but mostly goblins of various sorts." She licked his hand as she settled onto her haunches and watched the wall next to him.

"What about my sister?" He asked as he pulled up the quest information, suddenly worried that it might have changed.

"I don't know what she smells like," She answered with a huff. "I did find two people sneaking around the wall though, they were coming in this general direction. It was a man and a woman; the woman could have been your sister. I hope not though; she smells weird like an infection that has started to rot."

"I'll wait for them here if you want to start taking out the sentries and any other easy enemies that you might run across."

"Yes," She drawled, a wide doggy grin crossing her face as her tongue lolled out. "I need more practice with my Shadow-Walker abilities, the better I get with them the more people we can save in the future."

"Speaking of, how are the abilities? You seemed to be having some kind of difficulty with them yesterday." Charles asked her as he scratched lightly under her chin, teasing her more than anything.

"Oh, yeah. Right there," Alli panted as her back leg rose into the air and kicked repeatedly, only just keeping herself from thumping against the ground. She shook her head and backed away from him, needing to concentrate. "The ability is fine, it was a matter of it draining my stamina and energy too quickly. I think I might have figured it out now, though."

Charles turned away from the wall, facing her with interest. "And what have you learned?"

"It's in the name, I'm a Shadow-Walker. I walk through shadows, the more shadows there are in the area, the easier it is for me to move through them. The problem yesterday involved me going through fields of grass and using the small shadows inherent in everything to move through the area. Using shadows that small while possible, takes a lot more energy, not to mention when I have to cross an open space with no shadows." The first drop of rain fell on her nose as she finished telling him her thoughts. "The injured woman is almost here." Alli bumped her wet nose into his hand and stood to her full height. The shadows on the building they were against reached out and enclosed her in a dark film, and then she was gone.

Charles remained still as he waited for the people she had been talking about to enter his view.

"There has to be another way in besides the front gate," A male voice Charles thought he recognized said around the corner of the grocery store.

"We could get in easily enough using the sewers," A female voice that Charles knew he recognized answered back.

"We already discussed this; we can't risk letting your infection get any worse. The inside of a sewer is nothing but a breeding ground for nastiness..."

The voice faded as the boom of thunder rolled overhead. Charles stood beneath an overhang as he listened to his sister, arguing with her boyfriend. He didn't have anything against Scott; he had always been a nice enough fellow the few times they had met in the past. He also knew that his sister's first boyfriend was likely to be her last, the two of them fit together in just the right way.

A hollow feeling spread through him as he realized that unconsciously he had forgotten that Scott even existed until that moment. The man who had pursued his sister for over a year before she would even agree to go on a date with him. The man who convinced her that she needed to give dating a try when all she had needed before was Charles and her projects. The man who he knew his sister was desperately in love with.

He had forgotten him.

Charles shook his head as the words Scott has spoken reverberated through his skull, his sister was hurt, she had an infection and Alli thought it smelled like it was rotting! He stepped out from under the overhang and into the pouring rain, rushing to the corner of the building where their voices had been coming from. He needed to help his sister first.

His feet splashed through the rapidly expanding puddles noisily as he ran. "Charlotte," He called out softly, just before turning the corner.

There leaning against the side of the building for support, knives that had been scavenged from goblins in both hands stood his sister. Her face was red, and her eyes glazed over with fever, standing next to her, eyes full of worry was a tensed and battle-ready Scott.

"Hi sis," Charles said in a deadpan voice as he approached carefully, with his hands in view of them both.

"Scott, I think you were right, the fever is getting worse. I swear I see and hear Charles right now." Charlotte pushed away from the wall, the knives falling from her hands as she reached towards her brother on unsteady feet.

"Fever dreams aren't contagious," Scott said stupidly, seeing the same thing as her.

"I'm really here," Charles said as he engulfed his sister in a hug. "Come on, let's get out of the rain first and then we can talk." He was already sending a small stream of mana into his sister to see what was wrong with her.

Water dripped from their clothes in dirty rivulets, helping to wash away the stench of people who hadn't been able to wash themselves properly in over a week.

Heat radiated from Charlotte's body as he pushed her around the corner and then under the overhang, he had been standing under earlier. Charles could feel the infection that had taken hold of his sister, the meat on the inside of her thigh had started to necrotize and kill the flesh next to it.

He would still be able to help her, but it would take a lot out of him. His understanding of healing magic and how to use it effectively had been growing recently, but without the glove to aid him, he just didn't have that much magic at his disposal.

His eyes closed, he sent a party invite to Charlotte and Scott. He needed to use the potion on her, and he could only do that if she was a member of his party. He didn't trust the potion, but he wasn't going to let his personal feelings get in the way of saving her.

Charlotte mumbled incoherently as she sank to the ground, Scott holding tightly to her hand.

"What happened?" Charles asked as he waited for them to accept, praying that his sister wasn't too delirious to do so.

"Goblin knife to her thigh," Scott told him as he accepted the invite. "She didn't even tell me about it until yesterday, but it's gotten worse fast."

Charles winced at the thought of what the nasty filth covered knives he had seen the goblins using could be carrying infection wise. The potion would save her, he knew that, but it might also change her as it had him.

"Charlotte, I need you to accept the invite," Charles whispered to her, holding her hands in his.

A spark of something flickered deep in her eyes, as they focused on a message only, she could see. She blinked accepting the party invite, her eyes glazing over once more the next second.

"Hold her steady," He commanded Scott as he pulled the potion from his hip. With a quick flick of his wrist the cap came off he pushed the potion into his sisters' mouth. "This will heal her, but she needs to be quiet while it works."

Scott opened his mouth to argue but felt the woman he loved stiffen in his arms her mouth opening in a soundless scream.

Charles ignored the messages popping up in the corner of his vision, telling him that he had earned experience. Alli was out there killing any goblin she came across outside of the wall.

The potion fell to the ground and a moment later appeared on Charles's hip without anyone noticing. The area around Charlotte's thigh darkened as the infection was pushed from her body, the skin closing behind it. The smell of the infected fluids was awful as her mouth snapped shut and her eyes opened wide. A pained whimper escaped her mouth before a blissful smile appeared, indicating that the process was almost over.

With a deep shuddering breath, Charlotte blinked and looked at her younger brother. "What was that?"

"We have a lot to talk about," Charles told them both as Kira approached with her sister and parents.

Chapter 10

Charles took a moment to look at the newest message that had appeared as Kira and her family introduced themselves to his sister and Scott.

Congratulations you have completed a challenge issued by the gods and have found and rejoined your sister. As a reward for completing this challenge part of the curse has been lifted, you may now sleep once every fourteen days. Complete additional challenges to lift more of the curse.

With a barely contained growl, he dismissed the message only for another to take its place.

The gods have issued you a challenge, create a town in the location of their choosing. As the first challenge has now been completed the location of the town will now be revealed along with its purpose.
Create the town in the location formerly called Kansas

City, Missouri. This town will act as the guardian and
controller of the dungeon, as such the town needs to be built
where it can control any who wish to enter the dungeon.

Charles closed the newest message with an angry mental swipe. He couldn't say he was all that surprised. He had been expecting that to be the location ever since the challenge had appeared. It was just one more example of the gods playing with his life, sending him halfway across the country and then forcing him to return.

He listened to everyone talk for a few minutes before breaking the news to them. "I just got a new challenge from the gods; they want me to build a town back in Kansas City. They want it to serve as a control point for the dungeon that was created there."

Kira was the first to respond, sliding to the ground with a chuckle her back to the wall and just barely under the overhang. "Of course, they want us to go back there after coming all this way."

Kate sank to the ground next to her sister, a complicated expression on her face. "I like the thought of having a place where I can learn from you that isn't always on the move, but I have to agree with sis it's not cool for them to send us all the way back after coming here."

Kory held onto his wife and watched his daughters as he responded, "We have nowhere else to go, we all may as well keep following you. You've proven to have the abilities to keep the people around you alive, and in this new world we can't ask for more."

Charlotte looked at her brother with narrowed eyes. She knew what her brother was like. The way these people were acting around him was odd. Then again, he had somehow just saved her. Before that, though they had to rescue the people that had been captured inside the walls before it was too late. The goblin encampment hadn't even begun to stir yet, the storm kept them inside their hovels.

"We have to save the people inside the walls first," Scott said, beating her to the punch.

"Why?" Charles responded coldly, causing everyone to wince.

"Because Charles, they were part of my group," Charlotte said with a long-suffering sigh. She knew what her brother was like, people he didn't know were of no importance. It was part of the reason seeing the people with him had been such a surprise.

Charles glared at her for a minute before turning away. "Alli," He called softly, trusting that she would still hear him, regardless. Her ears were truly sensitive, or maybe it was just part of the bond they shared.

"Coming," He heard back seconds later.

"She's coming," Charles informed them before turning to look out into the rain. Behind him Charlotte looked even more puzzled. He had another companion? What had happened to her brother, that would have so many people flocking to him?

Alli trotted over to them, her silvery body glistening wetly in the rain. "Oh, I guess that was your sister. I'm sorry." Alli was quick to apologize, her ears laying flat in shame.

"It doesn't matter. I was able to help her, and she wasn't being attacked. There is little you could have done," Charles told her.

"What is that?" Scott asked before Charlotte elbowed him in the stomach.

"Don't be rude." She watched as her younger brother petted the large dog. "She's beautiful, but why is she so big?" She pushed her way up the wall until she was standing, making sure her legs could handle the weight that minutes before had made them tremble with weakness. She stepped to her brothers' side and reached out to touch her. "Is it alright if I touch her?" She asked at the last second.

Everyone but Scott smirked at the question, their eyes all on Alli.

"Well, Alli, what do you say, is it alright if she touches you?" Charlotte caught the mirth in his voice as he asked the question.

Alli pushed her nose into Charlotte's hand. "It's alright if you want to touch me. I'm glad that Charles was able to find you. He's been looking for you since the world ended."

Charles coughed in embarrassment as Charlotte stepped back in shock. "She can talk?" She asked wondrously, Scott perking up at her words.

"Alli's super smart like that," Kate said from behind them.

"We really need to talk about everything that has happened," Charlotte whispered to her brother, as she again reached for Alli.

Charles nodded at her but spoke to Alli. "Have you taken care of all the goblins and monsters outside the wall?"

She nodded. "There weren't many of them, so it wasn't hard." Only Charles and his sister could hear her reply.

"Charlotte says there are some people inside the wall. Could you smell them?"

Alli stilled, thinking over her reply. "Yes, there are many people inside the wall. Most of them are uninjured as far as I could smell, one person seems to have been separated from the rest however and is severely injured."

"The professor," Charlotte cut in. "He's part of my and Scott's group. He followed us from MIT since he knew Scott. We managed to look through a section of misaligned wall yesterday and saw that he had been tied to a table and was bleeding pretty badly from his arm."

"I want to save them, but there are many goblin monsters inside the walls and one of them smells different. Like they are rotting from the inside out, but still perfectly healthy on the outside." Charles closed his eyes at her words, whatever was in there must truly be bad otherwise Alli would be going on about trying to save them.

"Please Charles, my group is in there along with the surviving members of this town. Help me figure out a way to save them, they can all come back with us and help build this town you were talking about." Charlotte asked, knowing that if anyone could convince him to help it was her.

Charles knew they didn't have a lot of time, regardless of what he decided. The goblins inside the wall weren't truly awake for the morning just yet, which made it the perfect time to either attack or run away. "Why were you holding the goblins knives earlier?"

Charlotte's eyes unfocused as she looked into her inventory. "Crap, they're gone. That was my cleanest pair too." She pulled out another pair of knives before answering him. "Goblins drop their knives as loot a lot of the time, and our group discovered early on that monster weapons did more to them than our guns or knives did."

Everyone in Charles group looked at her in surprise and then regret, as they began to realize just how many weapons they had been passing up by not looting everything properly.

Alli looked at Charles over everyone's head using the moment while they were all distracted. "I have many of their little weapons in my inventory if you would like." She told him, confirming what he had long suspected. That she had an inventory. "It's not as big as yours, but it is larger than everyone else's it seems and can stack up to ten of the same items. I believe it to be a consequence or effect of our bond." She informed him quickly, guessing at the question he wanted to ask but couldn't with so many people around. They were her secrets to share, and he would not take them from her in that way.

He nodded, and she moved around the huddled group of people that were still talking about lost opportunities. Charlotte looked up at Alli's movement but didn't say anything when her brother caught her eyes and subtly shook his head.

Charles knelt next to Alli so that it looked like he was the one pulling them out. "Two for each of them just in case." He hesitated and then added, "Two for me as well, I damaged the glove yesterday and can't rely on it to get me through anymore. I still have my regular magic, but without the glove augmenting the mana cost I can only fire a few times before I'm out of energy." He told her quietly as she pulled the filthy weapons from her inventory. "Thanks, Alli. You really saved us here."

Alli moved to the side with a wide doggy grin and relaxed as she watched Charles work.

"Charlotte, why don't you and Scott toss your weapons into this pile," He called out just loud enough to be heard over the talking. Everyone's attention snapped to him and then the pile of knives at his feet.

"Alright, what for though?" Charlotte asked as she tossed her own dirty knives into the pile, knowing her brother had a reason for asking her to do so.

Charles waited for Scott to do the same, before raising his hand over the pile. He grabbed the magic in his body and spoke the simple control word that activated the spell. "Clean." A ball of water appeared above the knives and began to spin before it even touched them. The spinning ball of magical cleaning water sank onto the knives and began to scour them clean. Charles noted that using the cleaning spell worked differently on items than it did on people, he had never seen a ball of water appear above their heads in the past.

Scott stared open-mouthed while Charlotte grinned in excitement. "You can use magic? How, how did you learn it so quickly? Are you the one the manual kept referencing in the updates? Can I learn, can you teach me how to use magic?" She shot off the questions in rapid fashion, barely taking the time to breathe. "More importantly can you do that spell on me?" She looked at the ground in embarrassment. "I haven't washed in a few days and the infection only made that worse."

Charles pointed his hand at her and cast the spell, and then at everyone else in the group including Alli. The cost of using that particular spell was minimal, allowing him to use it on everyone before he could feel his energy flagging. He knew his magical energy would regenerate over time, and they weren't attacking the walled compound just yet.

The spell completed on everyone else, cleaning their clothes and washing away their individual odors before it finished on the knives. The ball of water was almost black with filth as it began to finish, shunting the nastiness it had collected into a circle around the now gleaming and polished knives.

With a thought, Charles stared at the knives, hoping that some information would appear on them.

Congratulations, your ability 'Analysis' has evolved into 'Analyze'. Analyze has the same functions as its lesser counterpart but can now be also used on items and the world around you. Be sure to use the spell often, it may reveal hidden truths of the world to you.

Charles read the message with a small grin before dismissing it and looking at the knives once more. This time, a small transparent box appeared over the entire group.

A grouping of fourteen knives. These knives have been cleaned by magic and have had their durability augmented to show for it. The knives are far sharper than they should be and will slice through even regular Earth metal with a little effort.
Note: Secondary effects of the blades relating to poison and infection based debuffs have been removed as part of the cleaning process.

"The spell cleaned them, sharpened them, fixed them, and finally removed the secondary poison and infection effects from them." He told the group with a slight amount of awe. He had been expecting the spell to clean them, and that was it. He had no idea the spell could be used in this way.

Charlotte was the first to stand and walk towards the pile of now gleaming and clean knives. Her face was more even now that she wasn't scrunching her nose at the smell constantly. "We need to get ready," She announced picking up her chosen knives and then looking at the gathered group. "First how are we going to get inside?"

"The sewers," Charles said as he picked up his own knives and stored them in his inventory. "I heard Scott mention something about going through the sewers earlier."

"Storm drains, if that makes it easier to think about going through them," Scott said quickly noticing the looks of distaste at the thought of crawling through a sewer. He pointed to the road in front of the wall where they could see a round heavy metal cover. "Whoever created the wall created it above ground, but I have seen nothing to say that they did the same underground. We can enter there and pop up in the middle of the compound, or closer to the prisoners if we're lucky."

"You won't need luck; I can guide you by the smells," Alli told Charles.

"Alli can guide us through the sewer system and get us close to the people. After we get in, Alli will start taking out the lone sentries and any other goblins she finds that are alone." He could feel the energy-returning slowly to his body and prayed that his magic would be back to full by the time he needed to use it. "We need to be quiet and quick while we are doing this. Our goal is to rescue the people inside not fight the goblins. There are too many of them and too few of us that will be armed. Get something to eat or drink if you need it, we'll leave in a few minutes." Charles took control and laid out the plan.

Charlotte pulled out some bottles of water for everyone and passed around a large bag of jerky as they prepared. Scott had a resigned look on his face, as though he was scared of what they were about to do but knew he would do it, anyway.

Kate clung close to her parents, knowing that they would be doing less of the fighting.

Charles stood as his sister stored the last of the jerky. "All right, let's do this, there's no point in delaying this any further than we need to and psyching ourselves out. Kira, you take the lead in front of me in case there is anything down there. I'll relay Alli's instructions to you as we go. Everyone else, just be as quiet as you can."

Kira nodded and leaped to her feet, stepping into the lightening rain next to Alli. Together they walked beside the building until they reached the road and the heavy metal plate inset in the ground there. Kira bent over and stabbed her fingers into the holes and lifted with a grunt. Her increased strength allowed her to lift the heavy metal disc with ease, but the pressure on her fingers was enormous as she did so.

She shifted the plate to the side and carefully set it on the ground, making as little noise as possible. Charles stood and hurried over to her as Alli used her class abilities to melt into the shadows and entered the sewer ahead of them.

Standing above the hole he used a small light spell to dispel the darkness below and followed Kira as she climbed down the metal rungs that had been placed in the wall of the opening. Alli was waiting for them further in, the ceiling well over a foot above her head. Pennsylvania had enough rain and runoff that their sewer system needed the extra space to prevent flooding during the rainy seasons.

Charlotte followed her brother into the sewer, and then everyone else came in after her. Ahead of the group, Alli sniffed the air and vanished. "Do not move," She commanded him.

Charles dared to reach out and touch Kira's shoulder, motioning for her to remain in place as she whirled away from him. Everyone else getting the message to remain in place and not make a sound without an issue.

Kira glowered at him but remained in place as a flicker of regret flashed across her face, leaving only the sadness in her eyes behind.

The water in the sewer that streamed past their booted feet rippled as something unseen took a heavy step. In the corner of his vision, Charles saw a message pop into being telling him that he had earned experience. He had figured out how to place the messages there earlier, ensuring that they wouldn't get in his way if he couldn't dismiss them quickly enough.

The influx of experience and the lack of being able to move had Charles opening his status sheet and quickly assigning the points he had gotten from his last level-ups. Now that he was able to sleep again, even if it wasn't often, he needed to start paying attention to those gains and assigning them as soon as he had the chance.

Alli had dark black blood dripping from her muzzle and the fur around her claws was quickly being washed clean by the water rushing by. "I've taken out one monster down here, but I smell more. Walk quickly and remain quiet." She told Charles, trusting that he would relay her words to the rest of the group.

Together with Kira in the lead, they followed her deeper into the sewer, trusting that she would lead them to the correct place.

Chapter 11

Alli led them through the twisting tunnels for over half-a-mile, turning into different tunnels as needed. Occasionally she would vanish, and the group as a whole would stop, waiting for her to reappear. Each time she did, she would have more of the dark blood covering her, and Charles would have a new experience message show up.

Charles kept the orb of floating light dim enough to not attract attention, but light enough they could use it to see.

They had been underground, for a little over fifteen minutes when they saw Alli pause beneath an opening.

"I think this is as close as we are going to get, more than that I can hear the goblins and other monsters beginning to stir above us." Her voice held a hint of pain in them, letting Charles know that she had been injured during one of her unseen fights. She knew how weak he was without being able to rely on the glove and it killed him to not be able to heal her right away. They would need all his magic if a fight erupted. He took solace in that the injury couldn't be too serious or she would have asked him to heal her, regardless.

Charles shifted the ball of light away from the opening and motioned for Kira to climb up first. She would need to shift the metal covering the opening before any of them could leave.

"Alli says this is as close as she can get us to the prisoners, but that we need to be careful the monsters are beginning to stir." He told the group as Kira carefully climbed the metal rungs.

There was a soft grunt and then the shifting metal could be heard as Kira pushed the cover to the side. A little light trickled in along with the rain, as the cloud-covered sky kept the sun from shining through.

Alli vanished into the shadows, taking the opportunity to go above and start hunting goblins.

"It's clear, come on up," Kira called down softly from above.

Charles was quick to climb up and join her, grateful to be out of the dim sewers. He knew that Alli would keep them safe to the best of her abilities but being in a dark enclosed area like that still messed with your mind. There had been a number of occasions in the short amount of time that they were down there, where he had thought he could see eyes in the darkness or hear voices whispering.

They had climbed up onto a sidewalk next to a crumbling brick building. A battered sign in the rubble claiming that it had been a brewery of some kind. Charles took the chance to look around as the rest of the group joined them aboveground. They were closer to the wall than he had been expecting, with the closest section only a few streets over.

From this side of the wall, he could see just how raggedy and pieced together the wall truly was. It was sturdy though if only because of the sheer amount of stuff they had piled against sections of it.

Charlotte studied the wall for a moment before pointing in the section they had been heading in the sewers. "The prisoners should be over there if I remember correctly. I'm not sure how close they are, though."

Kira took the lead again, holding the knives in her hand instead of using her larger and far more dangerous hammer. Every time she had called it in the past, it had produced a flash of light as it transformed from a bracelet to a weapon. They could not afford to be noticed, so she kept the knives in her hands and crept along.

The messages continued to appear on the side of his vision as Alli went about her work. She had used hit-and-run tactics to take care of enemies since the earliest days of their bond. Now that she had the ability to move through shadows, her ability to strike unaware opponents had shot through the roof. If she could find them alone, and they weren't too high of a level she could kill them quietly. She would leap from the shadows and clamp her jaws around their throats, preventing them from calling for help. Then she would rake their backs or bellies with her claws until they died.

Her attacks lacked a certain flair in their continued use, but no one could deny how effective her sneak attacks were.

Kory and Krystal kept their eyes open behind them, as they took the rearmost position in the group, making sure that nothing snuck up behind them. Kate walked in the middle with Scott, her sweaty, nervous hands struggling to maintain their tenuous grip on the knives. Charles walked behind Kira with his sister at his side.

Just past the building that had once been a brewery was an open space parking lot, and across from that, it opened up into a small park. Trees had been torn up by their roots and thrown to the side, in the effort to clear enough space for their prisoners.

The clearing that had once contained grass and trees now contained nothing but metal cages packed full of people. The smell of unwashed bodies and bodily fluids filled their air in a suffocating miasma that even the rain had been unable to wash away. The people had been forced to urinate and release their other bodily functions where they stood, the sheer number of people in each cage keeping them from moving.

The monsters had had enough decency to separate the males and the females but nothing more. There were ten cages scattered around the area, each packed with thirty or forty people.

Behind him, Charles heard Kate gasp in shock and then gag at the smell.

In the middle of all the cages plainly visible from the wall they were closest to was the professor Charlotte had mentioned. He was tied to a table and his shirt ripped from his body, revealing the pale flabby flesh of man in his later years of life that sat behind a desk most of the time. His face was swollen from where he had been hit, and it was clear even from their position across the park that his nose had been broken.

Rivers of red ran down his body, the rain loosening and washing away the blood that covered his body. Underneath the red water, they could see the markings that had been carved into his skin. The angry red, and likely infected lines covering his arms and torso, leaving a blank circular section on the skin where his heart was.

Scott cursed softly as he saw his professor. "What did they do to him? He wasn't like that when we saw him yesterday."

"It's a ritual," Charlotte guessed. "That's why they haven't killed or eaten these people, they needed them for whatever ritual they're trying to do."

Charles felt that now familiar creep of dread as he remembered the monster he had seen sitting in the tower. Something was wrong about this entire situation, he could feel it, but he also knew they were too close to turn back now.

"Everyone be careful," He began. "Something feels off about all of this, we're going to free those people as quietly as we can and then leave while remaining silent."

He waited for them to nod in understanding before giving the signal to Kira to continue forward. Her steps were sure as she stepped onto the cracked pavement of the parking lot, her feet splashing lightly across the watery ground.

The area around them was quiet, save for the soft moans and muffled whimpers of the starved and thirsty imprisoned people. The few that were awake had their eyes closed and their mouths open towards the sky. Their dehydrated bodies thirstily drinking any moisture that deigned to fall into their mouths.

Charles saw another series of messages appear in the corner of his vision as they stepped onto the grass. Knowing that Alli was out there keeping them safe helped the bunched together muscles in his neck and back relax slightly.

One by one, the people in the cages began to notice his approaching group, wisely choosing to keep their mouths shut as they nudged their neighbors. The cages were constructed of a dark wrought iron like material, with the doors locked by hunks of metal molded to the frame where a padlocked should have been. It looked as though the door was never meant to be opened again, lending weight towards Charlotte's ritual theory.

Kira ignored the door, knowing she couldn't do anything about the lock. She gripped the bars with her hands and forced them apart, her arms straining from the pressure. Regardless of how she tried to force them, however, she couldn't get them open enough for a person to wiggle through. More than that, every time she let go of the metal, the bars would spring back into position, sealing any gap she may have made.

"Use the knife," Charles whispered to her. "The information I got said they should be able to cut through normal Earth metals now. With your strength, it shouldn't be a problem."

Kira bent over and picked up her knives from where she had dropped them in front of the cage. "I'll try it, but do you really think these bars are regular Earth metal still? Wrought Iron is soft and springy, but I've never seen it bounce back into position and shape like these bars do."

Charles shrugged, unsure of what to tell her.

Kira pushed the edge of the knife to the bar and with both hands gripping the handle began to saw it back and forth. Within seconds she had cut through the bar and had begun working on the one next to it. She had to cut through three bars in total, once at the top of each and then at the bottom.

The people pushed through the hole, the first through picking up the bars of metal to use as weapons.

Kory had hurried over to another cage after seeing his daughter using the knife to cut through the bars. It took him longer than her, but he was still able to cut through them and release another group.

The freed people quickly set up a perimeter around the edges of the park, making sure to remain quiet. Kira moved from her second cage and then from her third before anything changed. Her father was cutting through the third bar on his second cage at that point.

Kira was working on her fourth cage when Alli called out to Charles. "The goblins are beginning to move, I'm not sure what changed but I see groups of them hurrying your way."

"Hurry up, we have incoming," Charles hissed at Kira, before waving over Kate and her mother. "We have monsters incoming, take everyone who isn't armed and get them into the sewers."

"What about the-" The dying scream of a person on their perimeter kept her from saying more.

"Never mind, get them behind the cages where they aren't in the way!" He quickly ordered, already knowing that a lot of people were about to die.

Groups of goblins appeared in front of them, knives and spears held at the ready as they marched ever closer.

Kira and her father continued cutting through the bars, while the people around them began panicking. One of the people inside the cage, a male, grabbed at Kira's arm in a desperate attempt to hurry her along. With a cry of rage, she dropped the knife and punched the offending man in his face, shattering his nose and pushing the people closest to him back several steps from the force of the blow.

"DO NOT TOUCH ME!" She screamed, silencing everybody in the area and focusing all attention on her.

The goblins were the first to shake off their shock and began to scream and howl alerting all the monsters in the area. Whatever had first alerted the monsters to their presence had now been confirmed.

The goblins rushed the group, knowing that reinforcements would be arriving shortly. Together they beat down the people, using the handles of their knives or the blunt edges of their spears to knock their victim's unconscious instead of killing them.

Scott rushed to the side of his professor and cut him loose, pushing his unconscious and injured body off the side of the table. Grabbing his arms, he began to drag him across the muddy ground away from the fighting, where he would be safe.

Kory had run over to his daughter in the ensuing confusion and was working to calm her down, further delaying the freeing of the rest of the prisoners. Charlotte had taken control of a group of people she seemed familiar with and had passed out several dirty knives. Together they were working to stab and cut any monster they came across, the group expanding as more weapons became available.

Kate and Krystal rushed behind them with another group of people, moving the unconscious and injured humans out of the way. The area at the back where Scott had dropped the professor quickly filled with still bodies.

Charles cast 'Icy Lance' whenever he had the chance, the moisture in the air making the mana cost for the spell negligible. Waves of 'Frost' coated the ground in front of the running monsters, causing them to trip and fall. Their movements were further slowed when they fell onto the frost, their rain-slicked bodies growing cold as the water changed to ice impeding their muscles.

Alli appeared behind the current wave of goblins and distantly Charles could see her bite down and kill a straggler. His experience ticked up again from her kill and his own, tipping him over the edge needed for level 15.

Congratulations, you have leveled up. You are now level 15;
you have gained 5 status points for distribution. The class
system has now been unlocked; you may now pick a class

Congratulations, the god who has chosen you as their
champion has locked your class selection. You have been
forced to choose the class: Archmage.
The Archmage class is a class only given to those with the
potential to use all elements and all forms of magic. This
class helps to further your understanding and control of
magic, further abilities may be unlocked with time and by
completing specific actions.

You have a message from the god 'Bob', 'The Archmage class
is particularly well suited to the training of others in the use
of magic. P.S. We really need to have a talk sometime.'

Charles dismissed the message as quickly as he could, not wanting to get attacked while he couldn't see. He would look it over carefully later when he had the time.

Kira was cutting through the last cage alongside her father when the message came, blocking each human's vision for several precious moments.

Congratulations humans an Archmage has joined your race
once more, seek out the Archmage to learn the secrets of
magic. Know, however, that the Archmage is able to deny
your desire to learn magic. He or She, (You will have to

discover which yourself) is under no obligation to teach you,
so if you want to learn magic you had best be on your best
behavior when meeting new people.

Those precious seconds where the message blocked everyone's vision were all the goblins need to retake control of the battle.

Two flashes happened in different parts of the muddy field in rapid succession. First Kira finished cutting away the last of the cage's bars and ran towards the enemy dropping her now dulled knives. The bracelet on her wrist flashing with a bright white light as her hammer formed in her hands.

Second Charlotte was engulfed in a familiar pillar of light that marked her as having been chosen as a champion. The light that engulfed Charlotte was bright and eye-catching, distracting all who saw it. The rain paused in the area around her, refusing to fall to the ground. The wind followed the example of the rain and stopped, as though nature itself was watching with bated breath.

The pillar of light tightened around her and a deep thrum that could be felt in your bones swept through the air. The rain scattered outwards with the thrum and then it was over; the world went back to normal. The wind went back to blowing, and rain once more fell on everything.

The pillar of light continued to shrink around Charlotte before it condensed around her eyes and then rose into the sky. On Charlotte's face where the light had condensed sat a pair of silvery glasses that rather annoyed Charles. His sister had never needed glasses before, and more than that when Kira had been chosen, she had gotten a weapon. What was his sister going to do with the glasses? Glare at them!

The ground trembled and the puddles of water jumped into the air, as something big and heavy made its way toward them.

Several people had fallen due to being distracted by the pillar of light, the goblins more interested in beating things than paying attention to such things.

Charles braced himself as he saw the puddles jump, having an idea of what might be approaching them. He began to collect mana in his arm, ready to cast a spell at a moment notice. Alli looked behind her and then vanished into the shadows only to reappear next to him a second later.

"It's a troll, a large one." She told him, her legs trembling from the effort to stay upright. The constant stepping through shadows and the fighting had taken all her energy, leaving her running on fumes before the fight had truly begun.

Charles nodded and let the bolt of fire form above his hand. He added as much additional energy to the spell as he dared. Holding the fully formed spell in place he used his control of mana to make the bolt spin faster and faster as he waited for the troll to appear.

With a roar that shook the crumbling buildings and the water to dance away from it, the troll appeared. Charles focused on the monster and let 'Analyze' scan the monster.

Troll Lv. 15, beholden to the Goblin Lord.
This troll has gone through several modifications due to the
experiments of the Goblin Lord's shaman. Its skin is now
dense and resistant to fire on the outside, the inside,
however, remains as susceptible as ever. At the cost of its
intelligence, its strength and willingness to obey the orders of
its holder has grown significantly.

Charles blinked away the message and suppressed the surprise he felt at the information his ability had provided. He had never seen that much detail on a monster before. That said, it also revealed that his bolt of fire was not going to be as effective as he hoped.

"I need it to bleed," He said to Alli as she swayed exhausted next to him. "Sorry, I know you're tired, but I need you to do this one last thing. Find Kira and tell her to make the troll bleed."

Alli took a hesitant step forward followed by another as she went to follow her nose towards Kira.

Charles grimaced as he looked down at the rapidly spinning bolt of fire hovering above his hand. The pressure of holding the spell in place was starting to strain him and adding the spin to the bolt was preventing him from absorbing the energy back into his body.

Carefully he lined up his arm and let the bolt of fire streak across the space to the troll.

Chapter 12

With a scream of terror, the troll stepped back as it saw the bolt of fire coming towards it. The troll may have been resistant to fire now, but it was still afraid of it. Fire had always been one of the troll's primary weaknesses, and the monster's every instinct was telling it to run away.

At the last second, the troll picked up several goblins and threw them at the bolt of fire. The spinning bolt cut through the first goblin, turning it to ash instantly, while it created a hole through the second and merely set fire to the third.

The troll was safe from the fire for now.

Charles saw Alli stumble away from the group and collapse to the ground, thankfully in an area where Kate and her mother would find her. The troll waited for the fire to finish killing the goblins in front of it and die out before taking a large lumbering step forward.

Its small beady black eyes could barely be seen under the bony jutting ridges where its eyebrows should have been. It walked with a stoop, with one arm longer than the other dragging on the ground as it walked. The shorter arm was a mass of flab and muscle and had been the arm it used to throw the goblins.

With every step, it took, its beady eyes remained on Charles never wavering even when it stepped on a still-living goblin. The goblin screamed as the troll's massive foot came down on top of it; the sound cutting off abruptly only to be replaced by a wet popping sound as it was turned into paste.

Charles felt at the mana in his body quickly gaging just how much he had left, and how much energy his changed firebolt spell had taken. He had enough for two more of those shots and then he would be out. He would become a useless liability on the battlefield, in a battle that hadn't even truly begun. He had yet to see anything but low-level goblins and the one troll. He knew there were shamans inside the walls, and he had seen something sitting on a throne in the tower earlier.

They were being toyed with, and there was nothing he could do to change that. Without the glove, he was too weak. Charles turned away from the troll and began to run. The troll followed after him just as he hoped it would.

The sounds of battle faded away as Charles began to run, his eyes constantly moving as he ran through one group of goblins after another. The troll stomped after him, crushing goblins left and right in its all-encompassing desire the kill the puny human. Desperately Charles ran on, sending little healing bursts to his lungs and legs in order to keep going. He was hyperventilating, and the fear he felt coursing through his body was keeping him from breathing properly.

Kira winked at him as he ran past, the goblins around her had all been smashed to bits. Her normally bright silver hammer was now encrusted with drying blood, making it look like an unholy weapon of death. Charles twisted his head to watch her as he slowed, a bolt of fire already forming above his hand once more.

She had the hammer cocked behind her with her hands spread over the length of the handle. He saw the muscles in her back bunch up as the troll ran towards her, its single-minded focus preventing it from seeing her.

With a cry, Kira swung with all her might, her right hand sliding down the handle to meet her left as she did so.

The troll was tall, and the head of her hammer hit what it could reach. The head of the warhammer smacked into the beasts' kneecap with all the force she could muster, toppling it instantly as it bellowed in pain. Her hammer had crushed the thing's knee but hadn't broken through the skin.

"I need it to bleed," Charles shouted at her as he launched the spinning bolt of fire at the troll. The bolt hit it in the face, causing it to screech in terror and scratch at its face. The longer arm smacked against its face uselessly while the shorter inadvertently gouged out one of its eyes. The shrieks grew louder, but still, there was no blood that he could see. The rain and tears coursing down its ugly face washing away any that might have come from its destroyed eye.

Kira kept hammering at the leg of the troll, not paying any attention to its wails of pain and terror. Her sole objective was to destroy its leg, and with each successive hit, she was doing just that. The leg she was hitting had turned into a pulpy pile of mush that resembled a tube of sausage more than it did a leg.

The magical fire died out on the trolls' face and whimpers replaced its screams of terror.

Kira seeing this held her hammer above her head and swung with all her might. The hammer hit it in the thigh, and with a snap, she felt thighbone give way. Tiredly she swung one last time at that same spot, with the sound of tearing leather its skin gave way and a jut of bone poked through with a burst of foul-smelling blood.

"Charles," She called instantly, already backing away from the soon to be torch.

Charles heard her call his name and with the last of his mana formed a ball of fire, not even having enough extra to make it spin. The bolt of fire hit the ground beside the troll and ignited the blood that had spurted there.

With a whoosh, the flame followed the trail of blood to the troll and then climbed inside its body. The troll's natural healing ability had already started to fix portions of its leg when the fire entered its body. The monsters changed skin kept the fire inside, while its healing ability worked to seal the open wound.

Charles felt his eyes widen in understanding. "Run," He screamed to Kira before following his own advice.

Behind him the troll began to swell in size, the fire having already killed it was devouring the last of its flammable blood. The pressure continued to build inside, as the skin the shamans had changed held the fire inside. The body began to distort, looking more like a balloon than a corpse.

Charles had managed to run ten steps when the body exploded with the force of a small bomb, sending him head over heels into the side of a cage. There was a snap as his left arm broke against the bars and then popped out of its sockets as his shoulder hit metal next.

A wave of pressure extended away from the blast downing everyone nearby. The prisoners were the first to recover and were quick to seize the opportunity given to them. The goblins that hadn't died in the blast were swiftly taken care of. Of the nearly four hundred prisoners they had freed, less than a hundred were still standing. Thankfully, only a few of them had actually died, as the goblins had been trying to subdue them and not kill them.

Charles remained curled around the bars of the cage for several moments as he waited for his hearing to return. The world was silent save for the annoying ringing in his ears, using the little amount of mana he had gained since the blast he sent a burst of healing to his ears. The ringing stopped and the sound of the world returned. The gentle patter of rain as it fell all around him, the soft gurgling of blood as a goblin's throat was cut.

"Your arm looks weird," Alli muttered to him as she collapsed next to the cage, careful not to disturb him until she knew how injured he was.

"Yeah, I can't feel it right now, but I'm pretty sure I heard it break and then felt it pop out of the socket." He muttered back as he began to move. His left arm dangled uselessly at his side, sending bursts of pain through his body whenever it was jostled. As carefully as he could he held it to his side with his right hand and then with his back to the cage, he stood, his feet crab-walking backward and his back inching up the rough metal.

Alli watched him from where she had collapsed, her breathing heavy and fast and her expressive eyes lidded with exhaustion.

"Come on," He said to her, pushing away from the cage. "We need to find everyone; this isn't over yet."

"You are right, little man; it isn't over yet. It has only just begun."

Charles felt a feeling of dread come over him as he turned to look at where the voice had come from. The largest hobgoblin he had seen yet was standing on top of the next cage over, his intelligent eyes taking in the remains of the battlefield.

"It talks," Alli said fearfully as she dragged herself to her feet next to him.

"You can talk," Charles parroted aloud.

The red lines that all hobgoblins seemed to have stretched taut as it moved to the edge of the cage and sat down his legs dangling over the edge. The monster was a vision of relaxed authority, as he rested his head on the palm of his hand. He looked past Charles and then waved at something he couldn't see.

"Of course, I can talk. I am a champion after all." He smirked, his eyes roving over Charles form dismissively. "Unlike the champions on your side of the game, we actually receive certain perks to being chosen. That's not to say that we can't normally talk; however, my shamans, for instance, are actually rather intelligent. Though none of them have mastered any of the human tongues."

"What do you want?" Charles managed to ask; his mouth suddenly dry.

"To kill you." He paused, and his eyes went out of focus. "Apparently, I'm not supposed to do that, however. You see, the game that we have been chosen to participate in has not officially begun, there are a few more days until that happens. Until that time, interacting with and fighting the champions on the other side is forbidden." His eyes had shifted from yellow to a deep red as he spoke, revealing the rage he was feeling at not being allowed to attack the enemy in front of him.

"What do we do then?" Charles asked his tongue flicking out to catch the rain dripping from his lips.

"Oh, you still die, I'm just not allowed to participate directly. So, here is what is going to happen. I'm going to leave with my shamans. Once I have left the area, the remainder of my troops are going to attack and crush you along with the rest of the humans. I will have to start over with another group of humans, but such is life. You, you will either be crushed by my troops or live." He looked at the scattered remains of his troll. "Likely you will live; you will then run far away from here and hide. And when the game has begun, I will come to find you. It may not be the first day or even the first week, but I will come for you, and when I do, I will crush you into dust and pee on your remains." He tilted his head upwards and let out a loud sigh.

"It pains me to let you live. You know that, right? You are the sole magic-user among the humans. If I was to erase you from existence here and now, the rest of humanity would not stand a chance of surviving for long." He growled and jumped to the ground in front of Charles, towering over the injured human.

He stepped closer and leaned over to look Charles in the face. "I heard you already have had a run-in with another champion on my side. My goddess wishes you to know you got lucky. It won't happen a third time." The monsters' breath smelled of death and rot, as though his very insides were rotting away.

The large goblin turned and jumped to the top of the cage, leaving him with those parting words and not looking back.

Charles quickly focused and activated his 'Analyze' ability.

Gabreen the Goblin Lord Lv. 20
Chosen Champion of an opposing god.

"He's a level 20 goblin lord and champion," He whispered to Alli, not daring to take his eyes off the goblin's back.

"He's dangerous," Alli said simply, before nudging him weakly with her side. "We need to prepare everyone, there's no telling how long we have before they attack again."

To the sides of the clearing, goblins could be seen slowly backing away and then disappearing behind the houses and rubble.

Kira came to a stop next to him. "What was that? I could have sworn I heard that monster talking."

"You did." Charles felt his legs tremble as the last of the adrenaline he had been running on left his body. "I'll tell you more later, but right now we have to prepare. They're going to attack again, and we need to be ready." He closed his eyes and pulled a bottle of water from his inventory, guzzling down the contents in one go. "I have a broken arm that is no longer in its socket, have little mana left and can't trust my glove. This is going to suck."

Kira reached out with quick hands gripped his arm, and with a quick thrust popped his arm back into the socket. The nerves in his arm came alive at the abuse all protesting at once at the rough way they had been treated.

"Now it's only broken, can't help with the mana though. And you're right. This is going to suck." Her eyes held a deep weariness in them as she looked away. It didn't escape his notice that this was one of the few times she had touched him, he wondered if hurting him at the same time had made it easier for her to do so.

"Where's my sister? Where's Charlotte and your family?" He asked, forgetting about Scott again.

"They're all together, back there," She said pointing over her shoulder with her thumb. The hammer in her hands flashed and ran down her fingers, forming the bracelet around her wrist once more. "Your sister is scary. I don't know what her level is, but I haven't seen anyone using two knives like that since this all began. I think she and the group she had with her are the reason we won, most of the goblins fell to them."

Charles cradled broken and throbbing arm as he turned and headed towards where Kira had pointed. "Come on, we need to get everyone together while we can. Maybe open up the wall with your hammer and let them out or something?"

"I can do that." She cracked her neck and rolled her shoulders. "We might be able to save a few of the more useless ones that way, doesn't fix our issue though."

Around them the former prisoners that were still conscious stumbled after them, the lack of food and water having finally caught up to them. They would be useless in the coming fight, even if he fed and gave them all water now it wouldn't do any good. They needed time to recover, time that they obviously didn't have.

Charlotte was sitting on the muddy ground her back pressed against a cage. Kate was sitting wearily next to her. To their left, Kory and Krystal were working together with Scott and others to lay the unconscious out.

Charlotte looked up at him and groaned. "It's not over yet, is it?"

"No," He said as he stopped in front of her, wanting to do nothing more than relax on the ground and not-sleep. That would come in fourteen days, or sooner if he was lucky. He missed sleep, the embrace of sweet oblivion. Charles shook, jostling his arm in the process, the burning pain in his arm serving to help him refocus.

"They are playing with us; we get a short little break and then the real fight begins." He turned to look at goblin corpses spread all across the ground. "This was nothing more than them keeping us in place so their real warriors could get into position."

Charlotte pushed off the ground and helped Kate to her feet. "We need to prepare then." She turned to look at the cage behind her, lightly biting her lower lip as she did so. "These cages have metal bottoms and tops, if we can get enough people together then we can move them around. Line them up and then tip them over, use them as a barricade, maybe even leave an open spot for them to come through. We can control how many get through that way, while still giving us a chance to whittle their numbers down."

"Make sure all the goblins are looted then, we can use their weapons. Regardless of whatever we do, we need to do it fast." He said weakly. "I need a few minutes though; my mana is gone and I'm running on empty energy-wise."

"Kate, find him a place to rest. Kira, you are with me, we need to get these people organized and prepared." Charlotte ordered them, taking control when she saw her younger brother was barely standing and in no position to do so.

Being extra careful to not jostle his arm Kate led him away and over to a tree that didn't have anyone near it. Alli plodded along behind him, her own energy flagging from the overuse of her abilities. Kate helped him sit down with his back to the tree before running off to help everyone else. He could hear his sister ordering everyone about, as he discretely pulled some food and water from his inventory. It would do no good to get the starving people thinking about food when they needed to prepare. He, however, had hopes that it would revitalize him and Alli, or at least let them function for a while longer.

Chapter 13

Alli gobbled down pieces of beef jerky hungrily as Charles emptied his third bottle of water. Storing everything back in his inventory for later use, he cast his healing spell on himself, guiding it to his arm and knitting his broken bone back together. It wasn't truly healed, not yet at least. He didn't have the energy to spare for that, but it would hold and keep it from hurting at least.

The jerky he had eaten had helped with his energy to a certain extent, but no more than it would have normally. It had done absolutely nothing for mana; however, he could feel it slowly trickling in at the same pace as before. Losing the ability to freely use the glove had truly driven home how screwed the curse the gods had put on him made him. He wasn't able to use the stats he had earned with his level-ups, leaving him weak and next to useless in a real fight.

The clang of a cage being tipped over brought Charles back from his melancholy thoughts. He had to keep his sister and friends safe!? He thought it over for a moment, yes; he considered Kira and Kate at least to be friends. They had been through a lot together, and they deserved his help.

Charles scratched at Alli's side as he stood. "Come on, let's go help them get everything ready." His voice was dull even to his ears as he spoke. He didn't have a lot of hope for them surviving the coming fight, regardless of what the Goblin Lord had said to him.

Together they shuffled over to where Kira was pushing a cage across the ground by herself, everyone else was afraid to be near her. The story of how she had hit the man who had touched her had quickly circulated and now no-one wanted to risk it. The man himself was lying on the ground unconscious with a smashed face.

Kira didn't necessarily seem to mind being excluded; however, and just kept working, Charles had a feeling she was used to this kind of treatment. Strangely, the thought of her being ignored or abused in some way sent a pang through his chest. He had never been very good with people in general and that was double for relationships. It was part of the reason he had always wanted one, actually. Even he could tell, however, what that pang meant; he was coming to care for the angry damaged woman.

The water on the grass and the mud helped the cages slid easier than they would have otherwise. That's not to say it was easy, because it wasn't. It took Kira and Charles with Alli helping several minutes to get their cage in position. When it was over, he just wanted to collapse again, moving the heavy metal cage had taken more energy than he thought it would.

The field around them had been cleared of goblin bodies, each vanishing into sparkles of light after they had been looted. The knives and spears the monsters had been using were now plentiful, arming those who could fight.

Twenty minutes after Gabreen the Goblin Lord left, the cages were in position, creating a barrier in front of the survivors. Ten cages, strategically placed, covered the front and sides, leaving the wall to guard their back. It wasn't perfect, even though the cages were large the area they were forced to protect was larger. They had done the best they could, but the gap in the middle they had left to funnel the monsters was larger than they would have liked.

The wall of cages was unfortunately just that in the end, a wall. Monsters could climb over it and into their midst if they took the time to think about it. They could only hope that the goblins and whatever else was about to come to attack them were stupid.

Charles stood next to his sister and Kira. Alli was laying at Kate's feet, eyes on the approaching wave of monsters, relaxing for as long as she could. They had appeared moments ago, a long erratic line howling in rage as they ran towards them.

Everyone with a weapon was in position, ready as they could be with the limited time they'd had to prepare.

Charles held his knives nervously and glanced down at his glove. He had not been in this position to fight in close quarters since the first day. He didn't like it, and as soon as he could have that conversation with Bob, he was going to learn how to fix it.

For now, he just needed to survive and keep the people around him alive as well.

The ground was slippery, and the mud began to deepen into a quagmire that pulled at the feet with every step. It left the attacking forces pulling against it, while the defenders could stand in place waiting.

Between forty and fifty goblins had attacked the first time around, this time it was closer to a hundred. The big difference though was that not all of them were regular goblins. The larger and tougher hobgoblins were interspersed among them, acting as leaders for each group. On the outskirts, four shamans could be seen, their feathered headdresses and long staffs making them apparent.

Thankfully, it was still raining and the moisture in the air kept the cost of using his ice magic to a minimum. He focused on the creation of his icy lances making them as dense as he could without going overboard. With a twist of his mana, he added a spin to all four, hoping that it would add some penetration along with the speed his firebolt had exhibited. Aiming at the four shamans on the outskirts, he let the lances fly.

Without delay, his lances went through the goblin horde, cutting down anything unfortunate enough to be in their way. Two of the shamans disappeared in clouds of pink mist, a line of dead goblins leading straight to them. The third was lying on the ground missing an arm and most of its chest, it wouldn't be alive much longer. The fourth however was still alive, at the cost of the hobgoblins life that had stepped unknowingly in the path of the bolt of ice.

In one single attack, Charles had eliminated three shamans, one hobgoblin and over twenty regular goblins. The ferocity of his attack made everyone pause and stare at him in awe and fear. The lull lasted for a single heartbeat before the remaining shaman screamed and the goblins leaped forward. Their long, thin limbs dragging through the heavy mud, while the screams of their shaman kept them focused on the thought of blood.

The larger hobgoblins railed at their backs, keeping them going and whipping them into a frenzy. The fear they had felt at seeing a fifth of their group disappearing in an instant hidden behind the promise of blood and meat.

Next to him, he saw Charlotte calmly reach up and tap the sides of her glasses. There were dots running all along the side and frame of her glasses, and it was one of these that she tapped. His sister gripped her knives and bounced lightly on her feet, a feral grin spreading across her face.

"It feels good to let loose every once in a while," She said, as she focused on the coming mob of monsters.

Kira gave a bark of laughter as her bracelet flashed and formed her massive hammer, that seemed to change a little every time she used it. It was learning from her fighting style, molding itself to best fit her.

Alli stood and stretched with a yawn, her large paws spreading as she did so.

When they were ten feet from the line of overturned cages, Charles cast one last spell emptying him completely. A wave of frost and ice extended outwards, coating the ground in front of the goblins.

Those in front lost their balance and tripped but were immediately trampled by those behind them. The sight of them tripping all over themselves would have been hilarious if their lives didn't hang in the balance.

It was only then that Charles remembered he had put all the guns back in his inventory after Tara's group had thrown them away. The guns still wouldn't do much if any damage, but with the ice shots at their legs could have at least tripped them. It was a wasted opportunity that would have delayed them for a few seconds at best.

To the side, the shaman could barely be seen waving his staff in the air and dancing in a circle. The ice on the ground began to sizzle and pop, shards of ice flinging themselves upwards into the goblins. Within seconds the ice was gone, no longer impeding their path in any way.

The battle had truly begun.

Goblins surged forward, those that had been trampled struggling to their hands and feet in an effort to keep from being stepped on again.

Charlotte leaped forward with Kira at her side in a move of recklessness she would never have tried before the apocalypse. Her knives flashed through the air, and each time she struck it was at a vital spot that would do the most damage.

Kira stood a few feet away, where her hammer wouldn't accidentally hit the other woman. Her swings split the air, and anything hit would go rocketing backward. Crippling blows was the best way to describe the two of them. They were crippling the enemy before they could do more harm.

The line was soon joined by everyone else that could still hold a weapon. Their arms were trembling from exhaustion and each of them only had maybe one attack in them. The days they had spent locked up without food and water had taken their toll, reducing them to thin, weak specters of their former selves.

They were not going to let that stop them; however, this was a fight for their lives. A fight they intended to win... if at all possible.

The two forces collided explosively, members of each side getting thrown back. The resulting clash was a mess of epic proportions as the humans tangled and fell, their inexperience showing as they fumbled with their weapons. Arms collided with arms as all thought left their tattered minds, leaving the struggling humans as little more than animals.

Few of them had ever been in a fight for their lives before now, and the sudden confusion of a battlefield proved that. All sense of cohesion or semblance of working together fell apart as more of them fell to the coordinated attacks of the hobgoblins. A few fled, more died as they tried to.

Alli used short jumps through the shadows to eliminate as many hobgoblins as she could, dragging them to the ground and then ripping their throats out.

The shaman danced madly to the side, cackling madly as balls of fire fell on the cages, melting them to slag after repeated shots.

The line broke completely with that, as the goblins were able to get around the group of fighters. A cry from behind distracted Kira and a goblin managed to thrust its spear through her thigh. She fell without seeing who had cried out, a passing hobgoblin smacked her head with his club and then moved on when she fell.

Kate went under a mass of bodies next, buried and unable to move after the first few piled on top of her.

They were being overrun by the more experienced goblins.

Charlotte had a ring of bodies surrounding her as she danced from attack to attack, and then she slipped. The rain had made the grass and mud increasingly slippery. Charles looked up from his own group of monsters in time to see her fall, goblin knives glistened in the rain as they plunged down after her.

And then everything went blank.

***

Kira watched through muddy, blood-filled eyes as Charlotte fell and saw Charles pause. His face morphed instantly into something else, turning the blood in her veins to ice. A rictus of pain and anger turned his visage into a mask that rivaled anything she had ever read described.

His eyes went blank, and his body began to glow with an inner light. A pressure washed over everything, commanding everything in its path to stop. Kira felt her heart stutter and saw the rain itself stop on its way to the ground.

The eyes of the goblins rolled in their heads, as they lost control of their bodies. Barely sufficient loincloths flapped to the side as the still living goblins all released a black sludge from their bowels at the same time. The smell was overwhelming, but no one could move to cover their mouths and noses. Every eye was fixed on Charles's glowing form.

His gloved hand extended out from his body as it pulled in the mana from the surrounding area. The speed of its attraction making the mana glow in multicolored hues visible by all as they collected around the hand.

In a voice that thrummed with power, deeper and older than his own, spoke a command filled with power. "Mists of Dispersion!"

Every monster still alive in the area immediately had their body turned to mist and then dispersed. They had been reduced to their basic elements; their very existence erased from the face of the Earth.

Charlotte was revealed on the ground covered in mud but alive, the goblins above her never having the chance to finish their strike. Farther away Kate could be seen covered in cuts and blood but also alive. Alli could be seen half in shadow and half out right behind where the shaman had stood moments earlier.

The glow suffusing Charles faded as he saw that his sister was alright. The last of the light surrounding him winked out, and the pressure holding everything in place vanished. The rain fell to the ground as though it had never stopped.

Charles wavered in place, and then his eyes rolled to the back of his head and he began to convulse. Kira pushed herself blearily to her feet, her sense of balance and equilibrium having vanished with the blow to her head. She stumbled over to him, her hands splashing against the mud and ground more than once as she stumbled to her knees. The fifteen or so feet that separated them felt like an eternity but was over in seconds as she rushed to his side.

A foam had formed around the edges of his mouth as he continued to convulse. The muscles under his skin shifting and moving of their own accord. Charlotte collapsed to the ground beside her, not daring to turn away from her brother.

"What is happening to him?" She asked the other woman not knowing what to do for her brother.

Kira remembered the last time she had seen his body doing something similar. "I think, he's leveling up. All the stats he has earned are coming into effect and changing his body."

Charlotte finally looked away from her brother to glare at Kira. "Don't be stupid, that happens when you sleep at night and it's nowhere near as violent as this!"

"Your brother hasn't slept since the apocalypse happened; he was cursed by the gods the day it started. Every single stat he has allocated from his many level-ups is coming into effect at the same time." Blood had started to flow in thin rivulets from his ears as she was speaking.

The veins and muscles underneath his skin slowly stop squirming around like they were trying to escape their fleshy prison. The flow of blood from his ears grew thicker and his breathing grew rapid.

Charlotte could only watch helplessly as her last living family member went through his changes. Scott came up behind her with Kira's parents and Kate and held her as they all watched him with bated breath.

The flow of blood slowed to a trickle and then finally stopped, the rain washing away the remnants seconds later.

His body snapped straight a moment later, his muscles rigid and standing firm underneath his skin. His legs tremored unable to move as his body locked up, then it was his arms fighting to free themselves.

"Look at his arms," Kate said, the first to notice what was changing.

He was wearing a simple leather jacket that had been torn and was now full of holes, his t-shirt underneath in even worse condition. The jacket had fallen open when he fell, leaving a portion of his upper bicep visible.

The silvery edges of a swooping rune could be seen snaking its way around his arm. No longer were the runes constrained to just the one thigh Kira had seen. She was sure that when he awoke, he would find them all over his body now.

"What is that?" Scott asked with wide eyes.

Charlotte tilted her head and answered before Kira could even open her mouth. "It's a rune." She turned to Kira as Alli barreled her way through the group and settled her body next to Charles, licking his face with a soft whine. "Why does my brother have metallic looking runes growing on his body?"

Kira shrugged not knowing exactly how to answer her. "The glove does it to him," She finally said.

They all watched as this process repeated itself several times. His body would relax, and the muscles would shift beneath his skin, then his ear would begin to bleed, and finally, his body would grow rigid as another rune was carved onto his skin somewhere.

None of them paid any attention to the people that had begun to wake up, leaving them to attend to themselves. Conversation ceased between them as they watched Charles, each hoping that he would survive the process and wake soon.

Chapter 14

Charles felt as though his mind were drifting on tall waves when he slowly began to regain consciousness. The tall waves would raise him up, and then drop him to the bottom at a speed, rollercoasters would envy.

His mind churned with the changes it had gone through, his body aching for the same reason. His back was wet, though the front of his body had dried underneath the gentle Pennsylvania sun. Gradually he became aware of his surroundings, people talking softly, mostly about him. His body refused to respond to his commands, leaving him to lay there and listen to the people. His world was dark, unable to even see a red tinge of the sun through his eyelids.

"Did you see what he did to those monsters? I've never seen anything like it before!" A voice he didn't recognize said.

"What if he turns that power on us?" Another voice asked.

"He might be able to keep us safe," Still another voice went on.

For several long minutes he lay there, listening to the voices of people he didn't know talk about him. The voices he longed to hear didn't make an appearance however, and as the memories of seeing his friends and sister disappear under piles of monsters, his breathing grew ragged and labored.

"It's alright, we're here and we're safe." The loving voice of his sister crooned to him soothing the ache that had started to form.

Something wet moved across his face, and it took him several moments to realize it was Alli's tongue.

"Stupid people, don't they realize we can hear them?" Kira asked distrustfully from the opposite side of his sister.

"Probably not, or they just aren't aware enough to care." Scott's voice came from somewhere beside his sister.

Kira snorted but didn't say anything more.

It took Charles several long minutes for his mind to calm enough for him to think properly. The waves were still throwing his mind around at their whim, but their height and force had been reduced. He went through his memories again and came up against a blank wall. He remembered seeing Kira and his sister go down, and then nothing more. Nothing that would explain, why he was on the ground apparently having passed out.

That thought clicked in his head, he had passed out, that explained why he was sore all over. He had finally managed to level-up properly. His joy was short lived however as he remained unable to move, the lingering effects of his body undergoing such a massive change keeping him from moving.

He lay trapped in his body, listening to everything the people they had saved said about him for several long minutes.

He had been awake for over thirty-minutes when his eyelids twitched and then opened. The sun hung high in the sky, denoting how long he had been out. The final fight had started around eight or so, it was impossible to tell with the way the clouds had covered the sky. Either way, it was closer to noon than eight, meaning he had been out for hours.

He blinked again, several messages and notifications coming into being in the corner of his vision. Charlotte's head appeared above his own, her shoulder length dirty blonde hair tickling his cheeks. Her stormy green eyes were darker than his own pale green and were filled with clear relief that he was awake.

"You're awake," She said softly, tears creeping into the corners of her eyes. "Don't you ever make me worry about you like that again. Do you understand me?"

Charles grinned and nodded, still unsure of what had happened. The messages in the corner of his vision blinked distractingly, but he ignored them for the moment as he was pulled to his feet. Kira gripped one hand tightly, Charlotte the other. Kira seemed reluctant to drop his hand as she stepped back, a look of confusion and wonder on her face.

"What happened?" He asked as he wobbled on his feet, his body feeling different and unfamiliar to him.

"You tell us," Kate said with a laugh.

"Yeah man, you started to glow, and everything stopped moving. You spoke a single word, 'disperse', and then all the monsters turned to mist and disappeared." Scott spoke up, his normally intelligent demeanor falling away, leaving him dumbfounded at what he had seen.

Kira chose to remain silent about what she had seen for now, she would discuss it with him in detail later.

Charles shook his head, putting his questions to the side for the moment. What Scott had said made no sense, but at the moment they had bigger things to worry about.

"We'll talk about that later." He looked at his sister and smirked. "Just another thing for us to talk about when we have the time. Right now, we need to be going, there's no telling how long we will need to get back on the road."

"We're just waiting on part of my group to return," Charlotte informed him with a scowl. "Kira gave us some gas to put in our truck, so they left to retrieve it a while ago. As soon as they return, we can leave, their vehicles have all been found next to the river. A couple of them were damaged, but they're all still drivable. So, don't try to distract us, we have everything well in hand. Tell us what happened!" Her voice left no doubt that her request was actually a demand.

"I don't know." He began with a feigned, carefree shrug. "I remember Kate getting buried in bodies, Kira getting stabbed in the leg and going down, and then you, slipping and falling. Everything after that is blank. Speaking of which let me look at your leg Kira."

Kira stepped timidly forward, tilting her leg towards him even as the rest of her went rigid.

Charles touched her leg and closed his eyes, feeling the magic in his body jumping to obey his commands. He didn't even need to speak the spells name for it to begin healing her, a soft green glow surrounding her thigh. The damaged muscles and the slightest nick on a vein that would have torn, if she wasn't careful, repaired themselves. Her skin knitted back together, a thin white line of scar tissue the only reminder that she had been injured, before it too faded.

Charles kept his eyes closed even after he had finished healing her, feeling at his mana and his body. His entire body glowed green as he healed everything he found, muscles that had torn with all their rapid movements. Skin that had stretched a little too thin in another area, the nerves around his shoulder socket that were inflamed from their earlier abuse and his barely healed arm. Countless little things that had happened during the battle and afterward.

He healed them all and felt only the slightest dip in his available mana, the potency of his magic and sheer amount he had access to, was several magnitudes greater than before. He felt great, his body responding better and faster than it ever had before. His thoughts were smoother and more organized.

"I've finally leveled-up," He announced to the group softly in a self-satisfied smile. Even without the glove, he was no longer helpless.

Kira was standing in front of him, her hand pointing to her thigh. "Your healing has gotten faster."

"Gather everyone up, I'll heal everyone before we leave," He told them, reveling in his newfound power and wanting to keep using it. The amount of mana he had used to heal himself and Kira had already come back to him, leaving his magic energy full.

As one, the entire group growled at him. There were things they needed to talk about, and he was ignoring them.

"Everyone gather up if you want to be healed!" They all yelled out before standing together in front of Charles, forming a line with them at the front.

For the next thirty-minutes Charles healed each person in line, their cries of astonishment falling on deaf ears. Finally, everyone had been healed, and the group that had left to retrieve Charlotte and Scott's truck had returned with it in tow. The back was piled high with non-perishable goods.

The rest of her group pulled their vehicles forward, the professor still unconscious in one of them. Charles had been unable to fully heal the wounds inflicted during their ritual. The scars gleaming white all across his chest and arms, several of them resembling bastardized versions of the runes Charles had inscribed on his own body.

"Wait, where are you going?" One of the original inhabitants of the town cried out.

"Kansas City," Kory yelled back to them, as they left through a hole in the wall Kira had smashed with her hammer.

"But we need you, he's the only one who can heal us, and keep us safe!"

Charles ignored their pleas and continued on. He didn't belong to anyone, and he certainly didn't owe those people anything. He had healed them because he felt like it, that was all. They were unimportant to him, and he cared little about what happened to them after he left.

He had a town to create.

His steps stuttered and stopped at that thought. "Tell them that we are creating a new town there. If they want to join us, they can help us build it." He said thoughtfully. Constructing a town required people, and the little group that was following his sister was not going to be enough.

Alli padded at his side and climbed into the back of their truck first. Charles tossed the keys for it to Kory as he caught up to them after relaying Charles' message.

Together, Charlotte and Kira piled in the back of the truck with him, Scott driving their truck just behind them.

Charles held up his hand before they could get started with the questions. "Hold on, I have a lot of messages and notifications that I need to go through first. After that we can talk."

Charlotte folded her arms and glared at him, her fingers tapping impatiently on her arm as she waited. He had told her 'later' consistently since finding her that morning and she was tired of it, she wanted answers, and she wanted them now. Kira had her back to tailgate and was studying her fingers quietly, her mind somewhere else.

Charles quickly dismissed any notifications relating to experience, looking for the important ones.

Congratulations, you have learned your first Digh@# Eot^esl spell, 'Mists of Dispersion'. Mists of Dispersion is a high-grade Digh@# Eot^esl spell that changes enemies to their base elements and then disperses them. Spell is currently unusable due to not meeting certain requirements.

Congratulations, due to the use of a high-level spell, advanced runes have been inscribed on your body.

Congratulations, due to the advanced runes inscribed on your body reaching an acceptable level, high-level magic can now be used.

Congratulations, through the use of inscribing your body with advanced runes your understanding of magic has increased. Further secrets relating to magic will be revealed through the use of meditation.

Congratulations, the effects of meditation have been increased due to the runes inscribed on your body. As a result, Mana Usage has been upgraded to Mana Control. The mana in the world around you can now be felt, in time you may be able to access some of it. Spells no longer require words to be used and may be shaped for additional effects depending on your understanding of the spell itself.

He was puzzled over the existence of another garbled message. The message at least made a little more sense this time though than it had the first time. The existence of a spell he couldn't use, but apparently had also confused him. The effects of 'Mists of Dispersion' matched with what he had been told he had done to the goblins.

The runes messages were the most troubling; however, he only had the runes inscribed on his skin when he used a lightning spell. According to what everyone had said that hadn't been the case this time, which meant it was one of the side-effects he had been warned about.

It had worked out okay this time, in that he had been unconscious at the time. The sheer number of messages relating to the runes was daunting. He was scared to look and see just how much of his body was now covered in odd silvery runes.

Closing the last of his messages he pulled up his stat sheet next, suddenly glad that he had taken the time to distribute everything before the second battle had started.

Charles Byrne || Level: 15 || Exp to next Level: 53421

Class: Archmage

Strength: 30 (+8) || Intelligence: 70 (+31)

Dexterity: 30 (+2) || Magic: 47 (+20)

Constitution: 40 (+10) || Agility: 32 (+4)

*Cursed by the gods with 'Sleepless' * || Available Status Points: 0*

A new item had been added underneath his name indicating his class as 'Archmage'. His new stats were shown on the left, with the amount they had increased by on the right. He had allocated the bulk of his status points to intelligence and magic, with the leftover spread out on everything else. He was no longer a weakling in danger of dying constantly because he could no longer use the glove. For the moment at least he was normal for someone his level.

With a thought he dismissed the stat sheet and focused on his sister and Kira whose hair was blowing wildly in the wind.

"Alright then, I think I know at least some of what happened to me now. What do you want to know?" He asked loud enough for them both to hear.

Kira scooched closer so she could hear easier but looked to Charlotte to begin.

She lifted her hands in exasperation. "I don't even know where to begin with what I don't know. Just tell me everything from the beginning."

So, Charles did just that, he told her of waking up to a goddess in his bedroom, of her telling him about the fate of his parents and his sister. He told her of how he found Alli, and then how Kira found and helped him, how she left them behind. Everything, many of the things he explained were new for Kira as well, as he hadn't told her everything before.

He finished off with the message about the unknown magic 'Mists of Dispersion'. "That's everything that I can think of."

They had stopped for gas once an hour into him talking and were due for another stop soon judging by the position of the sun.

Charlotte had remained silent the entire time, absorbing his words. "I think you and I might be different from everyone else. You slept through the apocalypse, and I likely only awoke for it because I was sleeping lightly in the lab at school. If I had been in my own bed with Scott, I probably would have slept through it as well. I saw what everyone around me went through during the change, but for me it was more like a relaxing massage it was nice, not painful. Then there's our inventory, I haven't told anyone but Scott this but it's different from everyone else's. It's like yours, size and ability to stack included."

"So, we're what, mutants?" Charles asked with a forced laugh when she had finished.

She shrugged in defeat. "I don't know, but I have a feeling it has something to do with those garbled messages of yours. They're hiding something important, something you shouldn't have access to." She pushed her glasses farther up her nose as she spoke.

"I have to ask, who chose you as a champion, and what is with the glasses?" Charles burst out at the subtle reminder.

Charlotte cocked her head with a smug smile. "Unlike you with the nameless god, I actually got someone important enough to have a name. I was chosen by Saraswati, she's the Hindu goddess of learning and knowledge. I think it's a good fit." Charles could only nod, he had never heard of that particular goddess but trusted that his sister had. "As for the glasses, they're not a weapon per-se not like Kira's at least. They are mostly geared towards learning and experimenting, that I think work with my attribute 'Magitech'. I'm pretty sure that after you teach me how to use magic, they'll become invaluable with whatever that pertains to." She paused with a mischievous grin. "In battle they do have a function that highlights weak points and high damage locations. I don't know if it helps me hit them, but in the battle earlier I was certainly hitting those locations more often than not."

"That's handy," Kira spoke up for the first time in a while, having been content to listen. Alli was asleep against her side.

Charles could already see some of the things his sister would be able to do once she learned magic. Her attribute had the potential to change everything.

"What do we do now?" Kira asked looking at them both.

"Now, now we use the barrels of gas in my inventory to get us back to Kansas City as quickly as possible. I don't know how long the Goblin Lord is going to wait before he attacks again, and I want to be ready. We have limited time to get the area in front of the dungeon livable and safe, and we need to make the most of it. We have what another three, four days before the game is supposed to begin." Charles stopped speaking as Kory took them off-road and into the woods, avoiding the plane crash up ahead. They had made good time and were already about to cross the state-line. If they hurried, they could be back at the dungeon sometime the next day.

They were each lost to their own thoughts for a time as the miles rolled by.

"Do you think we'll run into Tara and her group on our way back?" Kira asked with a slightly sadistic grin, breaking the silence.

Charles laughed at the question and shook his head. "That reminds me we need to figure out how to keep the undesirables out of our soon to be formed town."

Interlude 2

"There, that right there can be our boon!" Shiva yelled with a laugh.

Saraswati looked intrigued at the idea. Now that she had a champion of her own, she was trying to participate more. "How would it work exactly? Would we set it up or let them?"

"They will," Odin decided for them, as the ravens perched on his shoulder squawked in agreement. "We will merely give them the ability to make it an automatically enforced oath, that all who live there must take."

"Are we talking about giving them a contract type ability or is this a one-time thing for the town?" Brigit asked, her nose scrunched as she thought through the possibilities.

Bob who had been distracted for a while at the point looked up, the conversation pulling his thoughts away from Charles. "What are we talking about?" He asked, steepling his fingers together.

"We're talking about what we're going to use our boon on, we're thinking of allowing them to create a contract that would enforce the town's laws." Shiva's voice boomed throughout the room, his exuberance getting the better of him.

Bob leaned back in his high-backed chair, the cushion on the back supporting him just right as he thought. "I'm alright with this idea, let's say it has a maximum of five tenets that each person has to agree to live by and swear to. What kind of punishment were you thinking for those that break their oaths?"

Brigit positively bounced in her chair at the question. Her kind were forced to live by oaths and having the chance to inflict their misery on others was a delightful prospect. "They can decide the punishments as well, but the foundation of the oaths should be connected to each person's elemental core. Even for those that can't touch or use mana yet, it would still be a binding oath that their own core will enforce per the oath made."

Arinna the sun goddess who was one of the three gods yet to choose a champion spoke up, her voice filling everyone in the room with warmth. "Why is it so important to have the town guarding the dungeon?"

Bob pointed to Alaria who was standing next to the door with an amused expression. "Would you like to handle that question, goddess from another world?"

"My world creates mana constantly, and very little of it gets used by the current systems I have in place. The humans and other species on my world have grown complacent with merely surviving, not taking advantage of these systems to their full potential. Recently, however, a boy from Earth appeared on my world, and I believe he will soon begin to change everything. As a form of thanks, I opened negotiations with Bob and learned that this world is desperately in need of mana. I have agreed to help supply the Earth with mana through my dungeon here. The town Charles has been tasked with building is insurance to keep it safe from those that might wish it harm."

"A little long-winded but you get the idea," Bob said leaning forward with his elbows on the table.

"Well, sorry!" Alaria apologized sulkily elongating the words. "There is very little opportunity for a goddess to have a decent conversation on my world."

Zeus roared with laughter. "You won't suffer from that problem here. There are already too many of us gods for it to ever be quiet."

"I don't mean to interrupt this... enlightening conversation, but how are they going to construct the town in time?" One of the gods not playing but was watching from the walls asked. "There's no telling when that goblin champion is going to attack them, building anything traditionally would take too much time."

Everyone in the room looked at Bob for an answer.

"About that, there is actually a system I put into place before we began that they can use. I was planning to unveil it when they got to the designated location, as currently, Charles is the only human alive who can use it." Bob paused for effect as they all listened with rapt attention.

"The system is simple; it uses magic to take the supplies they provide to build. I put a series of different blueprints for everything into the system that he can choose from. All they need to do is provide the materials and have Charles provide the mana."

"What about facilities and electricity?" Zeus asked, feeling that the electricity part fell under his purview.

"The facilities they can use will be basic until they design a system for electricity, which shouldn't be difficult. There are several rather smart individuals in their group. However, certain radioactive elements have become inert with the introduction of mana to the world once more. They will never be able to use nuclear materials for electricity or weapons again." Bob calmly explained.

"What about the enemy champions?" Another voice asked from the walls, everyone was slowly starting to get into the game they had created.

Bob waved away the question. "They won't be a bother right away, they'll be busy gathering monsters for their army and then moving across the county. Depending on how they go about it, the town could be safe for several weeks after the game begins. Of course, they might make it there within a couple of days as well."

Chapter 15

They drove late into the night before stopping at an abandoned rest stop. Charlotte had gone back to her own truck with Scott hours earlier after they had finished talking. They had stalled on the idea of how to keep the town safe, while also having laws that could be enforced. Ideas had been bandied back and forth; in the end, they hadn't been able to think of anything that would work.

Three old station wagons followed behind the two lead trucks, with the rest of their group from MIT in them. The professor lay in the back of the first car, awake but catatonic. His body may have been healed by Charles, but his mind was ill-prepared to sort through what had happened to him.

"How many people do you think will follow us from that town?" Kate asked after she had finished training with Charles. She was making progress with assimilating her core but had only managed to finish a single hand.

Charles had noticed when they began training that night that his abilities in teaching her had changed. He was now able to activate meditation for her without her needing to touch his glove or even act as a guide. Now that he had shown her the way to her elemental core until she completed this first part of her training, he was unable to teach her more. The class Archmage had come with enhanced teaching abilities, and he could only assume this was one of them.

"All of them," Alli told her, touching her wet nose to the teenage girls' arm. "I heard them talking as we left, the power Charles controls terrifies them, but they also realize that his power can keep them safe. They were going to get as many working vehicles as they can and then ransack the town for everything usable. I expect they'll be a couple of days behind us."

Alli leaped from the back of the truck and ran up to the building of the rest stop. She sniffed and then sneezed, "I can't tell if there is anyone alive in there, the smell of the restrooms is over-whelming."

Charles relayed what she had said to everyone else, leaving the decision of where they wanted to sleep to them. He would be fine wherever since he couldn't actually sleep, he would use the time to meditate and no place was comfortable after meditating all night long without moving.

Charlotte and Scott pulled the catatonic professor from the back of the car he had been laying in while the rest of their group swept the building. The professor's eyes were wide open, but he only seemed to blink once a minute regardless of what was going on around him.

The people inside motioned that it was all clear and everyone but Charles and Alli hurried inside. They were all tired and worn out. It had been a long exhausting day. Charles leaned against the uneven brick exterior of the building and looked up at the green-tinged night sky. Alli was curled up next to him, her paws held ineffectually over her sensitive nose, enduring the smell for his sake.

Charles closed his eyes and brought up the ever-growing number of partitions in his mind. There was a partition there for each element he had learned, including the nameless garbled one that shone with a warm golden light. He let partitions fully form and then retreated into the depths of his mind and body. He had been making progress feeling and to an extent controlling the mana inside his body before today. Now with his body having finally leveled up and the new runes inscribed in his flesh he wanted to see how it responded.

Just like when he had used the healing spells earlier, the mana in his body jumped to respond. It was almost eager to be used and shaped in any way that he desired. The concentration of mana in his body had also grown thicker and denser.

The mana running through his body had felt like a gaseous cloud the night before and now was approaching a liquid state. There were still sections that were a thick gas, but there were also the denser sections that now had a weight to them.

All night long he manipulated the mana in his body, evening out the flow and density until it all matched. When he was finished, he noticed that his body was absorbing the mana in the air around him at a slightly faster rate than before.

The sun was creeping over the trees when he opened his eyes. He was glad they had not been disturbed during the night, but it felt wrong. The sudden absence of monsters everywhere had his nerves on edge. They were acting strangely, and he had a bad feeling in the pit of his stomach that it was related to those two enemy champions showing up. They were taking control of the monsters around them; they were building their armies.

In the short term, it was a good thing as it meant they were probably mostly safe for the moment. In the long term, however, it meant they were screwed, there was no way they could stand up to two different armies of bloodthirsty monsters. He had seen how large the Bugbears army had been days before, how much larger would it be in a few days or in a week.

A shiver ran through him as he began to fully realize how much work they needed to put into this town. It was going to need a very strong wall among other things, and it all needed to be built from the remains of buildings. This was not going to be a quick project by any means, which he was beginning to think it needed to be.

Alli ran off into the woods for a few minutes when she felt him stirring; it was going to be another long day in the back of a truck. She needed to take care of certain things before that.

The professor was still in a catatonic state, though he was beginning to at least blink semi-regularly now. Everyone got into their respective cars after having Charles fill their water bottles and were off.

It was another quiet day that lasted until they reached St. Louis. The people that had seen them drive by days before had blocked off the road and were waiting for them to return. A few of them held knives, but most were armed with guns that were ineffective against monsters. Depending on the person's level and attributes, they could still hurt humans, however. Meaning that these people were prepared to hurt humans and not looking for monsters.

A large woman with bulging muscles and gloves made for punching stood at the front of the group with her hand held up.

Kira jumped from behind the wheel and got into the woman's face before anyone could fire. "What do you think you are doing?" She demanded harshly, obviously prepared to fight them.

The larger muscle-bound woman took a step back with her hands up. "We just want information, not trouble."

Kira relaxed slightly at her word. It wasn't that she fully believed her, but if they wanted information first, then they had time before they would attack. "Information on what?"

The woman looked behind her at the group of men and woman blocking the road; it was apparent that they had not thought this far ahead. "Everything, especially where you all got working vehicles."

"No," Kira said with a hard edge to her voice, making it clear she was done with this farce. "We are not going to tell you anything, now either get out of our way or pay the price."

Charles activated his ability on her, getting her information.

Donna Pruett Lv. 8 Age 35

She was nothing great, her level was too low for her to offer much of a challenge. Alli had originally been paying attention, but as the other groups' intentions became clear, she had turned away ignoring everything.

Donna tried to look innocent for a moment before giving up the pretense. "Fine, we'll do it your way. Give us the vehicles and all your supplies and we'll let you walk away."

Kira pretended to think, before looking back at Charles, "What do you think? Should we do as the muscle-bound idiot asks?"

"Up to you, she's far too weak to hurt us though." He said dispassionately, he was quickly losing his patience and Kira could tell that if she didn't act, he would.

With that thought in mind, her bracelet burst into light, the metal turning to liquid and flowing down into her hand forming her hammer. Donna stared, stunned by the display of something she had never even considered possible until that moment. With a grunt, Kira twisted the handle and swung, the head of the hammer turned to the side and Donna was hit with the flat middle section of the hammer. Several of her ribs cracked loudly as she was blown to the side of the road.

She would live, but it would take her a while to heal properly. Kira pointed her hammer at the rest of the people in the road. "Any of the rest of you want to try?"

With emphatic shakes of their heads, they scattered, leaving the road clear for them to drive through. Kira let her hammer reform into a bracelet and climbed into the passenger seat of their truck. Her father was driving; while her mother sat next to him, Kate was in the back spending her time training with Charles.

The number of cars and trucks on the road had noticeably decreased from when they had come through the first time. Newer vehicles had been shoved to the side of the road, while older cars and trucks had disappeared entirely. Large semi-trucks had been broken into the large trailers pillaged for food and items.

The people of St. Louis had been hard at work since they had seen the lone truck pass through. The knowledge that others were alive and still had working transportation had reinvigorated the despairing survivors.

They sped over the bridge and left the broken city behind them, the presence of abandoned vehicles growing as they left the city further behind. Kate remained focused throughout the day, never stopping her training for long. She was pushing herself and Charles could already see the strain it was having on her. She was not leaving enough time in-between sessions, and it was causing the mana in her body to be uneven and stagnant in many places. It was something that would need to be fixed painfully later on or less painfully now.

Through her impatience, Charles learned why these in-between sessions time was so important. It allowed the mana to circulate properly throughout the body and seamlessly join the pool of power the user would someday have access to. By ignoring what was supposed to be happening and pushing forward carelessly, Kate was causing the energy inside her to build up in ways it was never meant to.

Fixing the damage and rearranging the flow of mana in her body was going to be painful enough that he knew she would want to sleep the effects off. With that in mind, he let her continue throughout the day. He would inform her of her mistake that night before fixing her.

Hours after crossing the bridge, they neared the same rest stop they had left Tara and her group at. The sun had disappeared an hour earlier, though that didn't mean much in the fall. Watches had all stopped working, but it couldn't have been later than eight in the afternoon.

The washed-out yellow of their headlights illuminated the road as they pushed to reach the rest stop. They would stop there for the night, and the next day they would reach Kansas City. A city that they could only imagine had been wrecked by the storm, but also a city with survivors that were unknowns. They might attack them or attach themselves to the group and help rebuild. The unknown was causing everyone to worry at least a little.

Each time they stopped for gas, Scott and Charlotte had talked with the rest of the people in their group, explaining what they needed to do. None of the brainiacs were exactly excited at the thought of hard manual labor, but they also weren't willing to leave. Each and every one of them had dreamed of using magic at some point in their lives, and Charles was the only person that could make that dream a reality.

Kira had taken over the driving for her father earlier and slowed the truck as they neared the exit for the rest stop. The headlights bounced as they went over some bumps and then turned to go under the highway. Together the group rolled through a stop sign that no longer had meaning and pulled into the parking lot. The large canvas-covered back-end of the transport truck faced them, stuck in the same position they had last seen it in.

The doors to the building opened and a tired and slightly bloody Tara poked her head out. Looking closer, they could see dark splotches near the door, but no bodies were in sight.

Tara opened the door all the way and walked into the night, a distinct limp affecting her gait as she walked towards them. No doubt she had recognized the sound of the truck and its general shape. In the truck bed, Alli stirred and poked her head above the edge looking at the woman as she approached.

"You came back," She said with a grimace, her hand falling to the gash on the outside of her thigh.

Kira shut off the truck and stepped from the cab, slipping the key into her inventory as she glared at the other woman. The other vehicles shut off in turn, plunging everyone into darkness.

"See if whatever attacked them is still around," Charles whispered to Alli, before throwing an orb of light into the air.

Alli disappeared into the shadows as the light flared above their heads, allowing everyone to see Kira glaring at the older woman.

"Not for you," She finally answered coldly before turning and walking away.

Tara's eyes turned downcast as she remembered how they had parted, what she had tried to do. Truthfully, she didn't blame Kira for reacting the way she did. She had been in the wrong; she knew it then, and she knew it now.

The thud of air being forcefully displaced echoed in the night followed by the flap of wings.

"Everyone inside," Charles yelled, recognizing the sound like something that had chased him at night before.

Scott ran to the last car in line and hauled the near-comatose professor over his shoulder. Kory ran past a frozen Tara, Krystal, and Kate directly on his heels. Charles sent the orb of light ahead of them and into the building. With each passing second, the sound grew louder; yells could be heard from inside the building as they ran inside. Charles pushed Tara ahead of himself. He was to be the last inside. He wanted to see what was chasing them as he had never gotten a clear look of the flying monster in the past.

With a thought and a flick of his wrist, he created the brightest orb of light he could and threw it into the sky. In the past, creating an orb that bright would have taken several seconds along with him overcharging the spell. Now, it was the work of a split second and nothing more, the mana in his body leaping at the chance to be used.

The voices in the building cut-off all at once as the bright light surged into the sky revealing the monster that hunted during the night. The new monster that would haunt their dreams, knowing that this one was undeniably real.

A screech that caused their blood to freeze and large leathery wings scraped the top of the transport truck. There was another screech this time the tearing of metal as a razor-sharp claw on the end of the wing cut through the old military truck's cab. Before they could fully see what it was, the monster had retaken to the skies and was gone.

Charles looked away from the sky and to the ruined truck cab, the roof was slit cleanly down the middle. The metal wasn't jagged or anything, but smooth with a rolled edge where the cut had occurred. He let the orb of light dissipate and sat on the floor next to the door. It was the first time they had seen a monster roaming in days and it had to happen at night.

The dull sound of people talking in the background filled the interior of the building. He ignored it all and motioned for Kate to come over to him.

"I learned something today," He began. "There is supposed to be a period of time between each training session for a reason."

Kate looked uncertain but didn't interrupt him.

"By not allowing for the full integration period, the mana in your body is not working the way it is supposed to. It is supposed to be smooth and full of movement, because of today it no longer looks like that." Fear that she had screwed up something that couldn't be fixed crept into her eyes as she listened to him. "I can fix it," He said hurriedly before she could panic. "It is going to be very painful, however."

She settled into position in front of him. "What do I do?" Her muscles were rigid as she was already imagining the pain and bracing for it.

Charles sent the lone orb of light that had guided everyone into the building to the ceiling and settled back against the wall. "Touch the meditation point on the glove. I'm going to need the barrier for what I'm about to do."

Kate took in a deep breath and before she could psych herself out, touched the raised rune on his glove. The light blue barrier formed around the two of them, giving off enough light for them to be clearly seen.

Chapter 16

The barrier had functions that he hadn't fully known the use of before, as they had impacted her training. Now, he believed he knew what one of them was for. The barrier allowed him to see the movements of mana through her body, something that he could do now with his own abilities. What he couldn't do on his own however was control the way her mana moved, by entering into her body like he had the first few times they had trained he was able to enter her mana streams.

Charles felt his mind expand as he joined with the mana flowing through her body. He could now physically feel the areas where something was wrong. It gave him hope that in the future Kate and any others that learned to use magic would develop abilities to sense the flow of magic in their bodies.

He could feel the girl stiffen and grimace in pain as he went through her body, fixing the little things first. Smoothing the edges, boring through the smaller bottlenecks, getting her mana to flow just a little better for what was to come.

Slowly Charles withdrew his consciousness from her body and opened his eyes. The orb still hung from the ceiling providing light, but everyone had long since gone to sleep, leaving only the two of them awake. Alli was sprawled outside the door guarding them, her tail flicking against the door as she had a happy dream.

Kate pulled a bottle of water from her inventory and quickly swallowed several mouthfuls. "That wasn't so bad." Her straight face broke with a grimace at the end.

"That was the easy part," Charles told her, somewhat sadistically enjoying the way she paled at his response. "I was fixing the little things just now, making the flow as smooth as I can before tackling the major problems. We'll do the rest as soon as you're ready."

She took a long drink of water and set the nearly empty bottle at her side, learning magic was a thirsty business. Kate flexed her hands and breathed deep. "All right, let's do this." With that said she reached out and touched his glove, the barrier popping into being right away.

Charles dived right in, feeling his mind expand once more. His mind was focused on fixing the remaining issues and with a firm, smooth hand, he began to manipulate the mana in her body. First, he finished opening the areas he had bored through earlier, strengthening them so they wouldn't collapse a second time. When that was finished, he headed to the area in her chest where the mana had gone stagnant.

It appeared as a small pond of unused mana sitting in her chest leading away from her core room, where her growing well was. Mana spun through the room and then exited without ever doing more than skimming the surface of the pond. The entry and exit points were too high for now.

Looking at the room closely, Charles was interested to find that this was not something she had caused in her rush. This pond like room was not something new, it had been there all her life collecting little pieces of mana that were unusable. He had no doubt that the pond had been much smaller back then, but her body had changed to create this space and was still adding to the pond for some reason.

The fact that the mana was in a liquid form was the worrying part. His mana density was much higher than hers and was approaching a liquid state. He wasn't sure what would happen to her if he introduced this dense, liquid mana into her system. With that in mind, he manipulated the room and created a new floor above the pond, this one skimmed the bottom of the openings. The pond would still exist but at least another wouldn't be created. When she was ready, he would show her how to open the room fully and integrate the liquid mana into her own.

It did make him curious as to whether he had a similar pond in his own body, and if he did, then did everybody? Shaking his head to clear it, he resolved to look later and then got back to work.

The last area he had to fix was actually in her brain, she had accidentally created a bottleneck of sorts here. Part of what she was doing when she touched her core was allowing the mana to spread throughout her entire body. Currently, the amount was too thin to be used for anything. When it had built up enough, she would be able to feel it and then later use it.

Her body needed the downtime between training sessions to expand and strengthen the mana channels in her body. By not giving her body time to do this she had weakened them, which led to the collapse of several of them that he had already fixed. It also led to what he was facing now, the channels running throughout her brain hadn't expanded enough leading to the bottleneck he now faced.

This was the main issue that had made him leery of fixing her in the truck. Playing around with someone's brain was delicate work, and no matter how he looked at it, it was going to be extremely painful.

He gathered up the excess mana that had built up and connected it to himself. He would need to feed it into her body as he went. With that done he followed the small channel into her brain.

Distantly he could feel Kate shuddering and crying softly as he worked, blood dripping from her ears and eyes.

He worked as quickly as he could, increasing the pressure on the channels so that they expanded and then fed her mana into the walls to strengthen them. One channel became two, and two became many. Thankfully, it had a replicative effect as more mana began to flow through the rest of her channels they slowly expanded and strengthened themselves on their own.

As he worked Charles thought through what could have happened and came to the conclusion that what had happened with her brain had more to do with when she began rushing, than the rushing itself. If she had begun to rush later on in her training, then the channels in her brain would have been wide enough to prevent a bottleneck from occurring. He decided he wasn't going to tell her that though; she needed to know that she couldn't rush this. She was getting a very painful lesson to that effect right now and he couldn't afford to undermine it.

Kate was pale and her face caked in dried blood when he finished. Without a word he cast his cleaning spell on her and handed her a fresh bottle of water. She blinked her eyes slowly and tilted the bottle into her mouth. She was tired and lethargic as she drank the bottle dry and then collapsed on the floor. She was asleep before her head hit the once white linoleum.

Charles put a pillow under her head and then settled his back against the rough brick wall. He had put her through a lot that night, more than he thought in all honesty. He hadn't expected the damage to be so bad this early on, but then it was because of how early on the training was that it was so bad.

Closing his eyes, he delved into his body searching for a pond of mana similar to the one he had found in Kate. He didn't have one, he couldn't even find a place where one might have existed. He would have to wait for more people to start learning magic before he would be able to tell if she was special or if he was just different. Another possibility floated through his mind before he could start meditating for what remained of the night.

Just how much did he believe the potion changed him and was it possible this was one of the things it had changed?

He looked over to his sleeping sister as he thought. She was the only other person besides him who had drunk the potion and he knew she wanted to learn magic. If everyone else had a pond of some kind, but his sister and he didn't then it would be proof. He felt excitement at what he was thinking, finally, he would have a chance to confirm whether or not the potion was doing more than just healing those that drank it.

Suddenly he couldn't wait to start teaching other people how to use magic.

***

Kate was still passed out on the floor in the same position when the sun flooded the building with light. People began to stir, making noise and grumbling about how much they hated mornings. Charles let the partitions in his mind fall away and then stood to go outside, Alli had been left alone out there all night long. He hadn't wanted to disturb her earlier since she was already asleep when he saw her, now though he just wanted to spend some time with her.

He had grown used to talking with her, and over the course of their journey, she had become more than just a friend or companion to him. She had become family, and it hurt to see family left outside as she had been. She was always by his side, and it felt odd to not have her there where she belonged while he meditated, and she slept.

As Charles walked through the door, he began to think of what they needed to accomplish and how much time they had to do it. They had been given a time limit of two weeks to the day of the apocalypse before whatever game the gods were playing started. Adding up the days in his head, he wasn't sure if they were on day twelve or thirteen. Regardless, it meant that they had little time to prepare and build their town.

He shook his head and sat on the cold cement next to Alli, they could only do their best and hope that the gods had something in mind that wouldn't screw them over.

"I missed you last night," Alli whispered to his mind as he sat next to her, raising her head she placed it in his lap.

"I did too. I would have opened the door to let you in earlier, but you were asleep when I finished with Kate." She nuzzled against his hand as he began to pet her ears and scratch her neck.

"I know, I saw you helping her last night. It seemed she was in a lot of pain?"

"She's been rushing her training, and it was causing problems to the way mana worked in her body. I had to go through and fix everything last night," He gave a hollow laugh, "Just be glad you were asleep for the last part, you wouldn't have been able to help her and it would have caused you some distress."

Alli lifted her head and turned to look behind them at the still sleeping girl. "You're right it would have, and it did. I may have been out here, but I could still hear her whimpers and smell the blood." She turned back around and placed her head back in his lap. "Speaking of blood, I followed the smell into the woods. It was a good thing we came back when we did, they were attacked by a lone monster I hadn't seen before. It was testing them I think after it killed one of the humans it took the body and went into the woods. I found a pack of them there and took care of them. If we hadn't come back, then they would have killed the rest of Tara's humans last night."

Charles looked to the corner of his vision and noticed that there were indeed notifications from last night there. He ignored the ones telling him he had gotten experience for fixing Kate and focused on the messages concerning Alli. He felt his insides clench at the name associated with the monster. It read 'Shug Monkey'.

The Shug Monkey was a creature from mythology that shared the features of a dog and a monkey. It was a being that he only knew about because of his sister and one of her weirder hobbies when they were younger. What made him clench, however, was that the time had already come for monsters from myths and legends to appear.

He remembered what a passage in the manual had said.

As the mana in the air grows thicker, new and dangerous monsters will come into being alongside beings from myth and legends.

If a creature like the Shug Monkey could appear already then, the mana in the air had already grown thick enough for more dangerous monsters to begin appearing. He hadn't expected the stronger monsters to begin appearing for a while yet. In the end, there was nothing he could do about it, but it was another reason to create the town and walls that could protect everyone as quickly as possible.

Charlotte came out to stand next to him. "The people inside are worried about the monster that attacked them coming back."

"They don't need to be. Alli took care of them last night." He lightly pushed Alli's head from his lap and stood, looking his sister in the eye. "It was a group of Shug Monkeys."

She inhaled sharply knowing instantly where he was going with that, "It's too soon for them to start appearing." She stamped her foot in anger. "Besides the Shug Monkey is from Cambridge. Does this look like England to you?" Unsurprisingly she seemed angrier at the fact the gods weren't going to follow facts from mythology.

"No, but it does means it's open season on where creatures from mythology might appear. Yetis won't just appear in the Himalaya's but also in Japan, and that Kappa's or nine-tailed foxes could appear here." Charles calmly said.

She growled and kicked the ground again before sighing in exasperation. "I suppose it's better to know something like this now rather than later when we aren't prepared or expecting it."

"Do you think some of them will be intelligent at least?" Alli had perked up when he mentioned the nine-tailed fox. They weren't dogs, but at this point, that was probably for the better.

Charles shrugged. "I don't see why not, we've already seen that the goblins can be intelligent enough to speak English. From what I remember in the stories, nine-tailed foxes were often depicted as crafty, intelligent beings that possessed the ability to shape-shift."

His sister raised her eyebrows as he spoke but understood quickly that he was speaking to the large silver dog standing behind him. Reaching forward she put her hand on Alli's muzzle so that she could hear her talk. "If you want Alli, I can tell you about all the creatures from mythology and legend that might be intelligent and similar to you."

Alli froze in excitement, her dark blue and bright green mismatched eyes going wide. "You'd do that?" She asked shyly, despite the excitement she was feeling. This might be her chance to find a being like her.

"I'll ride in the back with you today and tell you all about them," Charlotte told her with a smile, glad that she was able to make Alli happy. The dog was important to her brother, and that meant she was important to Charlotte.

Alli stepped around Charles and licked Charlotte's face. "Thank you, thank you. Thank you." She repeated happily.

Charles grinned at his overly happy companion, maybe the appearance of the Shug Monkey's was a good thing after all. It had given Alli some hope for a future she had all but given up on. It still might not happen but she had hope now.

"Is there anything you can do to help us with the truck?" Tara stepped out of the building, a step behind Kira.

Kira blinked and stopped her annoyed expression quickly morphing into a dark grin. The golden flecks in her chocolate brown eyes glittered in the morning light as she bent over and picked up a rock. "Here," She said as she thrust the rock at the tanned woman. "When all else fails, smack it with a rock."

Kira quickly turned away from the dumfounded woman and hurried over to Charles and his group. "Will that actually work?" He asked her in a whisper.

Kira smirked and nodded, "If she tries it on the bad starter it can help it start once or twice, assuming, of course, the starter isn't too far gone already."

"We're going to have to give them a jump again, aren't we?" He asked as Charlotte looked on feeling lost. The two groups hadn't mingled much the night before and she hadn't heard how the two groups even knew each other yet.

Kira nodded and folded her arms before speaking in a snotty voice, "They want to come back with us, apparently getting attacked without being able to defend themselves opened their eyes somewhat."

"Do you think we should take them with us?" Charles asked her while deliberately not looking at Alli. He already knew what she would say, and indeed he could hear her saying it in his mind though he ignored it for the moment.

Her fingers tapped against her arm as she took the time to think through her answer before responding. "I think we should. I'm not saying we should trust them or anything but looking at it from a sheer logistical perspective more bodies to help build the town is a good thing." She bit the inside of her mouth and nodded agreeing with herself.

"Alright then, let's get the cars and trucks all gassed up and then get everyone loaded up." Charles pulled two of the large barrels full of gasoline from his inventory along with the red hand pump. They had taken the time to siphon gas at each stop, but they had still fully emptied two of the barrels.

Kira picked up the first barrel and hand pump and walked over to the closest car.

Charles, for his part, pulled out Alli's watering tub and orange circular water cooler. He filled Alli's tub with water first and then pried the lid off the cooler before filling it as well. The cooler had been a lucky find at one of their gas stops, as it allowed everyone to fill their water bottles easily.

Twenty minutes later, Kira held a still sleeping Kate in her arms as everyone climbed into their respective vehicles of choice. Charlotte climbed into the back of the truck with Alli and Scott, and Kira passed her sister to her mother in the cab. Charles would be driving Scott's truck with Kira at the front of the group.

Red and black jumper cables ran from the hood of the transport truck to the truck Kory was driving. Kira had produced a tire iron from one of the cars and gave the offending starting a soft rap, careful not to hit it too hard. She was too good to use the rock she had given Tara.

Inside the large truck, Tara turned the key, and the engine rumbled to life on the first try. Quickly Kira unhooked the cable and closed the hood, her ears hurting from the loud exhaust.

Finally, everybody was ready to go. Kira climbed into the truck with Charles and rolled down the window. "Let's go. If we're quick enough, we can get started on the town today." She said as she clicked her seatbelt into place.

They didn't know where exactly the town was going to be, just outside the dungeon. What they did know was that they needed to plan for expansion. This town would continue to grow, and it was better to design it with that in mind from the beginning. None of that could happen until they knew the exact location, however.

Charles pressed on the brake and clicked the old automatic transmission into drive, it was time to drive.

Chapter 17

Charles snorted in annoyance as another gust of wind threatened to take the truck off the highway. The backend was filled with supplies that kept catching the constantly gusting wind. Kira felt the truck shudder across the road and gripped the handle hanging from the roof next to the door.

They had been on the road for over three hours making small talk when Kira suddenly fell quiet and then asked in a serious voice, "How much of the forest do you think ended up burning?"

Charles looked at her in amazement. "How should I know? Besides, why do you care?"

Kira pointed into the distance, "I don't care, but with how hot and large the fire was when we left it should still be smoking right? A fire that large would have continued to rage for at least a day or so, so why don't I see any smoke on the horizon?"

Charles was quiet as his face screwed up in thought, his foot gradually increasing the pressure on the gas pedal. "That is a very good question."

They should be nearing the spot where they had been attacked, but she was right there was absolutely no sign of smoke anywhere. Thankfully, the number of vehicles on the road in this area were few and far between allowing them to pick up speed. Constantly dodging parked and abandoned vehicles was not inducive to going fast.

The vehicles behind them sped up to match his new speed. Within minutes, the edge of the forest could be seen stretching in the distance. It was too far to make out details, and since he was driving Charles didn't feel comfortable enhancing his vision.

The truck slowed to a stop at the tree line, undamaged trees lining the torn and damaged highway. The forest itself was in perfect condition, and no one would believe that a fire had raged through that area only days before. The ruined road was the only proof that they were even in the right area.

"How are we getting past that?" Kira asked her eyes focused on the road instead of the undamaged trees.

"You're not curious about the trees apparently having grown back within days of the fire?" He asked incredulously.

Kira cocked her hip and smirked. "I would have thought you noticed it before me." She pointed down the line of trees. "Look at the trees farther down."

He took a few steps back and looked down the line, noticing for the first time how they gradually grew in height to tower over the ones in front of them. "They're growing!"

"The manual did say that everything would begin to grow faster as the mana increased in the air, but I wasn't expecting this." Kira was looking behind them as her father brought the truck he was driving to a stop behind their own.

"Still this is incredible, they've grown to their old height in only a day or two." Charles felt a grin spreading across his face as he thought of how fast crops might grow.

Charlotte and Alli were the first to leap from the back of the truck and join them.

"Why did you stop?" Charlotte asked before seeing the ruined road in front of them. Entire sections of the road were missing, making the road impassable.

"I set this section of the forest on fire when we came through a couple of days ago, but it's all grown back already," Charles explained, not feeling the least bit ashamed at having burned down part of a forest.

"Take a few steps back and look down the line of trees," Kira urged her before she could respond.

"That's fast, much too fast. How many monsters were killed during your attack?" She asked quickly catching on to what had happened.

Charles shrugged. "I don't know, a lot. Why?"

"Mana is released into the air whenever something dies, if a lot of monsters died here then it would have increased the mana in the air by leaps and bounds. I'm thinking it was all absorbed by the environment to fix the damage you caused." She calmly explained with a thoughtful expression.

"There go our daily crops," He muttered petulantly.

"Not by much." Charlotte tapped her lip thinking. "Crops would probably be finished growing within a week and harvestable by the end of the second week. That's likely to change though in the years to come, but I wouldn't expect by much."

"Why not?" Kira asked as she reached out to pet Alli.

"How much more death can we cause?" Charlotte snorted. "Charles said something like three billion people died that first night alone. How many of that five billion do you think still remains? Just from our little jaunt through the states, I'm going to say not many. Point being, if we say that it took four or five billion lives to reach the density we are at now, then it would take the rest of humanity for there to be a noticeable increase."

Charles left them talking together as more people joined them in the middle of the road. Alli remained by his side as he walked into the forest and stopped at the edge of the damaged road. Looking at it from up close, he could see that there was no way they were going to be able to make across the numerous ruined sections. Cracked and broken pavement stuck into the air next to large, several foot-deep holes. It was a mess and if he didn't think of something, they would have to backtrack several hours to get around this area. Unfortunately, the trees grew too close together for them to drive through.

"Can you fill them in with magic?" Alli asked, trying to be helpful when she saw him growing despondent.

He thought that over for a moment; he had unlocked earth magic. It wasn't one he had been concentrating on as much as the others, so he hadn't learned any spells for it. He seemed to only learn spells when he had a specific idea in mind before he began meditating. If he didn't, then his mind would delve into the magical mysteries of the element in question.

He had done a fair bit of meditating on earth magic in general without a spell in mind, leaving him at least familiar with what to do. Supposedly he didn't need to depend on actual spells as much now that his understanding of magic had gone up. Now might just be the perfect time to test out using magic without a spell to back it up.

He held his hand out over the hole and looked to Alli. "Maybe you should back up. I'm about to do this without a spell to control it. I have no idea what is going to happen."

Alli shook her head and stepped closer to him, making her point clear. She went where he did, and if he was going to blow himself up, then she would be there getting blown up with him.

He gave her a warm, thankful smile and closed his eyes concentrating. He wasn't actually sure what he needed to do since he had never cast spells this way before. Remembering how he used magic with the different elements, he let the magic flow through his body. He felt a connection form instantly with the earth and sent his magic down into that connection; he envisioned the hole filling itself in.

He felt a rumble and opened his eyes. He could see the ground filling in the hole until it was level with the road. Keeping his eyes open this time he reached for the connection with the earth and pushed. The road trembled, and the pavement shifted, only a little bit a first and then faster as he pumped more mana into the connection.

A ripple rolled down the ruined road, fixing the ground as it passed. The pieces of pavement sank into the ground and the many holes filled themselves, leaving a smooth even dirt road in its wake.

Alli was quick to catch him as he tottered and collapsed onto her back.

Casting a spell of that magnitude had taken everything he had, leaving him exhausted and barely coherent. Alli kept him balanced across her back as she carefully turned around and carried him back to the trucks.

"What happened?" Several of the gathered people asked as she carried him into view. They hadn't been able to clearly see what was happening down the road in the woods. The bright morning sun and the dim shadows of the woods had kept much of what had occurred hidden.

Alli stared as the idiots who had asked made no move to touch her so she could talk to them. Charlotte pushed to her side along with Kira and Scott. She exhaled with relief when she saw no wounds on her brother.

"What happened?" Charlotte asked, being the sole person of those who had asked her, smart enough to touch her.

"He exhausted himself fixing the road for us to drive through and he did it without a proper spell to control everything!" Alli couldn't decide how she felt about it right then. She was proud of Charles because he fixed the road for everyone but seeing him collapse after doing so... was unpleasant.

Scott lifted Charles from her back and set him on his feet, catching him as he almost collapsed again.

Charles looked around them at the gathered group of people. "Road's fixed, let's go." He turned to look at Kira. "I think it's your turn to drive now."

***

Charles was breathing deeply as he felt the mana coming back to his body. He had used such an enormous amount fixing the road that it had been a shock to his system. With this experience under his belt though he now had a clear idea of why spells existed in the first place. They were training wheels of a sort. When you used a spell, you knew what you were getting into. Everything was automatic, and the result was more or less always the same.

That wasn't the case when you used magic without a spell to guide it, it was primal and powerful. He had felt the connection to the earth in a way he never had when using spells. The cost of doing so was intense, however. Spells kept the cost reasonable in terms of mana. Straight magic without the spell had no such limiter however, it was stronger sure, but it also costs three times as much or more.

"You still alive over there?" Kira asked after a while, trying to lighten the weird mood in the truck cab. She cleared her throat and continued before he could answer. "Alli wasn't very happy with you, you know?"

The flat land of Missouri rolled by as he nodded without turning away from the window. "I know, seeing me collapse or hurt is never easy on her."

Kira firmed her grip on the old fake wood covered steering wheel. "You need to change the way you are doing things; we all do. We need to figure out how everything works and quit acting like we already do because we knew how it worked before. A great many people are going to depend on you in the future, and they can't do that if you collapse at the wrong time."

"And what about you? Are you ever going to let anyone besides your family in?" He asked, knowing the question would hurt but needing to know the answer.

She inhaled sharply. "I'm trying, I've been angry for so long because of what happened to me, and because my friend betrayed me. I believed it meant that I couldn't believe in anyone if they weren't family."

"And now?"

A sad smile graced her lips. "Let's just say the appearance of monsters hasn't been entirely bad. I've found it rather therapeutic to take out my anger on them, and it makes it easier to know who you can or can't trust now. You can trust those who stand by your side in a fight and help. Those who runaway can't be trusted."

"Who do you trust?" He asked looking at her from the corner of his eye. He had a feeling she would stop talking if he looked at her right then.

"Alli, your sister, you…" Her right hand let go of the steering wheel and trembling lightly she placed her hand on top of his own. "I'm learning that I can trust the three of you." The tremble in her hand grew more pronounced, and she withdrew it. "It's a long gradual process, but the point is I'm trying."

"What do you think I should do?"

"Just be more careful. As the current sole human magic user in the world, your life is not your own. If you die, then it has lasting effects on everyone."

He could feel his strength coming back to him as they talked, and the miles rolled by. She wasn't wrong he knew that, but it also didn't make her entirely right either. His life was his own, he didn't care about the rest of the world. He didn't know them, so they meant nothing to him.

What he cared about was keeping those close to him safe, and for those few, there was little he wouldn't do. So, while he regretted making Alli worried, it was something that was liable to happen again in the future. He had the power to keep them safe and he would use it to do so.

Charles pointed to a turn off ahead of them. It was for a long dirt driveway that ended at Tara's house. "Do you think she is going to go back there or stay with us?" He asked in an effort to change the subject.

Kira sniffed. "I don't care, either way. Her entire group has already proven that they are worthless wastes of space. If we didn't need people for this town of yours, then I would have left them at the rest stop."

They could barely see where the land had been ravaged first by the storm and then by countless monsters afterward. The grass had grown taller, weeds taller still. It left the area looking more than a little wild.

"Where are we going?" Kira asked as they crept closer to the once vibrant city. She knew they were going to be near the dungeon, but that was it. Which really didn't tell her anything, she had seen how big the dungeon was when it was formed. It had been huge, easily engulfing the entire city and more on its side of the river.

Charles pulled up the information on the challenge and saw that the majority of the message had remained unchanged there was one thing that was different. Underneath the rest of the message a glowing arrow had formed, that seemed to practically scream touch me.

With a mental prod, he gave in to the temptation and 'touched' the glowing arrow.

Kira jerked the wheel to the side as a glowing green arrow popped into existence on the hood of the truck. The arrow shifted with the jerk, telling them to stay on the highway for the time being.

Charles had a slim idea of where they were going to end up, but until they were closer to the city he wouldn't know for sure.

Soon enough, the first buildings of Kansas City could be seen. The skyline had changed from when they left; the storm had done a number on the more damaged buildings. Thankfully, the road was clear for the most part.

People could be seen everywhere doing their best to salvage everything that might be useable. They worked in groups of five to seven people and each person was armed with knives and a gun of some kind. Their weapons may not have been the most effective against monsters, but Charles was inclined to believe that they were for monsters of a different kind. Whether that was previously domesticated pets or humans he didn't know.

They looked up as the convoy of vehicles passed, the loud broken muffler on the transport truck alerting all to their presence. Most did nothing more than watch as they passed by, looks of defeat lifting a little at the signs of the working technology. Others ran away gripping their weapons, terror, and distrust showing in equal measure on their faces.

Charles ignored it all, they weren't his concern yet. In the future, they would either join his growing town or they wouldn't, either way, they weren't his concern. What did concern him was how closely everything was packed together. This section of the city had little in the way of open spaces, leaving him wondering about where they would find the space to create a town.

"We're back where we started," Kira remarked as they neared the river.

They were indeed almost back to the warehouses where they had watched the dungeon form. It was where Charles had thought they might end up. It was the location with the bridge after all, and while there had been others before they all disappeared this had been the biggest. If they were going to guard access to the dungeon, it made sense to do it in a location like this.

Kira slowed the truck and turned it off as the green arrow began blinking at them. They had arrived at their destination.

Charles climbed from the truck, the glowing arrow detaching itself from the now stationary truck as he did so. At the edge of the highway where it had formerly joined together with the bridge, a large green circle was pulsing, clearly waiting for him to step into it.

Without a second thought, he walked towards the circle. It was time to get some answers. Even if the only answers he got pertained on how to create a town in the middle of the city, it would be more than he had now. Every little bit of information helped him get a clearer idea of how the world worked and to what extent the gods were influencing everything.

Information like that was infinitely valuable and useful. He was nobody's plaything, and not even a god had a claim to him. His life was his own, and he would find a way to prove it someday if it was the last thing he did.

Charles turned around to look at the people that had gathered around, most of them belonged to the group that had been in the vehicles. Some of them were just people that had been scavenging in that area of the city at the right time to see them stop.

He locked eyes with Alli, then his sister, then to Kate and finally with Kira. He gave them each a small smile and then stepped backward into the pulsating green circle.

The lines of the circle thickened and grew until they were over a foot wide all-around. The pulses flashed faster and brighter as this was happening, and then when it finished it transformed into a ten-foot-tall pillar of green light obscuring the person within.

Chapter 18

Charles stood still as the walls of green first surrounded him and then began to change. He could feel something being built around him, the constants little shifts in the air leading him to believe it was a small room of some kind as the presence of the wind vanished.

The green pillar slowly flattened and then disappeared, revealing a black building with a single door and no windows. Inside the building, Charles found himself standing in front of a large table with a 3D model of the city spread across its top. Most of the city was gray and lifeless with little detail beyond the existence of the building being shown. Closer to the river and where the bridge had been, more specifically closer to where the building now stood things were different.

He couldn't judge the distance for certain, but everything within maybe a half-mile of the building was filled in with color and detail. He could even see little miniature people walking through the ruins and gathered in a clump in front of the vehicles.

Charles took all this in for several seconds before paying attention to the prompt that had come into being along with the map.

Congratulations, on being the first to create a 'Town System Building', this building will aid you in the development and guarding of your town.
As a reward for being the first would you like to reclaim all materials damaged or otherwise on your land? (Note: That normally this procedure must be paid for in mana.)

Charles clicked yes without thinking and immediately regretted the action as the buildings closest to them on the map disappeared.

Congratulations, all damaged materials have been successfully reclaimed and sorted. These materials can now be used to begin construction on various buildings and structures. (Note: All construction must be paid for in mana.)
Would you like to see a list of available buildings, structures, and other items that may now be built?

He clicked no.

Congratulations, a great many items of various natures have been reclaimed along with the building materials. These have been sorted into their appropriate categories and stored in the town's inventory.
Would you like to see a list of items in the town's inventory?

Unable to squash the intense curiosity at the thought of what else had been reclaimed he clicked yes.

An interface similar to his own inventory but with tabs appeared before his eyes. The tabs were named for what they contained, Weapons, Food, Clothes, Dishware, Utensils, Electronics, Misc. He closed the interface without looking further; he had his answer.

When he had commanded the interface to reclaim everything it had done just that. Everything that had been inside the buildings and the buildings themselves had been reclaimed and sorted. The area showing on the map now had a large blank section that abutted the river and ran in a half-circle around them.

He reached out and touched the wall of the dungeon next to the river, wondering what the map would feel like. It was hard and cold, but utterly smooth, and the action prompted another notification to appear.

The dungeon is currently closed to all delvers, it will open at the same time as the game begins. A bridge will form from your town to the newly created opening at that time. (Note: Should this bridge be destroyed, access to the dungeon will be cut off until it can be repaired by human hands.)

Charles waved away the words and took a step back as he thought. The purpose of the town was to guard and likely explore the dungeon, by having the sole access to the dungeon form in the middle of the town the gods would certainly be accomplishing what they wanted. The town would have no choice but to act as a guard for all who entered or left the dungeon. The question was, were they guarding the dungeon against people that wished it harm? Or were they guarding against whatever came out of the dungeon when it opened?

The entire room suddenly shuddered and the door to his back thudded with an explosive force bulging inwards. The door was barely staying on its hinges as Charles whirled around in a panic as his heart rate spiked.

Distantly he could hear yelling through the cracks from the now misshapen door, apparently, the room was very soundproof.

The handle turned, and the door opened partway before getting stuck.

"See I told you it would open." Kira's voice drifted through the opening.

"I don't care," Alli howled as she bowled into the door, smashing it wide open and revealing a sea of green grass behind her. Everywhere where concrete or pavement had once been was now filled with flowing green grass.

"Uh, hi?" Charles began unsure of why they had barged in like that.

"Are you alright?" Alli asked as she ran over to him and began sniffing him.

"We were uh, worried when you didn't come back out right away. Then the buildings all disappeared, which made some people angry by the way, and then the grass appeared. So, uh yeah, she, we, were worried." Kira was speaking oddly as she scratched at her cheek and refused to look him in the eye.

"Sorry," He told them while scratching Alli's ears. "I got absorbed in here." He motioned to the table and the map of their surroundings on it. "This table and map seem to be the key to building the town. It absorbed all the buildings in the area for supplies." He began explaining enthusiastically. "I'm not sure how it works just yet, but apparently it can use mana to construct buildings for us."

Kira snorted in disbelief. "If it can then it will be the first decent thing the gods have done for us."

He froze as he processed her words. "That's kind of true, isn't it? I wonder what changed?"

Alli sat back on her haunches convinced that he was unharmed. "We need a wall first. If we are going to be attacked then we need a wall to protect us."

"A wall?" Charles repeated aloud for Kira to hear. "The problem with building everything through mana is you still need mana to do it. I highly doubt I have enough mana to build a building let alone a wall." He looked at the map with a thoughtful expression.

"I'll tell your sister everything and together we can start getting everyone set up into groups. Hopefully, we can get a decent camp set up. While we're doing that, why don't you go through everything in here and learn what you can? Maybe there is an option to share the cost or pay it in stages." Kira walked out the door, having taken control of the situation.

"What about you, what are you going to do?" He asked Alli.

"I'm going to watch and guard you, make sure nothing bad happens." Her voice in his head was hard and possessed a somewhat fragile undertone to it. He could only guess that seeing him engulfed in that green light and thinking he had been taken from her had left her wary of letting him out of her sight.

He smiled fondly at her and then turned back to the table; it was time to work. He would spoil her later.

Congratulations, the menu system for your fledgling town has been unlocked. Reach a milestone of 10 buildings and have a wall built to name your town. Once the town has been named, people may then formally join the town. Additional features including a list of enforceable oath-sworn tenets will then be unlocked.
Would you like to see the Town Menu? (Note: The Town Menu may only be accessed while in this room and by you alone.)

Selecting 'Yes' opened a menu with different options relating to the maintenance and construction of a town. About halfway down the list was an option labeled 'Taxes' that was glowing faintly. Selecting that option opened another interface as well as a message.

Congratulations, you have decided to inflict taxes on the people currently occupying your land since they are not yet citizens of your town; they have no rights. Tax away.
Taxes are used for the upkeep and general maintenance of the town and can be paid in either coin, mana or both.
(Note: Every person has mana regardless of whether they can use it, taxing a person's mana can help them become aware of its existence. This can help them learn to use magic in various ways faster should they pursue being taught to do so.)
Would you like to set a tax?

Charles quickly set a heavy tax on mana for everyone but himself and Kate, since they couldn't actively use it, they wouldn't miss it. That said, he remembered how exhausting it was when he used all his mana; he kept it to a reasonable fifty percent of each person's capacity. Taxed once daily, for members of the town it would happen while they were asleep. It would take it from visitors in increments, however. The longer they were on the land, the more of the fifty percent would be taken.

Alli grunted and looked up at him. "That feels weird. What did you just do?"

He quickly added Alli to the list of exclusions before answering her. "I just set a tax on mana for everyone, the taxed mana is used for the upkeep of the town." He stopped before hitting accept of the menu, to the best of his knowledge she wasn't using mana for anything, but it made sense that some of her shadow abilities would use it. He would need to teach her how to use magic later and keeping the tax on her would help with that. He exited the menu without adding her to the list.

"Can it be used in the construction of buildings as well?" She asked while stretching.

"That's my hope, apparently it does have the effect getting people used to feeling their mana. It will make it easier to teach them how to use magic as a result." He exited the tax menu and went back to the main screen. A set of blue glowing numbers were now sitting above and to the right of the menu.

He focused on the numbers and they expanded with an explanation.

You currently have 750 units of mana in the town bank. These units may be used for construction purposes to offset personal mana costs.

The description was somewhat helpful but left him with more questions than he had before. What was a unit of mana, and how many did he have? It was nice to have definite numbers to work with instead of feeling it, but he needed to know what the conversion was.

He did some quick math in his head while trying to remember how many people they had brought with them and then decided it was pointless. People that had been nearby and within bounds of the town were getting taxed as well as the people that had come with him. It was impossible to get a baseline without knowing the exact number of people and their levels.

His eyes glazed over as he thought. Opening the construction menu, he saw exactly what he needed.

Complete Wall = 600 UM
Basic One-Story House = 50 UM

The list continued on with options for larger houses and other buildings, but it was the basic house he was interested in. It was immediately useful, and the cost seemed to be low enough that he could build it himself.

Selecting the house, a small glowing representation appeared on the table that he could move around. Deciding he wanted the house to be built next to the building he was in. He selected the option to pay for the construction with his own mana and accepted the location. Mana was pulled from him in a rush, forcing him to breathe deep even as less than a fifth of his total mana was pulled from him at once. He rested for a second before going outside. As a level 15 Archmage with he thought high intelligence stats, he had around 250 UM it seemed. That certainly helped to put the number received from taxes in perspective. Fixing the road without a spell had cost him more than building the house.

Outside what he could now see was a dark black building, materials were appearing and then flying through the air. Great chunks of concrete appeared and then settled onto the ground, forming one whole when it was done. Pillars of wood followed by planks settled into their places, forming a frame and then walls. In no time at all a one-story house had appeared, glass glinted from the windows and a sturdy unpainted door stood closed.

Everyone had gathered around at the sight of the small house being built by magic. Charlotte was the first to step up to the house and open the door, her brother right behind her. Inside was revealed to be a barren area, two doors at the back opened into a small open-hole toilet and empty bedroom, respectively.

Charles raised a hand before his sister could say anything, "Follow me, I need to get a wall built and then we can begin planning how to build the rest of the town."

Inside the Town System building, he quickly selected the option to build the wall from taxes and put the order through. Outside great chunks of concrete once more appeared in the air and began stacking themselves to build a wall 4 meters tall and just over a meter thick. A section would flash as it was completed, all seams and cracks vanishing as it became a single whole piece.

Charlotte pushed Kira and Scott into the room with the map and closed the door behind them, as the wall continued to build itself outside.

"Explain," She demanded while glaring at her younger brother. Kira found a place on the wall next to Alli and leaned on it while Scott remained in front of the closed door, blocking it.

The room was quiet save for his voice for the next several minutes as he relayed everything to them.

Kira was the first to break the silence after he had finished explaining everything. "I think we should use the rest of the available taxes to build a few more living spaces today and then revisit the options tomorrow with fresh eyes."

In front of Scott, Charlotte was mumbling quickly to herself. "I'm guessing these buildings don't have electricity since I didn't see any outlets or lights in the house. We'll need to find a way to generate some in the future, possibly from the river. Certain appliances should still work like lamps without needing to be fixed. That is an issue for the future; however, right now I need a lab. I have so many interesting things that I need to take apart and examine. I wonder if the professor can make something from troll's blood?"

Charles smiled indulgently at his sister, knowing she was already lost in her own world. "She'll be like this for a while, let's make some more houses for now and then we can review the rest of the options tomorrow, as Kira suggested. For now, space is going to be at a premium so I'm just going to build the houses right next to each other, we can change them in the future if we need to."

Scott nodded and pulled his girlfriend into his arms, well used to her oddities. "Why don't I take her outside, we can scope out a spot for her lab next to the river while we're at it."

He opened the door, letting the full sound of clamoring people invade the small room.

"We should probably fix that door?" Kira remarked after they had left.

Alli sniffed and turned away. "It's not my fault the gods were dumb enough to put a knob on the door instead of something I could operate."

Charles coughed and hid his smile underneath his hand as Kira let her warhammer form. The heads of the hammer were flat with slightly rounded edges, perfect for hitting the door back into shape.

While she was busy abusing the poor door, Charles quickly selected three more houses and lined them in a row away from the current buildings. He didn't want there to be too much traffic around the building he was in.

He saw the number counter above the menu tick down to zero. They were out of mana in the bank, anything more that was created from this point on would be from his personal mana. With that in mind, he placed two more houses on the map, next to the ones that had just been made. He felt a greater amount of mana being taken from him this time, leaving the mana channels in his body with a pleasant ache in them. It felt good to exercise them without damaging them like he had been doing lately.

He turned away from the map and watched as Kira finished bashing the door back into shape. "I have a lot of camping supplies that can be passed around to everyone that needs it. Currently, there are only six houses so there is not even close to being enough unless everyone packs themselves in. The first house that was built, I want only your family and my sister staying in it."

Kira looked at him with mirth filled eyes. "You just did it again. You forgot to mention Scott with your sister."

"He goes where she does. I don't need to mention him." He pulled the largest sleeping pad he had from his inventory and tossed it into the corner along with some pillows and a sleeping bag. "I'll stay in here, with Alli tonight. Later on, before we all go to sleep, we need to figure out what to build next." He ran a finger along the edge of the table containing the map. "We're in the town building stage now, and we need to make sure we do it right."

Kira opened the door as her hammer reformed back into a bracelet. "Come on, let's go empty your inventory. Then we can round up everyone to plan for the future."

Alli was the first out the door as they left, Kira right behind her. Charles closed the newly repaired door, listening to it click shut satisfyingly. The click was then followed by the sound of a lock they hadn't even known existed sliding into place. Before he could grow worried, a message appeared in front of the door.

> *This building is owned by 'Charles Byrne' and is currently locked, only the owner or those they allow may open this door.*

Unless they're Alli or Kira, he thought dismissing the message. He remembered how they had busted open the door, regardless. It was good to know that he hadn't just been locked out of his own building though. Spinning on the fresh grass he hurried after Kira.

Behind them, Alli sidled up to the closed door, squatted in front of it and peed on it.

Chapter 19

The wall had finished building itself by the time everyone had gathered together. It had a single opening for a gate they would need to add later on. The large concrete walls extended over the river and into the water, currently preventing anything from approaching that way. Twelve people, counting the professor, had come with Charlotte and Scott. Tara's group of twenty had shrunk to nineteen and then there was his group of six, counting Alli. That meant that they needed to provide for thirty-nine people right away.

It would only get worse as more people trickled in from the surrounding areas. They needed to find a way to sustainably feed everyone quickly, salvaging food from their surroundings wouldn't work forever. At the back of their group stood a separate grouping of people that didn't belong, made up of people that had been in the area. Anyone that had been salvaging nearby when everything was reclaimed stood in that group.

Charles waited for everyone to stop talking before beginning to talk, unsure of what he was going to say until he had said it. "We are going to build the town here. The wall will keep us safe from most monsters. Anything that flies will still be a problem, however, until we can figure something out for them. In the coming days, I will have more houses built, until then just do the best you can. We need to start thinking long term for our survival, winter is only a couple of months away and we need to have food stocked up. I'll see about creating some greenhouses to grow food, but our numbers are going to swell as word of us gets out." He looked up to the sky, noting the orange-colored clouds streaked with gold as the sun began to set. "Get some rest. Tomorrow is going to be a long grueling day."

At the back of the group, someone could be heard asking why Charles was in charge? The answering reply came fast as the sharp crack of a slap echoed through the air. "That man is the sole magic user in the world and is scary strong, everything that was just built is because of him." Charles turned away from the group with a barely concealed smirk. He was alright with the people fearing him. It would keep them from questioning him in the future.

He dumped the excess camping equipment from his inventory into a large pile and walked over to the house he had claimed. He pushed open the door and sank to the floor against the back wall of the room, Alli at his side as they waited for the rest of their group to join them.

Kira was the next one through the door with the rest of her family close behind Charlotte and Scott came next and closed the door behind them. "Alright," Charles began as soon as the door was closed. "We need to start planning out this town, where we want everything built. More than that, we need to discuss what we need to have built. Do we just build houses, or do we build a large communal bunkhouse? What about warehouses for supplies and do we need to build some kind of forge or blacksmith? We've discovered that the monster's weapons do more damage than our old pre-apocalypse weapons. What happens if we melt them down and re-forge them into weapons we are used to?"

Charlotte was the first to speak after him. "I would like a lab near the water, where Scott and I can work. I have several ideas about generating electricity from the river I want to try. I also have all of my lab equipment in my inventory taking up space. Most of it is likely fried, but not all of it.

Also, you need to start teaching me how to use magic tonight after your session with Kate."

Kira and her family seemed surprised by his sister's quick thinking and already having some semblance of a plan for her future. Charles could only grin and nod at his sister. She had always been like that. Always knowing what she wanted and how to get it, Scott had been the only thing she had never expected. She hadn't realized she even wanted a companion in life until he came into her life. If anyone could figure out a way to bring back electricity and then make their lives better, it was her.

Kory and Krystal whispered back and forth for several seconds before Krystal spoke up. "We think that you can leave planning the town and general logistics to the two of us. We know that you young people have more to do than worry about little details like that. Charles, we'll need to know the specifics on what can be built and the costs as well as how they are being paid for. Everything has a cost, whether it comes from you or someplace else we need to know."

Kory started speaking after his wife had finished. "If we can find people who can use them, then we definitely want to build production facilities like a blacksmith. Several large greenhouses are an absolute must. With everything growing faster now they could provide a sizeable amount of food in a relatively short amount of time. "

"A garage," Kira spoke up next when her father had finished. "We'll need space to store all the cars and where they can be worked on. Teams that go foraging in the city can look for additional cars that are old enough and car part stores."

Kate looked on with a frown before speaking up. "All of that is just for us though, what about everyone else?"

Krystal rolled her eyes and hugged her daughter. "That's where your father and I come in, we'll talk to everyone in the coming days and learn what everyone is capable of doing. Once we do that, we'll know what buildings we need to make right away versus what we can wait on. For example, we want the blacksmith but if there is no one who can use it properly, then it will be built later."

Kate looked mollified at her mother's words and settled down with a nod.

"We only have a couple of days to prepare. I think that today is the twelfth day since this all began. That means we have another two days before the game the messages keep mentioning begins. We need to get as much done as we can within that time to prepare." Charles told them before looking to Kate. "Are you ready for another training session?"

A look of fear flashed across her face at the thought of the pain she had gone through earlier that day. With a shake of her head, she dispelled those thoughts and moved over to him. "I am."

Charlotte moved over to him as well, knowing he didn't need to monitor or control her training once she was started. She sat on the floor in front of her brother and waited for instruction on what to do.

Seeing that Kate was deep in her training, he turned to his sister and pointed to the rune on his glove. "Touch this rune here, and we can begin."

It was clear from the barrier that came into being around them that his sister was different from Kate or Kira. The barrier looked vaguely like metallic silver with lines of white running through it. The entire barrier was glowing with a soft golden color.

Charles processed this all in the second before he dived into the meditation with his sister. With sure movements, he guided them to her elemental core room and saw that his sister was indeed different from the others. It was a trait that they both seemed to share.

Her elemental core was an orb of floating liquid metal, the surface of which crackled with electricity. Underneath the sparking orb, drips of metal had formed a latticework of circuitry that spread across the floor. On the far side of the room, a golden sun illuminated the room, when they went to touch it however a barrier of some kind prevented them from getting near it.

Turning away from the barrier, Charles moved over to her core and touched it, feeling the same rush as when he had touched Kates. Turning to his sister he motioned her forward and grabbing her hand placed it on her core.

Right away, her fingers began to glow, slowly spreading to her entire hand. The progress she was making couldn't even be compared to Kate's pace. Kate would take days or weeks to finish with her core. Charlotte would be done in a single day maybe two depending on how much she needed to rest.

Trusting his instincts Charles backed away and left the training to his sister, minutes into her first session and she already didn't need him to control it. He remained in position, not willing to break her connection to the glove.

With a thought he willed the message forward, looking for the one he had gotten from touching his sister's core. There were several of them.

Congratulations, you have learned the spell 'Lightning Bolt'. Lightning bolt is a basic electrical spell that creates a bolt of lightning, and short-term paralysis is possible with this spell. Max range is variable depending on the strength of the individual lightning bolt.

Congratulations, you have learned the spell 'Infuse'. Infuse is a metal spell that sends your mana into any metallic object, allowing for the metal to become stronger or sharper for a time. Must be touching object for the spell to take effect. (Note at higher concentrations of power it is possible to permanently change the metal.)

Congratulations, you have learned the spell 'Plasma Bolt'.
Plasma bolt is a shared element spell combining electricity
and metal to create a bolt of super-heated plasma. Max
range is variable depending on the strength of the individual
plasma bolt.

He had learned three spell and two elements just from touching his sisters' core. He was interested to see that he had gained the electricity element from her; it seemed similar to the attacks the glove put out. What really interested him though was the 'Infuse' spell, it had the potential to be a game-changer. It made him curious as to just what his sister would be capable of doing once she learned to control her magic.

He passed the remainder of the time talking softly with Alli. Kira and Scott had disappeared outside after they began training. Kate managed to last a few minutes longer than she had in the past and was beaming with excitement when she finished. "It's going faster now. I finished up to my elbow!" She exclaimed with excitement, before jumping up eager to find Kira and tell her the good news.

Charles had wondered if that might happen at some point, progress tended to increase with time, not slow down. He rethought the timetable and bumped her up to finishing within a couple of days, and his sister would likely finish within a day.

His sister remained in place for another hour before the barrier surrounding them faded. "I finished the first arm and the fingers on the second." She told him with a strained, tired smile that he could only see because of the light orb he had thrown up to the ceiling earlier.

"Don't tell Kate that, she only just reached the elbow on her first arm." He paused, thinking about what to say. "Charlotte, there is something different about us." He finally said quietly, his eyes flicking to the closed bedroom door.

"I know," She replied in an equally quiet voice. "It was apparent from the beginning with the inventory, but now this. I looked at the manual earlier. People typically have one element they can learn, with some possessing a second minor element. You mentioned that Kate's core was ice with a puddle of water beneath it. I think she would be one of these, her main element is ice with the ability to learn some water spells. I have two main elements, not to mention whatever my minor element on the floor is." She took in a deep breath and spoke even softer. "That's not even mentioning the second core we saw behind the barrier." She shook her head and leaned back. "We need to be careful about what we let other people learn about us." She stood and stretched, groaning as she worked out the many kinks sitting in place for so long had caused.

Alli stood and shook her entire body before stretching her forelegs out and yawning a wide tongue curling yawn. "Time to sleep," She said simply before moving to the closed door and waiting.

Scott was sitting on the grass in front of the house looking up at the green night sky. "It's so different from before," He said without preamble as he heard them open the door and walk up behind him.

"You should get inside, there's no telling when a flying monster will attack at night," Charles said to the man. "I think I like it better this way. The green makes the stars really pop at night."

"It's pretty," Charlotte agreed as she wrapped her arms around Scott's head. "Come on, we'll grab the main room of the house."

Charles walked away, following Alli to where they would be bunking down for the night. Kira was leaning against the wall of the building talking to Kate. Both were staring in wonder at the new night sky.

"You finished?" Kira asked when she saw them approaching.

He nodded and Kira pulled her sister behind her to the small house; the inside was still lit from the orb he put up earlier. He waited for everyone to go inside before releasing his connection to the orb and letting darkness claim the house.

The building unlocked automatically as he reached for the doorknob; he left the door open since there were no windows. He wouldn't know when the sun had risen otherwise or if there was trouble since the building was soundproof.

He spread out the sleeping pads in the corner and propped the rolled-up sleeping bag against his back as he sat down. Alli spread herself out next to him and placed her head in his lap before closing her eyes.

Two more partitions rose with-in his mind as he began meditating, the wall separating electricity and metal possessed a small hole where they could interact. Taking control of each partition in turn, he set them to learning specific spells instead of just meditating on their specific elements. It was time to expand his repertoire of useful spells, specifically ones that would help in more than just battle.

Night had begun to lighten with the first signs of the coming dawn when the first screams ripped through the still air. Charles jumped to his feet and ran from the building, Alli hot on his heels.

"It came from outside the wall," She told him, her ears flicking wildly as she listened. "I hear wings, it's another monster like the one from yesterday."

The front door of the house next to him burst open and Kira ran through the door. The rest of the people that had stayed in the house hot on her heels. They ran over to Charles and then as a group headed towards the opening in the wall.

Thankfully, it seemed that everyone had managed to cram themselves into the available houses to sleep. A long wide-open field separated the wall from the area the houses had been built. Whoever had screamed had really needed to put their all into it for it to be heard so far away.

Alli pulled slightly ahead of the rest of the group, struggling to restrain her superior speed to stay with them.

"Just go," Charles spit out, focusing on running as fast as he could.

"I'll make sure it's safe then," Alli told him as she rocketed ahead, her sheer speed making the humans feel like slugs.

The screams had long since died out by the time they reached the opening, Alli stood there growling at something only she could see. Coming up behind her, the entire group saw the grisly scene at the same time.

The monster had large leathery wings with razor-sharp claws on the end. It had beady little eyes and a sharp hooked beak. Feather decorated the monsters' neck and short legs that ended in clawed talons. The beak and talons glinted wetly in the early light, stained with the blood and remains of the body in front of it. The stomach had been torn into, and the heart along with the lungs and other meat had already been devoured.

Charles took a moment to look at the dead man's face, noting that he was not part of their group. Nor had he been part of the group that had been there when the buildings and wall were created. He had no reason to be lurking near the wall in the middle of the night and had likely been sent to spy on them.

Dismissing the dead man, he concentrated on the monster using his ability to bring up its information.

Vulture Bat Lv. 17

He scanned through the rest of the information quickly before dismissing it. A shadow on the far side of the monster shifted and another human male came into view, tumbling from where he had been perched. He had been hiding in the shadows of the building this entire time.

The vulture bat looked up and screeched loudly as it hopped away from its still steaming meal. Its head twisted towards the noise and the small beady eyes instantly focused on the moving man. He was scrambling to his feet but having little success as he was trembling violently. His trembles were preventing him from placing his feet properly, and eventually he just gave up and began scrambling backward. His butt scraping the ground in his haste to get away, his eyes focused on the large monster as it hopped closer to him.

Alli continued to growl but made no move to attack the higher-level monster. Charles remained still as he watched, seeing no reason to help someone that was spying on them. Charlotte was looking on analytically behind him, while Kira had just folded her arms and watched. Everyone else had turned away from the grisly scene.

Abruptly Alli stopped growling and looked up the sky, her companions following her lead. Above them, a dark mass hurtled towards the ground, angled just behind the monster. The vulture bat perked up as it finally noticed the sound of something whistling through the air. It was too late.

Just before the mass would have impacted the ground giant wings covered in scales spread out arresting its fall. A mouth lined with sharp teeth spread open and bit deep into the neck of the monster as it flew by and then back into the sky the dead monster clutched in its mouth.

Charles regained his senses long enough to analyze it.

Immature Wyvern Lv. 20

"There are dragons," Kory whispered, sinking to the ground in amazement.

"Wyverns," Charles corrected before, sighing. "It might as well be dragons."

"Did you hear that? There was a dragon!" Voices filled the still morning air behind them as the people arrived in a swarm.

Charles looked back for the second man, but he had vanished, leaving a fading cloud of dirt in his wake.

Alli stood and shook her massive body, "I'm going to go explore the area, I want to make sure there aren't more of either of those monsters in the area."

Charles detected a hint of frustration in her voice. "Go, but be careful."

"I will," She replied before running off.

Charles turned to the gathered people and clapped his hands. "Since everyone is up, we might as well begin the day."

Chapter 20

Alli subconsciously stuck to the shadows as she walked, her mind in turmoil. So much had changed since she met Charles. He had changed her. He had changed everything.

She could remember those first few days clearly, everything before that was wreathed in shadows and unclear. Except for a few things that is, she could remember that she was loved. She could remember being part of a family with a little girl that she loved. She could remember the little girl vanishing into little wisps of light when everything began to change and her parents panicking.

All of that was before though, it all felt one step removed, like it had been someone else's life and not hers. In the early days with Charles, she had tried to find the little girl, that desire had slowly faded as she became more aware.

With every level that she gained, she changed. Her body, her mind, her connection to Charles, all of it changed her in different ways. She became stronger, smarter, and worst of all, she became able to understand the world of humans. Humans like the little girl were rare. Not just in the sense that all children under a certain age seemed to have vanished, but humans that were genuinely good.

During her time with Charles, she had seen the many faces that humans possessed, and it made her cling to Charles that much harder. He was simple to understand, if you were important to him then he showed it, he worked to keep you safe and protected. Others just wanted to take, they were desperate to survive in a world they no longer understood, and it had changed them for the worse.

Her paws padded softly across the pavement, ears on alert for noises, but her mind still occupied. She had noticed the bond with Charles changing the way she thought, and while she could choose to refuse the changes, she rarely did. It made things easier on her, as a dog's life had been simple, and she had loved her humans, especially the little girl unconditionally. That had become harder to do as she grew smarter, and every time they had interacted with other humans or passed those in need by, she had felt her heartbreaking. So, she accepted the changes, and she learned why Charles acted the way he did, for the most part. He still acted weird on occasion.

She was part of a family again, one that truly loved and cared for her, she could feel it. She'd had her reservations about Kira in the beginning, and they were still valid. The woman was a mess of anger issues that she could barely control, but she was part of the family now. It was the same with Kira's parents and younger sister Kate; they had become a family, even Charles thought they were important enough to protect.

Then there was Charlotte, Charles older sister and the reason he had chosen to go in the direction he had that first day. It wouldn't be completely unreasonable to say she was the reason Alli and Charles had met. She was not what Alli had been expecting. She was expecting a female Charles, but that wasn't her. She was slightly off as he was, not caring for people as much as could be considered normal, but she was able to fake it with most people. Something that Charles seemed unable to do.

There was an intelligence in Charlotte's eyes that frankly scared Alli at times, it was as though she knew how everything worked, and even the changes in the world hadn't changed that.

Alli stopped moving, her ears straining to catch the noise that had taken her from her thoughts. The shifting of rubble was soft beneath the chattering of young voices, but something about it had seemed wrong, out of place.

Gathering up the strength in her legs she launched herself forward, hitting her top speed in seconds. Shadows blurred around her, each one revealing different secrets to her searching eyes. That was another change, but this one she had chosen. She could walk through shadows, entering one and exiting someplace completely different. It was not an ability she enjoyed using since she had little control over it, yet. She much preferred to slide through the shadows, the world slowed down when she did that, allowing her to see everything in incredible detail. The ability took a lot out of her, however, always leaving her exhausted when she used it too much.

It was too early in the day to be tired, so she was running, whatever had drawn her attention wasn't urgent in any case. It had simply been a tickle that what she had heard was out of place, so she decided to investigate it. Besides, she always enjoyed seeing young people; they were more innocent than their older counterparts. Their intentions more pure, she needed that right now. After seeing that man almost be killed and not being able to do anything, she needed the innocent healing a child could provide. True children had all vanished, but she would take what she could get, she had to.

Her steps slowed as she neared them, using their voices to locate them. She stuck to the shadows and chose a place to watch them from. It was near the top of a pile of rubble from a destroyed building with plenty of shadows and it allowed her to look down at the young humans. Wrapping the shadows around her she vanished from view and relaxed while she watched them, her head on her outstretched paws.

It was a boy and a girl, maybe eleven or twelve, she couldn't tell. It was clear right away that they had both lost weight recently, their dirty and ragged clothes hanging off their emaciated frames. Their skin was dried out and the rasp in their voices revealed just how dehydrated the two of them were. They were both flushed and exuding heat, their eyes slightly glazed with fever.

They were digging through the remains of what looked to have once been a small store, two of the walls were missing and the roof had caved in.

"Jenny," The boy whispered weakly as he collapsed to the ground. "What are we going to do? We have no food, no shelter, and neither of us has had any water in the last two days."

The girl, Jenny swayed and then collapsed next to him her shoulders shaking, it was clear that she would have been crying tears if her body had any water to spare.

"I don't know," Her voice trembling as she spoke to the boy. "After what happened with mom and dad though we can't trust the adults, they'll just take everything and leave us behind again."

Alli felt her heart breaking for these two kids, it was clear that they had no one left but each other and wouldn't last much longer. She opened her inventory and looked at what she had stored inside; it had changed when she became level 15. Her inventory started with 25 slots, more than the average human, but still quickly filled. Every time she fought and looted the monsters, she had been forced to decide what to keep. That had changed with her latest level, items had stacked up to ten of the same items per slot.

It had opened up her previously cramped inventory, and she had taken to collecting certain things as she explored. Shiny things mainly, they were things that glinted in the sunlight catching her attention. They rarely had value, but she liked them. She had been lucky enough to find some cases of water though in Danville. She hadn't needed it since Charles could summon water easily enough, but everyone else was always searching for water, so she had grabbed it and then forgotten about it.

Now with these clearly thirsty kids in front of her she remembered, the problem was giving it to them. She was aware that she was a large and potentially scary being, and if she just popped out of the shadows, she would be sure to send them running. She didn't want that.

The soft sound of shifting rubble that had drawn her there in the first place came again, and right away she knew why it had sounded wrong. Not only was it not the children making the noise, but it was coming from beneath the pile of rubble.

Jenny reached for the boy and covered his mouth, her eyes going wide as fear forced the effects of the fever to the background. She had heard the noise as well and was looking at the pile suspiciously.

The boy wriggled away from her and wiped his chapped lips with the back of a dirty hand. "What was that for?" A small concrete block further in the store shifted and fell over silencing him.

The sound of rubble being moved underneath the pile was louder now. The kids scrambled to their feet and began to back away from the ruined store they had been digging through. They refused to look away from where the noise had come from, moving blindly backward.

Another block of concrete shifted from the back of the store. A scaled head peered above the pile before withdrawing and a series of hisses could be heard. A small lizard-like being sprang from the hole, Alli had heard Charles call them kobolds as they fled through the woods. A second kobold leaped through after it, followed by another and then more. Within a minute, the entire store was filled with the strange scaled monsters.

The kobolds were skittish with their eyes constantly moving, their clawed hands constantly gripping and re-gripping their poorly made weapons.

Jenny and James froze at the appearance of the kobolds, not daring to breathe much less move lest they draw attention to themselves. It didn't help.

The kobolds could see the young kids and were licking their lips in between tasting the air around them. The kobold that had left the hole last was wearing better clothes than the rest and holding a better weapon. Not that this truly meant much, they were still rags, just rags with less blood and gore on them. The weapon, a goblins' knife instead of a spiked club.

Alli couldn't tell the gender of the monster or if they even had genders, but it saw the humans and hissed to the rest in excitement. Keeping the shadows wrapped around her, Alli stood and prepared to fight the kobolds.

She didn't wait for them to make the first move, instead, she vanished into the shadows, slipping through them until she appeared inside the shop behind them all. Mere seconds had passed while she traveled, and without making a sound beforehand she attacked.

Her jaws snapped around the neck of one, while her claws ripped through a second. She tossed the first body into the middle of the group, tumbling them as confusion kept them from reacting. She spit the blood from her mouth and growled; she had had a lot of blood run through her mouth lately. All of it had been nasty, but the kobolds blood was on a whole different level of rank and foul. She wanted to scrape her tongue clean but didn't have the time as she sprang to the next monster.

The kobolds scattered after the fifth one went down, their scales afforded them no protection against her. Weapons were dropped in their haste to getaway. She managed to snatch a sixth before it could flee, crushing its neck and dropping it down the hole they had appeared from.

The kids had frozen in the open and never moved once she started attacking. Blood coated Alli's muzzle and paws as she walked calmly towards them. Jenny held James behind her back as the large bloody dog approached them.

Alli stopped in front of the two kids and dipping her head to the ground dropped a case of water bottles at their feet. She then retreated back a few feet and watched them.

A small hesitant hand reached from behind Jenny and struggled to pull a bottle from the plastic wrapping surrounding it. The girl kept her wide eyes on Alli as the boy she was shielding finally got the bottle free. Her mouth opened in longing as she heard the crackle of plastic being broken as the cap was twisted off. She still didn't move though making sure that her body stayed between the unknown dog and the boy behind her.

Alli let out an annoyed huff and stood before the girl could react Alli had pressed her nose to her forehead. "Drink little one," She commanded.

Jenny gasped but still made no move to stop protecting the person behind her and drink.

"I said drink!" Alli growled, letting her teeth show and her foul kobold blood-drenched breath waft over her.

"You can talk?" The frightened girl finally managed to rasp out.

James peeked out from behind her and placed the half-full bottle of water in her hands.

Alli nodded her head and backed up a couple of steps, allowing the girl room to drink. The arms inside her ragged and worn long-sleeve shirt were painfully thin as she brought the bottle to her lips, her wide eyes never leaving Alli's.

"Wh-what are you?" James asked in a small voice, as he surreptitiously grabbed one bottle after another and put them in his inventory.

Alli snorted at the boys' question, her tail that had been wagging coming to an abrupt standstill.

Thankfully, it seemed Jenny was to more intelligent of the two, or at least the one with better manners. "She's a dog you idiot," She hissed after draining the rest of the water in the bottle.

"How was I supposed to know that, dogs aren't usually the size of horses," He rudely said while shoving another bottle of water into the girl's hands.

"Um, I'm Jenny, and this is my twin brother James. Thanks for the water and helping us with the monsters. I've never seen you around here before, are you new?" Jenny asked quickly in a single breath. Thankfully, she couldn't see the looks her brother was giving her, it was clear he thought his sister had gone crazy.

Alli stretched out her paw and placed it on the girls' leg. Usually, she touched people with her muzzle when she talked to them. She had noticed over the last few days, however, that people could still hear her as long as they were touching her body.

"Hi Jenny, it's nice to meet you and your stinky brother," Jenny giggled at the stinky comment, her feverish eyes twinkling with amusement. "My name is Alli. I'm part of a group of humans that just set up by the river."

"That was your group in the trucks and cars yesterday?" She asked while drinking more water.

"What are the two of you doing out here alone?" Alli asked remembering what she had heard them saying.

Jenny froze at the question, "Our parents were killed a few days ago, we were trying to join up with one of the groups in the area when they were attacked. James and I ran and hid when the fighting was done our parents were dead along with the monsters. The adults stole everything from their inventory and then left us and their bodies. James and I couldn't even bury them, we had to cover them with rocks." The small girl was sobbing at the memory, tears refusing to fall due to dehydration.

Alli made up her mind on the spot, she was bringing these kids back with her. They would become part of the town where they would be safe and not have to worry about monsters or mean humans. She crouched in front of them, lowering her body as close to the ground as she could.

"Climb on to my back, you can come with me. You'll be safe with my group of humans, they're good people."

Jenny's shoulders shook for a few more seconds, while her brother clung to her. "Okay," She said softly, she finished drinking her water and grabbed another bottle before standing.

Alli waited as they climbed onto her back, Jenny quickly explaining their conversation to James. Once they were in place and holding firmly onto her hair, she stood. After quickly looting each of the monsters, she turned back the way she had come and took them away.

She had been walking for a couple of minutes when she stopped, her ears twitching wildly. On her back, the kids were talking softly, but she could feel the feverish heat running rampant in their ill bodies.

Alli smiled happily and her tongue flopped out of her mouth as she heard Charles and Kira talking in the distance, turning towards them she began walking again.

"Charles," She called out, knowing that he would hear her. She heard him come to a stop before speaking again. "I found some small children that need to be healed of their fevers. I want to bring them into the town. Also, it seems they might know where some of the human groups are located."

"I know you can hear me, Alli, bring them here. Kira and I were just about to start looking for those groups. If these kids can help, then bring them here and I'll heal them right away." Charles spoke aloud, well aware of how sensitive her senses had become.

"I'll be there in just a minute," She told him, already on her way.

A warm feeling suffused her body as she hurried to meet up with her human. She had managed to help these kids. Charles was going to heal them and then they would be safe behind the walls of their budding town. She hoped someone was doing the same thing for the little girl she was having a progressively harder time remembering.

The girl's face was slowly fading, but the feeling of absolute love the girl had felt for Alli, and Alli for her, that would never fade.

Chapter 21

Charles led the group farther inside the wall after Alli disappeared in a rush. He had sensed that something was wrong, but he would talk to her later when there were fewer people around.

Kory and Krystal immediately took control, doing exactly what they had said they would the night before. They quickly divided the people into groups and sent them out looking for anything of value. They kept one group behind for a few minutes as they talked to each person in turn, writing down what they wanted to do, and what they had experience in.

Charles let them do that while Charlotte showed him the area, she wanted the warehouse built. It was right next to the river, and just a little way away from the first house he had built. It was clear she wanted to get back to learning and inventing. She trailed after him to the Town System building eager to learn more magic while the building was built. Kira and Kate followed behind them, talking quietly amongst themselves.

Charles pulled up the town menu and selected the warehouse. He would pay the mana cost himself since it was for his sister and not the town. The warehouse cost twice as much mana to build but was still well within his abilities to handle.

With that done, and now in the process of being built outside, he turned to Kate and his sister. "Let's get comfortable and then we can start."

Charles quickly started the meditations for both of them and turned to Kira. "Let's go explore the area."

Kira looked back to her sister one last time as they walked out of the building and closed the door. It locked automatically but would still let the people inside out without a problem. They were safe from harm.

Charles, for his part, was looking at the large walls of the dungeon across the river, thinking that they appeared smaller than before. Shaking his head, he saw Kory and Krystal sitting at a table that someone had dragged in. Their heads were pressed together, and several sheets of paper were spread on the table in front of them.

"What is it you're hoping to learn?" Kira asked as they walked past her absorbed parents.

Charles was silent for several minutes, only stopping when they had reached the opening in the wall. "I'm going to be honest with you Kira. I'm not good with people, in case you haven't noticed." The look on her face said she had clearly noticed, not that she had any room to talk in that regard. In some ways, she was worse than him. "We need people though, if we are going to make this into a decent town, that is safe, then we need as many people as we can get. The more people we get, the more mana gets taxed and the more we can rebuild."

Kira nodded along as he spoke, what he was saying made sense to her. "How are you going to enforce the laws? Are there going to be police in our little town?"

Charles shook his head, smirking as he remembered something that would be unlocked with the full town menu. "It seems there is something already in place to keep people in line. It will become unlocked with the rest of the town menu later tonight." He planned to build the last three buildings needed for that to happen that night.

"So, what you're saying then is that we simply need people. You want to absorb all the little groups that are left in the area into our town?" She was curious about what he had said but could see he wasn't willing to say more for the moment. "What about the jerks or little tyrants that have undoubtedly popped up?"

"The jerks." He smiled at the immature choice of words. "Will have to follow the same rules as everyone else, or they will be forced to leave. The criminals, I guess it will depend on what they did on whether or not they can be part of the town. As for the tyrants, they'll die."

Kira nodded calmly in agreement, her sister and parents were part of the town and she would not allow anything to hurt them. "So, we're just going to what, walk around and see which groups are closest to us?"

"More or less," Charles shrugged. "Unless you have a better way of doing it?"

"We could have at least driven the truck," She groused, not having a better idea at the time.

"We need to save the fuel, who knows when we'll need it, and the supply is going to run out rather quickly."

Kira sighed but nodded, she had enjoyed working on cars for her job. It seemed likely that her skills would soon be of no more use to them, once there was no more gas to use it would be pointless to continue working on vehicles.

"I wouldn't worry too much about that though," Charles began. He had noticed the despondent look on her face at his earlier words. "I have a feeling my sister and her group of MIT people will come up with something that will act as fuel."

She perked up at that thought, even while wondering just how smart his sister truly was. She hadn't spent much time with the other woman, but it had been clear from the start that she was incredibly intelligent.

"Do you think she can really do that?" Kira asked hopefully.

"If not her, then Scott and the professor will probably be able to figure something out. Who knows, maybe she'll figure out a way to make everything run off of mana instead of fuel and electricity." Charles had absolute faith in his sister, that much was completely obvious.

"Charles," Alli's voice echoed through his head before he could say more. Kira looked at him curiously as he stopped and waited. "I found some small children that need to be healed of their fevers. I want to bring them into the town. Also, it seems they might know where some of the human groups are located."

He thought over what she had said quickly, unable to keep the small smile from his face at what she was doing. "I know you can hear me, Alli, bring them here. Kira and I were just about to start looking for those groups if these kids can help then bring them here and I'll heal them right away." He said aloud, knowing that she would hear him. She rarely said anything to him from a distance where she would be unable to hear his reply.

"I'll be there in just a minute," Came her reply. He could hear the happiness she felt knowing that she had helped those kids, and that he was willing to go along with her desires.

"Alli will be here in just a minute, apparently she found some kids she wants to bring into the town. They need some quick healing and then hopefully they can tell us where to find some of the groups around here." Charles explained to Kira while shaking his head ruefully.

Kira nodded but didn't say anything, there was nothing to say. Alli was helping people just like she wanted, Kira wasn't going to get in the way of her doing something that made her happy.

Charles waited patiently as he listened to Alli tell him what had happened and the dismal shape the kids were in. He had emptied a lot out of his inventory the night before, but all the food and miscellaneous items were still in it. He withdrew some jerky and protein bars for them all to eat as Alli came into view.

The kids were clinging weakly to her back, their small hands gripping her silver hair in clumps. Alli came to a stop in front of him and crouched to the ground, so the kids could climb off of her back. The kids looked uncertain of the adults and remained next to Alli, even after Charles pointed to the food in front of them.

With a small frown he stepped forward and touched the small girl's forehead. Her skin was hot to the touch. Everything that had happened to them that morning had only served to exasperate the fever, making their condition worse.

He gathered up some mana and let the healing spell circulate through her system, fixing little things she hadn't even known were wrong alongside the larger more obvious issues. The girl shivered and wrapped her arms around herself as her internal temperature dropped to normal levels, the sudden difference making the change clear.

The boy, James, Charles remembered, stepped forward when he saw the flush fade from her skin and the scratches on her hands heal.

Charles touched his head next and did the same thing before taking a step back and frowning. "There's an issue with your heart."

Jenny froze, a piece of jerky in her hand. "It's been like that from birth, it wasn't fully developed or something. He's had to have it fixed twice since then," She gulped, afraid of what she was about to ask. "Is it bad, is he going to die?"

Charles frowned, thinking about what the healing spells were capable of. They were already close to miraculous and using the intermediate healing spell while controlling it might make it possible for him to heal the boys' heart. The question was, was it worth it? The cost in mana to do a healing of that nature would undoubtedly be high, it would take him a while to regenerate the mana.

"How close or far is the group closest to us?" He asked, not looking up from the ground.

The girl opened her mouth and then closed it, thinking. "A mile or two farther from the river, I think."

Charles nodded at that, walking that distance would allow him enough time to get some mana back. Unless the cost was truly ridiculous, they would be fine. He saw Alli looking at him, her eyes pleading with him to help the boy. He gave her a small smile and nodded.

Pointing to the ground in front of him, "Sit, this is going to be a lot different, and likely far more painful than healing a simple fever."

Kira moved to sit next to Alli, her hand unconsciously reaching out to scratch her as she watched what was about to happen. Jenny sat next to her brother and grabbed his hand tightly, unwilling to let him suffer through this alone.

Charles breathed out and touched the boy's chest where his heart was. He closed his eyes and sent out the first wave of magic. He quickly mapped the boys' heart and could clearly see that the problem was from an undeveloped chamber in his heart. He didn't know what it was supposed to look like, however, just that it was wrong.

Opening his eyes, he looked to the sister and with a quick apology reached for her with his other hand. His mind split painfully as he concentrated on seeing both hearts at the same time. He saw what her heart looked like and how James' should look. Keeping hold of them both he took hold of his mana and began to heal the boy.

It required all of his focus to guide the intermediate healing spell, directing it first to finish developing the chamber and then unblock it. Once that was finished, he fixed the little holes around the overworked valves that were depriving him of getting all the oxygen in his blood.

Minutes had passed by the time he had finished and both Charles and James were covered in sweat. Withdrawing his hands, Charles opened his eyes and watched as the boy coughed up some blood before relaxing, his eyes full of wonder. Jenny was still holding his hand, the worry slowly leaving her face as she realized it had been a success.

The mana cost had been high, taking just under half of what he possessed to fix the heart. Fixing something broken like that was much harder than simply healing something that had been injured. He had to admit though, that being able to perform what would normally be considered a miracle like this was extremely gratifying.

Alli stood with a huff, Kira's hand falling from her ears. Coming over to Charles, she licked his face. "Thank you for healing them. I know it wasn't easy to do."

He shook his head and gave her a quick hug as she pulled him to his feet. "Which direction to we need to go to meet up the closest group?" He asked the kids after giving them a minute to hug and cry.

They had a job to do, and while he could understand their joy, they still needed to get moving.

The kids climbed back onto Alli's back with happy grins and extra food clutched tightly in their laps, their outstretched arms pointing them where to go.

Kira's face had softened during the time he had known her, slowly she seemed to be opening up to him more and more. The current expression on her face was not one he had ever seen before and wasn't sure what it meant or signified.

Alli growled suddenly and stopped. "There is a lot of blood ahead of us, and I can't hear any people moving!"

"Stay here," Charles ordered her, as he moved ahead with Kira at his side her hammer already in hand.

A small wall had been constructed around what had once been a three-story apartment building. It had managed to survive intact, becoming a base for one of the groups. The inhabitants had not faired nearly as well as the building.

At first, it was unclear what had killed the people only that their bodies had been dragged away, leaving trails of blood everywhere.

Kira knelt and touched a trail of blood with her fingertip. "It's barely tacky, whatever killed them couldn't have happened more than thirty minutes ago." She announced before rubbing her finger on her pants.

Charles led the way into the building before stepping back out with a gasp. Pulling the same scarf he had used against the ash from his inventory, he quickly poured some water on it and wrapped it around his face. Pulling a second scarf from his inventory, he wet it down and handed it to Kira.

Inside the building, the smell of death and rotting things had become overpowering. A blade of apprehension had crawled into his stomach as he entered a second time. The smell was far too strong for whatever had just happened, leaving him with a bad feeling of what they were about to see.

Thankfully, it was not what he had been expecting. A large hole in the floor next to the elevator was the source of the smell.

Kira and Charles stopped in front of the hole and looked at each other. "Do we go down or salvage what we can from the apartments?" Kira asked first.

Charles tapped his foot thinking, "Alli, leave the kids outside the wall and come here if you can stand the smell, please?" He called out.

"Coming," She called back.

Her eyes were already watering from the overpowering stench wafting up from the hole when she stepped into the building next to them.

"Can you hear or smell any humans that might still alive down there?" Charles asked quickly, not wanting to inflict the smell on her sensitive nose longer than he had to.

Her ears swiveled, and she breathed in, before erupting into a fit of wheezing and fleeing into cleaner air. "Any humans down there are already dead," She called back to him, once she had stopped wheezing.

Charles held his hand over the hole and used one of the spells he had learned during the night. A wave of fire clung to the walls of the hole and began moving downward quickly. It continued to cling to the walls as it moved, burning everything in its path. He pumped as much mana into the spell as he dared, the extra mana would keep the fire moving for a while.

He stepped back from the hole and raising his hand used another spell he had learned during the night. A pillar of dirt rose from the hole sealing it from being used again, he controlled the spell compacting the dirt into a flat surface that was level with the rest of the floor.

"I haven't seen you use those spells before," Kira said once she saw him relax.

"That's because I learned them last night." He cracked his back and moved over to the stairs, sitting while he waited to recuperate. "The first was called 'Flamewave' it adheres to any surface and moves along it in a wave, the more mana I put into the spell the hotter it gets and the longer it moves. The second is simply called 'Earthen Construct' and allows me to create any object I want with the earth."

Kira looked down at her hands, flexing them a couple of times before looking at the man in front of her. "I want," She hesitated and cleared her throat before trying again. "I want to try learning magic again when we get back tonight."

"Are you sure? You didn't exactly respond well to it the first time."

"I know, but I think this is something I have to do. Even if I don't learn any magic from it, I have to face my core." She looked at him and blushed slightly, her tanned skin and dim light helping to hide it from his eyes. "It's time I moved past what happened to me."

Charles stood and looked her in the eye. "If you're sure, then I have no problem helping you. Now, do we go through these apartments ourselves or send another group to do it?" He asked changing the subject before she could become uncomfortable.

Kira pulled a map of the city from her pocket and spread it across the floor. "I found this in the rubble yesterday. Why don't we just mark the location on the map and then send another group here tomorrow?" She asked without looking up to meet his eyes.

Charles turned to the wall next to the mail slots, a corkboard for announcements hung on the wall. A little-used yellow pencil dangled from a cord next to it. Ripping the pencil from the cord he tossed it to Kira. "Sounds good, let's mark it down and then move on to the next place."

She quickly marked down the location on the map before folding the map around the pencil and putting both into her back pocket. "My inventory is full," She explained when she saw him watching.

Charles opened his mouth to offer to carry some for her before closing it. He didn't want to step out of line and offend her. "Come on, Alli and the kids are waiting for us."

She nodded gratefully at him for letting the matter drop and followed him back out into the morning sun.

Chapter 22

Alli had the kids already on her back and was waiting for them as they walked through the small opening in the wall. The wall surrounding the building was pitifully small, standing only four or so feet in the air. It was too weak for monsters and too small for humans; it had been built to warn others and nothing more.

"Where's the next place?" Charles asked the kids before they could say anything related to people that should have been inside.

"Our parents only told us of two others," James said after a moment of thought. "But they only told us the general location of them."

"That's fine," Charles said, waving away the boys' concern. "Once we get close enough, Alli should be able to pinpoint their location."

The kids looked at each other and shrugged before pointing further into the city. "Mom and dad mentioned that a group that had been staying at a school building on the other side of the river were that way. They said that they had joined with a different group at another larger high school."

Kira glared at the ground and began muttering, "If that worthless group got out in time, then what are the odds that filthy cockroach of a woman survived?"

"Probably higher than you would like," Charles said softly next to her, overhearing her words even though she hadn't meant him to.

"Probably," Kira growled, her eyes going hard.

Charles barely held back a sigh at the look in her eyes, she had just admitted to wanting to move forward. He could almost feel her withdrawing into herself at the mere thought of the girl who had betrayed her.

The kids talked with Alli as they walked, little by little the horror of the last few weeks was pushed from their minds for the moment. Their eyes grew brighter and their smiles more real, only for their expressions to grow shuttered as a group of people appeared farther down the road.

"They're not part of our group, but they don't seem hostile," Alli told Charles, causing him to relax slightly. She had warned him of their presence well before they had come into view.

Kira stood her ground, her expression quickly shifting to murderous as the other group came closer. Charles wanted to grab her and get her to calm down, but he knew that him touching her would do the exact opposite.

"This area has been claimed by our salvager teams," A middle-aged man with a bit of a paunch announced as they drew closer. The belt on his pants had been tightened several times recently, the wear mark near the end hinting that he had once been a much bigger man.

"We're not here to salvage," Charles said before Kira could react to them. "We're actually trying to meet up with each of the groups in the area."

One of the men held a finger to his nose and blew, releasing the curdled yellow mass on the side of the road. "You part of the group that came through and set themselves up by the river?" He asked.

"We are," Charles confirmed.

"How did you all get that wall built so fast?" The chubby man who had first spoken asked.

"Magic," Charles replied bluntly, not actually willing to tell them more.

The other group began laughing, slapping their thighs and relaxing. "Haha, that's fair. It seems like a lot of stuff happens by magic these days.

Well come on, we've got no reason to stop you if you aren't salvagers. Follow us and we'll take you to our leaders." The fat man laughed again, fully relaxed now. "Man, I've always wanted to say that."

Charles felt his eyebrows rising in surprise. He had not been expecting this rough group to welcome them so readily. Truthfully, he had been expecting the need to fight everyone, his experiences with people since the apocalypse had not been kind. Still, he remembered his last interactions with the group when they had been across the river. He did not expect their level-headedness and cool thinking to last long.

The place they led them to was only a ten-minute walk, and it ended in front of a two-story high school. There was no chain-link fence surrounding it this time, but there were visible patrols walking the grounds. The football field could partially be seen in the back, the ground and been torn up and separated into rows. They were going to start growing their own crops there.

They were brought to the entrance and asked to wait as the group that had found them went inside.

"Let's tell them we're in the area, make the offer to have them join us and then get out of here," Charles told his group firmly. Something about the way the group was acting seemed off to him, what wasn't clear was why. They seemed normal, and they hadn't been aggressive, but something still tickled at the back of his mind.

"This place is wrong," Kira told them softly after looking around for a minute.

"I know, I just can't figure out why," He said in frustration.

"It's the guards in the patrol groups, most of them are looking inwards. They act like they're more worried about people escaping than monsters attacking them." The kids began looking around intently when she said that, while Charles could only sigh and start preparing to fight.

"Let's go, there's no point in staying. We're not inviting people who treat others like this into our town." Charles told them firmly while turning to walk away.

The response to him turning was immediate, all the groups that had been patrolling the area rushed towards them. Alli growled and crouched low, the kids on her back-laying flat where they wouldn't be seen right away.

Orders of 'Halt' came in from every direction as they continued to walk away. Kira's face had gone back to being a cold, emotionless mask. While Charles had decided that one of the next things he needed to learn was a shield of some kind.

"Decided we are good enough to host the newest group in the area?" A grating voice called out from behind them, the odd echo accompanying it telling them the speaker was still inside the long hallway of the building.

"You were taking too long," Charles called back while continuing to walk away. "We have other groups we need to talk to today, and that means we can't stay at any one place for very long."

"Stop!" The grating voice called out at them, the lack of echo this time indicating the speaker had finally joined them outside.

"Why should we?" Charles asked harshly as he spun to look at the speaker. "Oh, it's you. I see you survived thanks to the warning we gave you before. I'm assuming you already know what happens next if you continue to try to stop us?"

Kira followed his eyes at that and saw the woman who had been leading the group at their previous location. They may have only just recently joined up with the group here, but it was clear from the glance everyone was giving her that she was high up the food chain.

The woman inhaled sharply, indicating she had not recognized Charles. "You're the magic user!" Her voice had gone shrill and her face pale.

The people that had continued to slowly surround them abruptly stopped and took a step back. They knew he was not someone they could afford to insult or get on the wrong side of.

At Charles nod, the woman stepped forward. "I was told that before you left that day, you were able to heal one of the people in the gym. Is that true?"

"It's true, it was Kira's younger sister." He pointed to the angry woman at his side as he answered.

The weaselly woman licked her lips, looking unsure. "Would it be possible to get you to heal some more people? We have a number of injured people inside that will die without advanced care."

Charles opened his mouth to respond but didn't say anything for a moment as a possibility sped through his mind. "That is actually one of the things I will be offering to the groups we meet with. Even if they don't decide to join us, if they bring their injured to us, I will heal them. That said, anyone who attacks our group will obviously not be getting any healing." The surrounding people took several hurried steps back at those words.

A grin threatened to cross his face, the twitching of his lips the only visible sign he hadn't managed to hold in. The town needed an influx of taxable mana in order to continue to grow, by having people come to them, he could artificially add more people that would be taxed. They wouldn't get the full amount from each person since they wouldn't be actual members of the town, but every little bit helped.

The woman had a constipated look on her face as they turned and walked away.

"Where's the last group you know about Jenny?" Charles asked while walking beside Alli.

"I'm not really sure," She said quietly, her eyes flicking to the group of people they had left behind. "We never actually went there, but mom and daddy called it a hotel of iniq... ity... of sin!" She struggled with the word before changing to something more familiar.

"What was the place called? Did they say?" Kira asked, speaking for the first time since the school.

"Ameri something, I think. It's supposed to be close to the river." James spoke up, the remains of a chocolate candy bar stuck to his mouth.

Kira sighed in disgust. "I know the place. It is close to the river, but it's further down than the town is. It will take us a while to walk there, the trucks would be faster." She turned to the little boy and the silvery hair sticking to his chocolaty hands. "And you, don't get any more of that on Alli!"

James looked startled before looking down at his hands and then at Alli's smudged back. Tears crept into eyes as he realized that he had made a mess of her.

Alli glared at Kira for making the boy cry, "It's fine, Charles can clean me later without any issues," She told them all, brushing lightly against Kira as she spoke.

Charles just nodded at that and together they began to head back towards the town. "You can stay at the town when we get there," He informed the kids. "Kira's parents are there. I'm sure they'd be willing to look after you until we return."

"Will you really heal everyone that shows up?" Kira asked, stepping close to him.

Charles gave her a calculating grin. "Only if they show up at our town, that's the key thing. If they are in the town, then they will get taxed and we'll get more mana for building everything. By having everyone be forced to come to us, I'm creating more traffic to the town. Once they see the things we can do there, they will spread the word and more people will start to join us."

The rest of the walk back was made up of small talk between everyone, the kids gradually opened up around the adults. The kids stopped talking abruptly as the tall wall came into view, through the opening where the gate would eventually be a field of green grass could be seen. It was like nothing they had seen since the apocalypse happened. The entire area felt safe, and the people they could see inside seemed happy. There was none of the wariness or fear that had become so prevalent.

Kira hurried over to Kate while Charles led Alli and the kids over to her parents, they were still at the same table as before with papers spread out before them.

"Kory, Krystal," Charles began, making sure he had their attention. "Alli found these kids all alone out there and invited them to stay with us. Would it be possible for you to watch over them, while we go visit the last group that we know the location of?"

Jenny and James slid from Alli's back onto the ground shyly, their eyes wide as they continued to look around the area.

"What about their parents?" Krystal asked Charles softly after pulling him to the side.

"Killed a few days ago, they've been on their own ever since," He explained in a whisper.

"Was it humans or monsters?" She had to ask, the pity and sympathy she felt for the kids palpable in her eyes.

"From what Alli told me, it was monsters, but there were also humans involved in a way." Charles softly told the older woman everything that Alli had relayed to him about the kids.

"What have the people of this world come to? It seems like most of the people we've met since the apocalypse have thrown at least part of their humanity away," Krystal muttered softly to herself.

***

Kira was sitting behind the wheel of the truck staring at the building that proudly proclaimed itself to be an Inn and Casino. She had been in an odd mood ever since they had left twenty-minutes earlier and had refused to say anything to either Charles or Alli. The truck was idling softly in the road a couple blocks down from the building in plain sight.

"Are you going to tell me what is wrong?" Charles asked the tense woman.

Kira clenched her teeth and put the transmission into gear. "Just remembering things," Her voice oddly strained.

"Have you been in there before, or something?" Charles asked as she quickly drove them to the front of the building.

"Or something," The growl in her voice telling him to drop it.

"There are a lot of people in that building, and some of the surrounding ones as well," Alli told him, her head stretched above the cab in the wind.

Charles nodded but didn't say anything, only making sure that Kira had the key for the truck as they climbed out of the cab. Taking the key was not really a deterrent on a truck as old as the one they had, but it would still give them a few extra seconds.

"At least I don't smell any blood or hostility from these humans," Alli said as she leaped from the back of the truck and stood next to them.

"That's encouraging at least," Charles said aloud to her, his words drawing Kira's attention.

The doors to the inn section of the building opened and a large towering man stepped through them. Dark eyes hidden underneath bushy eyebrows took in the two people and large dog standing in front of him, the truck at their backs.

"I take it you're the ones I heard about moving in farther down the river? They seem to be the only ones with working vehicles so far." A clear deep voice asked.

"Not the only ones," Charles began with a small grin. "But certainly, the only ones out here it seems."

The large man grunted but stepped to the side of the doorway, "You might as well come on in, I'm sure you didn't just stop by here for no reason."

Kira took the lead while Alli stayed at their rear as they walked inside the dim building. Small candles decorated the area, providing light to the corners farthest from the broken windows.

Their host seemed surprised that Alli had followed them in but didn't say anything regarding it as he led them to a large table in the atrium. People were gathered around the edges of the room and on the wide stairs towards the back going up to the second floor.

The man pulled out a wooden chair and sat across from them; the chair creaking in protest against the weight of his large muscled frame. "I guess I'll go first. My name is Ray I'm the leader of the people here. I'm 43, a Virgo, and I love long walks on the beach." His eyes glinted harshly as a menacing aura flowed out from him. "Good, now that we have that done and over with, tell me what you want?"

"We're just here to talk," Charles said defensively, spreading his hands on the table so they could be seen.

"So then talk," Ray demanded, leaning back in the creaking chair.

"We're creating a town, a safe place for people to live."

Ray snorted derisively, "Right, and what makes you think you're so special? What makes you think you are the only ones who can do this?" His deep voice was thundering by the end of his speech.

Charles stood having lost the last of his patience, "What makes me think I can do this?" He raised his hand palm up and let an orb of light float to the ceiling before a bolt of fire formed above his hand. "What makes you think you can do it without me?" His voice was deathly calm as he pushed away from the table, the people having been silenced by his demonstration. "Come on Kira, we're leaving."

"Kira, wait!" A female voice called from the stairs at the back of the atrium.

Kira's face was carefully blank as she turned to look at the speaker, "Sierra, I see you made it out alive," Under her breath she continued speaking, calling the other woman a 'filthy cockroach'.

Sierra stepped into view, her long blonde hair lanky and unwashed, her clothes no longer sparking clean. It was a large difference from what she had looked like the week before. She still possessed the same regal bearing that had people almost unconsciously looking to her for guidance.

"Please, Kira, we need to talk. There is a lot you don't know about what happened back then. Please, just give me a few minutes."

Kira clenched her teeth, glaring hatefully at the other woman. Abruptly her eyes changed, and a mean look appeared in them. "Fine, I'll give you a minute, and if I don't like what you have to say then I get to do to you what they did to me back then. Deal?"

Sierra went pale, looking visibly sick at the thought of what had happened to Kira happening to her. "Deal, as long as you let me explain fully."

Chapter 23

S ierra followed them calmly outside the building and to the shadowed overhang near the truck. They were being left alone for the moment, and Ray hadn't said anything since Charles had used his magic in front of them. Despite her best efforts Kira couldn't help but notice that Sierra was acting vastly different from when they had last seen her. Gone was the entitled princess act, now she was acting like an actual human, that had to work for a living.

Charles sat next to Alli, giving Kira and Sierra a little privacy to talk. Not that it was actually doing them much good as he had Alli repeating everything they said to each other word for word.

Sierra was the first to speak, "I need to apologize for not recognizing you when we met last week," Kira growled, and her knuckles could be heard popping as she squeezed her hands into fists. "Just hold on, I promise this is going somewhere," Sierra continued before she could be interrupted.

She cleared her throat and began again. "As I was saying, I didn't recognize you at first and when you told me who you were, I reacted badly. I've been trying for years to forget what happened to you, and you suddenly appearing like that reminded me of how badly my family not only failed you but also hurt you."

She stopped speaking for a moment and Charles saw her swipe at her eyes. "Do you remember what we were like back then? We were inseparable, even after my father bought the new house. You were my closest friend, practically my sister!"

Kira snorted in derision, "A fat lot of good it did me that day, and we were not inseparable, not by that point. You had begun to change, the money and status that went with it had already started to go to your head."

"That's what I'm trying to explain to you. I wanted to help you that day. You may have thought we were growing apart, but you were still my closest friend even then. It was my father that prevented it."

"Don't lie to me!" Kira shouted at her while surging to her feet. "I know you never reported me going missing to the police. I was kidnapped and tortured in your place and you did nothing to help me in return!"

"Would you shut up for two minutes and let me talk?" Sierra shouted back, starting to lose her cool. "I know what happened to you back then. You don't have to remind me. When I escaped, I immediately called my father for help. I told him everything, and he said he was going to take care of it, that he was going to make sure you were safe. He lied.

"He sent me away that same night, assuring me that he would help you. It wasn't until I returned months later that I heard the truth. He had never done anything to help you, he had in fact obstructed the cops from reaching you earlier. I had told him where we were taken, and though I know they later moved you if he had just told the cops everything I had told him, you would have been found sooner."

"Why, why would he do that to me? I was twelve years old; I had never done anything to either of you." Kira asked sinking to the ground next to Sierra, her eyes held traces of tears and though it was apparent she didn't believe everything she was being told, a glimmer of doubt had entered her being.

"I don't know, he never said." Sierra closed her eyes and pulled her knees to her chest, turning her head to the side. "I stopped talking to him myself after that when he refused to explain why he had refused to help you like he said he would, he stopped being my father. The damage had been done by then; however, I knew that you must have believed I had abandoned you, and truthfully, I felt like I had. I had trusted my father to help you, but never properly followed up when he dismissed my questions afterward. I felt as though I had failed you, and I had. I didn't have the guts or the answers I needed to have before I saw you again, so I stayed away, and tried to forget about the friend I had hurt."

"I don't know what to believe," Kira said softly, much of the hostility she had felt for the woman fading from her body leaving her exhausted.

"She's telling the truth, both of them are," Alli whispered to Charles. "The way Sierra's heart is beating, the way she smells. She is either the worlds most accomplished liar and a sociopath, or she truly believes what she is saying."

"It doesn't seem like they are going to hurt each other at least, let them talk in peace for now," Charles stood and led Alli away from the talking women.

"What's the plan now?" Alli asked once they had stepped away from the truck.

"Now? Now we go back and start building up the town. The people know we are here now, and word will spread, about the town and me using magic. I expect people to start showing up on their own soon enough. As far as I'm concerned, I've done what I needed to. Now it's time to make sure the town is safe." Charles bent over to pick up a rock and sent it skipping over the cracked pavement with a quick throw.

"What about the people that don't come?" Alli asked, her paws padding soundlessly at his side.

"I don't know what to tell you, Alli, I can't help everyone. This town will help ensure that people will be safe, but those same people still need to help. We'll keep expanding our roving teams and have them helping those they come across. When this place is safe and secure, maybe we'll be able to go around helping others. Changing the towns, we come across, changing them to use the town system. Besides, there are people here that you need to look after."

They continued to talk aimlessly for a few more minutes, as Kira and Sierra wrapped up their own discussion.

"Charles, Alli, come on we're leaving!" Kira called when they were done talking, she stood in front of Sierra awkwardly. Neither of them was making a move to leave, both frozen in uncertainty. Kira was the first to reach out and touch the blonde woman's shoulder before stepping back and hurrying to the truck.

Sierra stood in the road as the truck drove away.

"What did you decide?" Charles asked after they had been driving for several minutes.

Kira's lips thinned into a tight line. "I want to believe her, but I just... It's a lot to take in. I've hated her and blamed her for what happened to me for so long. Hearing her side... was... is confusing."

"If it helps, Alli believes that Sierra was telling you the truth," He said, revealing that they had been listening in.

"That actually does help. Thanks," Kira replied thoughtfully, some of the tension leaving her face.

There were several groups of people milling about when they returned, supplies were spread across several tables. Each table seemed to have a dedicated theme, one held camping supplies, tents, and sleeping bags. Another held dried or canned fruit, while another held weapons of all kinds.

Kira's parents stood to the side directing the groups, far behind them the doors to Charlotte's warehouse were open. "Go there first. I want to see what my sister is up to," Charles said, pointing with a grin.

Kira turned the wheel without saying anything. Inside the large warehouse, long tables filled with equipment could be seen next to the walls. In the middle of the floor, several motors could be seen in various states of being taken apart. Charlotte stood just inside the doors, talking to the no-longer catatonic professor and Scott.

His sister looked up as she heard the truck approaching and went outside to meet them. "Go talk to Scott. I'll meet you inside in a minute," She told Charles as soon as she laid eyes on Kira, noticing that something had changed with her.

With Alli by his side, he walked into the warehouse and over to the two men, inadvertently hearing the end of their conversation. "We've been able to salvage enough parts to fix at least one of the motors fully and scrape together an old-style water-mill generator. As soon as we get the electricity situation settled, then we can start focusing on other things. Char thinks she has a way to fix the electronics in the lab equipment, though she won't tell me what it is."

"Don't let her hear you call her that," Charles said with a wince, coming up behind them. He knew his sister was not exactly fond of the nickname, even though it had been used for much of her life.

"Charles, you're back," Scott started in surprise, having been too engrossed in the conversation to hear the truck approaching. He looked to the professor and back to Charles. "Uh, Charles is Charlotte's younger brother, Charles, this is James Wagner. He was my chemistry professor at MIT and one of the department heads. He woke up earlier and wanted to get to work."

The professor extended his hand towards Charles. "I have been told that I owe my recovery in large part to you. I truly appreciate the help and would like to discuss some things with you later, if that is alright?" Thin white scar lines were all that remained from his time in the hands of the monsters.

Charles understood that the man was likely trying to forget everything that had happened to him by throwing himself into his work. "Of course, don't let me keep you from your projects."

James nodded appreciatively and scurried off.

"He said he doesn't want to talk about what they did to him, and none of the other will talk about it either." Scott seemed to deflate and leaned against the warehouse wall. "He hasn't stopped moving or working since he woke up this morning. I want to help but I just don't know what he needs right now. Does he need time to sort through everything or does he just need to lose himself in a challenging project?"

"He'll have plenty of those soon enough," Charlotte informed them with a grin as she walked up to them with Kira at her heels. "As soon as the lab equipment is repaired, I expect he'll find a number of interesting things pertaining to the monsters when viewed under a microscope."

"Are you going to tell me how you're going to manage this little miracle?" Scott asked in exasperation.

Charlotte shook her head, "Not until I've tried it out, I probably shouldn't have even said anything, but I was too excited at the time to keep it to myself." She turned to wave an arm at the inside of the warehouse, speaking to her brother. "As you can see, we have been busy since you made the warehouse for us this morning. Thank you for doing that by the way. For now, we have been separating the items that will be useful from those that need to be repaired in the future, while also separating the interior into our own separate spaces."

Standing inside the warehouse itself allowed Charles the opportunity to see things he hadn't from the outside. There was a second floor running above their heads, with walkways running from rooms that hugged the walls. Stairs occupied the corners of the warehouse leading up to the second floor.

"We each have our own space, up there," She said following his eyes. "The rooms are big enough for us each to have a lab and sleep in them, for now, at least. With much of our equipment either missing or not working, our labs don't actually contain much, for now."

Charles smiled at how happy she was. "I just wanted to make sure you have everything you need before I go and speak with Kory and Krystal."

"Don't worry little brother, we're doing fine." She looked out over the warehouse floor, gently biting at her lower lip. "I have a few idea's I want to run by you later pertaining to electricity and such, but I'll do that tonight after we do another training session." With that said she waved them off and pulled Scott by the arm into the depths of the already cluttered warehouse.

"Is everything alright?" Charles asked Kira as they walked back to the truck.

"Yeah, it's fine." Her shoulders slumped, and she glanced quickly behind them. "Your sister is kind of scary. She knew just from looking at me for half a second that something had happened. I found myself telling her about Sierra and some of our history before I even realized it." Her brows furrowed, and a line appeared in the skin above them. "I've never opened up to anyone that quickly before." She muttered to herself.

She drove them back to her parents, parking the truck next to the house they had stayed in the night before. Alli had vanished as soon as she saw the kids, rushing over to play with them and Kate who was watching over them for the moment.

"Good, you're back," Kory stated as soon as he saw them walking towards him. Krystal was seated at a table with several stacks of paper. "We've managed to get everything mostly organized for the moment, thankfully the current lack of people made it fairly easy. We have a list of buildings we need built, along with a rough approximation of where they should go."

Krystal looked up at his words and pulled a hand-drawn map of the area from her inventory, spreading it on the table in one smooth move. "Since all the streets and regular markers for the area have obviously vanished, we decided it would be easier to just make our own map for now." She said while pointing to the marks that had been drawn for each of the buildings that had already been built. She laid another paper atop the map, "Here is a list of buildings we need first, at this point it is really just more houses and another warehouse. All the items found will go in the warehouse for now. One of the teams did manage to find a supply of seeds so the greenhouse has been bumped up the list as well. Of course, we know that this is all dependent on the cost of the buildings."

Charles looked closer at the map and noticed the penciled in marks for where the new buildings should be built. "I'm expecting people to start visiting us within the next day or so, so the mana cost shouldn't be an issue for much longer, with any luck." He pointed to the list, "Assuming we can afford it I can have two of the items on the list built right away, the third should wait until tonight though. The town system that builds everything becomes fully unlocked after we have ten buildings, and the system-building doesn't count. In other words, we have seven buildings right now and need three more to fully unlock the system. When that happens there will be a number of changes and buildings added to the area."

Kory tapped his fingers on the table, deep in thought. "We will need more houses if more people appear, and since I don't think you are wrong, let's make two more houses first."

Kira was looking at the map as they were talking, "Where are you thinking to put my garage?" She asked, twirling the key to the truck around her finger.

Krystal pushed her husband to the side and pointed to a spot on the map that was halfway between them and the opening in the wall. "This is the area we've been thinking that we'd have it. Several groups have already returned and told us of vehicles they have found that might work. We were thinking it would be a large warehouse that could hold them all, with a side dedicated to tools and other equipment." She loved her daughter, but she wasn't sure where her mechanically inclined nature had come from. Krystal knew enough to start a car and fill it with gas. Kory knew enough to check the oil level occasionally, and that was all.

"I'll need help transporting the equipment and tools, but that should be fine," Kira said after thinking it over.

"There were a lot of tools and equipment absorbed by the town system already. The warehouses around here had a little bit of everything in them. I might be able to get the system to include them when building the warehouse." Charles informed them, wanting to be helpful.

"Houses first today, then the greenhouse tonight. The warehouse/garage can wait until tomorrow." Kory reminded him firmly.

Charles hurried over to the black system building and went inside to the map. Knowing what they wanted made it a simple thing to select two more houses to be built and placed next to the others. The taxed mana count above the menu dropped by half, the amount the town had gotten today was far less than it had been the day before. All the extra people that had been hanging around when the town came into being had really helped them out.

He stepped out into the evening sunlight and watched as the houses seemed to build themselves farther down the line. The people that had been milling around the area doing their own thing all stopped and watched the impressive sight. Charles knew that someday seeing magic in use would be commonplace and not something to be gawked at, but that day was far in the future.

Chapter 24

After making sure the houses had been built Charles went back inside the town system building and spent the next few hours going through the menu. Certain options remained locked and somewhat hidden until he finished unlocking the system. Taking the time to go through and learn everything the system had to offer was worth it.

He was able to see what buildings and defenses they had available, and how it was possible to upgrade many of the buildings. Once they had working electricity adding it to the buildings would be a cinch.

The item that grabbed his attention and refused to let go, however, was one that was also currently locked. It gave him minimal information but was called 'Town Tenets' and appeared to work as a kind of automatically god enforced law. He had seen it before, but his little jaunt outside the walls with Kira and Alli had reinforced what he already knew. Civilization had fallen and chaos now ruled, he was not going to let that happen in his town.

He was determined to make it so his sister and their friends had a safe place to live and having automatically enforced rules or laws would go a long way towards making that happen.

The light outside had begun to fail when Kira walked through the open door of the building and pulled him from his musings. "Everyone is back, time to make the greenhouse." She held the map her parents had made in her hands.

"Alright, let's do this," Charles said with a grin, excited to see what would happen. He placed the greenhouse where they wanted it and ordered the system to build it, draining almost everything they had left in the taxed mana counter.

Together they ran outside the building and stood with her parents and Alli as they watched the greenhouse being built in the distance. Charlotte and Scott hurried over to them, while Kate came from the direction of the river with Jenny and James in tow.

The greenhouse finished construction, and everything was silent for a moment before a notification appeared in front of their eyes.

Congratulations, the first town in the world has been created.

Closing that notification revealed a new one behind it.

Congratulations, the full 'Town System' has now been unlocked. Please stand back as the town center and other applicable buildings will now be placed.

He dismissed the message and watched as the gathered people looked around, uncertain as to where they should move. Flashes of golden light gathered around the area, pushing the oncoming gloom to the furthest reaches of the distant wall.

Walls made of light gathered in front of them, outlining and shaping a multitude of buildings before they came into being with one last flash of light. In the center of the clearing directly in front of the black town system building was a covered gazebo with a pedestal in the middle. Behind the pure white gazebo stood a tall honey-colored building with a plaque that read 'Town Hall' sitting above the doors. Two other buildings had appeared as well, one on either side of the town hall. The one to the left had a plaque reading 'Store' above the doors, while the other read simply 'Post'.

Currently, the doors were locked on the smaller buildings, while the town hall could be used right away.

"Well, the manual did say the shop would be available when the game begins, I guess we'll have to wait another day," Charlotte told the group quietly as they watched the people try to open the doors to the store.

As the last of glowing light faded from the area, another notification appeared before Charles's eyes.

Congratulations, you have completed a challenge issued by the gods and have successfully created a town at a location of their choosing. As a reward for completing this challenge, you may choose from two rewards. Have part of the curse lifted, allowing you to sleep once every seven days. Or, you may allow your companion Alli to choose a reward for herself. (Note: Choosing not to have the curse partly lifted may have lasting effects in the future.)

Without a second thought Charles chose to give the reward to Alli, she had done so much for him, and all he had done for her was make her lonely.

Alli looked up sharply, her large mismatched eyes shaking as she read a message that only she could see. "You didn't have to do that; I know how much not sleeping is bothering you." Her voice was thankful, but her words reproachful came to him.

"Yes, I did," He explained, looking her in the face. "You've done nothing but help us all, meanwhile the only thing I've truly done for you is make you feel alone in the world. You are part of our family Alli, and I want you to be happy if that means that I can never have the curse fully removed then so be it."

Alli leaned forward and licked his face as soon as he finished speaking, thick watery tears already forming at the corners of her eyes. She nodded appreciatively and licked him again before closing her eyes as though preparing herself. Her eyes were clear and determined when next she opened them.

"I want to speak to everyone, without them needing to touch me," Charles heard her say in his mind, a second later her eyes went out of focus and her mouth dropped open. "It says that I already possess the ability to project my voice to others, but that I need to learn magic to unlock the ability. It says that I should choose something else."

"We can start on that tonight! What are you going to choose then?" He asked, reaching out to ruffle the hair around her ears.

Alli closed her eyes and leaned into his hand. "I don't know, it says I can choose later though so I think I'll spend some time thinking it over."

"Just make sure it is something that will make you happy," He told her before backing away, Jenny and her brother immediately taking his spot and her attention.

Charlotte sidled up to his side. "I should be finished infusing myself with my core after one more session," She told him softly.

Charles shook his head with a wry smile. "Make sure you keep that to yourself a little longer, you'll single-handedly have destroyed all of Kates confidence otherwise. Let's find her and then we can start, Alli will probably join us later as well."

Kate was speaking with Kira, her face going deep red with anger the longer they spoke.

"We might as well just get started," Charles told his sister, he had a feeling he knew what they were talking about and it was going to be a long conversation. "Kira met someone from her past earlier today, and they had a somewhat complicated history."

"Oh, was it a man or a female?" Charlotte asked, looking at him slyly.

"Female and they were childhood friends, so it was nothing like what you were thinking."

"Pooh, you're no fun," She said with a sulk, before pushing him towards the building.

They settled into a corner next to the open door and Charles began the meditation process before letting his sister take control. Kate stomped in a few minutes later and glared at him before plopping down next to his sister without a word.

Charles was going through the 'Town System' menu when Alli finally came through the door, her head hanging towards the ground. She could run at speeds rivaling a car for miles on end without getting tired, but a single day playing with two eleven-year-olds was enough to exhaust her.

"I'm ready," She told him as she went to the corner they had claimed for sleeping, resting her head on the pile of blankets.

He closed the menu and went over to her. He would let the others worry about coming up with specific laws for the town. He put his back to the smooth hard wall and slid to the ground next to her.

"Just put your paw on the meditation point here, and we can begin," It took them a few seconds to maneuver her paw correctly, making them both glad that she only needed to touch it the first time now.

A shadowy barrier sprang into being around them, assuring them both that her element was shadow. It wasn't clear if she had chosen her class well, or if the class had changed her element to suit it better. Regardless, Charles spent the time to show her what she needed to do, making sure to touch her core for a few seconds while he did so.

It was interesting seeing her work, unlike humans who had arms they could use to touch their cores, she used her head. Doing this made her head the first thing to be infused, followed by her heart without her needing to move. It was much faster for her than it had been with Kate and only slightly slower than Charlotte.

Charles made a note of this, determined to have people start with their heads in the future. Quietly and taking care not to disturb her, he exited her core room and meditation.

The notification he had been expecting sprang into being as he opened his eyes next to Alli.

Congratulations, you have learned the spell 'Shadow Spike'. Shadow spike is a shadow spell that uses your mana to create a spike made of hardened shadow essence. The more mana used to create the spike the harder it will become and the longer the range of the attack.

Congratulations, you have learned the spell 'Shadow's Grasp'. Shadow's grasp is a shadow spell that uses your mana to control the shadows in the area, using them to grab and hold enemies or items. The more mana used to infuse the desired shadows, the stronger their grip will become and the longer the range of the attack.

He closed the messages and grinned; it was always nice to learn new spell and elements. The two he had just learned from Alli seemed especially useful in controlling the battlefield. Making people afraid of their own shadows would be glorious in the middle of a fight.

Closing his eyes, he snuggled close to Alli and began his own meditations for the night.

He was alone with Alli when he opened his eyes the next morning; she had shifted positions slightly but had clearly been exhausted when she finally fell asleep. His back cracked and popped as he stood, the uncomfortable and tight feeling in his back muscles disappearing with a burst of healing magic.

The world outside the building he was using as his home was dark and still. The green of the night sky had begun to fade with the coming dawn. The barest hints of the sky lightening on the horizon. The wind that seemed to always be there on the Kansas and Missouri plains absent for once.

"One more day, and then the game begins for real. It kind of feels like the world is holding its breath," Alli said reverently as she came up behind him. "That is probably just me being silly though."

"No, that is exactly what it feels like." Charles pulled out her water tub and some food for them to eat and drink while they waited for everyone else to awaken. "How far were you able to get with your core last night?"

"I was able to finish my head, my heart, and part of my chest. So, there is still a bit more to do, but I think I should be able to finish in another three or four sessions. If we stay around this area, then I should be able to do three sessions today. One after we're finished eating, one at midday, and then one tonight before going to sleep. That should allow me enough time to rest in-between each session." She told him while thirstily drinking the water. If they were going to stay in the area today, then he would leave the tub out for her drink from whenever she was thirsty. He had been storing it in his inventory because they were always on the move, he didn't need to do that any longer.

Charles started Alli's meditation session when she was ready and then got up to walk around.

A dim yellow light could be seen through the warehouse windows his sister was using for a lab. Intrigued at who could be up and that the MIT group already had working electricity had him walking in that direction without another thought.

Pushing open the small door to the side of the larger doors and looking inside told him all he really needed to know. His sister was sitting on a tall stool in front of a cluttered table in the middle of the warehouse floor. Several lamps had been set up around the area, extension cords littering the floor.

"You managed to get electricity running rather quickly," He said as he stepped through the doorway.

Charlotte started in surprise. "With what we know these days, generating a little amount of electricity is fairly easy." She waved her arm to the five lamps spread around the area. "These lamps currently take all the juice the system is generating. If we added one more, they would all go dark." She leaned back on the stool and stood, stretching her muscles after sitting for so long. "I finished infusing the magic from my core into my body last night and managed to unlock an ability when I did. These glasses," She tapped the glasses she had gotten when she became a champion, "are incredible and help to increase my control, while letting me see the mana as it works! My ability lets me use my mana to repair technology, and at later stages I will be able to infuse the items with mana as well, increasing their potential exponentially." She had started to wave her hands around in excitement as he crept closer to the table to see what she had been working on.

Various electronics were placed to the side of the table while a laptop was resting in front of where she had been sitting. Charlotte saw his interest in the items and pulled him closer.

"I've already managed to fix an old Gameboy, an iPod, and Kindle, though it lost all the books stored on it when I did. Just imagine if I can get this laptop working again and then infuse it with mana. It will work so much faster." Charlotte began talking faster in her excitement.

Charles smiled indulgently before grabbing her arm. He was used to her getting lost in projects like this. "That's great sis, but how is one laptop being faster going to help us now?" Growing up with her had taught him exactly what he needed to ask or do to break the cycle and bring her back down to Earth.

She froze, her face screwing up in thought. "It won't but having running computers will allow us to conduct experiments more effectively while passing on information to future generations. We need to have people start collecting computers and other equipment on their salvage runs."

"Agreed, have you already fixed your lab equipment?"

She shook her head. "Not yet. I wanted to have a better control on the ability before I touch anything that complicated." She pointed to a pile of different items on the floor next to the table. "I already ruined a bunch of different things just to get to this point." She looked around the warehouse really quick and leaned closer to him. "This isn't even my laptop, it's Scott's. I'm not risking destroying my own until I know I can do it."

Charles covered his eyes with his hand and rolled them when she couldn't see. "And what about how Scott is going to feel when you destroy his laptop?"

Charlotte looked at him blankly for a second before her eyes widened in understanding. "This isn't his research laptop. He uses this one for playing games. Since we no longer have internet, he won't miss it as much."

Charles grabbed her arm and pulled her through the warehouse and outside. "Or and I'm just spit balling here, you can use something that your boyfriend doesn't care about at all."

"I would if I had one, but all the other laptops we brought with us have research material on them!"

He continued to pull her along until they had reached the system building. Pushing her inside he opened the town inventory and withdrew several older model laptops. "Here use these. When everything in the area was absorbed, that included countless laptops and other electronics."

"What else does it have stored?" She asked after taking the computers and throwing them into her own inventory.

"It has some of everything I imagine. The warehouses in this area were used for shipping, plus there were plenty of businesses as well. Why, what are you looking for?" He explained and then asked, wondering where she was going with this.

"Plenty, I'm looking for plenty. We could use parts for windmills, little electric motors, generators, really anything along those lines we can use or salvage. Not everything broke in quite the same way, with enough of the same item we can make a whole working piece. Right now? Definitely the generator, the professor has some thoughts on making a new form of fuel and needs something to test it on. I figure you would rather we destroy something like that instead of a car."

Charles opened the town inventory and began looking through it again. There was so much listed in there that even with the tabs he hadn't managed to read through it all. Thankfully, the interface would add new tabs at his discretion, he just needed to set the right parameters after finding an initial item.

"Well," He began after several minutes of going through the list. "There are several generators, and hundreds of little electric motors. We also have a lot more gas now than I realized," He shook his head, refocusing on the task at hand. "Point is, make up a list and I'll start looking through it for what you want. If I find something, I'll take it out and put it outside next to the building for one of your minions to come fetch later." A single generator on the smaller side appeared in front of them along with a box full of different motors.

Charlotte stored everything in her inventory a second later and began twisting her hands, "Thanks for stopping me from ruining Scott's laptop, I was just so excited and kind of got lost in the moment."

"Hey, what are younger brothers for, if not stopping their obsessed and slightly crazy older sisters?" Charles asked with a wide grin.

She punched him in the shoulder and spun on her heel. "I'll send someone up later with a list, it's going to be a busy day if we're to be ready for whatever tomorrow brings!"

Chapter 25

Kory was the first up, leaving the little house behind just as the morning sun made an appearance. He rubbed his arms and shivered, seeing Charles standing there without his usual leather jacket. "Aren't you cold?" His breath misting with each word.

"I wasn't until just now," Charles said, withdrawing his jacket from his inventory. He wasn't lying. He hadn't noticed how cold it was until it was brought to his attention.

The event he had been anticipating happening finally occurred a while later, with all the students from MIT rushing to learn magic from him. They had been waiting for Charlotte to finish and after seeing what she was capable of up close had them chomping at the proverbial bit.

To a person they had all been gamers or fantasy lovers, magic to them represented everything they had ever wanted. Charles was honestly surprised that they had shown the restraint they had and waited this long. He had been expecting them to mob him on the trip back, and when that hadn't happened, he had been expecting them to ask after the town was started.

Alli stayed by his side as he began training them, each person took a few minutes to learn what they needed to do. He had the first few people begin by touching their cores with their heads instead of their hands. He learned that Alli was as much of a freak as him and his sister, but that beginning the infusion process with the heads still made the process faster.

Kira had long since disappeared with her sister, having left to talk with Sierra by the time he had finished. Thinking on the future made him glad that he only needed to do this convoluted process once with each person now. Future sessions would be much faster.

He had taken the time to touch each of their cores as he showed them what to do, only one person had a new element. She was a botany major at Harvard that had hooked up with the group at some point. She had a nature element that was a calming green, he learned the nature spell 'grow' from her. One person had been able to learn healing magic, fitting since they had been going to school to be a doctor. Everyone else had element cores for either fire or water, with a couple that had earth instead. Those three elements seemed to be the most common among everyone.

What he found interesting, however, was that each person had a small pond of varying size of liquid mana near their core. Each time he blocked it off just like he had with Kate, he would need to tell them how to fix it when they were ready.

Charles pulled Kory and Krystal into the system building while Alli was meditating for a second time that day. "There are a couple of things that we need to discuss about the town."

They studied the map of the area that was built into the table before responding; this was their first time inside the building and seeing it. "What's on your mind?" Kory asked while his wife pulled out their hand-drawn map and began making corrections to it.

"Two things to begin with, but there is plenty we could talk about." He took a deep breath before launching fully into the discussion. "Now that the system is fully unlocked people can now join the town, but it needs a name first. This leads into the other item when people join the town, they also agree to follow five basic tenets enforced by the gods or something.

I'm not actually sure how they will be enforced, just that it says they are and that I shouldn't test it personally."

"What are these tenets?" Krystal asked, looking up from her work.

Charles pulled up the list. "There are currently three listed, the last two are blank for us to fill in on our own. Number one, each citizen agrees to pay the tax as set forth by the town administrator or owner. I'm guessing that is me. Number two, every person regardless of gender, race, or other mitigating factors- that is mentally stable and able must contribute to the betterment of the town. And number three, inside the walls of the town, no violence or theft is permitted among its citizens, unless they are attacked or wronged by another."

"So, we need to come up with another two tenets and a name, by tonight so everyone can join the town before tomorrow?" Kory asked, closing his eyes in annoyance.

"Pretty much, although we could probably do other tenets later as they will still be enforced by the initial pledge, I think it would be better for everyone to know what they are agreeing to," Charles said as he closed the interface.

"We don't want to do that," Krystal said as she tucked a pad of paper into her pocket. "I wrote down the three you mentioned. I'll go around to everyone and ask for their input on the name and the two additional tenets we need. If they ask about the taxes, what should I tell them?"

Charles ran a hand through his shaggy hair, it had grown in the last two weeks. "The current tax is set for fifty percent of their available mana since the town needs it to build anything and I was the only one who could use mana at the time. Once we get more people, I'm more than willing to change it to a lower amount. Just make sure that they all know the tax on mana is actually beneficial to them, as it will make learning magic easier for them in the future if they choose to learn."

"You're willing to teach that many people to use their magic?" Kory asked in disbelief.

Charles shrugged, "I'm the only one who can at this point, there is no one else to teach them. Magic is going to keep people healthy and alive in the future until we can rebuild civilization. It will be one of the most important things a person can learn. I don't care if they use it every day or never again, that is on them. As far as I know every person has the ability to use magic now, at least to some degree and it is on me to teach them."

"Anyway, moving on to the next subject, here is a list of what needs to be built next, and where to put them. We already have people working in the greenhouse planting seeds. The warehouse for all the vehicles and Kira to work in is next." Krystal grabbed onto her husband and pushed him out the door after handing the paper to Charles. They had work to do.

Charles pulled up the construction interface and had the warehouse built near the entrance in the wall, making sure to include the equipment she would need. Then he had a short road built to it for good measure. Building just that drained most of the mana they had in store, leaving only enough in case of an emergency.

Alli finished meditating just as he finished and answered the question before he could he even ask it. "Tonight, I'll have finished infusing my core by tonight. What happens after that?"

"Control, infusing the magic in your core allows your body to get used to feeling the mana it had been deprived of before. Once your body has gotten used to this feeling, you'll have completed the infusion process. Next comes actively controlling the mana in your body, if you can feel it then you need to learn to control it. After that comes learning a spell for normal people at least. It seems my sister was able to bypass step two and three because of an ability but using magic outside of that ability will mean she still needs to go through them. Since you already have a class, I'm sure you already have at least one spell. You just need to learn control first." Charles told her as they closed the door behind them and looked up at the cloudless blue noon sky.

Kira was running towards them, her booted feet pounding into the soft green grass and leaving slight dents in the ground. Behind her, Kate could be seen walking stiffly next to Sierra, the truck parked in front of the new warehouse. A smooth paved road extended from the warehouse to the opening in the wall.

"It has everything!" Kira yelled in excitement, coming to a stop in front of them. Her arms were twitching at her side as a look of consternation came over her face. Stepping up to Charles she threw her arms around him and hugged him for several seconds before letting go and hurriedly stepping back. "Thank you." She said quietly before turning and running away. It was clear she wasn't equipped to emotionally handle what she had just done.

Kate was staring at her with wide impressed looking eyes, having forgotten that Sierra was next to her in the heat of the moment.

Shaking his head, Charles turned to look at the gazebo, there was something about it that had been bugging him. Now that it was light out, he was determined to find out what it was. He had a vague feeling that the pedestal in the middle was how a person joined the town, but that wasn't what was off about the oddly shaped building.

Stepping on to the wooden planks gave him an up-close view of every slat and post that made the gazebo. On every plank that made of the flooring, a name was burned darkly into the wood. The slats of the wall held names written in grey near the bottom, gradually shifting to become colorless the higher it went. The six posts that held up the roof each had one name written on each, Brigit, Odin, Zeus, Shiva, Arinna and Saraswati. More names edged with gold were written on the roof.

It was a list of each of the gods, those that were using champions and those that weren't. Countless names were written, many of them belonging to gods he had never heard of before.

Touch Brigit's name.

A message appeared in front of his eyes just as he was about to turn and walk away, his curiosity sated for the moment. A moment later the message drifted away on its own as though it had never been there. Mentally shrugging and not seeing the harm in it, he reached out and touched her name.

An image of the goddess appeared in his mind's eye; it was her but at the same time it wasn't. He had met the real goddess and knew what she looked like, and the image in his head was a perfected version of her. Along with the image came a deluge of information about who the goddess was and what she represented.

The gods had come up with a way that would ensure they weren't forgotten a second time, while also restoring the information that already been lost pertaining to them.

"She's going to get a lot of new followers just on her looks alone," Charles said aloud with a smirk as he stepped back from the post. He would look at what the other five gods looked like later. For now, he wasn't tempted to follow any of them, so it didn't matter.

Alli was looking at the ceiling where the golden-edged names were written. "Something up there is calling to me," She told him before turning to walk away with him.

"It's a listing of all the gods. More than likely there was a god up there that resonated with you for some reason. A divine animal spirit or something," He told her, the words feeling right as he said them. If it was a complete list of all the gods, or at least those that were left then he was sure such a god existed. She deserved to have a divine being looking out for her.

The sound of people shouting from the wall distracted them from the conversation and they set off running to the opening. A line of older model trucks and cars could be seen coming towards them, all caravanning together.

A rusty Chevy sedan was in the lead, its brakes squealing as it came to a stop just outside the wall. "Is this home of the magic-user known as

Charles? We met him in Danville, Pennsylvania when he saved all our lives."

Charles stepped into view of the yelling driver and waved, "Come on in, find a place to park near the warehouse and we'll talk." He called out while pointing to Kira's workshop and vehicle warehouse.

The rusty heap of a car the speaker was in rattled to life, a belt screaming under the hood as the engine got up to speed and then went silent. It drove cautiously past the gathered people and parked in front of the warehouse, the long line of vehicles following just as slowly.

Each vehicle was packed to the brim with people and supplies, everything from bedding to food had been stuffed into every nook and cranny. Charles could only look on in wonder as the overburdened vehicles drove past him one at a time. Many of them had boxes tied down on their roofs or the trunks of the cars. Every spot was accounted for and used to its fullest.

It had undoubtedly been a very uncomfortable drive, but they had made it.

Charlotte and Scott followed by the rest of the people that had been captured in Danville ran out of their warehouse. It seemed they had just been told who had arrived. They mingled with the new group, talking and laughing while Charlotte, Scott, and Kira joined Charles and Alli. Kate hung back with her parents, waiting for the initial excitement to be over.

"Mister Charles, Miss Charlotte, Miss Kira," A man who had clearly worked hard every day of his life walked toward them. He wore a grease-stained trucker's cap and a threadbare flannel shirt underneath a too large down-filled coat. His face was lined with wrinkles and his skin looked like leather from having spent too much time in the sun. "This is everyone that you saved in Danville. We also managed to pick up a few people along the way. We spread the word that the sole magic-user was making a safe town here. I imagine there will be plenty more people trickling in over the days to come." He seemed to be particularly proud of himself as he spoke, his voice held the gravelly undertones of a person who had lived a hard life.

A semi-truck with a cattle trailer came through the opening in the wall. It had been taking the last spot of the caravan behind another set of cattle trailers.

"Before we left, we managed to round up some cattle and other animals from the area." He smiled a yellow-toothed smile. "We found some rabbits and chickens as well. Though to be honest with you, the chickens have been acting kind of odd," He brushed off his cap and scratched at his thin wispy hair in confusion.

"We're going to need a gate, and a fenced-in area," Kira said as she watched the semi come to a stop on the road behind all the other cars.

"How did you manage to get all of these cars running?" Charlotte asked in surprise.

"Uh, about that." He placed the cap back on his head and looked away, a flicker of shame crossing his face. "Pennsylvania or at least the Danville area is rather poor, out there everybody has older model cars or trucks. The hard part was simply getting them started, but with so many old vehicles to choose from it was a simple matter of picking off the working parts and installing them in a different one. Actually, the hardest part was push starting the first car, after that we were able to jumpstart the rest." He yawned and swayed on his feet. "Truth be told, none of us have really slept since you rescued us, we've been either working on the cars or driving ever since. We've been driving in shifts, but even the people not driving have barely slept. After being captured, they know what is out there now and couldn't take their eyes off the windows. We were constantly on alert and searching for monsters." He shivered and pulled the coat tight around his body.

Krystal and Kory appeared as he finished speaking, Kate hiding behind their bodies. "We'll get our people to unload everything for you then and set it to the side of the warehouse. While we do that, why don't you get all your people and find someplace to sleep." Krystal looked back at the small number of houses they had and the hundreds of people that had appeared.

"As long as they have bedding, they can use the floor of the warehouse for now. We'll get regular arrangements taken care of later," Kira stepped in, seeing her mother's dilemma.

The man who hadn't even thought to introduce himself turned around and began gathering his exhausted people. Sierra had cranked open the doors enough for the people to walk beneath them and into the dark depths of the warehouse.

"I'll get an area set up for the animals and then see what we can afford to build. I know there were options for larger apartment-style buildings, but I never looked at how much they cost," Charles said as the noises of the alarmed animals began to trickle through the air.

Kory looked at the trailers. "That would be appreciated, I can only imagine the state those animals are in after being stuck in those trailers for so long."

"Not to mention the smell," Kira said with a mean grin, knowing she wasn't going to be the one unloading them.

Chapter 26

Charles ran away at the mention of the smell, Alli at his side. Her sensitive sense of smell could already smell the stench of the people and the animals, and she had no desire to get any closer than she needed to either group.

Safe inside the system building Charles set about getting an area built for the animals, making sure it was far away from the people. Next, he had a large swinging gate made for the hole in the wall, making it into a proper gateway.

The tax counter above the menu was slowly ticking upwards as the new people began unknowingly donating their mana to the town. It had a way to go before they would be able to afford any of the larger buildings.

With that finished he left the building and walked over to where Krystal was directing the unloading of the vehicles.

"The animal area is finished," He said as he came up behind her, pointing to where a large barn had appeared. A fence stretched from the side of the barn up to the wall and then down to the river. It was set at the very edge of their current property limits.

"Thanks, we'll start moving them over in just a minute. Before we do that though, can you check out the chickens? One of them is acting like a possessed demon. Use your ability and make sure it isn't a zombie chicken or something, please?" Krystal asked without turning away from the people she was directing.

"A zombie chicken, really?" Charles laughed.

"After everything we've seen so far, I'd rather be safe than have my brain slowly pecked to pieces," She retorted with a smirk. "Seriously though, I looked at it for a second and it just seemed off... it didn't act like a normal chicken."

"Sure, whatever, just point out the offending ankle-biter to me," Charles said not really caring, it wasn't hard to use his ability on an animal. If it helped set her fears at ease, he saw no reason not to do it, and on the off chance it was a zombie chicken it would be better to know now.

"Ankle biters are children," She corrected. "The monster in the shape of a chicken is in a crate by itself sitting outside one of the cattle trailers," She waved a distracted hand in the general direction of the trailers.

Alli sniffed and walked away from him, heading towards where Kate was standing out of the way and off to the side. Sierra was helping Kira and the others unload everything next to the warehouse, stacking the items in separate piles. Each pile was dedicated to a single car or truck, there were already more than ten piles.

Charles saw the trailer with a crate next to it and walked over to it. He was able to see the offending chicken through the many small air holes in the sturdy crate, and while it looked normal, it was glaring at him. He had never heard of a chicken glaring at a person before, on top of that it wasn't clucking but was instead moving its lower beak from side to side.

Charles activated his analyze ability and began to laugh uncontrollably. "Well it's not a zombie chicken, it's something even better!" He called out to Krystal, his tear-filled eyes roving over the message that had appeared.

Poulet-Garou (Were-Chicken) Lv. 1
This poulet-garou was formerly a rat that was infected by a chicken with the Were-virus. Anything bitten by this

monster chicken will become infected and turn into a
chicken themselves. This particular strain of the virus works
best on animals with little intelligence. (Note: Infections of
this virus-strain can be cured through the use of a high tier
Restoration spell. The monster will be stuck its current form
upon being cured.)

It was the most ridiculous thing he had ever seen or heard of, and it was absolutely brilliant! Assuming it could lay eggs and they were edible and not poisonous, then this would help with their food problem. They just needed to start collecting rats.

Kate was the first to join him by the chicken, drawn by his outburst and uproarious laughter. "What, is there something different about this chicken?"

"Just, wait for your mother." He gasped out, his cheeks and stomach hurting from laughing so hard.

Krystal joined them moments later, Charlotte and Kira coming up behind her. "What's so funny about the chicken?" His sister asked, not having heard anything about its strange behavior yet.

"It's..." He managed to gasp out before forcing himself to calm down. "It's not actually a chicken." He quickly recounted everything the message had said, feeling a smile tugging at the corners of his lips the entire time.

Kira shrugged and smiled. Charlotte looked like she wanted to dissect it, and Krystal and Kate stared at the chicken in the cage with morbid fascination.

"I was only joking about it being a zombie chicken," Krystal muttered under her breath. "To think, it would actually be something even stranger. What has this world become?"

"Let's just keep it in the cage for now," Charles said as Kory climbed into the semi-truck cab and started it up to move the first cattle trailer to the barn.

Kira followed Charles as he walked away from the hustle and bustle surrounding the now occupied warehouse. "How are things with Sierra going?" He asked suddenly, seeing that she was following him.

"I'm not entirely sure. It has been a while since I've really interacted with someone as a friend. I'm out of practice, and that's before we take our complicated history into the equation." Her face was screwed up in thought. "I think I'm at least willing to try with her though. It may be because we used to be close when we were kids, but I found it easier to believe her side of things than I perhaps should have. Of course, hearing that Alli believed her words certainly helped."

Charles thought carefully before saying anything, "I must say from everything I know about you I expected you to be more reticent in this matter. You've come a long way from the woman I met a week ago, the one who left Alli and me at an abandoned hotel in the middle of nowhere."

Kira chuckled at the memory. "I know, I've only managed to make the progress as quickly as I have though because of you and Alli. The two of you have accepted me regardless of what I did to the two of you. More than that, you didn't shun me when you learned what had happened to me. Instead, you stayed by my side, quietly letting me know that you were there for me when I needed you."

"It's what you needed," He said softly, not entirely sure what to say to her. None of that was something he had consciously done, there had been plenty of times he had wanted to leave her behind. The fact of the matter though was that they had helped each other. That was not something he felt comfortable telling her now; however, besides his feelings when it came to her had become somewhat complicated.

"It may have been what I needed, but you were the one who did it, regardless. Not someone else." Another shout from the gate interrupted them before she could say anything more on the matter.

Several carts filled with injured people were waiting for them when they ran up. It was the first group of injured from the school group he had talked to the day before. Charles waved them in and directed them to a simple grassy area. He needed them inside for the mana to start getting taxed, so while it would be a simple thing to heal them all outside the gates, that wasn't what he was going to do.

None of them looked like they were going to die in the next few minutes, and since he didn't personally know any of them, he felt no compunction to letting them suffer. He was the one doing them a favor after-all, they could do this for him and the town.

Kory joined them after driving the other trucks with cattle trailers to the barn. He took control of the group after they had laid the people on the ground, he apparently knew some of them from his time living at the school. He quickly had them helping to unload everything from the remaining cars and trucks. The side of the warehouse was quickly being filled with organized piles.

As soon as they were finished unloading everything Charlotte's entire group headed back to the warehouse, they were using as a lab. The professor had been notably absent the entire time, stuck in one of his many experiments. He had done little else since he had regained consciousness.

Charles began examining the people that had been laid on the grass, finding everything from simple food poisoning to infect gut wounds. Krystal meanwhile had taken the opportunity to talk to everyone and while they had quickly decided on a name for the town, they were having problems with the tenets. Everyone had ideas and couldn't agree on something another person had suggested, resulting in zero progress.

Charles had just finished healing the worst of the injured when a loud explosion came from the lab and smoke poured from the open doors. Alli instantly vanished from where she had been watching everyone and reappeared in the lab warehouse's shadow.

She was the first to get there by a long shot, and seconds later people began to stream from the building. Only the professor had sustained any damage from the explosion, as it had been his experiment that caused it.

The skin on his arms had blackened from him covering his face, his chest, a mass of burns and peeling flesh. Charlotte took control of the group making sure everyone was out while Scott took care of the professor. In this case, taking care of him meant bringing the injured man to Charles.

Alli appeared at his side before he had a chance to look at the professor. "It was a generator that exploded, no fire, though some equipment will need to be fixed. He was doing whatever caused it to explode in the middle of the warehouse floor. Thankfully, no one was close enough to be hurt outside of himself."

"Small favors," He muttered to himself, before putting a hand on the professors charred and blackened arm. His healing spell quickly revealed just how lucky the professor had gotten, shards of metal peppered his chest like grenade shrapnel. It was only due to luck that none of them had gone deep enough to hit anything vital.

Scott held his professor in place as his entire body bucked and thrashed against the restraint. His burned skin tore and ripped open from the pressure as pieces of metal and plastic dug themselves out of his skin and fell to the ground. Skin reformed and damaged pieces flaked and fell off in dark sweet-smelling pieces. He was missing some hair from where it had burned off, but by the time Charles was done healing him, he was good as new once more. Except for the scars, the thin white lines of scars that now decorated his body. Leftover from his time as a carved sacrifice for monsters, no matter what was done to them they persisted.

"Going to have to dilute the mixture and change out the jets on the carburetor," Were the first words out of the professor's mouth after he had been healed.

"What were you making?" Scott asked in exasperation, not having the energy to tear into his careless professor.

"Gas, or rather something like it. Unfortunately, the mixture was far more potent than I thought it would be. I'll need to dilute the mixture before trying again and modify the carburetor on the generator, so it lets less fuel through."

"Focus on diluting it as much as possible, if we have to change parts on an engine to get it to work properly, we're going to run into problems in other areas as well," Scott told his professor in surprise, that was something that he should have already thought of. It wasn't something that should have been needed to say aloud.

The large doors to the warehouse were quickly opened, once they had determined there was no fire that they needed to be wary of. The smoke poured out of the larger opening in a sweet-smelling cloud and vanished.

Each of them stopped by the professors' side to make sure he was okay before going back into the slightly smoky lab. Their experiments and research awaited them, and there were many things just waiting to be learned in the world.

Charles knew just how single-minded their focus could be, his sister could be the same way at times.

Scott took Charles by the arm and pulled him away from the building, "I was looking at the pedestal in the middle of the gazebo, and it has a lot of functions besides just accepting our oaths to become citizens of the town."

"Okaaay?" Charles had no idea where he was going with this.

"Charlotte and I have talked about getting married in the past, but we never saw a true reason for it. Swearing our love for each other in front of a judge limited our marriage to while we were alive. With that limitation in place, there was no reason to go through with it." He wiped his hands on his pants and licked his lips. "The pedestal can conduct marriages as long as the couple involved have the town's administrator or owner's approval first. The ceremony is conducted by a god. I want to marry your sister there tonight. After we have finished becoming members of the town, I want to ask her to marry me."

"So why are you telling me then?" Charles asked, even though he already knew.

"You're her last living family member still alive. I wanted to make sure you were okay with me marrying her. I know it isn't the style to get the family's permission first before asking the woman to marry you, but since she and I have already talked about this in the past, I thought it would be alright. That and as far as I can tell you are the owner of the town and we would need your permission anyway," Scott was rambling slightly in his haste to explain.

"Calm down, as long as she wants it, I am fine with you marrying her. That said, I also realize she would still do whatever she wanted even without my blessing on the matter," Charles looked toward where his sister was standing outside, waiting for Scott to join her. "Just make sure she is happy and safe, that's all I ask."

Scott smiled as he followed his soon to be brother-in-law's eyes. "I would have done that, regardless."

"I have to finish healing the people that were brought. While I'm doing that why don't you keep an eye on your crazy professor?" Charles asked while walking away.

A couple of young people from the Danville group were moving about by the time he finished with his healing duties. They had likely not been part of the group doing the driving and had been able to rest for much of the trip, even if they hadn't slept the entire way.

Kory was talking to one of them and waved Charles over when he saw that he was finished healing the people. "Repeat to him what you just told me," Kory told the kid.

The kid shrugged and turned to Charles. "Alright, I was just saying that we had seen a lot of monsters gathering together in a group. They weren't doing anything when we passed them just before we reached St. Louis, but it was a huge group of them. We warned this big woman who seemed to be guarding the road as we drove through about them."

"Now tell him about the other part," Kory said nudging the boy who now that Charles was closer looked to between the twins and Kate in age.

"I joined up with this group alongside my parents in Indiana. They stopped there for gas and we were walking on the road nearby when they stopped. Anyway, what I'm saying is that what I'm about to say is just based on what they were saying at the time. No one else saw it but me, but they were talking about this weird tall goblin fellow that had captured them and how he had disappeared without fighting you," Kory nudged the kid again. "Uh, right, where was I?"

"The goblin monster," Kory reminded him, barely keeping his impatience with the kid in check.

"Right, that, I think I saw the monster they were talking about. I saw a group of weird-looking goblins camped out in the woods the night before we met the people from Danville. I remember thinking how odd the group of goblins was because they weren't hunting or eating people. They were just sitting around a fire, listening to another goblin that was wearing a headdress."

"A shaman," Charles interjected.

"Sure, a shaman, anyway they were just sitting there listening to it speak. I left them in peace since I didn't want to get eaten and didn't tell anyone what I had seen until now. My parents would have beaten my a—err bum, if they had heard about me going off on my own to explore."

Kory patted the kid on the arm and sent him away. "They're making good time if they were already in Indiana two days ago. Do you think they're coming here?"

"Yeah, but that isn't what worries me, it's the goblin lord he's already demonstrated how smart he is and he is clearly willing to work with other monsters. What worries me is what happens when he hears about this army that is being gathered. I think it is safe to say that the bugbear is leading that army if the two of them join together and attack us..."

Chapter 27

"Dungeonville," Kory said suddenly as Charles turned to walk away. "It was the name most people seemed willing to accept. Word has gotten around that we're here to guard the dungeon. People seemed to think it was appropriate to include it in the name of the town."

"Dungeonville?" Charles chuckled at the name intending to enter it into the system and make it official before anyone could change their minds on the name.

There were only a couple hours of light left in the sky before the effective hours they could work disappeared. The days of working long into the night hunched over a desk had vanished unless you belonged in the lab with his sister. They had desks and lamps and soon would likely have computers again. He needed to start preparing for what was to come.

What that kid had told them changed nothing. All it did was let them know they had been right. More than that, it let them know an approximate date on when the attack was likely to happen. In this case, it was going to be sooner rather than later, within the next few days, kind of sooner. There was a lot they needed to accomplish to prepare for an army of monsters.

Charles had begun his own preparations hours before; part of his mind had been meditating on a spell for a shield of mana. Once he had seen the need for a higher tier restoration spell, he had begun meditating on that as well. The partitions had almost come crashing down earlier before he had a chance to dismiss them, that had been when the explosion occurred.

Now it was time to make sure the town was ready to handle the sudden influx of people and monsters. He stepped into the town-system building and quickly set the town's name to 'Dungeonville'. Thankfully, there had been so many people entering the town that day that the taxed mana had skyrocketed.

Unfortunately, they didn't yet have enough to upgrade the wall in any way, they would have to try again the next day. It wasn't like people were suddenly going to stop showing up, not with a possible monster army appearing. While they didn't have enough to do anything to the wall, they had more than enough to make three large bunkhouse buildings. With a quick swipe of his hand, he placed them next to each other and across from the houses. The people staying in them would not have much privacy for the moment, but they would have a warm and comfortable place to sleep at least. More than that, once everyone became citizens of the town, they would be safe from other things and only town members would be able to enter them.

More of the people from the Danville group were out and about when he emerged from the system building. Their jaws were hanging low as they watched the three buildings being constructed in front of their very eyes.

Kory hurried over to him, a worried look on his face. "They all witnessed the monsters moving about as they drove. As the boy said they warned the people of St. Louis but none of them thought they really had a chance. They did have some vehicles running by the time they went through though so it's possible we might be getting even more survivors soon."

Charles pointed to the bunkhouses. "I can have more of these built without a problem and they'll house a lot of people. The problem lies with our defenses, we need to save as much UM as possible to shore them up.

There are a couple of changes that need to be made to the wall at the very least and trust me when I say they are expensive modifications."

The people that he had healed earlier had already left leaving only people that would be joining the town that night.

"Start rounding everyone up, we need to decide on the last two tenets and have everyone officially join the town," Charles told him, already making his way towards the gazebo.

Alli appeared first, all the various kids that were in the town following behind her. Kira and Kate were next, they had been moving each of the cars and trucks into her warehouse garage as the people woke up and vacated it.

Gradually the rest of the people began to trickle in, their number well over four hundred by that point. The area filled up quickly, and the noise skyrocketed as everyone began talking at the same time. Charlotte pushed her way through the crowd with Scott close on her heels.

"What are we doing all gathering here?" She asked once she had reached his side.

"Officially joining the town, as soon as we decide on the last two tenets," Charles told her. Kate was holding onto Alli's neck while they talked, Kira was making sure she was well away from the gathering crowd. Sierra skirted the edges of the crowd and made her way carefully to them.

They made sure to stay out of the way as Kory and Krystal calmed the crowd and started speaking. "We need to decide on the last two tenets for the town before we start swearing to become citizens of this protected and magical area."

The crowd exploded into noise and several loud minutes passed before they could get them to quiet down again. "If we are not able to decide on one now, then it will be decided on later after you have already become a member and can't refuse the new tenets!" Kory's voice echoed through the filled clearing, his words striking fear deep into their hearts.

One of the people stepped forward, a woman in her later forties. "I don't think we should enter anything into the tenets that aren't already there. The three that the gods put in already cover a wide range of things to help keep us safe. I think anything beyond those should become regular laws enforced by humans."

Charles could feel the beginnings of a headache forming as the woman spoke. They had been handed a gift, one that would have eliminated the need for a police force, and she wanted to spurn it and bring them back. Miraculously and rather sadly her idea quickly gained momentum, and soon enough the majority of the people were backing her idea.

He could almost hear the sigh of godly disgust as a new message appeared in front of everyone's eyes.

Due to humans being human, the remaining two unfilled town tenet slots have been removed.

It was a simple message that still somehow revealed the deep disgust the gods felt in the humans at that moment.

Kory turned to Charles his eyebrow cocked in a clear question of what to do next.

Charles was the first to step into the gazebo, not even waiting for everyone to calm down. He just wanted this to be over, he wanted to see his sister be married by a god. He placed the palm of his hand on the pedestal and a prompt appeared in front of his eyes.

Would you like to become a citizen of the town 'Dungeonville'?

He selected yes.

*Do you agree to follow the tenets as listed knowing that
they are being enforced by the gods and your own magical
core?*

He selected yes, a second time.

A swirl of golden light swept through the gazebo followed by a new message that only he could see.

*Congratulation, you have become a citizen of a town you
already own and administer. As the town now has a citizen,
all buildings will become locked to non-citizens. Only
members of the town may enter or use town facilities.*

That was a nice bit of insurance, it would make it easy to tell who was a member of the town in the future.

He stepped back and the rest of the people in his group stepped up one by one and became official members of the town. He would make Kory and Krystal the town administrators later as well. Sierra was the only one who stopped and looked back at him, making sure it was alright for her to join as well. He, in turn, looked to Kira who nodded without hesitating. She was the last of their group to go through the process. Even Alli had been able to join.

As soon as she stepped out of the gazebo a line of people formed and began to go through the process. It was clear that a few of them tried to refuse the tenets when they had to step back and place their hands on the pedestal a second time.

The line of people decreased rapidly as they were accepted one after another, the sheer number of people involved making it a time-consuming process. Only when it was over did Scott look to Charlotte and pulled her to the side out of earshot.

The sun had long since sunk below the horizon, leaving only a few streaks of orange in the sky. Clouds had begun to gather in small wisps at first but combined into larger and darker clouds as time went on. The temperature dropped naturally as more of the sky became covered in the writhing mass of dark moisture.

Charlotte was nodding speculatively as she listened to Scott speak. He was undoubtedly telling her everything he had told Charles earlier. What they were about to do was not a simple marriage that ended on Earth, but one that was backed by the gods themselves.

Kira was watching them as the rest of the gathered people began to disperse, leaving only their core group behind. Jenny and her brother had managed to join their group due to Alli practically adopting the kids. Kate and her parents knew something was about to happen and Sierra was looking on with warm eyes. Charles wasn't sure if his initial impression of her had been colored by Kira, or if she had merely managed to change in the last week.

The woman standing with them now barely resembled the woman he had believed her to be. Her manners and the way she acted were polished, befitting someone with money and power. Behind those manners and the emotional distance she naturally kept from those around her hid a somewhat shy and reticent girl. She was perfectly comfortable letting others take the lead, as long as she trusted them, and she trusted Kira. Even with the history between them, she trusted her more than anyone else.

Charlotte looked to the group with a wide smile on her face and tears in her eyes as Scott slipped an antique ring onto her finger. Taking her hand in his, he led her to the pedestal and together they placed their hands on it. Together they closed their eyes and linked their free hands together.

The now-familiar pillar of light that accompanied anything done by the gods descended from the sky and enveloped the gazebo. Charles and the others huddled together as the light coalesced into a female figure.

Everyone that had already left the area but had seen the light came running towards them.

The goddess that appeared behind the pedestal and was dressed in a pure white sari wrapped around her waist and with one end draped over her shoulder. A jade-green dress was worn under the garment. A book was in her left hand and a pink lotus blossom in her right, a white comb made of ivory decorated her dark brunette hair. She smiled beatifically at Charlotte and Scott and then began.

"I am Saraswati. I am Charlotte's patron goddess as I chose her to be my champion. I will be conducting your marriage ceremony today." The goddess placed her hand over theirs and a red string wrapped around their pinkies was revealed when she lifted her hand. Upon seeing the red string, her smile grew even more luminescent and warm. "The two of you are truly meant to be together, the red string of fate binds you already. Upon the completion of this ceremony, the string will become golden and your souls will be bound as one for all eternity."

Kira's face grew wistful and slightly fearful upon hearing the goddess's words, a feeling Charles could completely understand. Everyone wanted to be with their soulmate, but what if the person you fell in love with wasn't it? The knowledge held a certain amount of duality with it that made Charles sure there was more to it than they knew.

Saraswati conducted a simple ceremony similar in many ways to the traditional Earthly ones they were familiar with. The only real difference was that there was no mention of the marriage ending with their deaths.

The area was completely silent as the ceremony came to a close and they were allowed to kiss each other. The goddess looked Charlotte in the eye as she pulled back from her new husband, "I chose well," She said with a soft expression crossing her face, she tapped both of their hands once each and the now golden string vanished from view. With that done she stepped back from the pedestal and transformed into a pillar of light that was sucked back into the sky. The pillar cut through the thick layer of clouds that extended into the visible distance.

The crowd of people that had gathered around them was quiet for several heartbeats before bursting into noise dispelling the warm feeling the goddess had left behind.

Charles ignored them all, his eyes fixed on the dark roiling clouds above them. Carefully he sent a thin tendril of magic towards his vocal cords, amplifying his voice. "Everyone shut up!" His amplified voice thundering over their own and compelling them to be quiet as a sliver of magic unbeknownst to him crept into his voice. "I don't like the look of these clouds and tonight is the last night before whatever game the gods are playing begins. I expect a large storm to herald in whatever changes this means. I want everyone inside the buildings tonight. I'll lock the gate but everyone else please stay inside!"

At his words, everyone rushed to either the houses or the new bunkhouses, the last dregs of light vanishing as they hurried inside. The thick layer of clouds hiding the green tint of the night sky.

Charles threw a few orbs of light to different people in the group, the orbs would follow them until he dismissed them.

Charlotte put a hand on his arm before he could leave to close the gate. "I'm going to skip the training tonight." She pulled him into a hug. "Thanks for being here and giving him your blessing. I know your feelings about Scott are complicated."

"They're not that complicated. I just tend to forget he exists most of the time. I know he makes you happy, so how could I not give him my blessing?" Charles wrapped his arms around her tightly before letting go. "Now go enjoy your honeymoon in your lab or apartment, whatever it is. I know it was always your dream to vacation in Missouri!" His voice was mocking at their chosen locale, knowing they had no choice in the matter.

"That's where you're wrong. My dream was to be wherever my family was, and you and he are here." Charlotte released him and wiped at her misty eyes. "I wish mom and dad could have been here."

Charles looked away guiltily, he rarely thought of his parents. Their relationship had always been strained, leaving them somewhat estranged, especially in the last few years. "I know they would have been happy for you, they always approved of Scott."

With those parting words, he gently pushed her away and hurried off to close the gate. He needed some time alone with his thoughts, regardless of what he had told his sister. She was married now, and that required a mental adjustment on his part.

"What's wrong?" Alli asked as she fell into step beside him.

"Nothing, it's just going to take me a while to adjust to the thought of her being married. It feels like as soon as Saraswati pronounced them married a partition came down separating her from me. I know it's just in my head, but I've never felt that separation before. I could always depend on her, and her me, now it feels like I can't do that like I'd be the third wheel in their relationship." He struggled to express his thoughts as they walked to the already closed gate. He made sure that it was locked and could only be opened by a member of the town before turning and heading back.

"Well, you can always depend on me. I'm not going anywhere," Alli said, nudging him slightly with her side.

Charles barely held in the words 'Until you get married', but she still knew what he was thinking.

"Even if I was to somehow get married or find a mate, you would still be the most important person in my life Charles," Her voice hard and brooking no room for argument, she meant what she said.

Charles put his arm around her neck and walked silently back to Kira and Kate who were waiting for him outside the system building he called home. Sierra had vanished within the last few minutes, as had Kory and Krystal.

"Mom and dad wanted to talk to Sierra in private," Kate said, seeing him look around, solving the mystery. "I think they wanted to hear firsthand what she told Kira and decide for themselves whether she is truly innocent."

"I believe her, and I am trying to move past the blame I placed on her," Kira quickly looked at Alli before looking at the ground, signifying that her belief was not quite as strong as she would have them believe.

Lightning flashed through the clouds above them, followed by a roar of thunder a split-second later.

"Let's get inside," Charles told them, leading the way as the first drop of rain hit his neck and slid under the collar of his clothes.

Chapter 28

Charles dismissed all the orbs of light he could feel tugging at his mana and sent up a single one in the middle of the roof. It hung over the map, casting shadows across the small modeled buildings that sat atop the table.

Alli and Kate took a corner to themselves as Charles began their training for the night. Kira was sitting on the far side of the table waiting for him to finish. They had been talking to each other for over an hour by the time Alli had finished and came over to join them.

"I finished infusing my core, I'll need you to help me learn how to control my mana though." She settled down on the floor in front of them both. Her body close enough that their hands could reach her, which they immediately did. "Two spells unlocked as soon as I finished, they're apparently part of my class. One is called 'Shadow Spike', I think you mentioned learning that one as well. The second one is different though, it is called 'Shadow Shift' and it turns my entire body into a cloud made of shadows. It supposedly makes me faster, allows me to fly or glide for short distances, and while I am a cloud since I don't really have a body I can't be attacked."

"Can you attack while in that form or is it purely a movement type spell?" Charles asked as he brushed his fingers through her silky hair. The cleaning spell he used on them both each day seemed to moisturize their skin and hair as it scrubbed them clean.

"The description that came up for the spell doesn't say. I'll have to try it out tomorrow," Alli twisted and moved until her head was on his legs.

Kira who had heard everything since she began scratching her side spoke up. "What about that speech spell? Wasn't that why you first began learning magic?" She asked.

"That will come later," She told them as her tongue flopped out of her mouth. "I have to learn how to properly manipulate my mana before I can use that spell."

"Are you sure?" Charles asked. "It seems like that would be one of the spells you could automatically use."

Alli was silent as she pulled up the information on the spell. "Well, what do you know, you're right? I can start using it right away." She shuffled uncomfortably in place. "It will take some getting used to. I've never been able to freely talk to people."

Kate finished her session and joined them in their corner. "Two more sessions and I should be finished infusing my core." She said as she took her place next to her sister.

Through the partially open door, they could hear the pitter-patter of rain hitting the ground. The dark clouds had opened up and were releasing their wrath down upon the world as the booms of thunder and lightning began to reverberate through the buildings.

Conversation stopped as they listened to the elements rage upon the land. They sat there silently listening to the storm for hours until a countdown appeared in the middle of their vision.

Time until 'The Game' begins: 30:00

Kate started in surprise and inched closer to her sister as the countdown appeared. As she opened her mouth to say something a bolt of lightning hit the ground just outside and a pressure wave from the thunder threw the door of the building open.

Charles leapt to his feet and closed the door, eliminating almost all the noise instantly. A slight gap where the door hadn't quite been pounded into the right shape the day before letting a small amount of noise into the room.

"Are you all alright?" He asked as he tore his smoking jacket from his body. The metal zippers had become superheated from the electricity in the air.

Kira was gingerly holding the waistband of her pants away from her body, unwilling to touch the hot metal buttons. Kate had been wearing a belt and had a pained expression on her face. Her lips were locked tight to hold in her scream of pain as the smell of cooking flesh wafted around the room.

Charles rushed over to her and splashed her body with his water spell, cooling the offending metal instantly. His hand reached out and gripped her arm as he began healing the damaged and burnt skin.

Kate panted out in relief, the remembered pain keeping her from saying anything for the moment.

Kira pulled her sister into her arms wanting to say something that would disrupt the sudden tension in the air. "It's a good thing we got all the vehicles moved inside the garage earlier!"

Alli who far and away had the best hearing of anyone in the room and had covered her ears as the sonic boom sounded began to chuff with laughter. She could hear Kira's heart racing in terror and relief and knew what the woman was trying to do.

Charles collapsed next to her as the adrenaline rush left his body weak and shaky. A quick focused use of the healing spell restored the rest of Alli's hearing and got rid of that awful ringing noise that had appeared.

"I hope everyone else has the sense to stay inside," Alli said, using magic to project her voice to everyone in the room.

"I guess we'll find out when the storm is over," Kira began, sending a quick look to the closed door. "I'm not letting anyone through that door until the storm is over."

They went back to sitting silently, listening to the sounds of the storm that trickled through the door and watching the countdown. The storm grew worse the closer to midnight it became; the wind gusting fiercely and the rain coming down in a near solid sheet of water.

The river would be a raging mess in the morning.

"There's something out there," Alli whimpered softly, crawling on her belly to Charles. "I can hear it calling for me."

"Shh, even if there is something out there it can't get inside. Just ignore it, and it will go away," Charles whispered to her, making sure he had a firm hold around her neck just in case.

Kira ran her hand down her younger sisters' hair in a comforting fashion. She may have been dependent on Kate in the past, but she was well aware that she was the older sister. A position that she took seriously.

The countdown continued its inexorable work, ignoring the wants and desires of the people who saw it.

The storm continued to grow worse and then suddenly it was gone, the silence that existed in the eye of the storm. The countdown had reached zero, and there was no eye to this storm. It had simply disappeared.

"The voice it's gone," Alli said thankfully to him, still refusing to move.

Kira looked at him and then to the door, her question unspoken but obvious.

Charles shook his head and mouthed the word 'tomorrow' to her.

***

Kira and Kate had ended up sleeping in the building that night after the storm settled down, making use of the sleeping bag and pillows Charles kept in the corner. After making sure Alli was alright and asleep he had begun his nightly meditations, resulting in him learning two more spells.

One of them was 'restore', a higher-level restoration spell but not as high of a tier as he needed for the chickens. The second spell was the shield spell he had been wanting.

Congratulations, you have learned the spell 'Aegis'. Aegis is a metal spell that uses your mana to control a piece of infused metal and use it as a shield that hovers in the air. (Note: At higher proficiency with this spell, additional uses of the shield may be revealed.)

Sitting on the floor beneath Alli's hairy and furnace-like bulk, he pulled up the town inventory and removed several large pieces of flat scrap-metal. Using the aegis spell was a two-step process with him needing to infuse the metal with mana beforehand. He would always need to keep several pieces of the infused mana in his inventory until he learned how long they remained infused at the very least.

This was his first time using the infuse spell since he had learned it, and though he knew what was going to happen, it was still odd. The spell sent his mana into the metal and he could feel it crawling over the surface of the metal. Once it had covered the entire piece, the mana began to sink into the metal becoming one with it. He felt he could do the process another couple of times before it could handle no more.

Each time he did, the concentration of mana in the metal would grow. The bond between the mana and the metal grew alongside the concentration of mana until they were nearly one. The surface of the metal sheet in his hands had changed with each infusion, small imperfections were removed.

His hands glided over the polished and smooth surface in amazement before he placed the changed metal into his inventory. He did the same thing on three more pieces of metal, keeping only the last out to use as his shield.

Charles used his new shield spell to create the aegis and watched as the newly minted shield sprang into the air. It kept away from his hands not allowing him to touch it, but otherwise, it moved with his thoughts. He left it hovering above his head and carefully extricated himself from underneath Alli.

It was time to see what kind of damage the storm had wrought on their undeveloped town.

Not a lot had changed when he opened the door, letting in the chilly morning air. Puddles decorated the area, and behind the building, he could hear the river raging from the sudden influx of water. Blackened spots of burned grass were sprinkled liberally everywhere he could see, but that was the extent of the damage.

None of the houses or other buildings looked as though they had been damaged by the storm.

Stepping onto the soggy grass, Charles zipped up his jacket as the early morning chill began to creep inside. His boots splashed across the ground as he walked through the area, making sure nothing had been permanently damaged.

Behind the town system building a brand-new bridge extended across the roiling surface of the river. The dungeon now had a large arch above a set of dual doors that had been cut into the surface of the dungeon wall.

Alli joined him outside as he was walking across the bridge, leaping from one puddle to the next thoroughly soaking herself in the cold water. She shook the water from her body and ran across the bridge.

"I guess the dungeon is now open for people to enter and explore," She said, coming up behind Charles as he looked up at the decorated arch.

Swirling runes and Celtic knots ran across the surface of the arch and were inlaid into the doors.

"I guess," He answered in turn. "I won't be entering it though, but I have a suspicion most of the other champions will be going in. We don't yet have the weapons we would need to enter something like a dungeon safely. Heck, we don't even have the weapons we need to fight regular monsters safely."

Alli chuffed and turned away from the door. "And that is exactly why people will want to enter the dungeon. Don't forget I got some of your memories when I became your companion. The main reason people entered dungeons in the games you played was for loot and weapons."

Charles lightly kicked the wall that edged the road on this side of the bridge. This bridge led people to the dungeon, and that was it. "I'll heal the people that need it either way, but I have no desire to actually go inside."

Alli went to the center of the bridge and peered over the edge and into the speeding mass of muddy brown water below.

Kory and Krystal had managed to stumble out of their house by the time Charles and Alli had finished crossing the bridge a second time. Their hair was standing up in a case of prodigious bedhead and the constant streams of yawns made it clear that they had not slept well.

"Didn't sleep well?" Charles asked as he joined them.

"Kept hearing voices outside the house for most of the night," Kory managed to say while yawning.

"They kept inviting us outside, telling us that our loved ones were waiting for us," Krystal explained with a shiver.

Alli spoke up then, using magic to let them all hear her voice. "I heard the voice as well, Charles made sure I didn't listen to them. I don't think the girls could hear it though, with the door closed nearly all noise from outside is cut off."

"We don't need to touch you to hear you speak anymore?" Kory asked her in surprise.

"Nope! Once I learned magic, I became able to project my voice to anyone," Alli told them happily.

"We should probably go around and make sure that everyone is alright, and that they didn't go outside to meet whatever was speaking," Charles said, steering the conversation back before they could get sidetracked. "I'll go get Kate and Kira and then we can go around and make sure everyone is alright."

"Wait." Krystal grabbed his arm, stopping him from leaving. She licked her lips nervously and flicked her eyes to her husband. "We've been wondering, what is going on between you and Kira? At first, we thought there was nothing, but she seems, different the last few days. I'm sure some of it is from her talking to Sierra." Her eyes grew pinched as she mentioned the woman who they had believed hurt Kira for so long. "I don't think that's all though."

Charles looked away from them, unsure of how to respond. His feelings for Kira had become increasingly complex as he got to know her better and maybe understand what made her act the way she did. "I don't know how to answer that. We haven't really talked about it." He turned and fled before she could ask any more questions.

"What do you think is going on between them, Alli?" Were the last words he heard before entering the building and hurrying over to Kira's side.

Kira was lying on a sleeping mat, Kate's head resting on her chest and a sleeping bag spread loosely over their bodies.

Charles reached out and almost touched Kira's shoulder before changing targets and instead chose to gently shake Kate. Her eyes flickered open quickly taking in her surroundings before she even moved.

"Your parents are waiting outside. wake Kira up for me, please?" He asked, stepping back from them both.

Kate smiled softly and twisted her head to look up at her sleeping sister. "I think you could probably wake her, without her screaming at you."

"Maybe, I'm not sure if I'm ready to test that theory out yet though," He said softly before turning to look at the map on the table.

The walls would never hold against the swarm of monsters they knew were coming; they might look impressive to humans. But against monsters, it was nothing more than a pre-apocalypse wall that would fall without difficulty.

Charles pulled up the menu and looked at the options concerning the wall. He knew it was upgradeable. He had seen the options for it the day before. The problem was that the two options listed were incredibly expensive. Thankfully, both options changed the wall in specific and beneficial ways.

Kate had gently poked her older sister awake by the time he had selected the first of the two options. It was also the only option they could currently afford, and it raised the height of the wall another four meters.

Kira clambered unsteadily to her feet and put her hand on the wall as she swayed. "Light-headed," She announced simply, before heading for the door.

Charles made sure the order to make the wall taller had gone through and then followed them outside.

Startled shouts of surprise and screams could be heard by the gate as the people they hadn't known were there watched the wall grow. The sound prompted people to start waking up and soon doors were being flung open.

"There are a lot of people moving around just outside the gate," Alli told them all as Jenny and James ran to her, they had stayed in the same house as Kory and Krystal. Alli nudged them both with her nose and then joined Charles as he walked towards the closed and locked gate.

Every step brought more noise to their ears until they both could hear the people on the other side of the gate talking. "I'm telling you the wall is possessed, there's a devil inside the wall!"

"Shut up Earl, everyone knows the guy who uses magic lives here. He probably did something to the wall that makes it stronger. I bet you he's right on the other side of the gate listening to you bad mouth his magical wall."

"I am actually," Charles called out, not bothering to open the gate yet.

A series of curses were heard from the unseen people and Alli's eyes went wide.

"Wow, some of those were rather creative. They didn't need to bring me into it though," She whispered to him.

"I am almost certain that you were not the female dog they were talking about," He said with a muffled laugh while rolling his eyes at her.

"I better not have been. I never did anything to them or their parents," She said with a fake sniff. She would enjoy messing with the people when the time came for them to open the gate.

Interlude 3

"So how is this going to work exactly?" Zeus asked, the question silencing all the gods. It was a question that many of them had been wondering but none dared ask. It was the first day of the game, and they all wanted to start playing properly with their new toys.

Hermes was off to one side of the room with several of the other gods. Those that would be helping him run the shops and other services. Their part was easier to plan out and do since they didn't need to control any of the humans.

Bob tossed several dice onto the table. "You will be rolling for actions, of course." He waved his hand and a scene with Kira fighting side by side with the other champions appeared above the table. "Let's say I'm Brigit in this example." His voice changed into a flawless mockery of Brigit's own lilting brogue. "I'm Brigit and my characters keep dying." The gathered gods all laughed, while Brigit folded her arms over her chest and scowled at them.

Bob cleared his throat, his voice returning to normal. "Alright, so I don't want my champion, Kira, in this case, to die. Now I see that a goblin is about to stab her in the back, so I roll for a life-saving move. Assuming my roll is high enough, then Kira receives a little bump from us either telling her the monster is there through a sixth sense or pushing her out of the way. Since we aren't actually controlling our champions, this is the best we can do, for now, farther down the line that may change depending on them." As he spoke the Kira above the table suddenly dived to the ground, the goblin behind her tumbled over her body and into the face of the monster that had been in front of her.

Only three of the gods had chosen champions, leaving three who still needed to make their selections. Bob choosing a champion didn't count since he wasn't an active member in the game, and Charles was expected to be the same.

Alaria watched them all with a bemused expression as she went over to talk to Hermes and his group. They wanted to know what kind of items would be appearing in her dungeon and what they were traditionally worth to the humans.

Chapter 29

Charles let the people outside the gates sweat for a few more minutes before moving to open them. Alli preening herself at his side grinned and took the lead, making sure she was the first thing they saw as the gate opened.

"Now, who was it that said I was their mother?" She projected her voice to the entire crowd.

There were a few muffled screams as they took in the massive silver dog in front of them, Charles standing wordlessly at her side. He couldn't help the frown that came over his face as he saw just how many people were outside the gates. He placed a hand on Alli's neck, stopping her from teasing them more. It was more important that they find out why this large group of people were outside the gates so early in the morning first.

"What are you all doing here?" Charles asked, not moving from his spot at the gate.

Kira and her parents came up behind him as he spoke and saw the large crowd outside the gate. Each person was bedraggled and looked as though they had been walking for much of the night.

One person yelled, "We want to learn magic," While another yelled, "We want to use the town services."

Charles had actually forgotten about the store now being open. His larger than normal inventory had ensured he could carry everything with him. He hadn't had to worry about not having something like everyone else did. Seeing the odd looks he was getting, he dismissed the misshapen piece of metal that was his aegis shield, storing it in his inventory.

"Behave while you're here! Anybody that attacks or tries to harm another person while inside the bounds of the town will be dealt with harshly. This is your only warning." His eyes were flat and devoid of emotion as he spoke. These people were not members of the town and as a result, they were not constrained by the oath.

He would let them in regardless, the town needed the influx of mana and people. He would be watching them though, just waiting for the inevitable trouble to begin. There was always trouble when a large group of humans gathered together for the first time.

"The stores are next to the town hall building," He told them in a clear voice as he pointed to the buildings in question.

The crowd surged towards him as one giant mass of bodies.

"This is going to be one giant headache," Kory said as he pushed his wife behind him. "Why are these people all here this morning? Don't they know that everything changed again last night?"

Krystal grabbed hold of Kira and looked her in the eye. "Go find your sister and keep her safe. I don't want her to be around all these people, there is no telling what they might do."

"Speaking of which, I'm going to find my own sister. I have a few questions for her, about what their experiments are focusing on," Charles told them as he turned away from the refugee looking people.

Alli remained by his side as he hurried over to the lab where he knew she would be. It wasn't only that they were sleeping in one of the many rooms in the building. It had more to do with whom Charlotte was as a person. She was always working and was only ever rarely seen outside of her work environment.

Charlotte was sitting at the same table he had found her at the morning before. Lab equipment was spread across the table in front of her. Her eyes were closed, and her hand was pressed firmly to the plastic shell that protected whatever it was.

A moment later she inhaled sharply and opened her eyes, smiling in triumph. "That is one more piece that can be used again. It should be useful to Scott and the professor." She frowned when she mentioned the professor.

"What's wrong with the professor?" Charles asked coming up behind her.

She started in surprise, not having seen him or Alli come in. "He's being reckless is all, we're all playing with things we don't understand anymore. Normally, one would be cautious when experimenting with something new, he's not. He's acting like he has an idea of what is going to happen, but not how powerful the effect is going to be. I never had him as one of my professors, but Scott used to swear by the man. I find his current disregard for established scientific methods and beliefs to be deeply disturbing."

Alli went over to her and nudged her face with her wet nose. "We'll keep an eye on him then, but we can't forget what happened to him."

The professors' body was covered in the thin white scars of his experience, and they were strangely resistant to healing.

"Why are you here, anyway? Not that I don't like seeing you or anything. I just thought you would be busy preparing for the fight that is about to come." Charlotte asked as she rubbed at her tired eyes.

"I'm avoiding a crowd of people," He told her as he pulled a stool from one of the other tables and put it next to hers. "Apparently the people that don't want to join us and be safe inside our walls still want to use our services. A bunch of them wanted access to the store, that is now open, while others apparently want to learn magic."

"Are you going to teach them?" She asked as she moved another piece of equipment into position.

"I haven't decided," Charles said softly. "I had no problems teaching the people here because I knew they were going to be part of the town. The people that just showed up at the gates... I know nothing about them."

"So, make them join the town." Charlotte turned to fully look at him. "That's not everything. There is something else bothering you. What is it?"

"I'm just anxious to hear from the people around St. Louis. I know that there is a fight coming, and I don't know how to prepare for a battle of this size." The uncertainty he was feeling affected his voice as he spoke.

"Are you sure you need to?" Charlotte asked as she stood from her stool and pushed him towards the door. "What do you think people have been doing with everything they have salvaged over the last few days?" She pointed to a section of the wall away from the gate. A large pile of metal and concrete had come into being sometime during the last few days. Even as they watched, several people were taking blocks of concrete and carrying them towards the gate.

"You may be the reason that this town is as safe or as far along as it is, but others are doing their part to contribute. It's not up to just you to keep this town and the people in it safe, that responsibility belongs to all of us. Besides, Kory is doing a great job of making sure everything is running smoothly. He seems to have a good idea of just what needs to be done, and when," Charlotte directed his eyes to the gate where Kory and his wife could be seen directing everything.

"How is it you know so much more about what is going on out here than I do? You are stuck inside your lab all day while I'm actually out here!" He asked in exasperation.

Charlotte merely smiled and went back inside her lab, leaving Alli and him alone for the moment.

Alli watched her walk away with him before they both turned and began walking to the town system building. There was work to be done and Charles needed to make a couple of things pertaining to the town official.

"How did she know?" Alli asked suddenly, referring to his own comment earlier.

"I don't know," Charles said with a dry laugh. "That's just the way she is, she always knew more than she should have. Whether it was about the people around her or the way something worked, she just always knew more than everyone else."

"What are you going to do?" Alli asked, changing the subject when it became obvious that he knew no more than she about his sister.

"I'm going to make Kory and Krystal the town administrators. I'll still remain the owner of the town, but it should give them access to the system. It seems as though they have a firm idea of what needs to be done and are willing to do it. Right now, by having them go through me I'm just slowing them down."

"What about the remaining changes to the wall?"

"It's going to cost an enormous amount of taxed mana to infuse the wall. I'll ask them to hold off on building anything until then, once that is done, I'll more or less hand the reins of the town over to them."

"You trust them that much?" Alli asked curiously. She knew he had a hard time trusting people.

Charles cocked his head in thought, not replying for several moments. "I do, they've been nothing but nice and good to the people around them. It's more than that, though Charlotte seems to trust them. Kira obviously does, and you haven't said anything bad about them."

Alli stopped walking to stare at him. "My opinion matters that much to you?" Her eyes growing teary as she asked the question that should have been obvious.

"Of course, it does, how could it not?" Charles said opening the door for them both, his distraction causing him to miss the effect his words had on her.

Alli had known she was important to him, but for some reason hearing that her opinion mattered to him affected her deeply. The words he had told her numerous times since they had met were not just platitudes or meaningless words. They were real, and that knowledge was beyond precious to her.

"I," She swallowed and tried again. "I'll go tell them what you're about to do so they know for later." Her words came across in a rush as she hurried to get away. She needed time alone to settle her increasingly turbulent emotions.

Charles nodded after her already lost in the menu for the town. He made the changes and then closed the menu, a short message replacing it immediately afterward.

Congratulations, the town of 'Dungeonville' is now administered by 'Kory & Krystal Lourne' as well as the owner of the town.

Closing the message, he headed outside and found Kory and Krystal waiting for him with complicated expressions on their faces.

Charles held up his hands, stopping any talking before it could start. "The two of you are already pretty much-running everything. By making you town administrators, it should give you access to the town menu. Go ahead and look it over, just don't make any changes yet. I want to reinforce the wall, and it is going to cost more than we have currently."

"Thank you, but are you sure?" Krystal asked, being the first to regain her voice.

Charles awkwardly scratched at the back of his head. "I trust you both, and it is clear to me that you know far more than I do about what needs to be done if we are attacked."

Alli had Kira and Kate in tow as they all hurried towards them. "Sorry it took me a minute to find them," She said as they joined the group.

"It's fine." He hadn't really been expecting her to bring them as well. "This gives me the chance to say something that is probably obvious at this point. I don't trust many people, to be honest. The vast majority of humans confuse me. I trust everyone here though, along with my sister and Scott, of course." Charles stopped and suddenly looked uncertain. "My point is, please don't prove my trust to have been misplaced."

Charles waved to Alli and skirted the edge of the group. "Alli and I are going to explore the area around the town, follow the road for a little bit." He was feeling more than a little vulnerable after that confession and wanted to get away from everyone for a while.

He was sure people from St. Louis would be showing up soon, and he wanted to be the first to see and meet them. There was no doubt in his mind that they would come, either with news of their destruction or their triumph over the monster army. He doubted they would win, but anything was possible. His little town would be one of the next targets if they failed to eradicate the army. Gabreen the goblin lord had told him as much before he left his own little town of monsters in Danville.

Alli led the way through the gate, her large form cutting effortlessly through the crowd of people. More people had continued to arrive, as word spread of the shop being there. They may not have wanted to join the town, but they certainly wouldn't say no to the services it provided. Which Charles found he was alright with. He was not some superhero that wanted to save everyone.

He was a realist who would help those that helped themselves. If someone wanted to live outside the town walls, where judging by the group that had been killed in the apartment complex, it was more dangerous. Then more power to them, he didn't owe them anything.

"Where are we going?" Alli asked after they had been walking in silence for several minutes.

Charles looked up in surprise. He had been lost in his own thoughts and had forgotten where they were. "Uh, I don't care, you take the lead. I just wanted to get away from everyone for a while."

"Was telling us that you trusted us, that emotionally draining?" She asked quietly, the worry in her voice obvious to him.

"No, not like that," Charles told her comfortingly while he played with her ears. "You have to understand though, the number of people I trusted even before all of this happened was limited to just my family. I knew they would never betray my trust, that's just the way my family was. It's different with Kira and her family. I'm exposing a part of myself to them that not many people have seen or will see."

"Hold on," Alli commanded suddenly, her entire body going stiff as she focused on one of her senses. "Get on my back, now!"

Charles dutifully climbed on her back and she took off running at full speed as soon as he was settled. The road and crumbling buildings streamed past them in a blur, the wind whistling through their ears. As they continued to run, he couldn't help but wonder just how good her senses truly were.

"I smelled a lot of blood on the wind," She explained as she began to slow. In front of them trundling down the road on fumes was an old open bed truck. The bed was filled with the barely breathing forms of injured people. The engine wheezed and died, coasting to a stop at their feet. The driver looking on with glazed eyes, unmoving for the several seconds it took his mind to determine that something had changed.

"Help," The driver rasped as Charles opened the driver side door and pulled him out. "St. Louis was attacked. Need to find the one who uses magic."

"Will any of them die in the next few minutes?" Charles asked Alli as he pulled a gas can from his inventory.

"Their hearts are all still beating, some of them weakly but they should hold for a few more minutes at least," She said after listening closely.

"Good, I'm going to fill up the truck with gas and drive it back. Can you go ahead and make sure everyone is standing by to help take care of the people?" He asked as he threaded the plastic nozzle of the gas can into place.

"Done," Alli nodded and took off running, leaving Charles and the unconscious man behind.

Charles tossed the empty gas can into his inventory and picked the man up off the road. "It's a good thing you're not a fatty," He muttered with a grunt as he muscled the fairly thin man into the cab. The driver's side door closed with a slam and his foot pressed on the gas pedal repeatedly. The truck had been run dry, and the fresh gas he had just poured into the tank needed time to reach the carburetor.

The engine turned over and coughed, catching for a second and then coughing again. This process repeated itself two more times before the engine started and Charles put the transmission into gear.

The drive back to the town was a short but tense five-minute drive. He was unable to go very fast or he would risk losing the people on the open truck bed.

"Get the people that are injured onto the grass where I can heal them," Charles commanded the group that had gathered as soon as he drove through the open gates and stopped in front of Kira's warehouse.

He pulled the man from the cab with him and splashed his face with a bottle of water, waking him with a sputter.

"What, where, who?" The man continued to sputter in confusion as his eyes rolled in his head.

"What happened in St. Louis?" Charles demanded, shaking the slender man to get him to focus.

"We were attacked," The man blinked and took in a deep breath, suddenly calm. "There was a storm and then a message saying the game had begun. As soon as we got the message we were attacked by an army of monsters, they had been waiting for it, I guess."

Charles shook the man again. "Focus, what happened to St. Louis?"

"Gone I think, it was still being attacked when we fled with the news. There is no way they could have survived those numbers."

Chapter 30

The people who had surrounded them all began speaking at once after hearing the man's words. Many of them had known about the presence of monsters near St. Louis. Word of what the groups who had gone through the area had seen had spread quickly after their arrival.

Kory pulled the man to one side while pushing Charles towards the group of injured that had been placed on the grass. "I'll get the details from him, go heal them and join us in the town hall."

The sun hung high in the sky over the burgeoning town as Charles healed everyone on the grass. He hurried from person to person, his magic working quickly and leaving each person in perfect health.

"Have them brought to the town hall once they're awake," Charles told the people that had gathered around. The drain he felt on his magic was more than he thought it would be and he was looking forward to sitting down for a few minutes. Everyone was waiting at the town hall, however, so taking a break would need to wait.

Charles pushed through the crowd that had gathered around the building and into the town hall. Kory was pacing in front of a long table while Krystal, Kira, Charlotte, and everyone else was seated. The man who had been driving the truck was seated across from them.

"How bad was the damage?" Kory was asking when Charles entered the building.

"The damage itself was minimal and limited to the buildings people were using. The loss of life, however..." He swallowed thickly and tried again. "The loss of life even before we managed to escape was near total, the people that were with me were the only ones we saw still alive. With that army of monsters taking over the city I can't imagine that many of those who might have escaped are still alive."

"What makes you think the monsters are occupying the city?" Charles spoke up, unable to contain the question.

The man paused and paled as he thought the question through. "They're coming here," He said, realizing it for the first time.

"They're monsters, beings from stories and games. You can't attribute human logic to them," Charles said, taking a seat at the table across from him. "For humans, it would make sense to take a place and occupy it, make it their own. For monsters, outside of a desire to kill humans and possibly other monsters we have no idea what drives them. In this case however, we do know that the leaders of the monsters are coming for us."

"How do you know that?" The man asked in confusion.

"Simple we've encountered them both already, and both of the leaders are champions for the gods. It makes sense that they would be coming to attack the human champions," Charles carefully left out other more pertinent details. He knew that many people who didn't know anything were listening from the open doors.

Kory coughed loudly getting everyone's attention. "The question is when they will arrive, not if," He turned to look the man in the eye. "You said that they attacked around midnight, right? When did you all manage to escape?"

The man nodded and closed his eyes in thought. "I can't say for sure, but the sun had only been above the horizon for a limited amount of time. So, it was probably only between seven or eight-ish."

Kory folded his arms and looked up at the ceiling. "It probably two or three in the afternoon now and it's only two hundred and fifty miles from St. Louis to here. If we assume that they didn't even leave the area until noon and that they don't stop at any of the smaller towns on the way. Then based on what we know of their travel speeds, it is possible they could reach here late tonight or early morning."

There were gasps and groans from the people pushing at the open door. He looked at them sharply, his expression unchanging. "I want groups sent out right away to warn all the humans in the area that the army of monsters will be showing up sometime tonight or tomorrow."

There were some muffled groans, but even more people separated from the crowd intending to head out as Kory had requested.

"For everyone else who stayed behind, we need to start preparing the area for the coming battle," Kory announced dismissing the last of the people outside the doors of the town hall.

Charles spoke up then before anyone else could say anything. "I healed everyone from the truck bed and directed the people watching over them to have them come here as they come-to."

The slender man from St. Louis stood from his spot on the opposite side of the table. "It's alright, I'll go to them. I'm sure there is a lot that you all need to talk about and go over."

"Do we have enough weapons from the monsters to arm everyone?" Charlotte asked as soon as he was gone.

Krystal pulled out some pieces of paper filled with information. "The short answer is no; the long answer is we have enough weapons for our original groups. There have been dozens of people who have joined the town from the groups that wandered in. We don't have enough weapons to arm them or the refugees that will seek safety behind our wall."

"What about using the dungeon?" Kate asked from beside her mother.

"No, it's too dangerous for now. The dungeon is a completely unknown factor, no one has gone inside yet. We can't risk losing people inside it before the fight even begins." The weary form of her mother pushed away from the table, seeming to age years as she explained.

"About the wall," Charles began, wanting to keep the discussion moving. "Right now, it is merely a tall, fairly weak barrier. The next upgrade the system can do to the wall is infuse it with mana, which will make it incredibly hard. It is only then that we can truly count on it to keep us safe, but that upgrade will take all the mana we have taxed and more."

"How long before we have enough?"

Charles thought for a moment. "With all the new people coming here, and the refugees that will undoubtedly show up. I think we should have enough before we are attacked, but it will depend on how many people survive to arrive here."

There was a knock on the closed door and Sierra poked her head into the room a second later. "Charles, there are a couple of people from my old group out here that want to talk to you."

Charles stood and trailed his fingers across the smooth surface of the table. "Kate, you come with me. We can start your training before I talk to them. This should be the last session you need to fully infuse your core." He turned to look at Kira and then his sister. "Let me know if there is anything I can do to help with the preparations."

Kate joined him and Alli at the doors as they followed Sierra from the building.

"Did they say what they wanted?"

Sierra shook her head at his question. "No, Ray is with them though so maybe he wants to apologize or something."

Charles couldn't help but snort at the thought of the brash man he had met apologizing for anything.

"I need to start Kate's training session really quick before I meet with them," He said already leading the way to the house her family had been using. There was no reason not to use it, especially since it now had furniture. She would be more comfortable there than on the floor of the system building.

Kate could barely contain her excitement at the thought of finally infusing her core fully. She was pulling on Charles' arm urging him to move that much faster. "Come on." She pushed open the door to the small house and plopped down on the first chair she saw.

Charles didn't even pause his steps as he began the meditation session, a translucent blue barrier springing into being around her chair. With that done he left her in peace, making sure the door was closed as he left the house.

"Alright, let's see what these people wanted."

Sierra led him and Alli to a group of people that were arguing next to the newly opened messaging shop.

"The service is pointless! It can only send messages to towns that have a messaging shop in it," Ray was arguing loudly with his group.

"It may be useless now, but it won't be in the future!"

Ray growled and threw up his large meaty hands in exasperation, catching sight of Charles group of three before he could say anything more. "You mister magic, I want to talk to you!"

"Uh, isn't that why Sierra brought me over here?" Charles asked confused.

Ray scratched at his forehead, his bushy eyebrows waving with the wind. "I didn't see her there behind your dog."

"Alli," Charles corrected the man. "Her name is Alli, and she can speak for herself."

Alli nudged his side appreciatively. "Hello," She projected her voice to the entire group.

Sierra hung back, purposely distancing herself from the discussion. She no longer belonged to Ray's group and didn't want to get involved further than she already had.

"So, what is it you wanted?" He asked, ignoring how they were looking at Alli in amazement. He was quickly getting used to that reaction whenever she first spoke to someone.

Ray blinked in surprise and shook his head to focus his thoughts. "I need to apologize for how I came across the other day. It had nothing to do with you and everything to do with how people have been acting. You showed up, and I thought you were nothing but talk and I was rude as a result. Sorry!"

"It's fine," Charles sighed. "I wasn't exactly acting understanding that day for similar reasons." They were both silent for several heartbeats. "Was that uh, all you wanted to talk about?"

"Yeah, there was no other reason. I just wanted to apologize before there was too long of a gap and things became awkward."

Charles shook hands with Ray and walked away before things could get awkward again.

Sierra gazed at him, blinked once and then went back to watching the people around them. "I wasn't sure what to expect. I never spent much time around Ray once my group joined up with his."

"What did you spend your time doing then?" They had drifted towards the system building while they spoke.

"Thinking, mostly about Kira, and what she believed I had done to her. I never thought I would see her again. I even tried to forget her for a long time. Then she just steps back into my life after the world has ended." The blonde woman was looking at the ground as she spoke, her cultured voice heavy with emotion.

Alli stepped in front of her, forcing her to look up as she stopped. "Just don't hurt her again. Kira has begun to forgive you, but if you hurt my friend, I'll end you!" Alli's words were chillingly final as her eyes flashed different colors.

Sierra nodded, her already white complexion going even paler.

Charles ignored them as they continued to talk, focusing instead on the town menu. The amount of taxed mana available had continued to climb throughout the day. The cost to infuse the large wall was six times what the initial wall had cost them at 3600 UM. They would be pushing it to get the wall infused in time.

A message appeared as he closed out the menu.

Congratulations, you have managed to successfully guide another person to their true core and helped them infuse it in its entirety. As the first being to ever accomplish this in the history of the world you have been given the special ability 'Disciple'. Using the disciple ability allows you to select up to five people that you have trained and designate them as your disciples. People thus marked are able to use a single spell from each element that you have access to once a week. (Note: The disciples' compatibility with the element will affect the cost and strength of the spell.)

A large grin spread across his face as he closed out the message and designated the three that had finished with their cores. Alli, his sister Charlotte and Kate, who had apparently just finished with her short session.

A whoop of joy trickled through the open door of the building as Kate ran past looking for her family to tell them the good news.

Sierra and Alli followed him out of the building, still talking quietly amongst themselves.

Charles spent the next few minutes walking to the warehouse where all the vehicles were stored. The inside was split into different sections, one to store them in, one for Kira and others to work on them, and a third smaller area to rest in.

The building was empty, but his interest lay in how full it was, not in talking to someone. They would need to build another warehouse soon if they continued to find vehicles to fix and use. The need would become even more pressing when everyone discovered that the professor had managed to create gas from trolls' blood. Not that he was quite there yet if the destruction of the generator was anything to judge by.

Kira was waiting for them outside the large rolling doors of the warehouse. "She finished infusing her core," She said happily, vibrating in place with excitement for her little sister.

"Yup, now she just needs to learn to control the mana in her body and then she can begin to use spells properly," Charles smiled back at her, glad to see she was excited for her younger sister. He didn't want to be the cause of any issues between the two of them. Though Kira was the one who had chosen not to learn magic. That didn't mean she wouldn't feel jealous or some other negative emotion when she saw Kate succeeding.

Kira looked past him to where Sierra and Alli were conversing. "Give me a few more days and then I think I'd like to try again. I have a theory about why my core was so violent and off-putting and I think it will have calmed down some by then."

Charles felt his eyes soften as he stared at her. "I'm ready whenever you are." He cleared his throat as she turned to face him. "Now, let's go grab Kate and your parents, Charlotte and Scott, and hold a congratulatory party for them all. We have a lot of work to do, and this might be our last chance to celebrate for a while."

"I'm not too worried, mom and dad have the preparations well in hand. They started drawing up ideas to defend this place days ago when we first arrived."

Charles's feet stuttered as he was reminded of something that had been bothering him. "Kira, what exactly did your father do for work?"

She looked at him for a second confused and then her eyes widened in understanding; she glanced behind them and stepped closer to him.

"You're wondering about how he knows all this stuff?" Her voice was pitched low so as not to have it carry. "He truly was just a normal guy; he was never in the military or anything like that. When I was kidnapped, he changed, he blamed himself for not knowing enough to track me down and rescue me on his own. He started learning as much as he could about tactics and securing one's home. Honestly, I think if everything hadn't gone wrong that first night they would have done fine at the house."

"So, he was what, a prepper?" Charles asked skeptically. He had met preppers in the past and they had all acted differently than her father did.

"No, at least not in the way you're thinking. He just wanted to know how to protect us in the future if something ever happened again. For him, that meant knowing how to secure an area against intruders and less about stockpiling for the end of the world." She gave a wry laugh. "I bet he regretted that for the first few days."

"Well, that explains a lot, either way this town would be much worse off without him and your mother directing everything."

"Thanks for saying that," The vulnerable looking woman uttered softly.

"Thanks for having awesome parents," Charles replied, aware that the conversation behind them had stopped.

Sierra stepped forward and threw her arms around Kira who stopped as a look of panic flashed across her face. "Sorry," Sierra said, realizing her mistake and beginning to remove her arms from around her.

Kira breathed in deeply, calming herself and placed a hand on her friends' arm. "Don't. It just took me by surprise is all. I need to get used to touching people that aren't my parents or sister might as well start with another woman."

Sierra looked away sadly, once more realizing just how damaged her friend had become from her father's inaction. "So, what are we doing now?"

"We're going to find the rest of the group and then have a small party. Kate finished infusing her core, and as soon as she learns to control the mana in her body, she can begin to use magic," Charles directed them towards the town hall as he spoke.

Inside, Kate was saying something to Charlotte, her hands waving expressively through the air as she spoke. Scott was standing bemused behind Charlotte, his hands in his pockets.

Off to the side, Kory was standing on one side of a small table while Krystal stood on the other. Spread across the table was a map that showed far more details than it had before.

"You must have spent a lot of time looking at the map in the system building to draw that," Charles remarked as he came to a stop next to them.

"Not as much as you might think," Krystal said with a smile looking up at him. "Kate already told us the good news."

"So, I noticed." He tilted his head with a smirk to where Kate was now talking to Kira and Sierra as well as Charlotte. "I was thinking we could have a quick celebration for her, Alli, and Charlotte before we buckle down for the night."

It was true most of the day had vanished while they all rushed about and dusk was fast approaching.

Kory looked out one of the many windows and noticed the darkening sky. "It will have to be a short one. There are a few more things I want to have done at the gate. If we get the wall infused in time, then that will be our weak point."

"Speaking of," Charlotte interrupted as she came up behind them. "The professor put together about forty of these little grenades." An oblong-shaped object appeared in her hands, and the jostling of a thick liquid could be heard inside it. "It uses a simple striker system to ignite the troll's blood inside a plastic pouch. The pouch is then surrounded by the metal from various monster weapons. We didn't use many of them to make these, but we still needed to use some as they would be the most effective." She handed the grenade over to the man and then pulled out several boxes full of them from her inventory.

"Make sure whoever uses them has a good arm," Scott remarked as he joined them, Kate, Kira, and Sierra lagging slightly behind. "The explosive force behind one of those grenades is equal to several sticks of dynamite at least. If we had tried to create them with regular metal it wouldn't have worked, the explosion would have vaporized the metal itself."

Kory smiled, a look of relief spreading across his face and causing his shoulder to sag. "This is exactly what I needed to hear right now. As long as the army of monsters is nice and compacted these will cause devastating amounts of damage."

Charles clapped his hands, getting everyone's attention. "Great! Let's have a quick celebration and food and then get back to work!" He turned away from them all and for the first time in over two weeks, yawned.

Truthfully that's all the celebration would be food and a happy atmosphere, but they would be together. Which Charles thought counted for a lot.

Chapter 31

People from all around the area began trickling in shortly after the sun had sunk below the distant horizon. Their arms were full of the goods they had managed to save and couldn't store in their inventories.

Krystal worked alongside Sierra and others to get them situated away from the wall. They chose to take those that couldn't fight across the river, filling up the area in front of the dungeon and the bridge itself.

Charles was inside the system building, watching the taxed mana rolling slowly in. He had changed the settings on it earlier to tax more from the people that weren't citizens of the town. The problem was, it did so slowly over a long period of time. He couldn't risk taking more from the citizens otherwise it might begin to affect their ability to fight.

Alli stood by his side while Kate huddled in a corner, Kira at her side comforting her. The pressure had gotten to her and a long round of vomiting had left her trembling and weak for the moment.

"Are we going to make it in time?" Alli asked not projecting her voice so that only he could hear her.

"It will be close," Charles whispered back. "It really depends on how long they give us before attacking." He tried to hold in the yawn he could feel building at the back of his throat.

It didn't fool Alli in the slightest.

"How are you doing?" Her eyes flicked over to Kira and Kate making sure they weren't looking at them as she spoke.

"Not good." He was going to say more but the yawn burst from his mouth, unable to be contained any longer. With the sinking of the sun his thoughts had grown sluggish and his body increasingly tired. There was only one way to stave off the oncoming sleep, the potion on his hip, however, he was even more reluctant to drink it than usual. They might need it for when the fight came, and honestly, he desperately wanted to sleep. He missed sinking into the sweet oblivion it offered and was looking forward to it even as he tried to remain awake.

"Then just sleep," His canine companion said compassionately. "I'll make sure we wake you when the time comes."

"What about infusing the wall?" He asked while yawning again, his eyes beginning to droop.

Alli pushed him into the corner where all the pillows and blanket lay. "You can infuse the wall whenever I wake you. I'll wake you quickly enough that it won't have been damaged."

Charles sank to the ground. His muddled thoughts escaping from his grasp preventing him from remembering what he had been trying to do. "Alright, do what you think is right."

Standing above his sleeping form, Alli saw the shudder that ran through his body and the trail of tears that followed. Unsure of how to help him, she chose to lay down next to him and wrap her fluffy tail around him.

Kira and Kate followed their example and chose to get as much sleep as they could before the coming battle.

***

The green of the night sky gave off more light than the stars ever had but didn't obstruct one from seeing them either. It was an odd but welcome phenomenon that the humans found themselves relying on in a world that was suddenly without night-lights. Old forgotten fears of monsters that hid under the bed or in the shadows had come surging back to life.

With no light to dispel those fears, some people found the suddenly lit night sky a welcome addition. The monsters who had enjoyed the lightless nights cursed even that small amount of light. Shadowy figures could be seen when they moved, stalking their various prey. Night had always been their domain, the cold empty void of darkness welcoming their enhanced senses.

That night the world was filled with the hisses, the growls and the myriad of other noises that the undisciplined army of monsters made. Their presence was announced to everyone and everything, sending them fleeing in terror. It was the reaction they desired; they ruled the night, or at least they were above the filthy humans.

At the head of the procession, Gabreen the goblin lord stood next to the unnamed bugbear champion. It was unnamed because its goddess hadn't deigned to give it a name. Whoever she was, she was making it clear that the bugbear was nothing more than a high leveled pawn. The bugbear was meant to be disposable, and it knew it, making the large monster's disposition worse than usual. Bugbears were known to be prickly monsters that liked to be left alone.

Gabreen was growling at the large bugbear, keeping one wary eye on the ridiculously large sword strapped to its back. The road in front of them was empty, save for the shadowy figures of their scouts flitting about ahead of them.

The bugbear believed it should be in charge because it had a higher-level than the goblin lord. Whereas Gabreen felt he should be in charge since he had a name and was clearly smarter than the brute next to him.

It was the same argument they had been having since they were forced to join forces by their goddesses. There had been no plan when they overran the last human settlement they came across. They had swarmed the area and paid for their lack of planning in loss of life. They had been victorious, but the cost had been higher than it should have been.

The monsters they forced to join their army along the way, barely made up for the losses they had suffered. The humans were slowly learning how to fight against the monsters.

Gabreen held up a long-muscled arm, stopping the procession in their tracks. The bugbear continued for several more steps before turning back with a menacing growl.

Ahead of them, a large dark wall extended into the distance. The eight-meter-tall wall was more than high enough to prevent them from simply leaping over it. Following the road, they soon found the closed gate and Gabreen once more stepped forward. He had words to say to the human who wielded magic before the battle began.

***

"Charles, it's time," Alli was roughly shaking his body as she tried to wake him. He had only been asleep for a few hours, not enough time to counteract the weeks of lost sleep. It would have to be enough, however.

He rolled over with a muffled groan, his face buried in a pillow. "I'm up," He slurred, his eyes still closed.

Kira snorted and kicked him gently with her booted foot. "Come on, your little goblin buddy is waiting for you at the gate."

It took several seconds for her words to percolate through his sleep-addled mind. Charles rolled over and opened his eyes, staring up at the dark ceiling. "The goblin lord is here, at the gates?"

"Yes," Kira growled in exasperation, kicking him again, a little harder this time.

"Why haven't you killed him or something?" He asked as he struggled to his feet.

"I think some of them tried, but when he began to speak, they stopped," Alli informed him as he stumbled from the building with a jaw-cracking yawn.

"Why? Just because he can talk?" It was Kate who asked the obvious question.

"No, I think it was because he asked for Charles specifically," Alli responded while shaking her head. She hadn't been there as it happened. It was only because they had left the door to the building open that she had heard anything at all.

Charles began to invite people into a party as he walked, the chilly night air helping to wake his mind. Soon people began to appear behind them as the word spread, the time had come to fight.

Charles sent up orbs of light as he walked. The crunch of brittle grass and the quick breathing of panicky people the only sounds on this side of the wall. Nearing the gate, he could hear the shuffling of countless feet alongside the growls, hissings, and muttering of unintelligible beings.

Standing just outside the gate, waiting for Charles to appear was Gabreen the goblin lord. "Finally, I have been waiting for you."

Alli sneezed as he spoke, her nose twitching furiously. "The rot inside him has grown worse, even without us killing him he will be dead in a matter of days. His goddess is truly cruel."

"What do you want with me?" Charles asked from behind the opened gate. There was a dent about halfway up the metal gate as though someone had knocked on it with incredible strength.

"My goddess asked me to deliver a message to you and the other champions before this battle," Gabreens' smile grew malicious as he spoke, his words sending chills down the spine of all who could hear.

Charles turned to look behind himself and saw the gathering of humans. "You have been nice enough to allow us the time to gather and prepare, say your message and then let us be done with this charade."

Gabreen gave a phlegmy laugh that had him spitting a wad of blackened mucus to the side. "As you wish, there were two messages, one for you and one for the champions. The one for the champions is as follows. 'You knew this was coming, accept your fate as the playthings of the gods!'" Gabreen stepped forward his arms spread as he waited for Charles to step closer, the other message for his ears alone. His voice changed, and the light went out of his eyes, as a harsh rasp with an odd musical quality to it spoke. "This message is actually for you and your sister. We have found you, at last, you don't belong on Earth," The goblin lord shivered as the light returned to his eyes, "I really wish she would quit doing that!" He hocked to the side, a ball of blackened and congealed blood with a tooth sticking out of it hit the ground with a sickening splat.

Charles stepped back as the realization of what the goddess had done to her champion rolled through his brain. Her words momentarily forgotten after that display.

"The rot inside him grew worse while she was in control," Alli told him, her own shock at the display evident in her words.

Charles looked around for his sister, catching her curious eyes for a second. He wondered what the goddess had meant. Why didn't he and Charlotte belong on Earth?

The hodgepodge gathering of humans pulled their weapons out and prepared. A few scattered prayers could be heard by the few who hadn't given up their faith with the apocalypse.

Gabreen walked backward, never taking his eyes from Charles as he was swallowed back into the depths of the monster army.

This was not how anyone had thought the battle would begin.

Kory pushed his way through the crowd to Charles's side. "We upgraded the wall while you were asleep, we only need to worry about them getting through the gate."

Charles smiled appreciatively at the man as he vanished back into the crowd of people. He wanted to smack himself; he had forgotten about the wall when he was jostled awake. It was a good thing someone was thinking clearly.

Kira stepped behind Alli and pulled one of the professors' grenades from her inventory. She tossed it lightly into the air once before pulling the pin and throwing it deep into the gathering of monsters. As soon as the dark object left her hands, the bracelet on her wrist flashed and formed her large hammer. The heads had changed again. One was the traditional head of a large maul like hammer, while the other was a long spike.

The humans who had seen what she threw inhaled sharply and readied their weapons.

Alli tracked the grenade as it fell through the air and disappeared into the mass of bodies. There was a sharp cry as it hit a monster in the face, catching the grenade reflexively. Then it exploded.

The metal of the grenade cut mercilessly through the monsters even as a wave of pressure pushed them to the ground. The number of monsters that died was barely noticeable when compared to the whole.

Countless eyes tracked the falling monster body parts as they arced through the air. The monster's eyes flashed crimson with rage and as a large chunk of arm hit the ground, they leaped forward. All thoughts of strategy or working together they might have had lost in the moment.

As the humans surged forward to meet the monsters, Charles remembered that he hadn't spoken to Alli, Kate or Charlotte about the disciple ability. He was sure they had gotten a message when he designated them for it and could only hope they had the sense to not use it right away.

For the first few seconds of the battle, the monsters overwhelmed the humans. The orbs of light overhead casting harsh shadows over everything. The humans rallied together, working with those at their side to take down the monsters.

The humans were mostly lower levels than the monsters, but by working together they were able to take them down.

Kira had waded into the thick of it, her large hammer and prodigious strength pulping anything in her way.

Charlotte spun through the monsters like the dancer she had never been, her knives flashing with deadly accuracy. Streams of red spurted through the air, creating a bloody tunnel in her wake.

Alli vanished into the shadows, appearing only to claw or clamp her jaws shut on something. Each time she appeared she was bloodier than the last, and soon her hair and fur was completely covered. Her normally silver form now a blood coated nightmare for the monsters.

Kory stood to the side with his wife and youngest daughter. Each of them had a knife in one hand and a grenade in the other.

Charles soon lost track of everyone else as he was pulled into the battle. He had taken the time to pull an aegis shield from his inventory and was using it to deflect attacks. The last vestiges of sleepiness were pulled from his body as the adrenaline began to flow.

His spells began to course through his left hand, he was still hesitant to use his gloved right hand. He was unsure if he could properly keep them separated in the heat of battle and he didn't need the glove going berserk while he was surrounded by monsters.

The glow of a firebolt filled the air as it flew from his hand and hit a particularly ugly orc. The bolt of fire cooking its stomach and sending a goblin tumbling from its back as it roared in pain. The orc flopped onto its stomach, trying to smother the superheated fire. It stopped moving seconds later.

The goblin that had tumbled to the ground stayed where it had fallen as another monster carelessly stepped on it. A hobgoblin stood on its back and maliciously ground its smaller species into the ground, momentarily distracted from the human archmage.

A stream of lightning sped from Charles's hand, skewering a line of kobolds and gnolls in front of him. He was burning through his mana quickly as he cast spell after spell. The cost for the spells had dropped as he meditated on their individual elements, allowing him to cast more spells.

Humans began to fall as they exhausted themselves, some were overlooked while others were mercilessly stabbed into the ground. Blood spread across the ground, making it sticky in the sections where it was able to dry and slick where it couldn't.

The hyena-like gnolls had no trouble traversing the slickened ground while the humans found their footing tenuous at best.

Charles could feel the exhaustion of burning through his mana so quickly beginning to build even as he refused to slow down. Monsters littered the ground all around him, and a small number of humans were making sure each was dead in turn.

Through the connection he shared with Alli he could feel her pushing herself, though thankfully she was still unharmed. To his side, he could hear Kira roaring in anger as she relentlessly swung her hammer.

The battle had only been going on for thirty or so minutes, but it felt like an eternity to the humans. They were each going all out in an effort to save their people and the monsters were just continuing to appear.

Charles caught a brief glimpse of Scott and his fellow students from MIT working together before more monsters swarmed him. He found himself looking to the glove more and more often in the minutes that followed. The glove had a wide range area attack spell that he desperately wanted to use. The urge growing stronger as his personal pool of mana continued to be used at a rapid pace.

It was this distraction that cost him, the swift thrust of a kobolds' spear found it buried in his stomach. It was pulled roughly from his chest as he stumbled to his knees, the tip of the bloody spear dragging a furrow across his cheek.

Weakly his hand fumbled at his belt, he had used too much of his mana and knew he didn't have enough to properly heal himself. The potion was his only hope of surviving, assuming of course that he was able to drink it.

Charles fell to his back, struggling to breathe through the pain in his stomach. The kobold who had stabbed him stood above his struggling form, it reptilian eyes glowing in the heat of the moment. A lizard-like tongue flicking through the air as though tasting his pain and reveling in it.

One of the humans who had been standing near him thrust their own spear through the kobolds' stomach and out its back. The monster's eyes lost their glow as it stared down at the spear and collapsed on top of Charles's legs. Someone pulled the monster off of him and helped him with the potion, not knowing why he wanted it but trusting it would help.

His hands were shaking furiously as he brought the potion to his lips and drank. He felt the familiar heat coursing painfully through his body, eventually centering around the hole in his stomach. The soothing icy cold wave spreading through his body as the last of the damage was healed. The fog in his tired mind disappeared as he was once more filled with energy and mana.

Chapter 32

T he sun had just peeked above an unseen horizon as Charles pulled himself from the ground good as new. Gasps could be heard from the humans and monsters alike as he stood. The gaping wound in his stomach had closed in front of their eyes.

Charles took the moment to look around and saw just how tired the humans were. It was time to stop holding back, extending his gloved hand he aimed above the army of monsters and released the spell 'Lightning Storm'.

Concentric circles filled with runes each noticeably smaller than the first time he had used the spell appeared in the sky. The runes began to spin clockwise, while the circles spun in the other direction. A bolt of lightning formed in the middle of the spell hanging above everything.

Humans and monsters alike had noticed the forming of the spell and stilled, momentarily stunned by the sight. That moment was all the time the spell needed to complete itself. The circles and runes spun faster as the lightning bolt extended across the sky and began to branch off into sections. Then, with a scream of the air itself being ripped asunder the runes and glowing circles vanished.

Lightning began to fall to the ground, thankfully centered on the monsters and not the humans. With each bolt of lightning that fell to the ground, the great branching bolt in the sky glowed slightly brighter. Monsters fell to the ground in steaming droves, their bodies burned and blackened by the power of the storm.

In seconds, the remaining number of monsters had been reduced considerably.

Charles felt his hand begin to tingle, noticing for the first time that the glove had not released the spell. Instead, it was continuing to feed power to the spell and was the reason the bolt in the sky had begun to glow brighter. No matter what he tried, he couldn't cut off the flow of power. His hand was forced to endure the mana that trickled endlessly from the glove causing his fingers to spasm painfully.

He tried one last desperate time to wrestle control of the spell from the glove, putting everything he had into it. He grabbed control and immediately cut the flow of mana to it, his hand was numb and useless by then. He bit his lip as the skin on his back began to wriggle and move as more runes began carving themselves into his body.

The lightning continued to fall to the ground for several more seconds, draining the last of the energy from the spell. The air was charged with leftover electricity as the last bolt fell to the ground amidst a pile of dead monsters.

People stood from where they had pressed themselves to the ground and cheered as they saw the destruction of their enemies. Then the monsters stood from where they had hugged the ground themselves. Their number had been greatly reduced over the course of the battle and in that single attack. Leaving the number still alive daunting, but doable.

The large bugbear that was also a champion to the gods pushed its way to the front and roared in defiance. Behind it the monsters rallied, throwing off the cloak of fear his devastating spell had caused. It pulled the large buster sword from its back and set its furry paws into the grass, sinking them an inch into the soft ground.

"Fight me!" It screamed while looking at Charles.

Alli vanished from where she had been standing next to Charlotte and reappeared in the bugbear's shadow.

Charlotte extended her hand and using her designation as Charles disciple cast the 'Shadow's Grasp' spell. At the same time that Alli stepped from the shadows, they began to writhe and twist around the beasts furred paws.

Alli leaped onto its back using her weight and momentum to push it forward. The great canine used her own disciple designation to cast 'Shadow Spike', the spell using the monsters' own shadow to create the spike. It fell face first onto the spike, the hardened shadows punching through its eye but stopping short of the brain.

Seeing this Alli ran forward, hoping to finish off the much higher leveled monster before it could move. With a scream of pain, the bugbear pulled its face from the dissipating spike and rolled to the side. The sword it held clutched in its hand waved through the air as it rolled. The edge caught Alli in the stomach, scoring a deep cutting line with its accidental movement.

Alli stumbled and disappeared into a nearby shadow, reappearing next to Charles a second later. The entire fight had lasted mere moments but had left both participants grievously wounded. Charles knelt next to his animal companion and dear friend, his magic working overtime to heal the damage the sword had caused. His lip was bloody and his back felt as though it were on fire, but none of that mattered.

Kira threw her last grenade at the bugbear in a rage before hurrying over to Charles and Alli's side. She didn't bother to watch as the grenade bounced off its head and into the air before coming to a rest on a large furry stomach.

The bugbear could only watch in horror as the grenade hit its snout and sprang back into the air. A fear it had never felt before causing it to freeze in dread. The grenade hit its apex and began to fall back to earth where it landed on the bugbears' stomach.

Everyone watching held their breath, waiting for what was to come. They didn't have to wait long.

The grenade rolled down the furry slope of the monster's stomach and past its navel, stopping in the dip above its crotch. The human males all closed their eyes and winced as the grenade exploded, mulching the monster's reproductive organs. Shrapnel flew in every direction and the bugbears fur was coated in flame, the oils coating it catching fire with a vengeance.

A high-pitched scream echoed through the area as the bleeding and fiery form of the bugbear rolled across the ground.

Charles ignored it all as he concentrated on healing Alli, having to focus completely as he worked to hold her stomach together. The damage to her inside had been extensive, with many of her organs sliced through or pulped from the pressure. His magic was the only thing keeping her alive for the moment and he regretted having used the potion on himself.

He controlled the spell as best he could, dimly aware that someone was standing above him protecting them both. Kira was panting above him, her hammer dragging through the mud and filth they had stirred up with every swing.

Gabreen chose that moment to step onto the field of battle, no longer content to stand waiting at the back. His shaman was at his side, gyrating and spinning in a dance only it understood. The staff held in its gnarled hands making complex symbols in the air. The shaman stomped once, and a firebolt appeared in the air above its staff. It stomped again, and another appeared. The shaman stomped one last time, causing a third bolt to appear.

With a mighty swing of the staff, the firebolts arced through the air and landed amongst the humans. Each bolt exploded, taking three or more humans with it each time. The shaman extended its leg into the air and then slammed it into ground, before started to wildly dance about for a second time.

It was Kate who stepped forward to take care of the shaman. One spell for each element she had access to through the disciple designation rocketed through the air. The shaman was thrown into the air first with a firebolt, then it was coated in a spout of water. A lance of ice pierced its abdomen, the water coating its body turning to frost from the extreme cold. Weighted down by the ice, it fell to the ground and onto a spike of shadows.

The shaman's screams were cut short a second later as the still suffering bugbear champion rolled over it. The last vestiges of the monster's life were squished from its mutilated body.

Gabreen turned to the bugbear and picking up its large heavy sword swung it through the monsters' neck, killing it instantly. Many of the monsters were shaken with the death of one of their leaders and fled, not caring that it had died at the hands of one of their own.

Kate, having used the last of her mana to cast those spells, collapsed at her parents' feet where they could pull her to safety. The cost of using Charles' spells in that fashion was far higher than it would be if the spells had been her own. It had been a close thing to cast that last spell.

With his revenge having been taken at least in part for the death of his shaman, Gabreen turned to face the humans. Charlotte chose that moment to begin her own attack on him, following Kate's example. She had only used a single spell in the fight, and since she was a higher level than Kate, she had more mana to use.

She began with a 'Plasma Bolt'. It was a shared element spell and as such acted as the single spell she could use in those elements. The bolt of super-heated plasma took in the last remnants of electricity in the air becoming stronger. The now glowing bolt of white-hot gas shot across the open space, hitting the goblin lord before he could even move.

Charlotte was using her glasses to pinpoint his weak points enabling even her lower-level magic to damage him. The ionized gas splashed across the goblins' arm and sizzled as it burned through the green skin to the tender meat below.

Gabreen roared with rage and focused on the woman who had managed to hurt him.

Charles looked up from where he was still focusing on knitting Alli back together. Kira stood by his side her hammer dripping blood of different colors, pieces of skin and flesh clinging to the spike. Alli coughed and opened her eyes. Her magically sealed stomach all that was holding her injured organs and blood inside.

Without delay, Charlotte began casting another spell, the ground around the tall goblin lord trembled and began to move. Walls sprang from the ground, trapping the monster inside.

Charlotte sprinted across the open space, her booted feet digging through the pools of blood and remains that littered the ground. She reached out and touched the trembling earthen wall and closed her eyes, beginning to channel another spell.

A wave of flame appeared inside the walls underneath the injured goblins' feet. With every second that passed, Charlotte pumped more mana into the spell, increasing the heat. A scream of pain and impotent rage sounded from inside the cage of earth.

Gabreen pounded desperately on the walls, his bare feet cooking in the hot flames. Blisters appeared all over his legs, popping almost immediately after they formed. One arm hung useless at his side, the plasma bolt had injured it badly and him trying to break through the wall had finished the job.

Charlotte swayed and collapsed in front of the walls. They began to crumble and return to the ground without her constantly feeding them mana. The flames inside the walls persisted for another second before they too guttered out vanishing without a sound.

Ray burst from the crowd of unmoving humans and picked Charlotte up before the walls could finish collapsing. With her secure in his arms, he carried her to the back where Kory and Krystal were cradling an unconscious Kate.

To the side, Sierra was working with Scott and the rest of the students to prevent any monsters from entering the town. Scott kept his eyes on his wife even as he thrust his knife blindly forward.

Alli looked down at her stomach and then up at Charles. "Go, you won't get a better chance to kill him than this."

"What about you?" He asked, his magic was the only thing keeping her alive for the moment.

"I'll survive on my own for a few minutes, just make sure you survive and come back to me," Her voice was raw with emotion and pain as she struggled to stretch her neck enough to lick his cheek. "Go."

Charles reached out and pulled on Kira's arm as he stood. The muscles in his back cramped and protesting from the abuse he had continued to put them through. The runes had thankfully finished carving themselves into his back, but the pain was still fresh and effecting his muscles.

The blood around his lip had dried, giving him a garish look of deranged madness.

The walls finished crumbling in front of Gabreen as he thrust his one working arm through the fragile packing of dirt. Monsters that had spread out began to congregate around their leader, and Charles saw his chance to hurt the goblin slip away.

Gabreen stood tall in the middle of the remaining monsters, his raw seeping feet doing little to visibly inconvenience him. The arm that hung limply at his side, the white of bone jutting through the plasma burns clearly visible. Hate-filled eyes gazed past his minions and into Charles's own pain and rage-filled pools of pale green.

Unable to feel his right hand, Charles let it hang at his side as he began to cast his own spells. Healing Alli, even to the incomplete state he had, had taken more than he would say.

The remains of humans and monsters alike covered the ground all around them. The cost of protecting the town and the people that couldn't defend themselves had been steep, and it would only grow higher.

Charles pointed at the ground in front of the monsters and spoke, his voice raspy and raw. "Flamewave," The spell flickered to life, extending in a line in front of the beings that threatened them.

One of the few remaining orcs picked up a kobold in a large fleshy hand and threw it across the line of fire. The kobold skidding and skipped across puddles of blood but was otherwise unharmed from the throw.

Charles grimaced and began pumping more mana into the hungry spell. The flames grew higher even as it began to crawl across the ground, pushing the invading army slowly backward.

"How long can you keep that up?" Kira whispered to him from the side of her mouth.

"Not long," He growled back, already feeling the strain it was putting on his remaining mana.

"Drop it when I'm close then," Kira turned to face the humans and raised her hammer, then she turned and ran towards the monsters screaming the entire way.

The rest of the humans burst into motion running after her, their weapons raised in readiness. The lone kobold was quickly stabbed and trampled to death as they rushed the line of magical fire.

Charles waited until the last second before cutting the flow of mana feeding the spell. The fire dropped in height and then vanished, a cloud of steaming blood all that remained where it had crept across the ground.

Kira changed her scream to a yell and pulling her hammer back all the way, swung it into the orcs stomach. The hulking green monster that had tossed the kobold minutes earlier bent double in pain. A line of drool running from its tusked mouth and onto the haft of her hammer.

Gabreen kept his eyes on Charles, not caring that the beings that had made up his army were dying or fleeing all-around him. Bending over he picked up a grime and filth covered knife, tossing it once in his working hand. Catching it, a gleam entered the goblin lords' eyes and before Charles could react, the knife was whistling through the air.

Charles screamed as the knife blade dug into his left hand, the force of the blow twisting his hand at the wrist and breaking it. The knife was buried to the hilt, his hand flopping about refusing to obey his commands.

He had experienced a lot of pain over the last two weeks. He had been stabbed or had his fleshed carved more times than he could count. This knife, though, was the last straw.

It was all too much, his sister lay exhausted somewhere behind him, Kate next to her with her parents. Alli lay on death's door, and Kira was fighting on the front line to keep them all safe. It was all too much; he refused to let Gabreen and whoever his goddess was, win this fight. He had one last card to play and he could only hope it would be enough.

His knees splashed into the ground as he collapsed to knees and raised his right hand. An audible hum filled the air as the glove he had been told to stop using but hadn't, began to run out of control. The mana grew thick in the air as people and monsters alike began to run away.

Only the goblin lord Gabreen remained, and Kira who stood just behind Charles.

The glove began to whine, and Charles was glad he could no longer feel that particular hand. A spell he had never seen before began to form in front of his hand and then shot out at the speed of light.

Gabreen leaped to the side as soon as he saw the spell form, resulting in only his lower half being hit.

A beam of compressed light extended from Charles's hand and into the seeable distance. It cut through everything, regardless of material. A hole a meter wide appeared in the middle of the ground floor of a building, not slowing the beam in the slightest. It created a tunnel through a distant hill before vanishing as quickly as it had appeared.

Everyone was silent as they stared at the destruction with wide fearful eyes.

There was a bang as the air in front of Charles exploded flinging him backward into Kira. The force of the blast sending them both sprawling to the ground stunned. A line of rippling fire followed the path of the beam, igniting the air where it had passed.

The glove began to disintegrate, flaking off in portions until only two runes remained, both etched into the skin of his hand.

Gabreen crawled towards them from where he had fallen. A knife in each hand digging into the dirt as he used them to pull himself forward. The entire lower half of his body missing, cauterized from the extreme heat of the beam. A trail of blood began to seep from the wound as he dragged it across the ground, reopening what had been sealed shut.

Charles lay on the ground stunned and unmoving, while Kira who had been behind him was in a similar state.

The obviously dying goblin lord continued to drag himself closer. While the humans who could have helped found themselves frozen with uncertainty. What they had just seen Charles do was beyond their wildest dreams of power. They had become afraid of the man who had done so much for them, and that fear kept them frozen in place.

Alli tried to drag herself across the ground, her legs too weak to hold her but knew she wouldn't make it in time.

Charles felt his mind clear as a gritty knife was plunged into his stomach. Gabreen was leering down at him using one arm to hold himself upright even as he thrust the knife down again with the other.

"This is only the beginning of my goddess's plan. You, humans, don't stand a chance!" Gabreen stabbed down again and coughed, a spray of blood and meaty pieces of his stomach splashing across the thrice stabbed human.

Behind them, Kira struggled to her feet and pulling back her hammer did her best imitation golf swing. The spike went straight through

Gabreens' eye and into his brain, his battered and barely alive state no match for her strength.

The former goblin lord flew backward, both knives still clutched in his hands. He was dead before his body hit the ground.

Kira collapsed on top of Charles, her weight serving to momentarily seal his wounds.

Alli crawled up to them then and laid her head on the ground next to Charles. She blinked slowly and then spoke to him. "I know how I want to use my reward. I want to use it to save you."

A message appeared in front of both of their eyes.

The reward may not be used on another person in this way.

A tear trickled from her eye, as she realized her last hope of saving him had disappeared. She couldn't let this be the end however, she cared for him too much to let that happen.

"Then I wish to tie my life with his, forever."

Granted. Status changed from 'Animal Companion' to 'Soul Companion'.

Was all the message said, Alli, relaxed slightly knowing that she would be with him in the next life at least.

Above him Kira stirred and looked down at Charles slowly whitening face, the blood finding a myriad of ways to leave his body.

"Don't leave me," She whispered, brushing the blood from his lips. "Please, you mean too much to me. I can't let you go, not like this."

A glow began to envelop Charles before spreading to Alli.

Alli painfully twisted her head to look towards where the bridge was hidden behind the people. Jenny and James had said they would wait for her there. "I'm sorry," Was all she whispered, the magic she had left projecting her voice for all to hear.

Kira clung to Charles tightly and for the first time in her life, she kissed a man. Pressing her lips tightly to his as his heart stuttered and then with a flash all three were gone.

Epilogue

Alaria was standing behind Bob, watching as the battle unfolded above the table. In the beginning, the gods had been boisterous, talking about how their champion was going to kill the most monsters. That excitement had quickly dimmed and then vanished completely as the fight dragged on.

"How did this happen?" Saraswati asked as she saw Charlotte collapse after using the spells.

"We're going to lose them all," Odin remarked with a grimace. His champion Sierra was doing well, but he was under no illusion that she would survive if Charles and Kira fell.

Zeus snorted and drank from his goblet. "Makes me glad. I haven't chosen a champion yet."

Brigit surged to her feet and threw the closest thing she had on hand at him, a pair of twenty-sided dice. "If you three had chosen your champions like you were supposed to, we might not be in this position!" She was taking the potential loss of Kira strongly. She had truly been hoping she wouldn't lose yet another character.

"The one I wanted to choose wasn't ready yet, she still isn't," Arinna whispered, feeling for her fellow gods.

Shiva frowned as he continued to watch the battle unfold. "For my part, I have not seen any worthy of becoming my chosen champion. That said, I do apologize. Their fate could possibly have been avoided had I chosen in time."

They continued to watch until the end, where each sighed in relief as they saw Kira finish off the goblin lord. A distant scream could be heard from a room nearby as he died.

Saraswati looked up to Bob, a sad smile on her lips. "I am sorry that your chosen was fated to die this day. It will make his sister most unhappy."

Bob pushed his chair back from the table and stood, "It's alright, it is for the best this way," An unseen glimmer of delight hiding in his eyes. "I think we need to make some changes to the campaign after this, it is abundantly clear that we have been rushing the humans. We need to give them some time to stabilize and become stronger."

"I think that would be wise," Odin said pushing back from the table, content in the knowledge that Sierra had survived.

The large door to the room banged open, hitting the god who had been leaning against the wall next to it. Hel stomped into the room and headed for Bob. The side of her body that was decaying threatening to slough off with every step. Her congealed flesh jiggled unsightly with every movement distracting anyone from noticing the other half of her body. It was a thing of beauty, but it was lost in the moment.

Alaria was pushed roughly out of the way, stumbling at the unexpected action. Her head hit the side of the table with a crack and she slumped to the floor as Hel walked uncaring past her body.

The roomful of gods gasped in unison as they saw Alaria fall and quickly scrambled away from the table.

"What just happened?" She screeched with a dry raspy voice.

Behind her Alaria stood and felt at the lump on her head, healing it even as she glared at the goddess in front of her.

Bob stepped back, having watched with relief as she stood. Hel following his eyes turned and saw the bottomless blazing eyes of Alaria.

"Who?" She began as Alaria raised her hand.

With a vicious crack Alaria backhanded the impertinent goddess, sending her flying across the room and killing her instantly. The blow erasing her very being from existence. Such was the fate of a god who dared to strike an actual God.

Alaria had already dismissed the now-dead god, looking inside herself towards where her power originated. Her control had suffered when she hit her head, she would need to spend a great deal of time going through everything she controlled. That lapse of control could have untold consequences otherwise.

All eyes but Bob's were focused on her, and as such, they all failed to notice the gleam of light that appeared in the corner of the room.

Book 2 End, Arc 1 End

Afterword

Thank you for reading the second book in 'The Game of Gods' series.

Book three and the beginning of arc 1 is already in the works. If you enjoyed either this book or any of my others, then I would really appreciate it if you took the time to rate and review it on Amazon and Goodreads. Amazon rewards writers when we get four or five-star reviews, so please take the time and leave a review.

I have heard many complaints from people that Amazon is making it harder for them to leave a review, so if you can't, I understand, but if you can, a brief short review is as useful as a full-on, in-depth analysis.

Thanks for reading and until next time,

Joshua Kern

Acknowledgements

I would like to thank my alpha readers, my family, who spend endless hours reading and re-reading everything I write as well as seeking out any plot holes and typos. It has taken me a long time to get to the point in my life where I can actually sit down and write like I have wanted to for so very long, to all the people that have encouraged me over the years and helped make this possible, I thank you!

About the Author

Joshua Kern was born in a little town situated somewhere in Ohio and raised in an even smaller town someplace in Colorado. He attended University for a time, where he discovered that while he enjoyed Electrical Engineering and Computer Science his true passion lay in writing. He lives primarily in Colorado but has been known to move around as the need arises. When not writing Joshua enjoys riding motorcycles, reading anything he can get his hands on, and anime.

Other Books by Joshua Kern

Other Books by Joshua Kern

Refton & Thomas

Forgotten Spies

Forgotten Child

The Game of Gods

Arc 1 – Human

The Beginning

The Death of Champions

Arc 2 – Demi-God

Fragments

A Tower Novella

Pieces of Divinity

Arc 3 – God

The Dungeon Alaria (Completed)

The Dungeon Alaria

The Creators Daughter

The Well Within

The Well Within: Part 1

Stand Alone

The Ridden

Duologies & Box Sets

The Game of Gods: Arc 1 Duology Box Set

The Dungeon Alaria: The World of Alaria Arc 1 Duology Box Set

Milton Keynes UK
Ingram Content Group UK Ltd.
UKHW010716180823
427095UK00001B/81